CENTERNIA
MARK OF THE CASTLE

BOOK TWO

Rose Catherine Khan

ACKNOWLEDGMENTS

The journey from *Return to the Castle* to *Mark of the Castle* was a crazier ride than I anticipated. There are many people to be thanked, including those who did not get proper acknowledgement four years ago.

Beta Reading Team
Therissa Alexander
Maria Bassett
Eric Ulrich
Chelsea Gill
Matt Shand
Ashlee Daniel

Editor for Mark of the Castle
Keith DeCandido

Convention Support
Jackie Nee & Ling Tang

Evangelists
Cathy Razim & Joe Pietruch

And of course, thank you to my parents, my husband, and the two little monsters who keep me up all night.

DEDICATION

To my four Italian grandparents.

You worked hard so I could spend my life chasing unicorns.

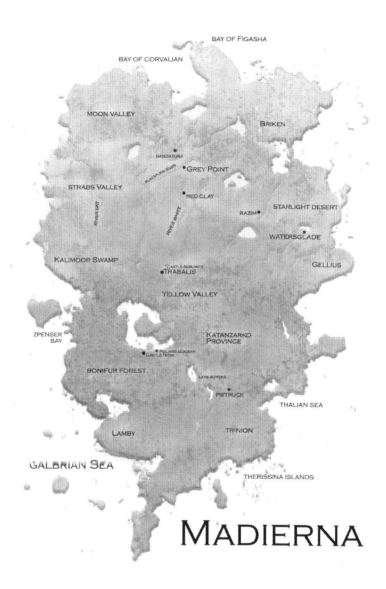

BAY OF FIGASHA

BAY OF CORVALIAN

MOON VALLEY

BRIKEN

BANDATURK

BLACKTURK BLUFF

GREY POINT

STRABS VALLEY

RED CLAY

RIVER SKY

RIVER WHITE

STARLIGHT DESERT

RAZIM

WATERSGLADE

KALIMOOR SWAMP

CASTLE AURUMICK

TRABALIS

GELLIUS

YELLOW VALLEY

ZPENSER BAY

KATANZARKO PROVINCE

POLARIS ACADEMY
CASTLE NOVA

BONIFUR FOREST

LAKE AURORA

PIETRUCK

THALJAN SEA

LAMBY

TRINION

GALBRIAN SEA

THERISSINA ISLANDS

MADIERNA

CHAPTER 1

Nico sat at a quaint breakfast table in the sun-soaked castle garden. His eyes traced the shimmering lace draped across its wooden surface.

"Glad you could join me. Would you like tea?"

Nico looked up from his daze, pleasantly surprised to find Misa seated across from him. Her curly hair cascaded down to her shoulders in ringlets.

"It's raspberry with a touch of gryphon's mint."

Misa's words were not atypical, but something felt odd.

Nico stared at the teapot in her delicate gloved hands, inhaling the grassy aroma mixed with the fresh sweet herbs of the tea. Dragonettes flitted behind Misa, chasing fat insects. Spring birds chirped brightly. The garden was very green, from the lush rose bushes to the layers of emerald tulle that comprised Misa's gown.

It was too green.

Everything *seemed* completely normal for breakfast in the courtyard of Castle Aurumice.

But Nico could not remember the journey back home.

"Misa, this is wrong," he scowled.

"I thought you liked tea?" Misa replied, pouring the steamy liquid into tiny red porcelain cups. Sunlight caught the beads at her neck. Each transparent gem was curved in the teardrop symbol of the goddess Aurora.

"You died," Nico stated coldly.

"Somebody woke up on the wrong side of the bed," Misa scowled in return, setting down the pot.

"I have not woken up yet," Nico stood. "This garden is a lie. You are buried in the woods beyond that wall!"

Misa sighed, then flashed her classic fanged grin. Her amethyst feline-like eyes glittered in the sunlight.

"Why must you always be miserable?" the young woman asked, carefully placing sugar cubes into her cup. Little lizards in formal jackets dashed upon the table, bringing plates of pastries balanced atop their heads. The weird lizards were definitely a sign that he was in a dreamspinner's dream.

"My sanity is tearing apart at the seams and this garden is proof!"

"It's fine to go crazy," Misa replied, "just stop being sad."

"The government of Trabalis won and I was sent to the Mines of Briken, my father is dead…and worst of all, you're gone. The tears the castlefolk shed could have filled the River White!"

Misa crossed her arms.

"At least you're still breathing."

The yawning creak of a metal door shattered the peace of the morning.

All vegetation vanished, replaced by the cold rock of Nico's subterranean hell.

Sitting up, the young ailurian man was surrounded by darkness and thick chalky air. His face was wet and salty with blood.

Nico blinked his left eye at the dim light of the guard's torch. His right eye ached painfully, swollen shut for weeks.

"Up!" a guard barked.

Nico scrambled to his feet, ignoring the wound on his face. He had been struck unconscious, the reason lost to him. It didn't matter. He had already lost two fingers and four toes for disobedience.

There had been a time he could have struck back with deadly magical energy, but somewhere in the darkness, Nico's fire-mage powers had evaporated. Before Briken, he didn't know it was possible to lose his mage strength, but the darkness had been relentless in taking away every fiber of his identity.

Sometimes he wondered if he had died and was trapped in the hell the Christians had written about in their holy book.

The guard jabbed Nico in the back with a rough blunt spear. The guards were faceless and nameless, always wearing protective brown masks. Nico had no such luxury to protect his lungs from the dense soot and caustic chemicals. He knew that the short time in the mines had aged him beyond his years. Had it been a year? Two? Ten? The mines were devoid of sunlight and all passage of time. Workers with picks struck the walls in a never-ending cacophony of metal scraping against rock. Wheelbarrows full of sediment were taken from one tunnel to another in a tediously inefficient process.

Nico grabbed a splintery-handled spade and took his place amongst the silent workers. Cautious not to drop a single pebble, Nico hefted the loose rock. Blue stones were later sifted from the dirt. He didn't know the name of the gem, nor did he recall seeing it traded on the Madiernian market.

Which made him wonder where the mineral went and why.

A needlewasp landed on his hand and he immediately crushed it. Its translucent body oozed a bioluminescent shimmer of blues and purples. The little bastards were drawn to the mineral they harvested. If Nico didn't hate the tiny deadly insects so much, he would have admired their ability to find the cerulean stones.

A guard approached before he was able to finish filling his wheelbarrow. Nico cringed, expecting to be struck again.

"You, follow. They have use for you elsewhere."

Nico set down the shovel, his head downcast. As they walked away from the other workers,

Nico's dread increased. They made their way through the narrow passages, his throat as dry as sandpaper. He wondered where elsewhere could be. The furnace? The grinders? The shovel pit was tedious, but the other caverns were far more deadly.

Walking up echoing metal stairs, they came to a wooden hallway lit by the gentle light of glowstones. Nico's palms were slick with sweat by the time they arrived at a wooden door. The air had changed; it was musty but sweet.

Opening the door, the guards led him into a large wood-paneled office. Nico's eye was overwhelmed as sunlight beamed through a large dirty window.

"To your knees," the guard growled. Nico immediately fell. Tremors radiated through his right leg and he prayed to Aurora they wouldn't strike him for the movement. His vision slowly adjusted.

9

Before him stood two people. One he recognized— Qara Umbrian, a humanoid purple leopardess and the apathetical magistrate of the Mines of Briken. The other was a black-haired woman. Her clothing was plain to the undiscerning eye, caramel brown tunic, tight black breeches, and dark cloak. Blinking, Nico could see that the fabric was well tailored, coated with an expensive layer of waterproof *bajundi* oil, enough to catch the light. She was likely well-armed, as her clothing had just enough give in the right places to hide a comfortable number of knives.

Nico found the tall woman interesting as she was sapien. Her skin was smooth, her ears rounded. Nico was very familiar with the people from the hidden dimension of Earth, and this stranger very obviously had no blood from Centernia.

"This is your third option," Umbrian commented to the woman. "He has the sort of look you asked for. He's still strong, don't let the lack of a few fingers concern you."

Approaching Nico, the stranger crossed her arms.

"Stand," she commanded.

Nico slowly got to his feet, wondering what cruel trick the universe was trying to play on him.

"He looks damaged and scrawnier than the others. I doubt my client will like that much. What do you know about this one's history?"

The woman's voice was so familiar. It was an unusual accent, close to Central Madiernian, a little like South Trinion, but not.

Umbrian flipped through a folder and selected a piece of paper.

"This is all the documentation we were sent. He came from Trabalis, was late on taxes, and owned an impressive amount of land. His family still hasn't paid off his debt. If you would like to purchase him, that debt needs to be settled."

Considering the information carefully, the black-haired woman continued to stare as if she could see into Nico's soul. Slavery had been banished across the continent of Madierna nearly twenty years ago, either the outside world had changed, or the black-haired woman was involved in something illicit.

The stranger looked at him carefully.

"Tell me, what language do you speak?"

"Central Madiernian," Nico murmured quietly. He wanted to ask her about her accent in turn, but held his tongue. He cast his eyes to the floor, watching a needlewasp crawl along the crevice.

"He is missing an eye."

"No, I believe it's still in there," Umbrian was unconcerned. "He is quite capable of work regardless."

"I want to examine these numbers more closely," the black-haired stranger glanced to the guards. "We are finished with him, you can place him with the others."

Nico was led from the room, not certain if his fate was improving or about to get worse.

CHAPTER 2

Frostfire whinnied with joy as she cantered across the field. Her sharp twin horns gleamed as she tossed her head. Her red-speckled coat glistened, heavy with sweat from an afternoon of racing in the pastures of Castle Aurumice.

Jessica, her rider, did not quite share the creature's seemingly endless desire to run. The teenage girl clutched the leather reins in her left hand, a staff gripped tightly in her sweaty right palm. Her legs clamped around Frostfire's barrel-like chest.

Spring sunlight blanketed the stable yard in warmth, and Jessica really wanted to nap instead of practice.

Across the field Wadjette faced her, deeply focused. The two teen girls could not be more opposite. Jessica was a sunburned red-head, a single neon pink streak dyed into her unruly hair. Wadjette was dark cat-like ailurian, skin coated with very fine velvety black fur. Her hair was plaited back into a tight braid atop her head.

Wadjette moved in perfect synergy with Racewind, the chocolate-brown bicorn. Racewind shook his head, his striped mane rippling. He was a heavier bicorn, much like a draft horse, colloquially referred to as a thunder ram. The name was apt, for as the beast galloped across the field, his heavy hooves struck the earth with a resonating force.

Luckily, Frostfire was undeterred by the larger creature. Fearless and brash, she owned the reputation for being one of the most ill-tempered bicorns in the stable. It was a notable achievement. Unlike horses, bicorns were intelligent omnivorous creatures known for eating rodents and occasionally taking a bite out of people.

Frostfire and Racewind sprinted directly at each other.

Both teen riders, the human and the ailurian, held long staffs ready for the game of Ribbons.

Wadjette signaled to Racewind with a subtle squeeze. Her equestrian skills had improved exponentially since returning home to Castle Aurumice three years ago. Jessica had arrived at the castle around the same time. Earth-born, the girl had a steeper learning curve, knowing nothing of bicorns, ailurians, or the land of Centernia.

As their mounts brushed by each other, Wadjette leaned in to grab one of the green ribbons at Jessica's right knee. Jessica held out her staff to block. Wadjette was deterred momentarily. Circling Racewind around Frostfire's hindquarters, she grabbed at Jessica's left ribbon before the girl had a chance to adjust. Dust rose into the air, mixing with the sweet aroma of spring pollen.

Slow, slow, too slow! Jessica berated herself. She always lagged against the ailurians, no matter how hard she practiced. Jessica longed for Wadjette's free time, and her and ability to be one person and focus on one purpose— serving Castle Aurumice.

Towering over the field, the great castle cast a cool shadow across the blooming stable yard. Soaring curved spires stretched to the sky. Grown by an ancient magic from the surrounding forest, the magnificent structure was a twisted elegant mass. Every time Jessica let her eyes travel across the hallowed, vine-covered structure and iridescent twisted towers, she couldn't escape the feeling the castle was alive. Like an ancient matriarch, she grounded all of the castlefolk to their home.

Taking a moment to glance at the castle was a costly mistake.

Wadjette circled again, grabbed the second ribbon, and leaned in just enough to shove Jessica off balance. Tumbling from Frostfire, Jessica struck the grass. She tried to roll with the fall, but took a face full of dirt instead.

Jessica rubbed the grit from her eyes. Blood streaked her hands.

"Jess, if you actually paid attention, you would be better," Wadjette admonished. The girls were the same age, yet Wadjette possessed a maturity that made her seem older.

"It's not that easy for me. I have a million things on my plate."

"There are no plates here, just you and Frostfire, me and Racewind. You let your focus get scattered."

Her rider lost, Frostfire took the opportunity as break time. Tossing her head, she trotted across the pasture to the water trough. Jessica glared at her rude mount. Other bicorns would wait patiently by their fallen riders. Frostfire never cared.

Wadjette dismounted and offered her friend a hand.

"How bad am I bleeding?" Jessica asked, taking Wadjette's palm.

Peering closely, the panther girl assessed the wound.

"Not bad, just a scrape."

"Hey Jessica! Jess!"

Penrik leaned over the fence. He was an ailurian boy, a few years younger than Jessica. His fur was white and spotted like a calico. He sported a distinctive brown patch of color surrounding one eye.

"How did that dirt taste?" he laughed.

"Come over here and I'll show you," Jessica brushed the dust from her sparring suit.

"No thanks. Your cousin needs you to come inside."

"See, this is what I mean," Jessica glared at Wadjette. "I couldn't even finish this practice session. Somebody needs me for something else."

Jessica whistled to Frostfire. The mare looked up at her mistress, then proceeded to graze on the tall spring grass along the fence.

"You mind taking care of Frost so I can go inside?" Jessica asked.

"Not a problem. Spar tomorrow afternoon, same time?"

"Yeah," Jessica said. "No, wait I have this summer college prep meeting."

"What do you need to do to prepare for college? Isn't your regular school enough?"

Wadjette tried to understand the customs of Earth and frequently questioned them. The ailurian meant no insult, but her question irked Jessica.

"If I could quit high school, I would, but my mother would kill me."

Penrik hopped the fence and approached. "I can help with Frost."

Seeing the young man, the red bicorn darted in the opposite direction. Penrik ran after the beast and Wadjette rolled her eyes in disbelief.

"You're going to get kicked," Jessica warned.

Wadjette took Racewind's reins and started walking towards Frostfire, whickering softly to get the mare's attention. Frostfire heeded the panther girl's call, much to Jessica's chagrin.

"I almost had her," Penrik frowned.

Wadjette shook her head with a tiny smile. Wadjette's smiles were always small. It wasn't that the girl was sad, she simply lived with a stoic expression. "You almost had a hoof stamped on your head."

Penrik shrugged.

Wadjette and Penrik had been friends for a very long time, both raised on the streets of Rockwood when the Castle had been locked under an energy field. Where Wadjette was serious, Penrik was always smiling. Wadjette worked diligently. Penrik was happy to find shortcuts.

"Where can I find my cousin?" Jessica asked, walking towards the equipment shed to drop off her gear.

"He's waiting for you in his library, but he's in a foul mood," Penrik warned her. "Really, really foul."

***

Jessica opened the heavy wooden side door of the castle, not too eager to speak to her cousin. She walked into the cool, dark back hallway. Stone walls transitioned to wooden panels, and then eventually to the white stucco of the two-story foyer. Spring breeze wafted through the open windows.

A little more than two years ago, the castle had been a dead dusty vermin-infested decrepit grave. With the return of the castlefolk, the halls were scrubbed clean.

Passing paintings and decorative sculptures, Jessica cut through the busy kitchen, hoping to pick up a snack on the way to Teren. Fresh baked bread enriched the air with its alluring aroma.

The impressive kitchens of Aurumice boasted a collection of three large yellow rooms. Exposed wooden beams bordered the ceilings. Massive brick ovens were built into the walls, with open grills and stone chimneys that stretched upwards. The room was filled with large tables of stone and wood, each a designated work area. Against the walls were metal basins and deep stone sinks.

Mixed amongst the Aurumician fixtures were an odd conglomerate of objects from earth. A fan from the 1950s occupied a rusty cart, always blowing air like a diligent workhorse. Three white Kitchen Aid mixers were lined up neatly on a stone table, plugged into a power strip that snaked up to an outlet.

In one corner was an orange porcelain electric oven with coil-top burners. Jessica had no idea how or why anyone would bother to bring such a large appliance across the dimensional portal known as the Gate.

The teen walked by trays of neat little loaves of bread. In a mock theft, Jessica grabbed a small hot fresh bun and hid it behind her back, grinning at Eve La'Roch as she passed through.

Aden, Eve's young son, was learning how to roll bread dough from Jiberty, who himself was doing a terrible job keeping the loaves a similar size. The tall lion-faced man was an expert craftsman, but a terrible baker.

Standing on a stool, Aden leaned over the table. He was barely eight years old, but he worked without question. It was the way of the castlefolk. Everyone had a job, but most people were placed on rotation to cook, clean, and stand guard. Even Jessica's cousin Teren, leader of the castle, spent time each week mucking stalls.

Jessica examined Jiberty's work.

"You know Cookie's going to yell at you when he sees that tray."

"Little girl, I'm not the one Cookie's about to yell at," Jiberty replied with a good-natured smirk.

"Jessica! Jessica! JESSICA!"

"Escape from Cookie while you can," Jiberty murmured.

Jessica liked the castle cook. Rotund and jovial, the tiger-man was the head chef and kept the kitchens constantly running. His recipes had been passed down from hundreds of years of Aurumician chefs. Most importantly, he had an impeccable eye for quality, overseeing every detail of every meal for over a hundred people.

"The freezer isn't cooling, could you take a look at it?" Cookie asked, "Also, can you bring me blueberries? It's blueberry season in your world, isn't it?"

"Yeah," Jessica said. The seasons of Earth and Centernia differed by one. Though it was Centernian spring, on earth it was the height of summer.

"How much do you need?"

"Three bushels?"

Jessica grimaced, blueberries weren't cheap.

"Maybe, that'll cost a lot."

"Well, if not, that's fine. What about my freezer?"

"I'm on my way to see what my cousin needs. I'll come back with my tools."

"We have a lot stored in there, it can't go to waste!"

"How much is a lot? Is the air circulating like it should?"

The freezer was a large walk-in cooler, cobbled together from six decades of refrigerator parts from Earth. There were so many places the system could fail.

Biting into the roll, Jessica pulled open the freezer door, gripping the heavy metal handle. Peering in, she saw shelves packed tight and crates of food piled high on the floor.

"Cookie! I warned you!" Jessica was dismayed. "Do you really need all of this in here?"

Jessica looked at the temperature gauge. The thermometer was from Earth, but years ago someone had written Madiernian numbers alongside the English ones. Cookie was right, the temperature was reading at thirty-eight degrees.

Jessica's eyes scanned the shelves.

"You really don't need to freeze the dried peppers, do you? And that butter can go down in the cellars, can't it?"

"Yes, but it's less work to have it up here."

"Cookie, you've got a dozen people in the kitchen every day! You've gotta use the freezer for the really important things, like the meat. So many of these things can go down to the cellars!"

"I know, I know…"

"Why is the wine in here? If those bottles are too full they'll shatter."

"Your cousin wanted a wine…thing...ah, wine slushy?"

"Ugh, why did my mother show him one of those things?" Jessica sighed. "Just try moving a few things, but I'll be back to see if there's anything actually wrong, okay?"

"But he asked for a slushy…"

"You tell my cousin I said no unnecessary things in the freezer, and if he has a problem, he'll have a problem with me, not you."

Jessica slammed the door with a resounding thud.

"I'll be back," she promised, grabbing two rolls and leaving the kitchen before Cookie could come up with another request.

If the freezer was a problem, she looked forward to figuring it out. Though Jessica had a steady rotation of chores like everyone else, fixing things was the one job she felt she excelled at. Her friend Nico had taught her basics for keeping the electrical system of the castle in repair. In his absence, she had learned so much more, and discovered that the work he had done was sometimes haphazard and questionable. But Jessica had access to tools and supplies from Earth, as well as the internet.

Strolling through the Rosewood hall, the teen passed the nautical-themed carvings and statuary. Her mother was walking in the opposite direction of the upper balcony, stopping short upon seeing her daughter.

"Jessi! What are you still doing here?!"

"What?! I know I'm supposed to find Teren!"

"Come here, I need to talk to you," Lily gestured quickly. Blonde hair greying with age, her mother was still a formidable warrior and a weather witch. Most people feared her, and for that reason, Jessica took a little bit of humor in being obstinate.

"What do you want?" Jessica called up.

"Come here, I'm not shouting across the hallway!"

Jessica sighed, trekking up the glossy wooden staircase, the soreness in her muscles protesting. She had hit the ground harder than she had thought.

"What?"

"Why are you still here?" Lily's voice lowered. "Your hair is covered in dirt, you've got blood on your forehead, and I'm supposed to drive you to your father's house in less than an hour!"

"You made me walk all the way up here to tell me that?"

18

"I couldn't exactly shout it, now could I? You want the whole castle to hear?"

"I really don't think people are going to care," Jessica quipped.

The people of Centernia had a prejudice against the idea of divorce. With the exception of death or incarceration, by their societal views, there was no way to break a marriage. Lily had lied to the people of Aurumice. She'd told them she wasn't sure who Jessica's father was and she had never been married. Being a bastard was less shameful than being divorced.

"They would talk more than you think," Lily snapped.

Jessica shrugged.

"Castlefolk gossip about *everyone*."

"I would prefer not to be the topic of rumor. Jess, please. You don't understand how the Aurumicians would look down on me. Now will you go home and wash up? You can't be late for dinner!"

"Okay, okay, I get it. Teren wanted me for something first."

"Quickly. Every time you're late, your dad asks too many questions. And clean up that scrape on your forehead. Cover it with a Band-Aid and say it's a zit."

Jessica ran her finger across the wound.

"I don't think that's going to fly. I can't say I was hurt sparring with Wadjette. Who kicked my ass again, because I don't have enough time to practice, because I have to spend my time going to stupid dinners back home."

"Dinner isn't stupid, your father barely sees you."

"And whose fault is that?"

"Keep talking, and you're going to need more than one Band-Aid."

"Castle rules, can't hit me outside of the sparring fields." Jessica smirked at her mother as she walked away. It was only a half-jest. Jessica's childhood memories were peppered with back-handed slaps. Her relationship with her mother was improving, but it was still antagonistic.

Traveling through several hallways, Jessica finally came to her cousin's door and knocked.

There was no need to even announce herself, Teren could sense her emotions and her presence before she even touched the door.

Sunlight radiated into the large circular room. On every wall was a tall bookshelf, stretching upwards to a ceiling made of a large stained glass dome. In the center of the room was a gleaming wood table surrounded by a dozen chairs. The cold blue marble floor shimmered with veins of copper and amethyst threaded throughout its speckled surface.

Jessica hoped her boots weren't too muddy.

As with all of Teren's private quarters, there was not a speck of dust to be seen.

Teren sat at the table, folders and papers arranged in neat piles in front of him. He was a pale gaunt man, his hair silvery white despite being only a few years older than Jessica. It was tied back neatly at the nape of his neck. He wore a dark blue jacket and tall black riding boots, a sign he had just returned from a trip or was about to leave.

"You called?" Jessica took a wooden swivel seat. Teren nodded, shifting through a few stacks of papers, not looking up.

Jessica twirled in the chair, looking up at the flower burst ceiling. If she spun just fast enough, the glass formed interesting colors like a kaleidoscope.

"Could you not do that?"

Jessica slowed and took a bite from the bread. Crumbs fell to the table and the teen herded them into a neat pile with her index finger.

Teren looked up, glaring.

"Must you try to irk me? You know I can wipe that smug smile from your face?"

"Yes, and I'm certain you won't."

Teren was a *Sinari*, one of the forbidden mages. The young man could sense and manipulate the emotions of others without their knowledge. He was the glue that held the castle together. Despite being so critical, his life was always in danger. If anyone found out his secret, Castle Nova and the mages would hunt him down.

"What did you need me for?"

"Vex Chezidian is leveling fines against Aurumice for our power usage, again."

"Can we just pay them? If we turned off the power, the castlefolk would revolt."

Teren pushed a piece of paper across the table into Jessica's view.

His cousin sat up, joviality gone.

"That's quite a large number for municipal fine."

"Yes, it is. And it will continue to grow."

Castle Aurumice had a tenuous connection with the surrounding city of Trabalis. Hundreds of years ago, its presence had built the city. Trabalis had once been prosperous land, electrified and modern. Graveerians had attacked, destroyed the power grid, and brought the city to its knees. Like many other cities in the continent of Madierna, the government chose not to rebuild. Instead, they outlawed all major uses of electricity.

"What did you call me for?" Jessica grew worried. "You don't want me to actually turn off the power to the castle?"

"Fighting Trabalis is pointless. I think it's time to revise our strategy. We need to convince Vex Chezidian and the council that they should overturn the law. We need to find a way to bring them technology that will be so irresistible, they could not refuse. What would it take to bring power to the city?"

"That's a bit of a challenge. You do understand our power source is magical, right? And I have no clue how it works. I've read Nico's notes a dozen times, it doesn't make any sense. It's not like the electricity from Earth. I think it just comes out of the foundation of the castle and somehow doesn't kill us."

"I know that, Jessica," Teren glared. "I'm asking what else could you bring us of Earth? A generator?"

"For enough power to be impressive, we would need gas. I'm too scared to try to bring gas through the dimensional Gate. Maybe we could do something with a wind turbine or a solar panel. The Earth coffers are a little low, but I could build them up for this project."

Every time Jessica needed to buy a supply of something for the castle, she would take something of Aurumice and list it on the internet. Anything would sell, the stranger the better. No one seemed to care for finely made blankets or decorative candles, but when she would post a 'miniature dragon skull' the money rolled in. Buyers had no idea they were purchasing real bone from a meadowdasher dragonette.

The same worked in reverse for Centernia. Velcro, zippers, and plastic gadgets all flooded into the Trabalis marketplace. It was

ROSE CATHERINE KHAN

frustrating all the same, no matter how much Aurumice earned, Trabalis always found a new way to tax the castle.

"We need something. I thought for sure by now we would have brought Trabalis to our side, but Vex Chezidian is a difficult man to convince. Think on it. We cannot pay fines like this over electricity. I don't want the daywatch trampling through the castle forcing us to turn it off."

Jessica heaved a sigh of frustration, not sure how to solve her cousin's problem.

"Well think on it."

The teen could feel a tension headache creeping across her forehead.

"Oh, I have something for you to sell," Teren turned the conversation. "It may catch someone's eye."

He set a folded piece of fabric on the table and delicately unwrapped it. Inside were three little insects with bright blue bodies shimmering like translucent jewels. Their wings had an equally eye-catching iridescence flecked in gold.

"Beautiful! What are they made of?"

"They're real. Dead, of course. I am not totally certain what they are, they look like needlewasps to me. Gross parasites, but these are simply beautiful."

"Yeah," Jessica agreed. Centernia would never cease to amaze her.

"You may want to ask Corwin what they are, but I'm certain if you mount them in a decorative box, they will catch someone's eye."

"I've never tried to sell an insect online," Jessica remarked. "I have no idea if there's a market for them, even ones this pretty."

"I would have never thought there to be a market for dragonette skeletons, but that proved surprising."

"I'll see if they sell, thank you," Jessica wrapped up the tiny insects. "I need to head out. I have dinner at my dad's house, which reminds me, no wine slushies."

"Excuse me?"

"That freezer is way too full. I made Cookie take everything out that didn't need to be frozen. Everything."

"But one bottle of wine…"

"No, you're not special, remember?"

Teren glared.

Her cousin walked a precarious line. Castle Aurumice was not governed by a monarchy. It was run like an estate, owned by the family of Nicoveren Aristo Verdian.

But Nico was gone, taken away to the Mines of Briken because of ridiculous taxes. He gave control of the castle to Teren, who ruled the estate with a careful balance. The castle needed a strong leader, one who was respected. To earn the castlefolk's respect, Teren could not let them think that he was above them.

Even if it meant not having wine slushies.

"Can you bring me a little freezer?" Teren pleaded.

"Yes, but I have bigger priorities, like a radio. This castle desperately needs communication. I'm trying to figure out how to build a big system."

"You have an extra fridge in your garage."

It was true, there was a little dorm-sized mini fridge in Jessica's garage on Earth. It was a gift from her stepmom.

"But that's supposed to be for college. If Carrie Anne knew it was for wine slushies, she would not approve."

Teren scowled.

"If you go to college more than a semester, I will eat my boot."

Jessica glared. "I'm going to college and I am taking my mini-fridge with me. Now, I really gotta go to dinner, but I'll see you tomorrow."

"Actually, I am leaving tonight."

"For the Mines?"

Her cousin nodded.

Teren had been working tirelessly to find a way to free their friend without causing a stir. The city of Trabalis expected Nico to work off the impossible tax debt accrued by Castle Aurumice. If Nico were to escape, the magistrates would be outraged and vengeful.

"Safe travels, I hope you find a way to free him."

"As do I."

CHAPTER 3

Two hours later in the suburbs of Pennsylvania, Lily's rusted Jeep Cherokee backed down the driveway as Jessica walked up the brick pavers to her father's upscale colonial. She punched in a code on the keypad. The lock whirred, releasing with a click.

She stepped into the brightly lit house, only forty minutes late.

Stephen Ravenwolfe's home was the latest in trendy suburban design, though Jessica was certain it was at the insistence of her stepmother. A classy brown ceramic tiled the floors of her father's house. There was something Italian about it, but Jessica could never recall the name. The carpets of the house were white, an achievement that wouldn't last an hour in Castle Aurumice. Somehow Carrie Anne kept all of the carpets bright and plush. Tasteful paintings of nature and inspirational quotes rounded out the décor of the home. Above the coat closet was a bible verse:

By wisdom a house is built, and by understanding it is established; by knowledge the rooms are filled with all precious and pleasant riches.
Proverbs 24:3-4

"Hello, I'm here," Jessica called. Her nose picked up the aroma of chicken.

She slipped out of her sneakers and set her bag by the door. Her father appeared in the hallway, drying his hands on a paper towel. Stephen Ravenwolfe was a tall thin man. His hair had once been pure black, but it was starting to streak in silver.

"Hey, Jess," he embraced her, kissing her forehead. "Got a little scrape there?" he asked.

Her father was always observant of her injuries. Which was unfortunate for Jessica, because she always got a little banged up in the castle.

"I tripped and hit my head on the countertop."

"Oh, goodness Jessica," Carrie Anne appeared in the hallway. Her stepmother was thin and tired. She was a mousy-haired woman, tall and always perfectly dressed. Carrie Anne was the kindest stepmother Jessica could have asked for. She was soft-spoken and polite. Ever since Jessica was a little girl, Carrie Anne had tried very hard to make her feel welcomed and loved.

"You need to be more careful," she warned, pulling Jessica into a tight hug.

Jessica shrugged, walking into the kitchen. Carrie Anne's cooking was excellent. Every meal she ever made was a balanced medley. Jessica paused, instead of Carrie Anne's usual organic perfectly-balanced dinner, the table was set with fast-food fried chicken.

"Your father was in charge of dinner tonight," Carrie Anne sighed.

Jessica's sister Ashlin sat in the living room, engaged in her handheld game.

"Ashlin, wash your hands for dinner," their father commanded.

Ashlin nodded, tossing down her game and walking past Jessica without acknowledging her sister. The younger girl was the mirror of her mother.

"Hey, Ash!" Jessica greeted.

"Hi," Ashlin mumbled.

"Wow, you're in a bad mood," Jessica commented, washing her hands in the kitchen sink. Ashlin was no longer a cute little energetic girl. She was becoming an obnoxiously irritable teenager. Jessica wondered if she had been so moody when she was Ashlin's age.

Carrie Anne served drinks as they all settled down for dinner. They embraced hands as her father led the blessing. Ticking rhythmically, the bamboo-framed clock punctuated his reverent words. The prayers had once annoyed Jessica, but she now found solace in them. It reminded her of the Holy Circus and the devoted followers of Goddess Aurora, the primary religion in Centernia.

Jessica took a large helping of mashed potatoes and three pieces of chicken when she noticed Ashlin hadn't moved. Her little sister just stared blankly.

"What's wrong with you?" Jessica asked, reaching for the baked beans.

Ashlin remained mute.

"Jessi, tell me, have you picked all of your classes for senior year?" Carrie Anne asked, oddly ignoring Ashlin's silence.

"Yeah, I decided a while ago."

"Did you decide to rejoin orchestra?"

Jessica shook her head, feeling an old wound ache in her heart. After she had destroyed her friendship with Felicia Lee, the orchestra room felt like an unwelcome territory.

"It would help with your college applications," her father said. "Speaking of which, how are those?"

"Not really making much progress," Jessica poked the chicken on her plate. "Still thinking engineering, can't decide which one."

"Are you applying to MIT?" Carrie Anne asked. "You really should."

"I'm sorry, my grades just aren't that good."

"Maybe if you had been a little better focused," her father stated, glaring at Ashlin.

"What? What are you looking at me for?" the girl balked.

"You spend so much time with games. I don't want to be having this conversation with you in three years."

"Whatever," Ashlin mumbled.

"I'm looking at some schools in New York, there's one in Rochester," Jessica said, "but I don't know about being able to afford it."

"Jess, don't worry about that part," her father said. "Just worry about getting in, then we will figure it out. Maybe you'll get scholarships."

Jessica was very torn. On one hand, the idea of going away sounded exciting. If she had a real job, she could help her mother pay off the mortgage and keep the Gate safe. On the other, it meant she wouldn't be able to travel to Centernia so easily. There was only one Gate she had access to and it was in her basement.

Her friend Jared had told her there were other Gates in the United States, but they were closely guarded.

"Ashlin, dear, please eat your dinner," Carrie Anne softly encouraged.

The young teen stabbed the plate angrily.

"You gonna tell her or keep lying?" Ashlin muttered.

Suddenly the fried chicken was cold and greasy.

"Ashlin, it's not a lie," their father became angry. "We were waiting until we had more information."

"More information?" Jessica asked. "More information about what?"

"Jessica," Carrie Anne said slowly. "This is really hard for us, but I have breast cancer."

"Oh," Jessica looked down. Her dinner became impossible to eat. "Is that treatable?"

"They'll try a combination of surgery and chemotherapy."

"Does that usually work?" Jessica asked.

"We are hopeful it will," her father replied, taking Carrie Anne's hand.

"It's seventy percent survival," Ashlin shoved away from the table. "I looked it up, it's terrible!"

Bursting into tears, the young teen ran from the table.

Jessica couldn't think of what to say. Carrie Anne did not deserve cancer. The woman ate healthy and went to the gym more frequently than she attended church. She was loving, kind and did everything for everyone.

Jessica suddenly felt guilty of not replying to Carrie Anne's constant text messages.

"Honey, I know this is hard," Carrie Anne consoled, "but I am really going to start looking to you to be more support for your sister. She's always had difficulty adjusting to things and this is going to hit her badly."

Stephen stood, frustrated.

"Ashlin, get back down here!" he shouted.

A door slammed in response. It was forceful enough to rattle the picture frames in the upstairs hallway.

"I'll go talk to her, just give me a minute," Jessica left the table to walk upstairs. As she ascended, her feet sunk into the plush beige carpet.

"Ash?" she knocked on her sister's door.

"Go away."

"Come on and eat, you're upsetting your mom."

"Exactly. *My* mom, not yours. Go away."

"That's not fair, Ash. I was five when dad remarried, I barely remember my life without Carrie Anne."

"Then why do you call her Carrie Anne and not mom?"

Jessica startled at the question, struggling for an answer that was truthful but not hurtful. Ashlin did not wait for a response.

"You don't understand, and you should leave me alone!"

Feeling terrible, Jessica knew she had to say something but didn't want to beg outside the door. No doubt their father would come upstairs and yell.

Instead, she took a more unconventional approach. She abandoned Ashlin's door and walked into her own bedroom, the room she hardly ever occupied. Carrie Anne had decorated it tastefully with bird motifs in neutral browns.

Opening the window, Jessica popped the screen off and climbed onto the roof. She inhaled the humid summer evening. Looking out, the suburban neighborhood was a picturesque sea of green with its pristine yards.

The roof was a little bit narrow and steep, but not the worst thing Jessica had ever climbed. If she was ailurian, like Savina or Wadjette, she could have jumped to the ground without much chance of injury.

Jessica walked across the roof to her sister's window. Her socks made it easy to grip the warm shingles. Peering inside, she saw Ashlin sitting on her bed, staring at her laptop. The window was open but the screen was securely in place.

Jessica took out her pocketknife and started to pry off the aluminum frame from the outside.

Ashlin startled at the noise

"Jessi, what the hell are you doing!"

Ashlin dropped the laptop and ran over to the window.

"The door was locked," Jessica explained, carefully prying the screen loose.

"You'll get in trouble! Or fall!"

"It's not too far down. You could just unlock your door and I won't need to break in."

Jessica popped the screen from its track, bending it a little in the process. She hoped her father wouldn't notice. She pulled it away, climbed inside her sister's bedroom and proceeded to wedge the screen back into place.

"Why do you always do these things?" Ashlin was pretending to be horrified, but it was obvious she was impressed.

"You wouldn't listen to me otherwise."

Jessica felt little roof bits stuck to the bottoms of her socks. She pulled them off and sat in the purple office chair, flicking the tiny bits of roof into the black trashcan. A white spray-painted skull was stenciled on the side of the metal basket, clearly Ashlin's work.

Ashlin's room had been redecorated again, it seemed to be a yearly project of Carrie Anne's. First the room had been baby pink rabbits, then sea creatures, a few years of princesses, followed by fairies, then fairy princess pirates, then space. Now the room was starting to take on a darker life suited to Ashlin's preferences, but still within Carrie Anne's rules. The walls were striped black and purple below a black chair rail. Jessica recalled the fight between Ashlin and Carrie Anne over the color. First Ashlin wanted black walls, which was promptly vetoed. The teen had counter argued with black and purple stripes. It ended in the chair rail compromise.

Jessica had to admit, the room looked like it came from a magazine. The plush carpeting was a deep purple and had the distinctive scent of fresh new carpet. Ashlin's desk was striped with a black and white Mackenzie Childs pattern. Jessica had listened to Carrie Anne debate which desk to purchase for an entire weekend, which is the only reason she knew the name of the designer. Carrie Anne would have been horrified to see Jessica's bedroom at Lily's house. It was vintage, and not in a good way.

"You're never afraid of anything." Ashlin lamented. "You even have a knife. It's not a pocketknife, that's like a real knife. Mom would freak out if I tried to carry a knife."

"I'm afraid of a lot of things," Jessica assured.

Sting lizards, starflower adders, mom's lightning....

"Robbers, spiders, airplanes."

"Jess, last month you squashed a spider with your bare fingers."

"I didn't mean to squish it! I was just going to pick it up, and put it back outside in its spidery home."

"You're not scared of spiders, Jess."

"Yeah, so? Want to go eat dinner and stop interrogating me?"

"I didn't want to cry in front of Mom again."

"Oh."

Jessica felt awful and struggled to say something helpful.

"Dad went and ordered the unhealthiest dinner imaginable. You can't miss this historic event."

"What am I going to do if Mom dies?"

"Gain twenty pounds from Dad's cooking?"

Ashlin did not crack a fraction of a smile. Jessica felt terrible. Somehow sarcasm always worked for her friend Jared, but Jessica lacked the gift.

"Sorry I sound like a jerk. What do you want me to say, Ash? This sucks, it sucks a lot. And you're right, she's your mom first, but she's my mom too. You just gotta be thankful they caught this thing before it was any worse, and the chemo works. A lot of people get cancer, and a lot of people beat it. Carrie Anne is fit, and we've got good health insurance. She has a fighting chance."

Ashlin rubbed her eye, trying to obscure a tear.

"But what if she doesn't? What if she doesn't see me graduate high school? What if she doesn't even live until Christmas?"

The girl's voice cracked.

Jessica panicked. She was bad at sarcasm and worse at being comforting.

She reached for her sister's hand.

"Ashlin, trust me. I have seen stranger things in this world than you can imagine and awesome things. Just don't focus on the bad, okay? You focus on the bad and then you're just going to get miserable, and your mom will be miserable. If your mom is miserable, she won't be able to heal herself as well. So, the best thing you can do is not be sad."

"But I am!"

Jessica's shoulders slumped. Her words of wisdom weren't much better than what her own mother would have said. Lily's life philosophy was to not show feelings, pretend everything's okay, and not talk about terrible things.

"You can text me when you're upset. I'll listen."

"Promise you won't vanish on me?"

"Where am I going that you can't message me?"

"College. You'll get busy with college and forget about me."

"I promise Ashlin, I'm here. Now, dinner?"

"Will you get me a knife?" Ashlin smiled.

I'll get you a knife, I'll get you a knife of the castlefolk.

The thought sprung to Jessica's mind, but she didn't speak the words. In Aurumician tradition, those who became castlefolk received a tattoo and a custom knife in an elaborate mark ceremony. Ashlin would be in awe.

"Yeah, I'll see if I can get you a pocketknife, but you can't tell your mom," Jessica knew she couldn't bring her sister across the Gate. Centernia was amazing, but it would be too dangerous.

CHAPTER 4

Toxic clouds stretched oppressively for miles over the hilly mining town of Briken.

Black soot coated the landscape, leaving a dark film on every twig and pebble. Spiny grass sprung up between the stones, their exterior a deterrent against the few mammals who struggled to survive in the harsh environment.

On the top of a hill sat a tiny decrepit house, hidden behind overgrown trees. A little trail of wood smoke wafted up from its chimney. It was early evening, but the sky was so grey it was impossible to see the sun.

Inside the shed, a blonde man sat, balancing a knife on its point.

Jared had spent far too many nights alone in this small cabin, and was eager to be gone. He had never lived in such a cramped space. Barren and poorly constructed, the hovel consisted of a common room, two small bedrooms, a privy and an indoor well. The water quality was poor and not much better than the air.

A tall beautiful mahogany woman paced in front of the twenty-one-year-old. Her ears were lynx-like and displayed a glinting sundry of earrings. Her shirt was as blue as the ocean, adorned with intricate gold piping, and cut in a manner not conservative by any stretch of the imagination. Jared didn't understand why Savina chose to dress as if on a beach vacation when they were stuck in a miserable hellhole. It was just another aspect of the woman's personality that irritated him.

"Jared," Savina's voice was rich with the accent of the Galbrian sea, "how far away is he? It's been nearly a day since you sent that message! Did you pay for the right courier?"

"Next time you do it yourself," Jared muttered.

Blinking, the young man reached out with his mind. He had the gift of being able to see through the eyes of others. In recent years, it had become easier for him to know whose eyes he was borrowing.

Jared squinted, he could *see* the little shed from the outside through the eyes of a visitor. He didn't bother to answer Savina, instead he put his feet up on the table, knowing it would annoy her.

A key jingled and the door opened.

A man cloaked in black entered the small cabin, his fine tailored black boots creaking ever so slightly. The visitor pulled back his hood exposing sand-coated glass goggles and a heavily wrapped scarf. He removed the goggles first, revealing striking amethyst eyes and a pale white face. He unwrapped the scarf carefully and set it on a hook next to the door. His hair was thin and long, tied back at his neck, in his ears were modest sapphire earrings.

Jared smiled. He had a lover back at Castle Nova, but their relationship was open, freeing him to browse. Teren was attractive, very attractive, and he had a reputation around Aurumice for being in many different beds. Jared and Savina were two of the small number who knew his secret abilities to sense and project emotions upon anyone around him. Which meant he obviously knew Jared's desires but chose to not act upon him. This confused Jared.

Savina embraced Teren, stealing a quick kiss.

"Praise the Goddess, you're finally here. *Za falla cal ca magali daya.*"

Teren seemed disinterested in her affections, and wordlessly he sat in the chair across from Jared. His eyes were hollow with exhaustion. Jared felt bad for the man, taking on the weight of the castle, always sorting out fights, convincing people to work together. Managing the castle robbed years from him, even though the young man was barely older than Jared.

"Nico's presence has vanished from the mines," Teren stated

Jared affirmed. "That's why I sent for you, I haven't been able to see through Nico's eyes for four days, or see him through anyone else's eyes. Is he there?"

For the past year, a steady rotation of their most trusted friends had cycled through the small hut, trying to fish information from the prison and mining town. Nico was trapped in servitude, and the castlefolk were not keen to wait for time to release him.

Savina and Jared spent the most time at the outpost. Jared used his sight abilities to see through Nico's eyes, assuring he was alive. Torturous horrors from inside the prison haunted Jared's mind and he tried to squash his recollection. Every day was a new coal black hell and he didn't know how Nico remained sane.

They had been trying desperately to free Nico from the mines without endangering the castlefolk. Certainly Teren could influence guards to let Nico go, but the city of Trabalis would demand another castlefolk suffer in his place.

For endless hours, Jared studied the Mines through the eyes of those who were inside. He watched the workers toil, excavating rock, sorting it, sending it to the furnaces where a blue mineral was extracted. The ore was turned into small blocks, then sent on its way by train.

There was only one piece of the process that Jared could not see. Whatever went on in a small nondescript grey building with a single blue door. Very few entered or exited, and those who did were difficult for Jared to follow with his mage powers. He just could not see through the eyes of anyone inside building.

It was a frustrating mystery.

Everything was frustrating.

Savina poured tea from the hot kettle. The lynx-eared woman set the porcelain cup in front of Teren, and kept silent. Jared watched the man carefully. They knew he was reaching out with his emotions, trying to find the unique signature that denoted their friend.

After a while, Jared grew impatient.

"Well, am I right. Is Nico dead?"

Savina shot him a venomous look.

"Oh come off it, Vina, you were thinking the same question!"

Teren took a slow sip of the tea, shaking his head.

"I do not believe so. When Misa died, I knew it. When my parents died, I knew it. If Nico were dead, I am certain even as far as Castle Aurumice, I would have known."

Savina brought her hand to her heart, making the sign of the Goddess. It annoyed Jared.

"But those others were your blood relatives," Jared pointed out.

"No. I am certain I would know it if Nico were dead. Anytime castlefolk have died, I sense the ripple. The castlemarks connect us, even at a great distance. It's a different feeling, but it's there. It feels like someone punched a hole in a wall and the cold air blows through."

"Well, if you're so sure he's not dead, then where does this leave us?"

"I already told you what we should do," Savina snarled. "We should have gone after the last train that left, the one that went south four days ago."

"We don't know if he was on that train. It could be as far as Gill Post right now."

"*Ma jar calla vi!* You could have tracked him. What good are your mage powers if you fail to use them? You are lazy, you just want to give up! You want Nico to vanish so you can go back to your stupid Polaris Academy!"

"Lazy?" Jared sat up. "Lazy? I was nearly expelled for helping Misa open the Gate! Polaris was my entire life, it was all I had ever known and I lost it all for your castle! I have given you the past year sitting out in this forsaken shack watching things I never want to see again, all for your stupid Lord of Aurumice. I'm not even castlefolk!"

"You rotten—"

Teren held a hand up, silencing Savina, and turned his glare to Jared.

"Why did you not follow the train?"

Jared chose his words carefully, fully aware Teren was reading his emotions. Jared had not signed up to live the rest of his life constantly traveling to this disgusting outpost for weeks on end, fishing for information in a decrepit town, inhaling chemicals likely to shorten his years by a decade.

"I didn't realize he was missing from the mines at first, he had been gone maybe a day before I noticed. I wasn't sure, you know he's been knocked unconscious before. If he's asleep or out, I can't see anything. I checked his cell mates, I couldn't see him through their eyes, but that's not always reliable. I waited for about a day before I sent word to you."

Teren looked to Savina.

"Do not blame him," his voice was quiet. Jared was relieved. Teren was always the smooth diplomat.

Savina crossed her arms and settled into a tall wooden chair.

"Fine. I will not blame him. What are we doing now?"

"No point staying in Briken any longer," Teren replied. "We know the route of that train, I could travel out, see if I can find him. My range has increased quite substantially as of late. You can go back to Aurumice."

"Can you figure out direction yet?" Jared asked.

Teren shook his head.

"It takes some trial and error, moving closer usually is all I need, but there are other factors that skew it. It's the best we have."

"I should go with you," Jared volunteered, "He could move a mile in one direction before you realized you've gone a mile in the other."

"Go back to Aurumice, you've done enough, and we're probably already too late."

"Teren, please, hope is not lost," Savina encouraged. "The goddess finds ways."

Teren remained silent. Jared knew his friend wasn't very religious, but likely he did not want to argue with Savina.

"We should tell the others of the change in plans?" Savina switched topics.

"Tell Lily and tell Kaity. No one else needs to know until we understand more."

"And Jessica?"

Teren had insisted they be cautious in what they told the teen. Teren's Aunt Lily was incredibly concerned that her daughter be kept positive and hopeful, so she could focus on graduating high school. The elder castlefolk didn't tell Jessica when Nico was tortured. They didn't mention the whips or the hot irons that seared into the man's skin. When two of Nico's fingers were removed, they kept their vow of silence. Jared had watched in agony through Nico's eyes as two dull metal shards wedged into each joint until they were separated and the fingers removed from each individual segment.

Jared had seen it all. Teren had felt it all. Between the two of them, they had a very clear understanding of the horrors of Briken.

"Well?" Savina questioned.

"I will tell her myself when the time is right. I do not wish to jeopardize all she has worked for."

"Shall we leave tonight?"

"No, I am too exhausted. Pack your personal belongings, but leave everything else, we may return to this place. We leave at dawn."

Teren kicked off his boots, abandoning them in the middle of the floor as he walked to the bedroom.

"I do not understand why you coddle that girl," Savina mumbled. "When I was her age, I knew the true nature of people. No one tried to dip the world in candy for me."

"Hope is a strong motivator." Teren stripped out of his shirt, not bothering to close the door. Jared did not mind.

"Once that girl graduates high school, you can have all the melancholy fun you want telling her all that we know. I want her to live in hope until that point."

"You never give me hope anymore," Savina muttered. "All I get is worry and misery and nightmares."

Teren stripped out of his dirt-coated pants and threw himself on the bed. He spoke, his face muffled by the pillow.

"Come here, Vina. I will take away your hurt, at least until you fall asleep."

"Oh, come on, this place is a shed and I don't want to go outside," Jared protested.

Savina stood, her skirts swishing. The tall woman abandoned her tea and walked into the bedroom, also not bothering to close the door. She took off her golden necklaces and bracelets, setting them upon the side table. Jared glared as she crawled into bed with Teren, nestling under the man's arm. She curled around him, her tail resting upon his chest. Jared watched curiously, arming himself with lewd comments, determined to sour any amorous behavior in the other room.

Instead, Vina relaxed into a calm state, a smile on her face.

It took Jared a moment to realize sex was not the end goal. Instead, Teren was using his mage abilities.

"Hey, *Sinari*, share the love, will ya?" Jared called out in jest.

37

Suddenly, Jared's melancholy mood and feelings of annoyance vanished. Jared felt as if he been presented with a triple layer chocolate cake, on his birthday, while standing on the tropical beaches of Therissina.

His heart trembled with the strange and wonderful elation.

Jared understood, gaining clarity to Savina's relationship with Teren. In the castle, she was always making her way to the man's bedchamber. If this was what he did for her, it was better than any carnal romp.

For long moments, Jared sat at the table, barely able to comprehend the joy in his heart. After a while, the feelings shifted from elation to warm fuzzy contentment. Now Jared felt the coziness akin to snuggling under a blanket with a book on a cold rainy afternoon.

The blonde man turned and looked in the direction of the tiny bedchamber. Savina was still curled around Teren, her eyes closed, her face serene as he wrapped his arms around her. Teren stared at Jared, his dark amethyst eyes catching the glint of the fire.

"Holy goddess, Teren," he whispered. "If I didn't know better I'd say I was stoned."

"I will warn you that I can't sustain such projections for long," Teren lectured. "It is truly like a drug."

Jared jumped to his feet.

"The Mages of the Consortium have it wrong, they should not kill your kind! There are so many lost and grieving souls who can benefit to feel a little bit of happiness, to remember what it feels like. Imagine the good you can do for the world!"

"I agree, mage," Savina murmured. For once, she stated the word *mage* without malice and spite. "Now you know why I hate Polaris Academy and your Castle Nova. They would kill the greatest joy in my life, for no reason other than their fear of him."

Opening her bright green eyes, the beautiful cat pressed against Teren's chiseled white chest. Her pupils were wide in the darkness. She beckoned to him with a single, elegant clawed finger. Jared was delighted, confused, and still aware that Teren's magic made the woman amorous.

"I am sorry I insulted you," she whispered. "You have given much to help Nico, and I regard you as a very close friend. Please rest with us."

Jared's heart was fluttering with warmth as he grabbed an extra blanket. He extinguished the tallow lamp and made his way to the cuddly nest, delighted to curl up in contentment for the first time in weeks.

CHAPTER 5

Nico awoke to a strange sensation.

For long moments, he did not move, caught in the haze of a dream.

Inhaling slowly through his nose, he realized the air was cool and light, not bitter like the Mines of Briken. His body was laid across something soft and cushioned. A sweet aroma of wood caressed his nose.

Slowly, he opened his eyes, waiting for the dream to shatter. Instead, he saw a wooden wall. Tilting his head ever slightly, he gazed upwards. Wooden ceiling beams stretched across the small room. For a moment, he thought he was in Aurumice, but realized the ceiling above his head was lower, the beams cut smaller and tighter.

His brain tried to piece together the recent past. He remembered the encounter with the warden Umbrian and the strange black-haired woman. After the conversation, the guards led him to a cell where he had sat with two other male prisoners.

Then the world became a hazy jumble.

Nico became aware of a swaying sensation, like the gentle pitch of a ship at sea. He sat up, his mind finally able to process his present surroundings.

It was a cabin, a ship's cabin.

Light filtered in through a dirty circular window. Nico found himself on a small bed set low in a wooden frame. The furniture was curiously bolted down.

Nico had not been on a ship since he was a boy. His parents would take him to the ocean, but when a ship carrying many castlefolk was lost in a storm, Aurumicians shied away from the sea travel. Nico had not thought of the lost ship in some time. With the reflections of the ocean, his mind rolled in memories of childhood and thoughts of Castle Aurumice. His sense of self crept back into his conscious along with a newfound hope.

Wherever he was, it wasn't the Mines of Briken, and for that he was grateful.

On the floor, next to the bed, sat a small basket. Inside was a crusty hunk of bread and a cup of a mead.

Nico reached out, hand trembling. It had been over a year since he had tasted bread. The ashen chunks of hard biscuits in Briken barely constituted food. Sniffing the small loaf carefully, he relished in the sweet aroma. He bit into the flakey crust, his battered teeth sinking into the soft sponginess of bread. As he chewed carefully, he could taste and smell the delicate herbs baked into the moist fresh loaf.

Unbidden, tears sprung to his eyes.

With his shaking left hand, he reached for the mug. Unable to lift it without spilling, he set down the cherished bread and with two hands lifted the mug to his lips. Fragrant and smooth, the mead possessed the sweet tang of summer fruit. He meant to sip, but instead he gulped it, his badly dehydrated body demanding the hearty liquid.

The cup emptied, he wiped his eyes and returned to the heavenly bread.

With a soft creak, the door opened.

Nico flinched out of reflex.

"I see you're awake."

It was the dark-haired woman from the mine office. She had changed into sapphire blue boots, breeches, and a blue tunic .

Nico watched her carefully, uncertain what to say. He knew social convention expected him to speak, but in the Mines, it was a punishable offense.

The stranger tilted her head, studying him as she took a seat. Crossing her long legs, she leaned forward in a wooden chair.

Nico realized that he was wearing real clothing, pants without holes, and a grey shirt with buttons. He looked down at his injured four-fingered hands. They were clean and his wounds bandaged. A hazy recent memory bubbled up in his mind, as he recalled the soothing humidity of a strange bathhouse, but the details were fuzzy.

"Any questions?" the stranger asked.

Yes, he had a thousand. Who was she? Where was he? Why did she save him?

Instead, Nico kept silent, looking down at the empty cup and half-eaten piece of bread. What if it was a trick? Perhaps Briken had developed new form of torture meant to break him further.

"Not very talkative?" she said. "Well, I will begin. My name is Zia, this is my ship. You are our temporary guest."

"Am I permitted to speak?" Nico asked, his eyes downcast.

"Yes, of course. I facilitated your purchase. I am a broker, delivering you to my client."

"Who hired you?"

"My client will prefer to explain things once we arrive. They are fairly private individuals I would say," she gave a little smile. Nico was still trying to place her accent.

Nico's stomach lurched as the ship pitched sharply to one side. The basket went sliding across the floor.

"That happens," Zia reassured. "You get used to it. Follow me, I will give you a tour."

Nico awkwardly climbed to his feet. His muscles were weak and he surmised he had been kept in a drug-induced sleep for some time. Steadying his hand on the wall, he caught his breath. Even though the air was much better than Briken, his lungs burned with embedded ash.

Nico wondered who had paid a small fortune for his release. He hoped it was Aurumice, but knew it was not. There were no bodies of water that easily connected Briken to Trabalis, it was all inland routes and a few rivers. It was unlikely they were heading towards Castle Aurumice.

"You move like an old man," Zia said. "I can't imagine you were any use as a worker."

Nico wanted to tell her that he worked every day until he could barely stand. He toiled, loading ore and heavy rock into the carts, pushing them to blistering hot furnaces, ever watchful of needlewasps.

Zia had no idea how hard he worked to evade torture.

As Nico steadied himself, he looked at the window, hoping to sneak a glance at recognizable landscape in the distance, or at least determine the climate. Instead of rolling waves, he saw blue sky and wisps of clouds.

It was strange.

Leaning forward, his curiosity overrode his sense of fear. A great flat plane of wood extended from the side of the ship. As he glanced downwards, he realized they were not on an ocean.

They were in the air.

Zia laughed behind him.

He turned around, bewildered.

"Your face!" she exclaimed. "Everyone has that reaction."

"An air ship?" he asked. "Those are…the stuff of stories…"

"Yes, they *were*."

Nico's mind reeled as he tried to grasp the scope of the ship. Zia gestured for him to follow her to the hallway. The vessel felt much like an aquatic ship, each compartment was narrow. Instead of staircases, ladders connected compartments.

Zia pointed out a small privy, followed by a tiny library with two chairs and a single window. The last stop of the short tour was a dining room, containing a small table able to seat about a dozen people.

"My crew eats two meals a day, so if you want a hot meal, that's when you get it. Listen for the chimes, the first signals the crew's dinner, you are expected to stay in your quarters and not interact with them. On the second chime, a meal will be waiting for you here. The chambers I have shown you are the extent of your access. If I find you, or hear word of you outside these four rooms, we will lock you up in an endless sleep until we reach our destination."

Nico felt no desire to cross Zia, and he actually found her to be likable.

"Do you have questions?"

Nico hesitated.

"Go on," Zia insisted.

"How long before we reach our destination?" he asked quickly.

"A few more days, and your second question?"

"How are we held aloft?" he asked. He cringed, waiting for a strike for his impunity to ask a second question.

Zia tilted her head.

"Air balloon keeps us aloft, but we are steered by nightflights," she explained. Nico knew nightflights were dragon-like creatures with leathery wings. They were very, very expensive.

Zia reached out, startling Nico.

"They really have hurt you, haven't they? Like a beat dog, the way you hunch, and shake and stare at the ground."

She placed a cool hand on his cheek. Nico instantly felt calm under her touch.

"Look at me," she said.

He hesitated.

"Look at me," she repeated.

It was the opposite of what he had been told in Briken. He had scars to prove his forgetfulness.

Nico looked up, truly seeing her face. She was younger than he had initially thought, perhaps ten years older than himself. Her eyes were beautiful and he found himself lost in their darkness.

"That's right," she soothed. "Breathe a little deeper, you are not going back to Briken."

"You will stay in these quarters? They are acceptable? Do they please you?"

Nico nodded in agreement.

"Good."

CHAPTER 6

It was only a game, but Wadjette was unrelenting on the field.

She attacked Jessica from the right, then left. Her staff was quick, and Jessica barely dodged it, rolling and drawing her knife. It had been nearly two weeks since finding out Carrie Anne had cancer. As much as the teen knew she should be supportive, she found herself spending more time in Centernia.

It was easy to ignore unpleasant problems when you had someone trying to beat you into the dirt.

The dust coated Jessica's face mask and she wiped it away with a gloved hand. It was a second too long as Wadjette was at her side again. Cringing, Jessica heard the familiar sound of a ribbon being ripped away.

She was down to one. Wadjette still had all three.

Jessica crouched as a surprising force grabbed her from behind, firmly gripping her throat. The teen couldn't focus on two attackers at once. Thrashing wildly, she fought against the second attacker. Her trachea spasmed under the intense pressure and she gasped.

Wadjette claimed the last ribbon.

The captor dropped her unceremoniously. Jessica ripped off the leathery facemask. Inhaling deeply, she sucked in a mouthful of gritty sand from the outdoor arena.

Glaring up at her second attacker, she coughed and spat.

It was her mother.

"Your spatial awareness needs work, Jessi," the older woman stated. In the sunlight, her face showed the wrinkles of stress and the years of fighting.

Jessica's throat ached.

"That wasn't fair!"

"Tell that to the next thief that corners you."

Jessica felt the sting of embarrassment as she recalled an incident from a few months ago. Teren used his unique abilities to sense her fear. Without her cousin, she may have been dead.

The teen punched the ground in frustration. The past two weeks had gone from good to sour. Carrie Anne's cancer was a heavy weight in her heart, she didn't know how to get rid of the Trabalis fines for electricity, and she hadn't won a single spar in over a month.

Wadjette extended her hand to Jessica.

"Do not let yourself be defeated," her friend encouraged. "You are better than you have ever been!"

"Yeah, well it's still not good enough," Jessica grumbled, taking Wadjette's hand.

"Lady Vance, it is good to see the years have not diminished your skill!"

They all looked up at the stranger's voice calling from across the sparring field. An ailurian man had walked onto the dusty earth. He was an aged cat, greyed and handsomely striped like a blue tiger. Leaning heavily on a cane, he carried a single satchel on his back. Behind him walked a strange pointy-eared hound, its skin white and covered in scales.

"Fentalon La'Roch!" Lily gave a wry smile. "What brings you back to the sparring fields of Aurumice?"

"There are rumors spreading across the far reaches of Madierna. They say the cursed castle has been freed of the energy field, and the castlefolk can go home. I see it's true."

The newcomer looked up at Aurumice.

"I have never been so happy to see those towers," Fentalon said. "And I am happy to see the Aurumician guard back at practice. Perhaps I have a chance at resuming leadership?"

"We already have a leader for the Aurumician Guard," Lily crossed her arms.

"Ah," replied Fentalon. "Then perhaps you should be kind to give me the honor of a spar?"

"Gladly," Lily smiled, gesturing to the rack of equipment.

Fentalon turned and gave a signal to the white beast. It sat obediently, as unmoving a statue.

Walking over to the rack, the old man shed his cloak. He was lean, and already wore plates of armor. Jessica got the impression that the older man was a little bit more than his initial appearance implied.

Jessica followed Wadjette off the field. The cat girl was strangely silent, still wearing her protective mask. They sat on the wooden bench with a few other competitors and members of the guard. Jessica silently hoped the tiger-striped cat would defeat her mom as payback for the sneak attack.

Lily rotated her knife like a pinwheel, letting the blade dance on her fingers. Sunlight glinted off the metal.

"Ribbons?" she asked.

"Stones," Fentalon replied. "Three."

Lily walked over to the supply rack.

The suggestion of stones made Jessica nervous and she began to regret her previous wish for Fentalon to beat her mom.

When sparring with Ribbons, the fighters wore three lengths of fabric, typically as long as a forearm. For stones, one wore an armor suit with special clips. Stones were placed at the heart, gut, and forehead. The goal was to remove your opponent's stones. Jessica had tried it once against Jared in hand-to-hand combat. It was impossible to grip the smooth orbs to release them from their clips.

Usually one played stones with knives and swords, making for a potentially deadly game.

"Weapon?" Lily asked.

"I have a preference for my staff," replied Fentalon, "and the stars of the goddess." He pulled out a set of sharp throwing stars. The metal was adorned in red jewels, catching the springtime sun.

"I will take my knives, and a long sword," Lily countered. She pulled a protective mask over her face.

"I agree on this arrangement," Fentalon replied.

A white cloud passed overhead, covering the sun and shading the field.

Jessica got the impression she was watching a well-rehearsed ritual.

Penrik ran out onto the field with a mask for Fentalon. The calico teen gave a little bow of respect and ran to the benches by the shed.

Castlefolk gathered at the fences, murmuring. Something about the fight between Fentalon and Lily was different, but Jessica had no idea why.

Birds sang and the insects continued to hum, oblivious to the games in the stable yard.

Lily and Fentalon met in the middle of the dusty training field, engaged in a bow, turned heel, and walked ten paces.

The two warriors rotated to face each other and the spar began.

Fentalon La'Roch moved faster than Jessica could have imagined. In mere seconds he threw a star at his opponent's chest, and sliced off the gem with an eerie precision.

Lily was not far behind, in a series of twists and turns, and a quick flick of the sword, she sliced the gem from his forehead.

Gripping the wooden bench, Jessica marveled at the skill of their moves. A fraction of an inch more and Lily could have easily come down with enough force to break Fentalon's nose— or worse.

Jessica understood why the castlefolk were eager to watch the fight.

Word traveled fast that there was a stranger in the yard. A crowd was starting to draw around the sparring field and finally the silence was broken with excitement and chatter. The castlefolk were a mix of cat-featured ailurians, human-like sapiens and a handful of horned caprasians. Cooks and scholars, bicorn trainers and farmers, everyone was excited to watch the impromptu match.

Fentalon and Lily moved in perfect synchrony, dancing with the weapons and their bodies. Fentalon flipped, twisted and kicked with an inhuman grace. Lily was not as flexible or quick, but she was calm and smooth in her attacks. Each move was executed with power and precision. Jessica had never seen her mother fight with such elegance.

It was clear both warriors were completely showing off.

A few quick jabs, and Fentalon lost his chest stone. A twist and a kick later, Lily lost her gut stone.

Finally, Lily knocked him to the ground and in a quick flick of her sword blade took out his gut stone. The shiny red gem flew in the air and Lily caught it, bringing her sword to Fentalon's throat.

Silence enveloped the yard, leaving only the sound of humming cicadas.

Both fighters breathed heavily, pulling off their masks. They were red faced and worn, their age visible.

"I missed you, old friend," Lily grinned.

Fentalon was chuckling to himself as she offered him a hand. He took it gracefully and the two embraced. Lily even afforded him a kiss on the cheek.

Jessica was stunned.

She had never seen her mother kiss any stranger.

"I have no qualms losing to the guardmistress," Fentalon said. "I am glad to see time has been kind to you."

"Oh, I do not lead the guard," Lily's arm was tight around his waist, leading him towards Jessica and Wadjette.

"I would like to meet the cat who bests you," Fentalon laughed.

Wadjette finally removed her sparring mask. Jessica didn't know Wadjette was capable of smiling so widely. The young woman absolutely beamed with pride and adoration.

"Father, I am the Master of the Guard."

***

Later that day, dinner filled the warm hall with laughter. Castlefolk exuberantly celebrated Fentalon's return. The man sat at a table in front of the grand fireplace, Wadjette at his right, Lily to his left. His scaled dog sat obediently at his feet.

Jessica approached slowly, there didn't seem to be much room at the long wooden table. She looked around for an open space elsewhere. There was one next to Savina, who had just returned from Briken. Jessica really wasn't in the mood to hang around Savina, but she sat across from Kaity Cosette, whom Jessica liked.

"Jessi! Join us!" Kaity shouted. Kaity was a white leopardess who was always full of smiles. A trained mage of Polaris, she gracefully led Aurumice in Teren's absence.

Her little grey spotted daughter Temi sat beside her. Standing upon a bench to eat, the almost two-year-old made a mess of her food.

Aurumicians didn't bother with high chairs. It was impossible to tie an ailurian cub down to anything.

Jessica took a seat at the open place setting. In Aurumician custom, platters of food were set upon the tables. They ate from shallow wooden bowls. Dinner always consisted of meat, vegetables, bread and cheeses. It changed with the season. Jessica helped herself to a meaty chicken drumstick and a heaping serving of the green leafy caboni root.

Temi threw her grease-covered hands around Jessica's neck. Impish and ever-curious, the child had wide eyes and a heart-melting smile. Her face was speckled with pretty little grey-brown spots and her brown hair hung in soft curls. Temi held up a chicken bone gleefully, making a cooing sound. Temi didn't speak yet, and they didn't know if she ever really would.

Temi was born deaf.

"May I take this seat?" Wadjette had left her place at the other table. It was a strange sight to see the woman happy, she never smiled.

"Of course," Kaity replied. "You must be ecstatic your father came home."

"It is like a dream," Wadjette sat next to Jessica. "I had no idea my father still lived."

"Where has he been hiding?" Savina asked.

"The north," Wadjette replied. "Far north, the reaches of the continent where they don't know what Aurumice is or care about the cursed castlefolk."

When the castle had been locked under the forcefield, the fleeing castlefolk had been looked upon with fear. In truth, there was no 'curse', just an invisible energy dome that caused anyone who touched it to flee in terror. Terror and rumor are a potent blend. For many years, it was dangerous to admit any association with Castle Aurumice.

The magic was supposed to last a day, not a decade, and Jessica's family was to blame.

"In the north, my father got work on the ships in the arctic seas. Word doesn't travel very quick up there, as soon as he found out Misa freed the castle, he came back."

Wadjette's words had been an understatement, it had been nearly three years since Jessica's cousin Misa had broken the forcefield that surrounded Castle Aurumice.

"I wanted to ask you something, Lady Cosette," Wadjette addressed Kaity. The pantheress was always very proper, and though she knew Kaity quite well, she wanted to demonstrate respect.

"Oh?"

"With my father returned, now would be an excellent time for the Ceremony of Bright Path. I have been waiting a while, but now with my father here, it feels right."

"Oh of course, Wadjette!" Kaity absolutely beamed. Anything that involved a celebration made Kaity Cosette happy. If the leopardess had her way, Jessica was sure there would be a party every week.

"What's Bright Path?" Jessica asked. It sounded familiar.

"It's an Aurumician tradition, akin to a graduation of sorts?" Kaity explained. "Young castlefolk have a choice, they take the role they have been apprenticing for, or they can have a bag of money and seek their lives elsewhere with the blessing of Aurumice."

"Are you leaving us?" Jessica asked, shaking her head. "No, I wouldn't believe that for a minute."

Wadjette smirked.

"It's tradition not to tell if she will stay or leave," Kaity said. "Until the ceremony, no one says which path they choose, because it's really their choice. And traditionally, one's parents give blessing that it is time for them to choose. I can't imagine Talon not saying yes."

"I already asked my father. He is fine with this as long as you or Teren sanction it."

"Of course," Kaity agreed. "We don't need to wait for Teren to return. We can host the ceremony whenever you wish."

"Thank you," Wadjette stood, giving a nod to Jessica. "Thank you, I will tell my father."

She left the table.

"Wait, she can really leave Aurumice forever? Just like that?" Jessica asked.

"Well, castlefolk can always come back. Once you're marked as the folk, you are one of us."

Jessica understood the weight of the mark. She had had the magic imprinted on her right shoulder, but her mother had burned away the tattoo when she had been a child. Now Jessica bore a scar with magic buried underneath. Most days she didn't think much of it, but she envied the castlefolk who could walk with their marks proudly displayed.

"Wadjette can leave, and if she comes back, we welcome her," Savina spoke softly. "It is the way of the 'folk."

Jessica continued to feel envious of her friend. Wadjette had so much freedom in her future.

"I'm so happy Talon returned. For Wadjette's sake and for ours. Do you know we're far past a hundred castlefolk?" Kaity grinned. "In the beginning only thirty-seven had returned. We're almost at the point where we are going to need two dinner shifts, just like the old days!"

"Still quite a few missing," Savina seemed grumpy, pushing her food around on her plate. The pretty woman was less bright and assertive than usual. Even her clothing was dull brown, a contrast to the scarlets and purples she usually favored.

"Yeah, I need to convince my parents to return," Kaity sighed.

"You think they're ever going to come back?" Jessica took a drink. Temi put the chicken bone on Jessica's plate, smiling impishly.

"I'm not certain. I mean now that I have Temi I hope they will," the leopardess shook her head. "And my sister is a lost cause. I hope she never returns."

A basket of bread floated to the leopardess' hand. Such occurrences were common around Kaity.

"Where's your sister?" Jessica's curiosity was piqued. She was unaware Kaity had a sister.

"I don't know, and I don't even know if she's alive," Kaity replied, her tone oddly indifferent.

Jessica chose to let the topic drop, it was a story for another time. Instead, she took the chicken bone and balanced it on Temi's little muzzled nose. It was a game they played, as the child liked to try to balance things on her tiny soft snout. The little leopard smiled in victory, then took the bone and reached up, trying to place it on Jessica's human nose.

It fell and Temi giggled as Jessica made a shocked face. Temi was always intrigued by Jessica's unusual nose. Most of the people who surrounded her on a daily basis had more cat-like features.

A round of riotous laugher exploded from Fentalon's direction. Castlefolk pounded the table, causing the silverware to clatter. Jessica watched her mother carefully, the woman was laughing to tears, her hand on Fentalon's shoulder.

Jessica turned back to her dinner, looking at the half-eaten chicken. Then she noticed Savina was staring blankly. Normally the woman had some sort of quip about something. She didn't seem to notice the outburst.

"You okay?" Jessica asked. "You don't seem like yourself."

"It is still strange for me." Savina stated. "I hate being out in Briken, it's dirty and disgusting and my lungs still hurt from breathing that air." She jabbed at the meat on her plate, her bangle bracelets jangling. "When I'm home, I still feel not right."

"I'm sorry," Jessica murmured.

She wanted to tell Savina thank you, but knew the woman would reply with a terse remark. Jessica felt guilty that her friends took turns going out to Briken, trying to figure out how to free Nico. Jessica was never allowed to go, she begged, argued, pleaded. Her mother and Teren were insistent she stay in Trabalis.

"It's like Misa all over," Savina gritted her teeth. "We're just waiting for Nico to die. If he's never coming back to Aurumice then I wish he were dead."

The unexpected words hung in the air awkwardly, causing Kaity to stare at her lynx-eared friend.

Savina realized her mistake and set down her fork, head bowed.

"I apologize. Goddess forgive my words."

Kaity reached across the table, setting a hand on Savina's arm.

Jessica felt trapped in a strange place. Kaity and Savina had grown up with Nico, and Jessica knew they both cared very deeply for the man.

But Jessica cared for him too, in a different way, and she was fairly certain he cared for her as well. Jessica always wore the necklace he had given her. The small pendant of Aurumice was her security blanket.

"Excuse me," Savina said, abruptly standing. "I cannot eat."

Her words echoed Ashlin's and Jessica felt uncomfortably reminded of Carrie Anne's illness. A guilt crept back into her heart.

Savina fled from the room as laughter erupted from Fentalon's table again followed by chanting.

"Ger ball, ger ball, ger ball!"

Kaity made no move to follow her friend, so Jessica likewise did not chase after Savina.

The outburst was a welcomed distraction.

"Why are they chanting gerbil?" Jessica was confused.

"Ger ball," Kaity sighed. "The game. No one's played it at Aurumice since before the forcefield. In fact, I think Nico's mother banned it before then."

Laughing and pouring generous amounts of ale, the castlefolk at the rowdy table stood and gathered their belongings.

"It's a game, played on the back of a bicorn, and they use a leather ball and three hoops and an empty barrel, and then a full cask. It's a drinking game."

"I can't wait to see this." Jessica forced a grin, trying to ignore Savina's words echoed in the back of her mind.

I wish he were dead...

"It's hilariously fun, and so incredibly dangerous, but fun." Kaity grinned. "I played it at the Mage Academy. But at least there we had someone to heal you if you really did anything stupid."

Jessica planned on following the crowd out of the dining hall, when she recalled she had kitchen chores.

"Why the face?" Kaity asked.

"Dishes. It's my turn for kitchen duty. If I don't, I'm pretty sure Cookie is going to report back to Teren, and then I'll hear about it worse, because Teren, Lord of the Castle, lets me do no wrong."

"Oh, well Jessi if you're staying in, can you watch Temi?" Kaity asked.

Jessica sighed, disappointed that she would miss the game.

"Sure..."

"Great! I really wanted to play too!" Kaity jumped to her feet. Kissing her little daughter on the forehead, the young woman smiled then ran to join the group.

Kaity always balanced between responsible mother and fun-loving imp.

Temi watched her mother leave the table, but was content to continue to make a mess of her plate. Jessica felt strangely isolated left alone with the child. The world around her spun with energy and laughter but she remained disconnected. Savina's outburst would not leave her mind.

Jessica stood and began cleaning up the mess.

***

After dinner and dishes, Jessica made her way out to the stable yard. The sun had set and the air carried the pleasant fragrance of wood smoke.

Music and laughter carried through the stable yard.

The castlefolk knew how to party.

Jessica balanced Temi on her hip, the child clinging to her like a little monkey. Ailurian children climbed and latched onto everything, fearless and bold.

She spied Temi's father, Corwin, standing at a fence post by the bicorn pen. Watching the festivities from afar, Corwin held a small book, jotting down notes. The quiet librarian was shunned by the castlefolk.

Two years ago, Corwin had fatally stabbed Nico's father Malachi. Nico was sent to the Mines of Briken instead of Malachi. Many people hated Corwin for that.

On the other side of the coin, Malachi had imprisoned Kaity, which was the only reason Corwin walked free. The whole situation struck Jessica as odd leaving too many unanswered questions.

As Jessica approached, the grey cat smiled, furrowing the deep lines under his eyes. He reached out for his daughter.

Temi was all giggles, hands outstretched. She clung to her father happily.

"Jessica, I looked into that insect you brought me the other day. They're called the *squamish crystalaticus*, colloquially known as a frost needlewasp. Very interesting creatures, some of the few that can withstand freezing temperatures without ill harm. I can research more for you, may I keep the insect a while?"

"That's cool," Jessica said. "No pun intended. Sure, you can hold onto it, the name was what I needed. Teren found it and I'm going to sell it back home when you're done. If it sells well, I want to get more."

Jiberty walked by.

"Better hide, little dung-bag mage. When Fentalon hears what you did to Malachi, you'll get your punishment," the lion-faced man spat at Corwin.

Corwin held his daughter, not responding.

"What the hell, Jiberty?!" Jessica generally liked the tawny man. It was strange for him to be so rude.

"His cub can't hear me." Jiberty replied.

"Yeah, but I heard you and you sound like an ass," Jessica crossed her arms, fumbling with a response. "Castlefolk don't talk like that."

"First, he ain't castlefolk so I can say whatever I want," Jiberty unsteadily waved a finger. "Second, your cousin isn't here for him to hide behind. You need to understand our ways better, girl. Fentalon does what's truly best for Aurumice. Fentalon wouldn't let a murderer hide in our walls, let alone one who stabbed his best friend in cold blood. Fentalon and Malachi were like brothers. You wouldn't know that, you and your mom vanishing into your portal."

"Malachi had Kaity locked up in the cellars, how the hell can you justify that?"

"No one knows why Malachi did what he did, and he didn't live long enough to say, now did he?"

"Jessi," Corwin whispered, "Don't argue with a drunk. You'll always lose."

"The castle was being ripped apart," Jessica ignored Corwin, too angry. "Malachi was an egotistical idiot and a crappy leader."

"Who was going to go to the Mines of Briken instead of Nico! Or did you forget this wormy mage is the reason Nico is gone? Just give Fentalon time," Jiberty addressed Corwin. "You'll be packing back to your ivory tower, if you're lucky."

"Go suck a maggot, Jiberty!" Jessica was furious.

"Don't think any of us have forgotten what your mother did to the castlefolk. Hiding in your demon world while everyone else lived on the streets. Everyone good is gone and every blight of a person is still here. Fentalon will fix that."

Corwin placed a hand on Jessica's shoulder.

"Just let it go," he held Temi tightly. "He is inebriated, just let him talk."

Temi was staring at Jiberty fearfully. The child couldn't hear his words but she could very easily read his body language.

Jiberty snorted. He was ready to speak again but distracted as the creaky side door to the kitchens opened. Penrik wheeled out a large cart piled high with pastries.

"Don't forget it, the old ways are coming back. The real old ways," he spat, leaving them.

"I'm sorry he said those things to you," Jessica apologized. "I'll tell Teren."

Corwin seemed unphased.

"Don't bother, I hear those things all the time. Usually it's in whispers, but I suppose hard liquors will bring out the worst in people."

"Is Fentalon really anything like Malachi?"

"Oh no, no very much the opposite," Corwin stated. "Malachi was all bravado and Holy Circus theatre. He was a terrible guardsman and a bad leader. Fentalon is sensible, disciplined, and a great strategist. He respects the hierarchy of Aurumice, so with Teren and Nico's pardons, I would assume he would have no cause to come after me. Though what Jiberty said was true, Malachi and Fentalon were good friends."

"Yeah, but Nico was Malachi's son. And Nico told the 'folk to leave you alone, so everyone needs to respect that."

"Let them say what they will." Corwin acquiesced, "I respect the castlefolk's ways of protecting their own. I am the outsider."

Corwin always seemed to be in an awkward place. He was not castlefolk, he was a Mage of the Consortium. The man had no castlemark. He chose not to become part of the castle, even though his wife and daughter were tied to Aurumice. The man's heart belonged to Castle Nova and Polaris Academy. Jessica could plainly see he tolerated Aurumice for his wife's sake.

"I will take Temi inside for the evening. If you see Kaity, please tell her we went in."

"Yeah, no problem."

Corwin and Temi walked away. Jessica felt awful for the man. One mistake would haunt him forever.

Folding her arms, the teen continued on to the party. The chilly spring night left her wishing she had a jacket, but happy she wore her tall soft boots. Walking closer to the bonfire, she could smell the aroma and the sweet warmth.

Wadjette tackled Jessica in a rough hug.

"Jessi, I'm so happy he's back!" the panther girl grinned. Her bright green eyes were glassy.

"Are you drunk?!" Jessica was shocked. Wadjette always possessed more decorum than any other teen Jessica had ever met.

"Happy," Wadjette replied. Jessica noticed the tankard in the girl's hand.

"Uh huh."

"Come play fiddle for us!" Wadjette laughed, yanking Jessica with her. Jessica raced after her friend, knowing it best not to argue lest her arm be wrenched from its socket.

Wooden tables filled the stable yard and lanterns glowed bright for the festivities. With Teren away and Kaity at the helm, there was very little to stop any impromptu event.

Wadjette led Jessica to a table where her father sat across from Jessica's mother. The two warriors threw dice, engaged in a riotous game.

"Ah, Jessica, join us!" Fentalon greeted her, gesturing to the bench next to him.

"Jessica plays violin as good as Teren," Wadjette sat at her father's right side.

"Yes, but I don't have my violin with me," Jessica tentatively took the seat next to Fentalon, still very amused at Wadjette's drunken behavior. Fentalon didn't seem concerned that his daughter had been drinking, he was very intent on beating Lily at the game.

His scaled hound obediently gathered at his feet, calmly ignoring the inebriated people. Warm orange firelight glinted off its white scales.

"Your pet, I've never seen the species before," Jessica said. "What is he?"

"He's a Lazuli hunter, his name is Bo. His true name is Davidbowie."

Jessica snorted. "Your dog is named *David Bowie?*"

"Yeah, your Aunt Beatrix gave him that name," Lily laughed. "Damn, I miss her way of naming animals."

"Aye, your sister was the most amazing beast speaker I ever met," Fentalon said. "Sorry she is gone. Little Misa too."

"Eh, as they say, the way of the goddess, the turn of the wheel, the tears of the time dragon," Lily replied.

Bo looked up. His eyes were a brilliant blue, one a little darker than the other.

"His scales are beautiful," Jessica said, not sure what else to say.

"And suited to a purpose. They're incredible swimmers, adept climbers, and the best trained hunters. Nothing stands between them and their prey once they're in the hunt."

Jessica wanted to pet the creature's smooth glassy scales but thought better of it.

"Jess does a lot for the castle," Wadjette interjected, the alcohol eroding her social skills. "And she does everything with electricity for the castle. Nico taught her everything and she is so good at figuring things out, and she's not a mage or anything, just like Teren, and that makes her even better."

Jessica giggled.

Wadjette was hilarious.

"Speaking of Teren, where is the boy?" Fentalon asked.

"My cousin is away," Jessica replied.

"Briken!" Wadjette filled in. "He is trying to find a way to free Nico from the Mines, and he's going to do it. Teren is the best leader of Aurumice, and he's so clever."

"All well and good but no one leaves that hell pit alive," Fentalon said flippantly.

Jessica scowled. Though the man quoted common knowledge, it seemed rude of him to say. Before she could comment, Lily pushed a large mug in her daughter's direction.

"Here, Jess, we broke into the good wine casks."

"Um, Mom?" Jessica raised an eyebrow. She had been allowed the occasional glass of wine, but it was always accompanied by dinner.

"Oh, lighten up, Jess."

"Uhhh…did you forget that I'm seventeen?"

"Jess, it's fine," Lily rolled her eyes. "I'm your mother, and I said it's fine."

Lily became distracted by the game. Throwing down her cards, she shouted. "Got you, ring-tailed bastard! Storm high, meadow low, and that is game!"

"Blood'ura, you cursed mage! I swear you're cheating!" Fentalon laughed.

"Again! Let's go again! Deal me in!" Wadjette giggled. She had apparently already forgotten she had asked Jessica to play violin.

Jessica's eyes traveled around the stable yard. People danced to an impromptu band of fiddles, horns and drums. It was a hell of a party, but many people were missing. Teren and Jared were away, Nico was imprisoned, Savina was in the castle, and Misa was long buried in the woods. With so many gone, Jessica felt a little alone.

Cookie approached them with a tray of green drinks. The cups were unusual, curved like little black horns. The shape reminded Jessica of the tail of a sting lizard. He set the beverages with a plate of dried meat in the center of the table.

"Slow smoked," he grinned. "Nice and spicy."

"Jess, you in?" Lily asked her daughter. "You know how to play killeuno?"

"Mom, I have that summer school assignment to finish."

"It's not every day Talon La'Roch returns to Aurumice!" Lily grinned, taking a strip of the meat.

"Ah, this is what I missed the most about Aurumice." Fentalon also took a bite. "Our cooks were always the best this side of Nova."

Wadjette dealt the cards and passed the dice. Jessica had never seen her mother so happy. Wadjette was laughing and warm.

Jessica hadn't been able to tell much about Fentalon, but he seemed like a nice old guy.

He offered her one of the green drinks.

Jessica placed the cup to her lips. The beverage smelled pleasantly sweet and she downed it like a shot.

And instantly regretted it.

The strange alcohol burned her throat and hit her stomach. A gush of stomach acid immediately burst up through her esophagus. Jessica leapt out of her seat, barely able to take three steps before she threw up. The green vomit struck the dirt in a putrid splash.

Cringing, she heard Fentalon's laughter. Nearby castlefolk cracked jokes about not being able to hold her liquor.

"Your daughter doesn't know not to drink green sap straight. Girl, you can't drink it like that. Lily, what do you teach your daughter?"

"That was rotten," Jessica stood. "You could have warned me, I didn't know what green sap was."

"Oh Jess, lighten up," Lily's face was flush with laughter.

"Mom, it wasn't funny. That tasted horrible."

"You were supposed to drink it with the dried *jobee*, it reacts with the sap and tames the sting."

Jessica's stomach tingled, barely giving her warning. She turned around and this time was able to dive behind a bush before she vomited again. Chills raced down her body as her arms shook. Tears stung her eyes. Wadjette was laughing and Lily wasn't very concerned. Fentalon made a flippant comment about Jessica being a bastard, with no father to teach her the important things in life.

Jessica clutched the wet grass and earth, waiting for the world to stop spinning. She didn't know what hurt worse, the burn in her stomach or the castlefolk's laughter.

Two hands gently gripped her arms, steadying the world.

"I can't leave you alone for a few days, can I?"

It was blonde haired, blue-eyed Jared.

"Jae, I drank some green sap and I feel awful."

"And I'm bringing you inside to get cleaned up," he said quickly. Thankfully, Jared didn't appear intoxicated. He smiled at Lily.

"I've got Jess, go back to your game."

"You just got back from Briken," Jessica stammered. "Is my cousin with you?"

"No, but we'll talk about that later."

"Now Jessi, you should come back to the table..." Lily continued.

"Lily, Lily darling, go back to your game," Jared reassured. "I've got your daughter, it's fine!"

Jared yanked Jessica away, whisking her through the stable yard.

"I left my puke in the middle of the party."

"Oh Jess," Jared laughed. "Believe me, the way they're going, by the end of the night it will be one of many."

"I've never seen Wadjette like that, or my mother, I can't believe them...my mother was stupid drunk...she never gets drunk...who cares if Wadjette's dad is back..."

"Let them have their party."

Jared led her to a water cistern. He turned on the faucet and Jessica washed her face. She shivered. They were far enough from the bonfire that the night chill reached her arms.

"You look a fright, girl," Jared was concerned.

"And I have a paper due tomorrow," she muttered.

"I'll escort you home," he wrapped a protective arm around her shoulders.

She nuzzled against his chest.

"Thank you," she slipped her arm around his narrow waist.

"Don't worry. I'll always keep my eyes on you."

CHAPTER 7

Jessica sat at the worn kitchen table, staring at her homework. Her stomach had finally settled, and now it was empty from losing dinner.

The clock ticked past ten in the tiny suburban home.

She should not have procrastinated, and the fiasco of the stable yard party only made it worse.

Jared rummaged through the yellow fridge, pulling out frozen burritos and a beer.

Jessica balked. "We just ordered Chinese."

"But I'm hungry now," Jared complained. "I didn't have any chance to eat at the bonfire, and I missed dinner."

Jared was quite possibly the strangest anomaly in Jessica's life. The boy was born on earth and raised with the Mages of Polaris academy. Some of his childhood was spent in New York, so his upbringing was an eclectic mix of city life and the wild lifestyle of a Polaris child. There was a lot in his life he shrouded in vague secrecy and sarcasm.

When Jared was seventeen, he struck a deal with Jessica's cousin Misa to help her destroy the forcefield that bound Aurumice. Unfortunately, the logistics of that deal inadvertently expelled him from Polaris Academy and nearly landed him in the dungeons of Castle Nova.

Luckily for Jared, he had an Aunt and Uncle able to get him out of trouble.

That Aunt and Uncle happened to be Kaity and Corwin.

How the cat-like Corwin was related to very human Jared still puzzled Jessica, but certain elements of Centernia she just shrugged at and ignored.

Jared unwrapped a pair of burritos and tossed them into the microwave. He seemed dismayed by the microwave's interior.

"When's the last time anyone cleaned this?"

"There's paper towels and soap if you've got a problem with it."

Jared seemed to consider it, but laziness won out as he pressed the keypad.

"What's your homework on?" the boy asked.

"The Red Scare."

"Isn't the Cold War part of the eleventh-grade curriculum?"

"How would you know this?" Jessica glared.

"Wait. What's the date here?" Jared searched for the calendar. "Isn't it August? Why are you doing schoolwork? You failed eleventh grade history, didn't you?!"

"Shut up," Jessica snarled. "I didn't fail it, I just failed the state exam. Which means I need to retake the exam and they make you do a remedial summer course."

"What you mean is you failed history."

"Sorry I was trying to learn how to fix the water issue at Aurumice, you know, the one that was making people vomit. That seemed a little more important."

The microwave hummed for a while, then beeped. Jared served the burritos on two small plates.

"When you going to fix the toaster? I like toasted burritos better."

"It'll get fixed if you learn what a soldering iron is."

"Snappy, snappy," Jared said. "Need help with your essay?"

"No," Jessica clicked through a few websites. "I can't believe the 'folk. I heard Jiberty say some really crappy things to Corwin."

"It happens Jess, when people have too much to drink the castlefolk always say stupid things. My uncle will be fine, he's tough."

"It's not right."

Jared popped open a beer. Jessica gave him a death-stare.

"I'm twenty-one, that's the law here," Jared asserted.

"Yeah, but I need your help."

"I have had a rough couple of weeks, let me relax. And I'm here helping you, aren't I?"

"I want you to tell me what's going on in Briken," she commanded.

"Who said anything was going on?"

"Where is Teren?"

"Trying to figure out how to help Nico, as he's always been."

"Savina came back and so did you. It's not Teren's turn, why is he still there?"

Jared took a drink and didn't reply.

Jessica continued to press.

"Savina is upset, and she won't talk about it. Why is she back?"

Jared took a long drink.

"Jae, why won't you tell me what's going on? I know you want to talk, you always want to talk. Who is telling you to keep secrets from me?"

Jared took a drink, then paused, then took another long drink, and paused.

"What are you doing?"

"Playing a drinking game."

"How?"

"Every time I think 'Teren will kill me if I say something', I take a drink."

"Now you have to tell me! What is going on?"

Jared took another drink.

"It's not fair!" Jessica threw her pen across the table. "Everyone expects me to be mature, and then they carry on like idiots, and when I ask questions I get nothing but the runaround and lies!"

"Just graduate high school, and you'll be fine."

"Somehow I doubt that. Is Nico dead?"

Jared took a long drink.

"Jared! You don't need to worry about my cousin because *I* will kill you if you don't tell me the truth!"

Jared released the bottle with a satisfying smack. "I'm kidding this time! No, no, he's not dead. Your cousin swore to that. No point thinking about it now anyways, you have an essay due tomorrow."

Jessica growled in frustration, resting her head on the table.

"I don't want to write this."

"Why are you frustrated with one essay?" he asked.

"It's not the essay, it's graduation, it's college, it's my whole life. Every assignment matters, because I need to graduate, but I don't know why."

"Because you don't want to work fast food all your life?"

"No, that's just it," she threw up her hands then clutched her head, burrowing her fingers through her red disheveled hair. "My mom and dad want me to go to college, but I don't want to leave home and Centernia for four years and I don't want to go to AVCC. And why take out that huge college loan if I find out I'm a mage and I decide to just live in Centernia? But then I can't, because we need to keep this stupid crappy house because of the Gate in the basement and someone needs to pay the mortgage and I don't think Mom will ever pay it off. The kids in Narnia never had this problem."

The doorbell interrupted their conversation

"Moo shu chicken!" Jared exclaimed, hopping out of his chair.

"I put the cash next to the door," Jessica told him, trying to refocus on her essay. It was impossible, between Nico, and Fentalon, she had too many unanswered questions.

"When will my cousin be back?" Jessica asked.

Jared spun around, grabbed his bottle, and theatrically took another drink in reply.

Jessica was not amused.

Jared answered the door.

There was an awkward moment of pause, and she realized she didn't hear the familiar rustle of a paper bag of deliciousness.

"Oh, hello, Mr. Ravenwolfe!" Jared was surprised.

It took a moment before Jared's words sunk into her ears, then Jessica panicked.

"Who are you?" she heard her father say.

He was *not* happy.

Jessica ran to the door, shoving Jared out of the way.

"Hi Dad, what are you doing here?"

"Hey, you didn't answer your phone. Carrie Anne had to go to the hospital, I thought I would pick you up. Ashlin asked for you."

"Oh, yeah, of course, let me get my sweatshirt, and my homework."

"Where's your mother?"

"Napping, upstairs, she had a headache."

"Who is this?"

"Dad, this is my friend Jae, and he's helping me with my homework."

"And now drinking is part of your homework? Is this why you failed history?"

"I wasn't drinking."

Jared took a few steps back away from the door.

"Your mother lets underage drinking happen in her house?"

"Dad, Jared isn't underage."

"Yes, sir, I just turned twenty-one."

"Your mother lets you hang around a twenty-one-year-old? Jessi, you are seventeen!"

"Sir, I was helping Jessica with her homework…" Jared tried to do damage control, but he understood how bad it looked to her father.

"We will discuss this later, right now I have too much stress to deal with you."

***

An awkward silence dominated the drive to the hospital. Carrie Anne had been at her book club, then collapsed and was whisked away in an ambulance. From what Stephen was told over the phone, they didn't know if it was a bad reaction to her medication or a problem with her heart. She was being admitted overnight for observation.

Ashlin wouldn't make eye contact and stared out the window of the car in sullen silence. When they arrived at the hospital, the trio walked through the emergency entrance. The large waiting room was full of coughing, injured, and the elderly. Jessica wondered what it would be like to have Teren's abilities, if mage powers actually worked on Earth. Would the room be full of fear, hope, or dread? Everyone's eyes were melancholy, and she imagined that hope was a scarce commodity.

After waiting in a long line at a desk, they were finally directed past a set of security doors to the wing were Carrie Anne had been admitted.

The middle-aged woman was sitting up in bed, pale, but in good spirits. An IV was connected to her arm, giving Jessica a ghostly memory of Misa. She did not want to lose her step mother as she had lost her cousin. Misa had handled too much magic to break the forcefield, throwing her into a coma for months.

Ashlin wrapped her arms around her mom, crying.

"Ashlin," Carrie Anne soothed. "It will be alright, I'm not going anywhere for a long while."

Wishing to run back to Centernia, Jessica said nothing. She would have rather dealt with her embarrassment at the bonfires than watch her little sister cry.

Their conversation was strained and shallow. Carrie Anne was focused on taking her daughters back-to-school shopping. Ashlin didn't care about the plan and Jessica made half-hearted acknowledgements. Stephen was silent as Jessica waited for him to explode about Jared.

A nurse came in and checked on Carrie Anne, monitoring her blood pressure. Stephen kept his arms crossed, glancing around the hospital room as if it was a cage.

Jessica wanted to break the awkward silence and talk about real things, like her cousin's absence, the bonfire, even Carrie Anne's cancer. It was all a long list of taboo. Jessica felt like a stranger in her family when she didn't want to be.

Ashlin calmed down and Stephen gave her some loose change, sending his daughters on a long walk to the vending machine.

Jessica sighed, and dutifully distracted her little sister into the hallway. The hospital was quiet, the air cold with the smell of disinfectant. As she followed Ashlin down the hall, Jessica realized she spent very little time with the girl anymore. She saw more of Wadjette than her sister.

"I hate this," Ashlin growled. "I hate this, I hate this, I hate this."

"I know," Jessica agreed, "I hate it too."

Jessica reflected on the strange way her family was structured, to her and Ashlin, Dad was dad, and no one could be another Dad.

But to Jessica, Lily was truly her mother. To Ashlin, Carrie Anne was everything.

"She's going to die," Ashlin said, "You're going to go to college, Dad's going to go on his business trips and I will have no one."

"Ashlin, that's not true," Jessica argued, feeling guilty for wishing to run away to Centernia.

"You're never around. You don't reply to my messages and you don't care about me."

"Ashlin, that's not true!"

Was it?

"Where were you all day?! I tried to talk to you and you ignored me!"

"My phone wasn't charged," Jessica lied.

They found the soda machine and Jessica handed the money to Ashlin.

She wanted to tell her sister about the ailurians, to whisk her away to her land of bicorns and castles. Ashlin was exactly the type of girl who would thrive on Centernia.

Ashlin I have a world that is nothing like this one. It won't save your mom, but it will take your breath away.

"Ash…"

Ashlin took her soda from the machine's tray.

"What?" the girl snapped.

Ashlin's anger gave Jessica pause.

Maybe I'll tell you when you really need it most.

"What?" Ashlin repeated.

"Can you hit the button to get me a root beer?" Jessica asked. Her sister obliged, and they took their sodas back to the room. Their father waited at the door, Stephen gestured for his younger daughter to enter, but held out a hand stopping Jessica.

"We need to talk."

Stephen led Jessica down a long white hallway to a foyer with a smooth grey stone fountain and small decorative ferns.

Walking up a frozen escalator, they arrived at a tiny hospital chapel. Jessica breathed a sigh of relief.

Prayer, much better than conversation.

They took a seat on one of the white wooden benches. A simple oak cross was the focal piece of the chapel. A statue of the Virgin Mary was displayed to the right side, adorned with fake plastic flowers. When Jessica was younger, she found churches uncomfortable and strange. After watching the Centernians worship the Goddess Aurora, Jessica found a new acceptance. She could see parallels between the two religions, and that made her feel happy.

Stephen bowed his head reverently to the cross, then he turned to his daughter.

"Who is Jared?" he asked.

"A friend," Jessica squeaked.

"A boyfriend?"

Jessica shook her head.

"A bedfellow?"

"No!" Jessica yelled, cringing at the way her dad said the word *bedfellow.* "Dad, it's not like that at all! I'm pretty sure he's very gay."

It was a half-truth. Most single, prowling Centernians seemed to hop to either side of the gender fence without concern. Jessica didn't honestly know where Jared's true preferences fell as she had heard of his exploits with both genders. Every once in a while, he mentioned another man in Polaris Academy with wistful longing.

"How sure are you that he's gay? How long have you known him?"

"Dad! Please! Jared is nothing!" she squeaked.

"Please, respect the chapel, lower your voice," Stephen was stern.

"Sorry, no, Dad I swear Jared and I aren't anything."

"Where is he from?"

"From New York."

"Is he one of them? The people from Centernia?"

"Dad, you're jumping to conclusions…"

Stephen held a hand up, "Just stop talking, I know the answer. He must be one of them, otherwise he wouldn't have been popping open a beer so casually in your mother's house."

"Friend of Lee's brother," Jessica replied.

"Quit the lies, Jessica," Stephen said. "I am going to say this once, and you listen good, because this situation with Carrie Anne has really, really worn my patience thin."

He took a deep breath.

"If you get mixed up with boys from that world, you are asking for nothing but trouble. God forbid you get pregnant, your life is going to be worse than you can imagine."

Jessica's stomach soured and she felt the urge to throw up again.

"Dad I wouldn't…"

Stephen held up a finger, silencing her.

"I also want to make it very clear to you, if you dare fall in love with one of them, and are stupid enough to get married, I will not even consider that relationship to be real. And if you have a kid with one of them, that child will not be my grandchild."

"Why do you always have to be an impossible jerk!? Carrie Anne is sick and you care about my non-existent future marriage? Jared is my friend, one of my best friends."

"Jessica, it is very easy to fall into a trap, just ask your mother about your Aunt Beatrix. She got mixed up with those cat people and never came home."

Jessica's hands went to her forehead.

"I can't believe you're even lecturing me on this in a church. We're done, Dad, my turn. I'm texting Mom. I'm going home."

It was a farce, Jessica didn't know who she would text to save her. Her mother was certainly still drunk in the stable yard.

"No, you can't go," Stephen grabbed her arm.

"Why not?" Jessica asked, "When I'm eighteen you won't regulate my schedule anymore. I won't be a ping pong ball between you and my mom, and if you aren't careful, I will bring Ashlin to Centernia and there is nothing you can do to stop me."

Stephen released her arm.

"I think she needs it," Jessica continued. "I wish you would see that." Jessica took a step back.

"I'm going to be with Carrie Anne now, and if you keep threatening me I just might tell her, too."

Stephen was dumbfounded by his daughter's response. The girl left the chapel without looking back.

CHAPTER 8

Life on the airship took on a strange surreal rhythm.

Nico spent his days traveling between his small cabin, the tiny library, and the dining room. Weeks ticked by. A younger version of himself would have found it maddening, instead he found the routine peaceful.

The ship landed several times, but never did Nico feel compelled to leave. He watched out the windows as featherwings were walked around the ship, led by white-furred caprasians. By his count, there were four grey featherwings, likely two mated pairs. They were dragons in all respects, but their wings were soft and downy like a bird.

Nico saw no one else, nor any other creatures. He had no desire to talk to anyone, so the arrangement suited him well.

Eclectic and odd, the books in the library were an interesting and haphazard mix. Most were classic literature, a few were financial advisory guides, three on maritime travel, a few on bicorns, and then one on steam engine technology. Nico read through the steam book first, and then slowly made his way through the other volumes.

Reading was delightful. He had forgotten how marvelous it was to step into a book and live in another world for hours.

The black gritty mines felt so far away, and his family in the castle were even further. At moments, he wondered if he was being drugged to make him an amicable passenger. Serenity overtook him, and his warmth and happiness seemed too persistent.

As soon as these doubts crept into his mind, they were squashed as he told himself to be grateful.

He also pondered if his powers would return in the calm, but there was no sign of the mage energy no matter how many times he tried to call it to his hands. This detail did not bother him, but only became a curiosity.

Zia came to visit him with increasing frequency. The woman said very little of herself, but was content to listen to Nico speak.

On a still evening, she appeared in the doorway and led him from his peaceful confinement to a tiny infirmary. At first he was nervous, but with soft hands, Zia peeled off the bandages, rubbing clean salves across his broken skin and beyond. Nico closed his eyes, trying to ward away memories of the Mines. The wounds were still unhealed, but they were not getting worse.

"What's this tattoo on your shoulder?" Zia asked, running her hands along the muscle.

It had been so long, Nico had almost forgotten about the convoluted design.

"It's a castlemark," he replied.

"Not many people have symbols like these," Zia seemed intrigued. "This isn't normal ink."

"It's not, it was put there by magic. It connects me to Castle Aurumice and the other castlefolk."

"Interesting..."

Zia's bandages were a bit sloppy, but Nico did not mind. Under her hands, his pain melted and he felt free.

Afterwards, she escorted him back to his room. He happily settled down into the bed. Sleep overtook him easily.

In the deep sleep, his dreams were a jumble of haphazard places and times. He stood on the beach in Therissina, watching the waves lap across the stones. A ship was far in the distance.

From the beach, he walked into the dining room of Aurumice, then into the kitchen of Jessica's suburban house. The red-head flipped through a book and eating noodles from a plate. The girl didn't look up and Nico felt as if he were intruding.

Abruptly, the house changed.

His feet were planted at the edge of a rocky cliff overlooking a starlit abyss.

Nico's senses became more acute but the dream continued.

A nightflight sat, hunched over a stone table, leathery wings folded. Winds blew across the cliff, moving tiny grains of sand. As Nico approached, he realized Misa sat across from the beast. Between them, on the rocky crest, was a chess board.

As the reptilian creature moved the pieces delicately with his hands, and Nico realized it wasn't a nightflight at all. Nightflights were animals, very clever, but animals nonetheless. True dragons were mythological beasts of wisdom. The chess player was a Time Dragon, a legend from the religious texts of the Holy Circus. The story stated that the Time Dragon was the cursed last of its kind. Throughout the tales, the beast repeatedly petitioned the goddess for a companion who would survive all of eternity.

"Join us," Misa turned to address Nico. For once, her clothing was demure— a long black and white striped jacket over grey pants. His friend was so vivid, Nico could see every ringlet of hair and the shiny little buckles on her boots.

"This is the game where the rules are like Beetles?" he asked.

"Yeah. I'm trying to see how many moves I can hold in my mind," Misa said. "You seem happy."

"Oh, I am!" Nico sat at third stone bench that had suddenly materialized. "I'm free of Briken."

"Teren rescued you?" Misa asked. "Please tell him I said hi, and to stop being grumpy. I know he must be grumpy."

"Not Teren, a woman, Zia. She has an airship, we're traveling across the continent."

"Traveling?" Misa seemed confused. "What about Aurumice? Have you been home?"

"No. No, not yet."

"Do the castlefolk know you're free?"

Nico shrugged, looking at the chess pieces. He wondered if it was possible to play a game with Misa, or if he would wake up before he could make a single move.

The sapphire Time Dragon reached forward, picking up a piece with his dainty claws. After he moved the horse-like figure, he turned and looked at Nico. His deep eyes possessed an intelligence and wisdom that was frightening. Nico was raised to be Auroriate, but he took his father's religion with a bit of skepticism. He suddenly felt he had made a grave mistake.

"Why don't you tell them?" Misa persisted. "Why are you flying away in an airship? Are they okay? Is Jessi alive? And Teren? Vina? Kaity? My aunt?"

"I have no idea," Nico said. "I haven't seen them."

"Why don't you go home?!"

"I'm happy!" Nico shouted, unsure of himself. "I'm happy, I'm content. I have books to read, and good food to eat. Zia is a lovely person, a good conversationalist."

Tilting her head, Misa addressed the Time Dragon.

"You'll have to excuse me, my friend is having a momentary lapse of judgement."

Grunting, the Time Dragon shrugged and leaned back. He crossed his arms and looked more closely at the board.

Nico bristled.

"I am happy," he repeated.

"Who is Zia?" Misa stood squarely in front of him. He knew the look.

"She rescued me," Nico said. He could be just as stubborn as she. "I am eternally grateful and indebted to her."

"Great, well, throw a party for her when you return to Aurumice."

"I am staying on the airship."

"What about my brother?"

"I do not owe him an explanation."

Without warning, Misa slapped him across the face.

For a dream, it smarted hard.

"What is wrong with you!? She must have drugged you. My Nico would never run away and not think to contact his family!"

"Drugged me?" Nico repeated, his hand still to his cheek.

"Yes! You're completely crazy!"

"Says the dead girl on a mountain playing chess with a Time Dragon."

"Not a Time Dragon, *thee* Time Dragon," she sighed. "Please, I know you're an idiot, but try not to be so insulting."

Misa turned and looked to her scaled companion.

"I apologize, my friend lacks manners."

She reverted her attention to Nico.

"This is all a dream, I'm dreamspinner mage, it's what I've always done, but this...this isn't you. I want you to promise me you'll go home. And stop eating whatever they're feeding you!"

"But I starved for more than a year!" Nico was furious. "These people are very kind and hospitable!"

"They tricked you," Misa repeated. "They tricked you!"

Reaching up, she knocked furiously on his head.

"They tricked you. Do you hear me?!"

Nico shoved her away.

"Will you stop that?!"

Misa paced angrily. The wind speed increased and Nico was reminded they were on a mountaintop over a yawning chasm of stars.

"Aurora damn you to hell! I hate this!" she grumbled.

The Time Dragon snorted, offended by the phrase.

"Sorry!" Misa apologized to the blue creature. "I want to just wake up and fix this!"

Snorting, the Dragon looked at Misa thoughtfully.

"I could," she said. She turned to Nico.

Her form melded into Teren, pale skin, hair white.

"Tell me you never want to see me again."

Nico felt uncomfortable, knowing it was Misa controlling a dream puppet.

"Quit it," he ordered.

"Tell me I am not worth your time. Tell me you would rather fly across the continent than sit down and have tea in the gilt lounge. Tell me you don't miss our endless debates!"

"You're not Teren. I won't tell you anything."

Misa melded into Savina, leaning forward, wrapping an arm around the back of his neck. Her bangled bracelets chinked with every move.

"You know I miss you. Life in Aurumice is not the same without you."

Nico shoved Savina away.

His old friend shifted into Jessica. The girl was a little older than he remembered, more woman than teen. "What about me?" she asked.

"When I crossed the Gate, you were the one who looked out for me while my family was caught up in their drama. You were my friend, and I need you."

Nico turned away, feeling guilty.

"Let me just have some time to myself," he told the apparition of Jessica.

"But how long? When will you come home?"

Nico began to question the airship, and Zia. But the black-haired woman was so kind, how could he be wrong?

When he looked up, a new form startled him.

Jessica had vanished.

Instead, a tall woman stood in front of him. Her hair was brown and smooth, half-pulled back and threaded with a thin gold circlet of ivy. She wore a lavender gown and gazed at him with sad brown eyes.

It was his mother, long dead.

"Nico, what are you doing here?" Elina asked. "Why are you forsaking our home?"

"Misa, this one is too much."

"No, you need to hear me," Elina stated. Her voice was too real, bubbling up long-dormant memories and feelings. When his mother had died, she had been crazy. This soft-spoken apparition was the best version of his mother, from the earliest recesses of his memory.

Elina brought her hands together.

"You are the last one of our family. No one can guide the castle like you can, it's what you were raised to do, to be. You know Aurumice has a power of its own, and you are in harmony with her. You have to protect all the castlefolk and the children of the castle."

"Misa stop this," Nico said. "This isn't right, you can't conjure an image of my mother!"

He began to cry. "Misa! Artemisa!"

"Please, Nico, break through the lies and go home. Please, you are torturing everyone by staying away."

"This! This is torture!" Nico's hands clenched in rage. He wanted to strike the vision, but could not bring himself to raise a hand against his mother, dream apparition or not.

Misa stood beside him.

"Then go home, and I'll stop, and if you don't, I swear I will find a way back into your dream, and show you things about yourself I *know* you don't want to remember."

Elina vanished, and Nico feared the next image Misa would bring forth.

"Wake up, and just stop eating and drinking," Misa ordered. "You'll thank me later."

"I want to wake up," Nico said. "I want to wake up! Wake up! Wake up!"

He was jolted into the darkness of reality. For a moment, he believed he was back in the Mines, but the reassuring details of the small cabin seeped into his eyes. In the darkness, his breathing came in quick rasps and his limbs trembled.

Jumping to his feet, Nico hobbled to the window. Beyond the glass the world was cloudy and black. The feelings of entrapment engulfed him. Gazing into the darkness, he wondered how far he was from Castle Aurumice.

Glowstones illuminated the hallway as he heard boot steps. Zia appeared in the doorway, wearing a red and black robe.

"I heard you shouting," she said. "Are you alright?"

"Yeah," he was unable to make eye contact with her. "Just a nightmare."

On a corner table of his room was a small bottle of spirits that Zia had brought a few days prior. Before the Mines of Briken, Nico was never a drinker, too much would cause him to lose control of his powers.

His powers. Why did he not care that they were still gone?! He looked at his hands, wondering if he could conjure the magic.

The tall woman carefully lifted the bottle and selected two glasses.

"Let me pour you something to calm your nerves."

"No," he declined, remembering Misa's warning.

"I can brew you some tea. Honestly, screaming in the middle of the night isn't good for the crew, so it's in my best interest to help you. Tomorrow we land and go meet with the people who financed your liberation."

"No, tea is not necessary."

"The quality of water on this ship isn't the best, or I'd offer you that."

"No, no,'" he furiously tried to figure out how to escape her. It was heartening to hear they were going to travel elsewhere in the morning.

Zia poured two glasses, took one, and sat on the edge of the low bed. Gesturing to the empty space beside her, she smiled warmly.

"Sit, tell me about your dream."

In the back of Nico's mind, a little image of Misa started hopping up and down, screaming at him. His hand went to his cheek on instinct, recalling the sting of her slap.

Zia gazed at him intently.

"You can stand there all night if you like, you know I don't bite."

Relenting, he sat next to Zia. She placed a hand on his shoulders.

"I dreamt of..." he sought out the words, "the Time Dragon."

He did not want to tell her about Misa, or his mother.

As he recounted the dream, he found the glass of spirits in his hand. Zia started talking about Time Dragons and Aurora, and spoke flippantly of some of her dealings with the Holy Circus. Nico had not told her of his father's association with the religious group.

As she spoke, Nico relaxed, and took a few sips. The more Zia talked, the more it drew him out to speak. He told her about Misa, Jessica, Teren and his mother. Zia placed her cup aside and began massaging his back with both hands. She was very skilled, and he felt his worries ease away. She asked again about his castlemark, and the magic of Aurumice.

A little mind glimmer of Misa swore at him, but then the image snuffed out like a candle.

Eventually he sprawled out onto the bed, sleep promising to overtake him again.

***

Nico awoke to an empty room and a pounding headache.

He stood and looked out the window, he saw trees and realized they were on the ground. Judging by the light, it was later in the day than he typically slept.

Gathering his clothing, he dressed and then made his way to the dining room. He was eager to be on his way, feeling very odd from the night before. He was having trouble separating dream from reality. His night with Zia hadn't been unpleasant, but it was all very odd and uncomfortable to him. He had crossed a line he had not intended to cross.

Shame and betrayal filled his heart.

Suddenly, the deck beneath his feet lurched and he steadied himself on the bolted dining table.

The airship was moving upwards.

Looking out the windows, he realized they were hovering.

Escape you idiot!

Nico frantically searched for a way to break open the window.

The ship tilted again, taking his chance of freedom. Tumbling across the floor, he slammed hard against a wall. He braced himself as the airship rose, jostled by the wind.

He cursed himself for sleeping too late.

Escape! Escape! Escape!

He repeated the word in his mind, praying he wouldn't forget.

When the wild motion ceased, a door opened and Zia walked into the dining room, carrying a large bundle. Her hair was disheveled, but she possessed all of her usual composure.

Nico felt like she could see right through him, though her face betrayed no hint of it.

Zia set the bundle on the ground. From the fabric, a gold and red gryphon chicklet emerged. He was the size of a medium dog, with the distinct lion-like body, feathery wings, feline eyes and a sharp little beak.

The critter was oddly calm for being in close quarters. Yawning, he stretched his wings.

Zianna announced. "Mind his beak, he bites."

Nico was dumbfounded. A gryphon chicklet was the last critter he expected to see in the airship.

The gryphon padded across the floor, sniffing at Nico.

Escape! Escape! Escape!

"My family raised gryphons," Nico commented, not sure what else to say. "How by the Goddess did you acquire a gryphon chicklet? After the Julibur virus they were almost completely wiped out."

"I rescued him from his previous masters. Plans have been altered a bit, I'm afraid, " Zia replied. "It will take us longer to reach the rendezvous point."

Nico drew his hand into a fist, allowing the gryphon chicklet to sniff the backside of his hand. The little beast was calm. Nico scratched under his chin. The critters fur was soft, blending into feathery down on his face in a unique texture transition known as *ploomuff*. Petting the critter allowed Nico to let go of his anxiety.

As the gryphon purred, Nico forgot his plans to escape.

CHAPTER 9

Jessica popped out of the cinderblock wall, clutching the heavy wooden crate. The momentum propelled her forward, and she tripped and tumbled to the musty concrete of the basement floor. She tucked as she fell, resisting the urge to use her hand to brace herself.

The crate was undamaged and she breathed a sigh of relief.

Jessica had never lost anything through Gate Travel, though she worried what would happen if someone did. Was it possible to drop something in the space between dimensions? She didn't know.

Jessica hefted the crate, pulling it up the basement stairs to her kitchen. She hauled it past the beat-up door onto the yellowed linoleum floor.

Glancing at the clock, she had a little time to change, finish her work, and then make it back to Aurumice for Wadjette's Bright Path ceremony. She was looking forward to the event. The castlefolk seemed to have forgotten her vomiting incident from the week before. There was a new air of joviality in Aurumice, one they desperately needed.

Stepping in to the living room, Jessica set the crate in front of the dark blue curtains. She pulled back the faded fabric and opened the window, letting fresh air and light.

Jessica and her mother lived in a small Cape Cod house in the suburbs of Autumn Valley, Pennsylvania. Their living room had been transformed into a makeshift warehouse, photography studio, and packing facility for Centernian goods.

Carefully untying the knots on the container, Jessica opened the rough wooden lid.

Inside, the package was lined with straw and fabric. She carefully unloaded the contents— two complete meadowdasher skeletons. Jessica set each bone on a card table with other projects. It would take her a while to piece the bones into display cases with the other sets, but it was worth it.

She returned to the box for the scaly hides of the dashers. Wadjette had luckily found the beasts, dead of natural causes. Though it would have been easy for the huntress to shoot a meadowdasher, it was considered bad luck to do so. If one found the tiny dragon dead, it was completely reasonable to dispose of the carcass, and someone's shelf was a better end than a dirt hole.

Jessica would deal with the meadowdasher skeletons later. She continued to pull objects out of the crate. She had brought a few wooden cups, carved by Musian. They were beautifully etched with dragons and bicorns. Jiberty had let her have a set of his handmade plates, glazed in rich purple minerals and ornately decorated in a wave pattern that seemed to move under the cast of the light. The last thing in the case were burch leather belts, fitted with handmade buckles.

Jessica set the straw-filled crate to the side. It could be used as part of the packaging material, adding to the allure of the unique products.

Slapping her hands together, she wiped the dust on her jeans. She stood, then settled into the desk chair, refreshing her online account to the various shops. In the overnight she had sold a 'handmade' unicorn horn and a leather satchel.

She calculated the postage, printed the packing slips and grabbed the items from their makeshift inventory. She and her mother had found old shelves at a garage sale and lined the walls of the living room with the tall metal units. They piled the goods from Centernia with some semblance of organization.

Bicorn horns sold as unicorn horns were also popular. Their bread and butter were the skeletons of unusual beasts. They advertised them as 'hand made with a proprietary plaster, delicately painted'. None of their buyers knew they were purchasing the real thing as they bought the skeletons for display in their offices and game rooms.

Fluctuating, but stable, profits weren't amazing, but they were enough to justify the work. Over the years, Lily had dug herself deeper into debt. Anytime a Centernian crisis arose, Lily would inevitably lose her job. Her car would break, or there would be a medical bill and the credit card debt would pile up. Jessica had quietly taken on the weight of the mortgage, knowing it was just as much her job to protect the Gate as her mother's.

The 'unicorn' horn packaged, Jessica focused on photographing the new objects. She arranged the belt with lighting, snapped a few photos, then uploaded the images. It had taken them a few months to figure out that imaginative descriptions were needed to sell the unique items.

Jessica had once asked Ashlin how she would sell a dragon skull online.

"Whether for your muse or for admiration, these dragon remains will remind you of their magical spirits. Each handcrafted with love and respect, each are perfect for any soul pulled to their song."

The language was flowery, but it worked. She couldn't tell Ashlin what she did with her words. Jessica kept the business a secret from her father's family.

Thinking of them reminded her of Carrie Anne's illness. Jessica searched the shelves for a gift to brighten her spirits. She found a little pendant, carved from a smooth jade stone she found in the River White. Her cousin Teren had taken a rare few minutes to carve a design into the smooth surface using a small drill. He was a masterful artist but rarely shared his work.

Jessica's cell phone buzzed in her jacket pocket. She pulled it out and read the message.

```
Carrie Anne
Will you be joining us for a Labor Day picnic?
I invited your mom, please encourage her to
join us.

Jessica
Pretty sure that would be awkward

Carrie Anne
I would love to see you, and I want your mom
to feel welcome. Let me know what you decide
:-)
```

```
Jessica
Thnx but we know my dad doesn't like to be
around my mom

Carrie Anne
With you going to school soon, I want you to
have your whole family together. Please tell
your mom to come to the picnic!
```

"You're too nice a person to be this sick," Jessica mumbled. "I wish I could invite you for a dinner in Aurumice."

Jessica sighed and slid the cell phone into her pocket. Carrie Anne and Ashlin would love dinner at Aurumice, but Jessica knew that was a hornets' nest she could not stir up. After the night at the hospital, her father didn't mention Centernia any further.

Glancing at the clock, Jessica realized she was running late. The teen changed into a carmel skirt, found her Centernian boots, then ran down the basement stairs.

Diving into the cinderblock wall, she was deprived of her senses, caught in a wild energy.

She emerged in a storeroom in Aurumice.

Her first experience with the Gate had been terrifying, but she learned to adapt to the strange transition. Occasionally she wondered what would happen if the magic of the Gate disappeared. Someday could the cinderblock wall become solid?

They really had no idea how the magic worked. It was like gravity, it was just there.

Jessica walked through a secret passage beneath a barn in the stable yard. She crossed through the passageways going through the hidden network of Aurumice. For every hallway, there was another route, hidden behind walls and through ceilings.

Ascending a wooden staircase, she arrived at her private quarters in the castle. The air was much warmer with the coming summer.

Pennsylvania was starting to feel like fall. Jessica enjoyed living in two seasons at the same time.

Opening a door, the teen emerged into the elegant castle suite. Like most of the private quarters in Aurumice, the center room was a large sitting area with a fireplace and seating. Two rooms with beds were positioned on each side, beyond curtained arches. The walls were textured in blue and green.

Lily stood in front of the mirror putting on a pair of red earrings. The older woman wore an emerald Aurumician dress and long jacket. She was smiling and humming to herself.

Jessica was surprised to see her mother.

"I thought you would still be at work."

"I didn't want to miss this," Lily said. "It's so important to Wadjette and Talon. Are you ready to go?"

Jessica was a little annoyed that Lily would leave work early for one of Wadjette's events. There had been plenty of missed concerts and school trips in Jessica's past. But perhaps it was a ceremony really worth seeing. The Aurumicians had many events, parties, and holidays that had a great deal of pageantry and sometimes, a bit of magic to them.

"Yeah, I'm just about ready," Jessica took a moment to look at herself in the mirror. She combed her hair, twisting it back while letting the small chunks frame her face. After she pinned the bun back, braided the two strands, pulling them back off her neck.

Her mother watched

"What?" Jessica felt her mother's gaze.

"Nothing. It's just you're getting good at braiding your hair, you're looking more Aurumician."

"Kaity taught me," Jessica replied. "I can add braids to your hair if you want."

"Nah, I'm fine. Let's go, don't want to be late."

Jessica pinned the braids back and selected a few orange beaded barrettes from her jewelry box. Teren had given her much of Misa's jewelry and she wore it often. The only piece that was her own was the Aurumician necklace given to her by Nico.

"Carrie Anne texted me before I left. She wants to know if you can go to the barbeque."

Lily shook her head.

"I just can't."

"Why not?"

"Don't take it personally, Jess. Your father and I will never be able to be friends again."

"Well, Carrie Anne seems to want it and she's sick. Living every holiday split is getting really tiring."

"Jess, it's just a picnic."

"But that's the thing. It's just a casual barbeque and somehow that's difficult." Jessica turned to face her mother. "What about when I graduate, or I get married, or have kids? Do I spend the rest of my life with split holidays between you and dad? Bad enough I'm split across the Gate."

"I know, but believe me, it's just for the best."

"It doesn't feel like the best. Seriously, if Nico forgave you for killing his mom, I don't get how you can't forgive dad for whatever you hate him for," Jessica evaded eye contact. She selected a large orange beaded firefly and added it to the bun on the top of her hair.

"It's different, Jess, complicated. Besides, I can't go to the picnic because I'm going to be taking a little trip, but I figured you would be okay."

"Trip where?"

"Talon and I are going to see some old friends."

"You have friends?"

Lily scowled.

"Kidding, Mom, where are you going?"

"To the south, towards the Olivi islands."

"Can you take me?"

"We're not bringing Wadjette either."

"If this is some sort of romantic getaway…" Jessica's voice faltered.

"Believe me, Jess, it's not. There are some castlefolk there, who are fearful to return. Talon wants me to go with him because if we run into trouble he thinks I'm intimidating."

"I would agree with him."

Lily shrugged.

Jessica's mother had an odd combination of powers. She could call lightning from the sky and slow down water molecules to ice. Not surprisingly, the lightning was wild and unpredictable, so Lily rarely used it. The ice powers were a little safer, but Lily didn't like using her ice abilities either.

Instead, Lily preferred traditional combat. It was likely the reason she got along so well with Fentalon.

"What's in the Olivi islands? But who are these castlefolk?" Jessica was concerned. "Mom, what if you get hurt? You can't even call and tell me where you are."

"I think I can take care of myself, I have for years. Besides, Talon has my back."

"And my cousin is okay with this?"

"Your cousin is not my boss."

"Um, pretty sure my cousin is acting as the Lord of Aurumice right now, pretty sure you have a tattoo that says your castlefolk. So yes, my cousin is your boss, and I don't think Teren is going to like this one bit."

"I can handle myself. I wanted to be honest and open with you about the details of this trip, Jess, I'm trying to build a bridge of trust here."

"Take Wadjette with you. I don't know if I can trust Fentalon, but I can trust Wadjette to look out for you."

"Jess, you can trust Talon. I've known him for years."

"Yeah, well, I bet Aunt Trixie thought she could trust Nico's mom and we all know how that turned out."

"Shut up. I don't want to think about it on a day that's supposed to be happy."

Jessica shrunk back in fear.

"I trust Talon, and this is the end of this conversation," Lily said. "If you would like to join me in the ballroom you are welcomed to. And you may want to put on a necklace that's a bit nicer, this is an important occasion."

Jessica was startled by her mother's comment. The teen no longer had a castlemark on her shoulder, so the necklace was the closest thing she had to looking like castlefolk. She didn't know if that was Nico's intent, or if his gesture was more romantic. There was no time to ask as the daywatch dragged him away.

"You look like I asked you to cut off your arm," Lily commented. "It's just a necklace. You're allowed to take it off every once in a while."

"I like it, it makes up for my mark," Jessica stated. "Which you burned off, so let me have this."

"I'm not making you take it off, I just thought since you have that entire box of jewelry from Misa that you'd like to wear something more formal to a ceremony like this."

"No, this suits me fine. I don't want to discuss it anymore."

Her mother shrugged, grabbed a scarf and walked to the door. Jessica took an additional moment and looked at herself in the mirror, wondering if she would ever see Nico again.

***

Nico stared out the window of the airship, as the wispy clouds grew dark and heavy with rain. As lightning reflected across the circular window, he slowly stood and tentatively walked to the dining room.

Thunder reverberated through the airship, vibrating anything that wasn't bolted down. He felt vulnerable and wished he could escape the aerial deathtrap.

Dark clouds continued to envelope the ship. Looking out, he could see the nightflight at the side struggling to steer the ship through the fierce winds. The tiny vessel lurched and Nico fell to his knees.

He crawled to the window as rain pelted the side of the airship. It was clear the nightflight was trying to gain altitude and fly above the storm, but the beast was helpless against the winds.

Lightning illuminated the side of the vessel with a blast of thunder.

Immediately, the ship plummeted. They were either hit or the nightflights had given themselves to instinct, seeking shelter on the ground.

In either case, they were in for a crash.

Pitching heavily to the left, the airship continued to descend. Nico's stomach lurched with the pressure change as he was thrown. He gripped the table leg as another bolt of lightning illuminated the large windows. The sonic boom threatened to tear the room apart with monstrous vibration.

Nico clenched his eyes as the vessel struck the ground.

The movement didn't stop, instead the ship rolled. Looking out the window, he realized they had landed in water.

There was no telling how quickly the ship would sink.

Nico ran for the exit door, hoping to find his way above deck. To his surprise, a short caprasian greeted him with a crossbow.

"Can you fight?" the goat-man barked at him, shoving the weapon into Nico's hands. Nico was bewildered, not expecting to meet a crew member in the hall.

"Fight? The ship is sinking!"

"It's airtight, watertight, our problem isn't the water. The mages are coming for Zia Casimirio. If you want to live, you'll fight with us."

"The storm…"

"It was a weather witch, the mages want to kill us. Are you fighting or not?"

"Yes, I can fight…" Nico agreed. The white caprasian didn't take the time to hear his response. He gestured for Nico to follow. Seeing no reason not too, Nico trailed after the man into a network of hallways. His mind raced. He had no desire to fight mages or stay any longer on this strange ship.

Escape. Take your first chance to escape.

The caprasian led Nico to a large room that appeared to be a formal dance hall of some sort. Nico realized he had misjudged the purpose of the airship, it seemed to have been an entertainment vessel from a bygone era. Accents of red and orange adorned the garish tables and chairs.

Zia waited in the room with three other caprasians. The gryphon cub stood by, tail flicking in a defensive posture. Bobbing and lurching, the ship continued its unsteady dance. The three caprasians wore helmets over their curved horns. They focused on readying their weapons and did not give Nico a second glance.

Zia turned, her eyes lasering in on Nico.

"You will fight the mages, or you'll die," she stated.

Nico felt the force behind her words. He had no doubt the mages intended to kill them all.

Zia gestured to a stairwell. The caprasians followed her, armed and ready. Nico took the rear of the guard, his senses sharply tuned.

They raced up the stairwell. Zia opened a door, letting in a gust of salty sea air and water.

Outside, the scene of chaos unfurled under lightning and driving rain. The grey nightflights of the airship were flying wild, tangling with black nightflights ridden by mages.

Four mages stood on the large deck, wearing the blue uniform of Castle Nova. Caprasian fighters, Zia's crew, leveled crossbows against them.

"You need to come with me," Zia told Nico. "Stay by my side, we're getting out of here."

Nico followed Zia out into the roaring storm, his clothing immediately plastered to him by the rain.

Letting loose a flurry of shots, the crew fought, but they were easily deflected by the skilled mages. The airship bounced and rolled, uncontrollable on the raging ocean.

One of the ship's nightflights flew low, focused on them.

"Here comes our ride!"

Just as the nightflight descended, a cloaked mage leapt forward and grabbed Zia by the wrist. Without hesitation, Nico leveled his crossbow at the stranger, squinting through the harsh rain.

He squeezed the trigger. Even with only one good eye, years of practice shone through.

The bolt sliced through flesh, impaling the man through the neck.

Zia smiled and stepped away from the mage.

The stranger fell to the slick deck, writing in pain as Zia climbed onto the nightflight. She looked back at Nico, gesturing for him to follow.

The mage gurgled and thrashed, hand to his neck. The color drained from his human face as he gritted fanged teeth in agony. Blood poured from his carotid artery, staining his uniform. It was a mortal wound.

A pressure blast knocked Nico back, slamming his head against a deck railing. His vision flashed white for a moment. As he regained his senses, Nico realized the mages had shifted focus to Zia and their fallen comrade.

The fallen mage had stopped thrashing, his body limp and white.

As the others closed in, Zia shook her head at Nico, then turned her eyes to the sky. With a powerful leap and burst of wind, the grey beast launched itself into the air, leaving Nico and the battle far behind. The nightflight struggled for a moment, but it regained speed quickly and remained aloft, climbing into rain clouds out of sight. The mages abruptly abandoned their fight with the caprasians, chasing furiously after Zia.

The injured mage vanished.

Nico panicked. Around him, Zia's crew was fleeing, taking the remainder of the nightflights with them. There wasn't enough room for all of the crew on the beasts, and some of the caprasians ran towards the edge of the ship, clearly with an escape plan in mind.

Nico chased after the crew, coming to the edge of the airship. Despite his fear, he marveled at the ingenuity of the barrel-shaped vessel as he peered over the side. Ladders curved around the airship. About twenty feet down, he could see tiny life boats.

Nico began descending down the side of the airship, trembling. His feet slipped on the wet rungs as he clung to the thin ladder.

He continued downwards and stepped cautiously into a small boat. Relief washed over him. Nico loosened the ropes and lowered the boat into the raging sea.

***

Far from the stormy ocean, the castlefolk gathered in the Grand Ballroom of Aurumice.

Majestic and massive, the ballroom's ornate carvings were as beautiful as they were difficult to keep free of dust and dirt. The ancient chamber was nearly six stories tall. It was made up of three levels, each one completely encircled with an elaborate balcony.

The apex of the ceiling held a stained glass star, newly repaired by Jiberty. With Kaity's levitation skills, the master craftsman was able to reassemble the stunning focal point.

With laughter and conversation, the castlefolk had gathered for the Bright Path ceremony. The crowd began centering on a small platform that was typically used for musicians.

Jessica's mind wandered. One snowy afternoon, she had followed Nico to repair the wiring in the chandeliers. A nest of fire doves attacked him, but Jessica had saved her friend from plummeting to the stone floor. It had only been a few years ago but it felt like another lifetime.

"Jess!" Kaity Cosette called to her through the gathering. Dressed in an elegant lavender gown, the leopardess wore a long jacket, trimmed in gold. In her hand was a heavy leather book. On her right arm, she balanced Temi. The speckled child seemed determined to pull a lavender ribbon out of her own hair

"Jess, I need you to do me a favor. Summer Fire Flight Fest is in a few weeks. It's outside, do you have time to talk about exterior lighting? I want to do something really fancy for it."

Leave it to Kaity, one event had barely begun and she was already planning another.

"Yeah, I can come up with something."

"Great!" Kaity barely acknowledged her response before dashing off to talk to someone else. The child dropped the ribbon. Jessica picked it up.

"What was that about?" Jared appeared at Jessica's left side.

"Something with lighting for the Fire Flight Fest, I don't know. It's Kaity."

"Do you know if they're doing any fancy food for this thing? I've never been to Ceremony of Bright Path, it's sort of an Aurumice thing. We don't have them at Nova"

"Jared, they make a buffet like three times a day here. How are you hungry?"

"But it's different when they have a party. They do the really decadent pastries, and the spun sugar, and the good wine and the extra tasty meat. I didn't know if this was a party or a ceremony or what."

"I've never been to one either."

"At least you're Aurumician."

"Barely," Jessica became self-conscious of her scar. She began to worry if the dress was a poor choice because it left her scarred shoulder exposed.

Across the room, her mother laughed with Fentalon. Jessica's feelings towards the man continued to be in turmoil. She twisted Temi's ribbon in her hands.

"You tend to stare at them a lot," Jared commented.

"Yeah, I'm not so sure I'm cool with this."

"You know they were at it in the barn loft the other night?"

Jessica punched Jared in the arm as hard as she could.

"No! No! No! Keep it to yourself!"

She *suspected* her mother had been sleeping with Fentalon, she didn't need to know it was true.

"I'm just saying she likes him, a lot apparently. You should be happy for them. Stephen has Carrie Anne, why shouldn't your mom have someone?"

"Because it's a weird combination," Jessica whispered. "And he's really...cat like."

"Do you have any idea how racist you sound right now?" Jared glanced around, concerned that Jessica was in earshot of other castlefolk.

"I didn't mean it that way, I meant it like he's never going to be able to visit Pennsylvania."

"Last I recall, you have a thing for an ailurian man."

"Had."

"Have."

"Jared, I was fourteen and he was the first guy who really treated me like a good friend, that's all."

"I read that book. I don't think that's how the story went," Jared mused.

Jessica crossed her arms, waiting for Jared to chide her for wearing the necklace. Yes, she believed Nico was more, but the past year had dulled her feelings. At first, Jessica had tried to silence her sadness around Teren, afraid her cousin would read her emptiness and echo it. She couldn't pretend to be happy, so she simply tried to feel nothing. The more time past, the easier it was to pretend she didn't miss him.

"Nico was different," she said. "He could pass for human on earth with a little costuming, if you recall Halloween. Also, those two are both old."

"Now you're ageist?"

She knew the statement would distract Jared from Nico.

"Will you stop analyzing my opinions? I don't like the idea that my mom is with someone, period, because she's my mom, and moms don't do that sort of thing."

"You realize you exist because..."

"Shut up."

Jared could not continue the banter as the castlefolk around them quieted. Kaity climbed up onto the little stage and stood by a decorative table. Its surface was covered in a heap of coin bags that reached to Kaity's shoulders. On the floor was a sword, positioned into a display base. Polished to a glassy obsidian finish, the hilt was stamped with the seal of Aurumice.

Kaity led many ceremonies traditionally practiced by the old monarchs. Aurumicians lived without royals, and were happy for it. Kaity was a perfect public figure in absence of a monarch, well-spoken, powerful and yet humble. The leopardess was born of the fields; her parents were Aurumician herders. By chance, Kaity developed mage strengths as a child, the first in her family.

At Kaity's left hand was a series of chimes on a stand, suspended on strings, each a different color. She picked up a little wooden mallet and drew it across the bells. Silence spread at the sound of the chimes.

"The Chrysalis Chimes have been rung, we are ready to begin," Kaity said.

"Oh my God," Jared murmured. "She's beautiful."

"Who…?"

Wadjette had entered the room silently. She walked up the steps of the dais, and Jessica's breath caught in her throat.

She had never seen Wadjette wear something so stunning.

In Jessica's mind, Wadjette was the warrior street girl, wise beyond years. On the stage, Wadjette was an elegant goddess. The pantheress' black hair was down to her waist, plaited with gold thread.

A gossamer web of earrings and necklaces trailed down her forest green gown. Each gold chain wove into a crisscross then intersected with tiny river stones at her waist. Shimmering, the skirt of the dress was a beaded matrix like nightflight scales.

Jessica grinned, happy for her friend.

This was Wadjette's moment, her graduation, everything she had worked for in her entire life.

Kaity nodded to Wadjette and the girl nodded back.

"People of Aurumice," Kaity began, reading from a small book. "Tonight, we gather for an ancient tradition, the Ceremony of Bright Path. I am Kaity Lin Cosette Evansi, daughter of Aurumice."

"From the earliest days of Aurumice, even in the time of the monarchy, we believed that each of the castlefolk may pick their own destiny. No one is bound to the life they were born into, and it is by the love of the Goddess Aurora and the blessing of Greenbriar that the people of Aurumice forge their own path."

"Wadjette Kristianna La'Roch, daughter of Fentalon La'Roch and most honored Desaryee Scarlett La'Roch, you are a child of Aurumice. You bare the signet of the castle with pride, and every day serve her will."

"All children of Aurumice are given a choice as they come of age. You have had time to study interests of your choosing. Now is the point in your life where you must decide your path. This path is not forged of stone, but it is born of the light of the castle. You may bend it at your will, and know you will always have home in these hallowed walls."

Kaity turned slightly, gesturing to the table.

"To start your life journey, you may take one of two paths. Wadjette, if you chose the coins, you may take your leave from Aurumice. You may purchase what you need to create a home elsewhere, and wherever that may be, we pray you carry us in your heart, and live according to our teachings."

Jessica glanced over at Fentalon. The man stood very proudly, hands folded.

Kaity continued.

"The second path you may take is the one of your greatest achievement. From the moment you returned to Castle Aurumice, you were determined to defend her, and all of the castlefolk. Relying upon the teachings of your father, you forged alone, bringing together a new guard. You trained tirelessly. You took on the honored traditions of Aurumice, working with every individual, making certain everyone had the knowledge to defend themselves against danger. You led when there was no one else to lead, and accomplished what no one would expect from one so young, and yet you did it with a determination that cannot be overlooked."

A little cheer went through the crowd, breaking the decorum.

Kaity waited until the noise died down before she continued.

"I know you have led our guard as Aurumice rebuilt. But now it is time to decide. It is because of your great feats, if you chose to remain in Castle Aurumice, you shall formally take the title of Vice Captain of the Guard, second only to Fentalon La'Roch, and you will continue to defend our home."

Kaity touched the coin pouch and the sword.

"You have two choices. Wadjette La'Roch, what Bright Path will you walk?"

Kaity was interrupted by a squeal. Little Temi ran up the dais, no longer content to stay in the crowd away from her mother. The child clung to Kaity's legs, trying to climb up and be held.

"Oh Temi, you are not supposed to interrupt," Kaity lifted her daughter, balancing the child on her hip. A little ripple of amusement went through the crowd.

Kaity glanced to Wadjette, whispering apologies.

Corwin stepped forward to the base of the stage to retrieve his daughter, but Wadjette outstretched her hands.

"Give her here, it's alright," the young warrior said.

Wadjette caught Temi's attention. The child was very much enthralled by the shiny braiding in Wadjette's hair. Leaning out of her mother's arms, Temi was determined to grab onto Wadjette and pull at the gold threads.

"Alright," Kaity seemed a little concerned to have formality eroded, but moved on. "Now as I just said, Wadjette, what Bright Path do you choose?"

Jessica smiled, seeing Wadjette's intent.

Wadjette carefully took the little girl from her mother and balanced on her hip. The pantheress then grasped the hilt of the sword, pulling it from its base. It sung as the metal slid against metal, ringing crisply through the ballroom.

She held the sword aloft.

"I choose to stay, here, in my home, and forever protect the children of Aurumice."

A chill ran down Jessica's spine as the castlefolk erupted into wild cheers and applause. Temi looked around and mimicked the clapping of the crowd. Wadjette kissed the child on the forehead.

"It is with great honor," Kaity shouted over the crowd. The noise subsided a little bit and she repeated herself. "It is with great honor that I present the Vice-Captain of the Guard of Aurumice."

Cheering burst through the crowd. Jessica glanced at her mother, the woman was beaming with pride.

The pantheress gently set Temi on the floor and placed the sword into a scabbard, affixing it to her belt. Bounding down the stairs, the child chased after older cubs as Wadjette followed into the sea of congratulations. The crowd parted a bit, allowing Fentalon the honor of being the first to hug his daughter.

Lily embraced the girl second.

Jessica understood that it was a special day for Wadjette, one she truly deserved, but she could not help but feel a sting of jealousy.

As the crowd milled around, a table was brought out with platters of confections. Spun sugar globes were carried on trays atop cinnamon cakes trimmed with candied nuts. Platters of cookies were brought in as well as large pies, four times the size of anything from earth.

"Oh, I knew there would be something good," Jared followed the tray of cinnamon cakes. Jessica joined the crowd and congratulated Wadjette, hugging her friend. She barely had a chance to say a word before Wadjette moved on to the next person.

The entire ceremony was interesting, like a graduation, but this one made more sense to Jessica.

"Oh, by the Goddess could this cake get any better?" Jared's mouth was stuffed.

Jessica picked a chunk of the spun sugar globe off his plate.

"Come on Jess, get your own!"

"FIRE IN THE EAST HALLWAY!"

It took Jessica a moment to process the words.

Fire?!

Fear jolted Jessica, but the castlefolk were quick to react to the shout. The crowd ran from the party, abandoning their plates with a clatter as they ran. They had trained and practiced for this under Wadjette's command.

Fire in the castle halls turned deadly quickly.

There were no firetrucks to save them.

Jessica ran after the mob, but a hundred people densely packing into the hallways made movement difficult. She was stuck, immobilized between castlefolk. The party was ruined and the tension high.

By the time Jessica reached the east hallway, clouds of steam were pouring out of the room. The air was hot and smoky with an acrid stench. A bucket brigade, plus Lily's freezing powers and Kaity's telekinetic abilities, worked as an efficient team.

Jessica looked for something to do, but the hallway was already drenched and partially frozen. Icicles hung off the light fixtures and encased the tapestries.

Which also meant Lily was sure to be in a foul mood. Though her mother had command over lightning and ice, lightning was far easier. Lily *hated* using her freezing abilities. It gave her awful migraine headaches.

Jessica looked for her mom. Her work was already done, and she rested a steadying hand on Fentalon's shoulder, exhausted. Jessica stood awkwardly by, the fire had happened so fast, but the castlefolk had controlled it.

"Wow, this looks like a mess," Jared again was behind Jessica, still eating his cake.

"They put it out quick, I didn't even get a chance to help...how can I help?"

Jared shrugged.

"Castlefolk never cease to amaze me. If this was Polaris Academy, they would have been standing around arguing which department should be getting the water while the whole castle burned."

Kaity and Wadjette delivered directives, sending tapestries and rugs outside to dry. The crowd of castlefolk started to go back to the party, the festive mood undampered. If anything, it was strengthened by their unfaltering comradery.

Jared went back to the ballroom. Jessica offered to help and found herself carrying drenched carpets out to the side yard to dry.

When she returned, the soot covered hall was mostly empty. Corwin and Kaity discussed the patterns of the smoke on the wall. Fentalon stood by, arms crossed, listening in curiosity. His white dog sniffed the floor. Jessica's mother leaned on a chair, watching in silence.

The fire centered around a panel of wall in a charcoaled twelve-foot patch.

Corwin touched the saturated wall gingerly. He was reading the history of the room, trying to detect anything unusual. It was puzzling. The only thing on the wall were a few paintings, no candles or lamps nearby.

"I know what it is," Jessica interrupted. She unhooked the brittle painting from the wall. It was heavy and cold.

Beneath the painting, the ice held frayed wires in a crystal sarcophagus.

"Damn, those wires feed a really large chunk of the upper castle." Jessica felt her stress levels rise. "I need to fix this."

"Will it take you long?" Lily asked.

"Probably not, as long as someone a hundred years ago put a breaker in a good spot. I'll figure it out. You can go back to the celebration."

"Are you sure you know what you're doing?" Fentalon questioned again. "This is dangerous. I wonder if you have the age or experience to deal with this."

Fentalon's words stung.

"I know more about these systems than the rest of the castlefolk put together," Jessica said. "They're old and there's vermin constantly chewing their way through the lines, but I make it work. Safer than it's ever been, that I can assure you."

"Jess brings things from our home," Lily interjected. "She is making it better."

It was rare her mother paid her a compliment.

Fentalon seemed content with Lily's endorsement. He excused himself to return to the party. Lily accompanied him, leaning on his shoulder. Bo obediently trailed at their heels. Kaity and Corwin followed soon after.

Jessica was left alone in the frozen, dripping hall.

***

The lifeboat brought Nico to a cold, rocky coastline. Climbing out of the boat, icy water welled into his boots. He trudged up the windy beach until he was out of the reach of the waves.

Nico's eyes traced the landscape, searching for any clue as to his location. Past the rocky sand, the forest was tall and dark. Evergreen trees filled the horizon for as far as he could see. Beyond them, mountains, but which range he couldn't discern.

Drinking in his freedom, he listened as seabirds cried in the distance. Even the overcast day was more sun than he had seen in over a year.

His elation turned to endless regret as he realized the gravity of his actions.

When Nico was sent to the Mines of Briken, it was an act of service and sacrifice. Neither the forcefield nor the back taxes were his fault, but as the last of his family, it was his burden to bear.

This was different, attacking the mage had been his foolish choice.

Feeling vulnerable on the open shoreline, Nico climbed up the beach through the tall grasses into the forest. Inhaling the pine needle aroma, he wanted to relax but dread wrapped its arms around him.

Seeking a path forged by animals, he saw no signs of people as he wandered into the forest.

He kept walking.

Bramble bushes cut into his skin, but still he pressed into the forest, needing to be as far from the sea and the memory of the dying mage as possible.

How was he so stupid?! He looked at his hands and his lost fingers. What had the Mines done to him?

Time slipped by him as he continued to walk, having no appetite, not eating. He walked for hours. If he had been thinking straight, he could have found adequate shelter, hunted for food, and truly rested. Instead, he picked berries and leafy herbs along the way as he continued to stumble through the dense forest.

Few in number, mages never responded well to an attack on their own. They were the ultimate law of the land. Local governments pretended to wield power, but everyone truly bowed to Castle Nova and Katanzarko, the City of Mages.

When Nico was a child, a dozen magic users arrived at the doors of Aurumice, vehemently searching for a mage killer. The fugitive had been one of their own, Savartos Sarkisian, a name that always stuck in Nico's memory. Beatrix fled to earth with Teren, afraid that a psychic mage would accidentally come upon the Sinari child.

If there was even one psychic in the fight on the airship, they would be able to find Nico and make him stand trial for a crime that was *truly his fault.*

He collapsed in the tangled root base of a massive tree, torture by the gravity of his crime. Disgust and self-hatred filled his heart. Trembling violently, he berated himself again and again. He couldn't return to Castle Aurumice. If the mages hunted for him, it would put his home, and Teren, in jeopardy.

Everything was destroyed.

Nico slammed his fists into the tree, furiously pounding until his knuckles were raw. Darkness strangled Nico's mind as the Mines of Briken leeched their black ichor outward to capture his soul. Ripping at his hair, he sobbed until he fell into a tortured slumber. Visions of past horrors resurged as his dreaming mind was sucked back into the subterranean hell. The blade tore into his digits again as they sawed off the last of his fingers in a river of blood.

His psyche was fractured.

CHAPTER 10

Jessica worked for days to restore power after the fire, running new wires through passageways. Castle electrician was a job no one was eager to do, so the teen took up the challenge. There was a fear of electricity in Centernian culture, but Jessica shrugged past it.

On a rainy afternoon, the girl stood in front of the blackened wall in the East Hallway, clutching a hand-made blue book. She flipped through the pages and carefully added her new circuits to the map of the castle wiring.

The book, cobbled together by years of castle electricians, was a precious tome to understanding the power system of Aurumice. Jessica couldn't read hand-written Centernian script very well, but she could understand most of the book.

It was the strangest mystery of the Gate, how two civilizations could share a verbal language but have a completely different text system.

The door at the end of the hall creaked, rousing Jessica from her muddled thoughts. Teren stood in the doorframe, haggard and soaked from the rain. He wore an open grey jacket, the top buttons of his white shirt undone. Her cousin seemed older, though Jessica had seen him a few weeks before.

"You're back!" Jessica exclaimed, embracing Teren. He smelled like bicorn and travel.

Teren returned the embrace half-heartedly.

"What happened here?"

"Barbeque," Jessica replied. "Something sparked in the wall. It created enough heat to catch the painting on the other side on fire, which is what caused this mess. I patched things up, but there's something here that you may find interesting"

"How so?"

She pulled a voltage tester out of her pocket and pointed it to an empty space in the blackened wall. It beeped, flashing a little red LED.

"Look. There's still current, flowing in a neat little line, but there's no wire."

"On the other side?"

"There's nothing there, I checked. This path, if you look up, leads right to that burned end. There was a wire there, but it's gone! I spent the past day looking this up at home, and there's no explanation. It's like there's an invisible wire!"

"Is your equipment wrong?"

"No, I tried different testers. It's magic, right? Ethereal magic? That's the type that persists long after the mage." Jessica was excited by the idea. "It's not that surprising. We've always known this electricity is different than what we have on earth. Before we assumed it followed the same rules. This doesn't."

"Do you think this patch is dangerous?" Teren raised an eyebrow.

"Well I'm not touching it."

"Seal the wall."

"Teren, it could spark again. We can't panic until we learn more. I need you on my side for this one, people have been complaining about how dangerous the electrical system is, and Fentalon is fueling that paranoia."

"Yes, Savina told me he had returned, is he well?" Teren's voice was tired and it was clear he was losing interest in the conversation.

"Yeah, he's back in charge of the guard. We just had the Bright Path ceremony for Wadjette, she's Vice-Captain of the guard now. That's when the fire happened."

"Oh unfortunate, and I am sorry I missed Wadjette's Bright Path ceremony."

"No, it was nice despite the fire. She's really happy. The 'folk are happy. My mom's happy. My mom's sleeping with Fentalon, which is annoying, and I also don't like that he's complaining when we already have Trabalis up our butts about the electricity."

"Fentalon was never a fan of technology, he thinks more like the old ones."

"Well it would be nice if he didn't spread his opinion around."

"Jessica, I cannot deal with this problem right now."

"I'm not asking you to. I'm telling you what's going on!"

Teren appeared so exhausted that Jessica was sure he would fall asleep standing up.

"Regardless," her cousin blinked. "I was coming to find you. I had something to show you."

"Another problem?"

"No, this is something I think you'll like, a gift."

"You seem really dismal about this gift."

"No Jess, this is important but I am very, very tired, and this wall," he gestured, "is concerning."

"You want to change, get some tea? Then I can put away my tools."

Teren thought about that for a moment.

"Yes, yes you're right. I will meet you at the staircase by the dancing bird statue."

***

Far in the dark forest, Nico took fang berries and set them into a tightly curved piece of bark. He mashed the red pulp, carefully extracting their liquid from the rough outer shell.

Madness ripped at his mind as every demon of his past emerged from the shadows.

He needed to escape.

The berries would give him a way.

The crimson juice would take his pain, perhaps permanently.

His muscles were weakened, his tremors were worse. His fingers were numb as the noxious juice collected in the makeshift bowl. Nighttime insects began their song as the darkness fell through the nameless forest. Mosquitos bit at Nico's face and his head continued to pound with pain.

Again, Nico wondered the name of the mage that he killed. Was he someone's husband, father? Did he say goodbye to the people that mattered before he left to begin his journey? Did he leave behind siblings? Nico did not know the answers, but he knew that whoever the mage was, he had plans for the tomorrow that never came.

Nico continued to drip the juice into the pod. The long skinny fruit were toxic in their native form, but more potent in a juicy pulp. Nico knew he might lose his nerve while chewing, gulping the liquid would be more effective.

He was done.

His life was one tragedy after another, and he feared what new torture would come next.

Staring at the pulpy liquid collected in the bark, he spoke aloud to the empty forest.

"Should I go back to Aurumice?"

The trees were silent.

Nico was already an escaped convict for tax evasion, but now he bore a real crime on his soul, one that deserved punishment. He had debated turning himself in penance, but remembered mages had a practice of reading the minds of felons.

If they peered through his thoughts and found Teren, his friend would surely die for being born a Sinari.

And that was too great a risk to take.

That single thought was reason enough to extinguish his own life.

Nico picked up the little bark boat, his mind resolved. Hand trembling, he brought the liquid to his lips. Closing his eyes, he drank the poison.

The liquid had a sharp tang to it. It was much like an alcohol with both a nutty and fruity flavor.

He waited in the still forest, wondering what would happen. He had read that fang berry poison was swift.

His stomach turned, and he thought he would vomit. His arms became numb and heavy, as if they did not belong to his body. Dizziness swirled the dusk forest around him.

Nico's face struck the soft wet grass, but he soon realized he couldn't actually *feel* the ground beneath him.

So this is dying.

He took consolation in the fact he was numb and not in pain.

Until he realized he wanted to close his eyes, but couldn't.

Then his lungs failed and he forgot how to breathe.

***

Jessica waited at the metal statue resembling a heron with elaborate head plumage. The beige hallway was in a quiet part of the castle that few people visited.

Her cousin appeared around the corner. His pale face was calm, but tears began to stream down his cheeks.

"Teren, what's wrong?"

He reached up and touched his face, a confused look creeping into his eyes.

Jessica grew uneasy, whatever he had to say, it was going to be bad.

"Why are you crying?"

Teren seemed perplexed, his hand to his cheek, confused as to why it was wet.

"That's strange. I have no idea why."

"But…"

"Cold…sad…regret…but not mine." His voice was soft, "This has never happened before. Sorry, Jessi, this is not the reason I asked you here."

Jessica knew a mage's powers evolved in unpredictable ways. Teren was an empathic mage, there was no telling how far his magic could reach.

Teren shrugged off the tears, and that indifference worried Jessica even more. The wetness continued to drip down Teren's face.

"Strange. Follow me."

"What happened in Briken?" she asked.

"I will explain," he said with such sadness Jessica feared to say another word. Jessica thought Teren was going to lead her to his study, but instead he took the small staircase up to the third level.

The silence was uncomfortable.

Rounding a corner, they came upon a red mahogany bookcase at the end of a hall. With surprising ease, Teren pushed the bookcase to the side, revealing a white corridor lit beyond.

"Huh…that wasn't there before," Jessica allowed herself to be distracted by the strange new doorway.

"There are always more secret passages and forgotten hallways in this Castle to discover. You can spend a lifetime in Aurumice and not know all her secrets."

"But I thought I had a good sense of all of them looking at the wiring maps."

"There's no electricity in this part of the castle," Teren explained, leading her past the bookcase to a stairwell lit by natural light. The walls were a rough tan stone, decorated with an ivy design. They ascended the staircase to a wood door. Birds were etched into the wooden panels. Teren rubbed his eyes, unable to stop the tears that obscured his vision.

"You're still crying for no reason!" Jessica accused.

"Yes, I know," Teren said softly. "This feeling is new. I don't understand."

"Someone else is in trouble?" Jessica asked. "It's Nico, isn't it? He's in trouble?"

Pushing the door open, Teren did not reply.

Jessica begrudgingly allowed him his silence and instead became caught in the grandeur of the room.

It was breathtaking.

A rounded octagonal atrium welcomed them, thirty feet wide. The ceiling was made up of intricately woven metal beams, creating a domed apex. Much of the glass was shattered, boarded up hastily. There was a narrow metal staircase on one wall. Rain poured down the remaining glass, tinking in a perfect little symphony. The air held the fragrance of an early summer storm.

"Are we high up?"

"Highest tower, save for the spires from the grand ballroom."

She looked at her cousin. How could he expect her to ignore the fact that he was *ignoring his own tears?*

"Teren, you're frightening me. Something isn't right with you."

Her cousin closed the door behind him, not wishing to be overheard by the casual passerby in the hallway.

"Jessica, I have no idea whose emotions I am sensing right now, so stop asking me!"

"But!"

"Stop asking or I will make you stop."

"Now you're being a jerk," Jessica crossed her arms, then took look around the room. The stone floor had been covered with shattered glass and a decade of dust, grime, and mouse carcasses . Jessica walked carefully, eyes drawn to the design in the center of the floor.

A tiled moon was at the center of the design, surrounded by a swirl of animal designs. The floor was glassy and transparent in some areas, like crystal. She realized that there once water beneath the floor, but now it was filled with a dried brown algae.

Jessica drunk in the details of the room. Teren was silent, arms crossed, looking downward. The cold feeling of dread did not leave Jessica's heart. She tried to distract herself with the room.

From the ceiling hung many bird perches and she realized it had once been an aviary. A small tree was off to the north corner, withered and dead. A fountain was built into the wall beyond the tree, its basin integrated with the floor. Jessica surmised that it must have aerated the aquarium housed beneath.

The room had a small stone fireplace, chairs, a table, and a desk. A dog bed was placed under the desk, covered in white fur. It was a sign that the room had once belonged to her Aunt Beatrix, who had kept a beautiful white wolf as a pet.

"This room belonged to your mother," Jessica stated.

"Yes, once it was a music room with an aquarium floor, but as soon as my mother became an animal speaker, birds came from all over and nested in this place. She turned it into an aviary. You would have loved those days. There was always some stray critter wandering around, and she would converse with them just as easily as I talk to you."

"Must have been magical."

"Actually, it drove everyone quite insane because we could only hear half the conversation and these were usually not domesticated animals. They would make a mess of the castle, but my mother never meant to cause trouble. She and Misa were quite alike, always on some grand adventure, some interesting new plan." Teren picked up various objects from the desk — a pencil, a mirror, and a metal clock decorated with cast ivy leaves. He set the clock back and took a step away, but as he moved, his foot caught the table's leg.

Before he could react, the clock tumbled off the table's edge. Jessica was quick, and grabbed the ornate device before it hit the floor.

Teren's expression was pure relief.

"Thank you, I don't need more bad luck."

Jessica gently placed the clock on the table towards the center.

"Is that a special clock?"

"No. It's just bad luck to break a clock."

He took a few steps away from the desk in silence, his hand resting on the back of a woven wooden chair.

"I thought you might like to restore this room," Teren continued, "and take it for your own. It seemed like your type of challenge, and you need your own space away from your mother."

"Really? This is mine?"

Teren nodded.

Jessica was overwhelmed.

"This space is so beautiful, I'll fix it, it will take me time, but I'll fix it."

"Do with it as you wish," Teren said. "No need to restore it to aviary. Make it your own."

Jessica took a deep breath, but Teren's tears still bothered her.

"Please, don't take this the wrong way, I appreciate the room, but please tell me the truth about what's going on. Teren, you are crying for him, because no one else in this entire world would make you cry."

"I think you are right," Teren whispered. "But I don't understand this magic. There are no books for the Sinari. We are supposed to be dead."

Hands trembling, he leaned against the white wooden table. He was fighting to control his tears. It would have been a humorous farce if Jessica had not been so worried.

"Please sit," Teren commanded, trying to take control of the conversation.

Jessica looked at her seating options, everything was covered in dirt. The cushioned furniture was particularly disgusting. She wiped off a white wooden chair, hooking her feet on the support rung. By the time she had settled, her cousin seemed to have stopped crying, though his amethyst eyes were red and puffy.

Teren continued to speak.

"I did want to gift you this room, as a terrible means to soften what I am going to say. As you are very aware, we have spent the past year trying to network our way through the town, and the mines, trying to figure out what would convince Qara Umbrian to release Nico. Around four weeks ago, Jared noticed Nico was missing. He called me out there, and likewise, I have not been able to sense him. We know supplies get transported out of Briken via train, I followed the line, but I found nothing. I have no idea where Nico is. I'm really fearing the worst."

"Oh." Jessica looked up at the rain as it ran down the broken ceiling. She could see churning clouds of the storm beyond the patterned glass.

"I wanted to keep you shielded as long as I could, so you can focus on school, but every time I try to lie to you I feel like you can see right through me. Few people can do that."

"That's easy Teren, it's because you lie all the time," Jessica smirked.

"I do not."

"Well, maybe not a true lie," Jessica backpedaled, "but every time you use your power to make someone change their mind about something. It's sort of like a lie…"

"I want to make them feel better, or to not fight amongst themselves, is that a crime?"

"No! Teren, I'm not saying that!"

"You have no idea Jessica, you have it so easy! You just walk through that Gate, and none of this is your responsibility. You have paradise in Pennsylvania, and you can't see it. Misa would have given up Centernia for our mother's world in a heartbeat, she said it so many times and damnit, I didn't believe her then, but she was right! You have so much in your home and you take it for granted."

Jessica looked in her cousin's hallowed eyes. Teren was so young, but he carried the weight of the castle on his shoulders. She tried not to argue with him.

"I do appreciate home," Jessica said quietly.

"No, you're just a kid, you don't understand."

Jessica bristled.

"Teren, I do appreciate home, and I appreciate Centernia, and it's really frickin' difficult trying to make everyone happy all the time! I'm not real castlefolk, and I don't have time for friends at home, and Felicia Lee won't even talk to me anymore! I don't have time for my father's family, and Carrie Anne is sick, and I'm supposed to go to college, and I miss Nico, and I try so, so hard to never be sad around you!"

"Jessica, you—"

His words were cut off as he doubled over and fell to the floor. Clenching his teeth, he gripped his chest in pain.

"What's wrong?!" Jessica reached for him, but as she knelt, she felt a strange tingle on her right shoulder. She paused, trying to understand the sensation. The scar of her castlemark stung, like a piece was being ripped away.

The argument forgotten, Teren leaned heavily against her, shivering and sobbing. She wrapped her arms around him, for the first time feeling how thin and bony he had become. Her left arm tightened around his chest, and she cradled his head in her right hand. As soon as she touched his skin, an intense sadness flowed into her veins like a heavy icy water.

Teren's nails dug deep into Jessica's back, further compounding her pain. She wanted to run away from the monstrosity that clung to her, but at the same time she feared leaving him. His pain was unimaginably deeper than her own and somehow, she knew he was teetering on the edge of hysteria.

"I can't...." Teren choked. "He's dying alone and I can't find him."

Jessica felt the wave of paralyzing grief. For a moment, she thought Teren was going to strangle her in his terrifying magic.

Jessica looked up to the broken skylight, trying to fixate on anything to take her out of the moment. Teren heaved sobs into her shoulder, biting into her skin in a vain attempt not to scream. The physical pain helped Jessica think.

She couldn't pull him out of the abyss, but she could focus on how much she loved him. Closing her eyes and holding her cousin, she hoped her feelings could keep him from completely succumbing to insanity.

***

The darkness was a tranquil velvety blanket. Nico floated through the calm until it melted into the rooftop of Castle Aurumice. Leafy forest canopy stretched out before him. Bicorns race in the pastures at twilight, their horns glinting. Fireflies twinkled across the meadows. Trabalis in the far distance, the River White flowed steadily, cutting through the landscape.

Standing beside him was Misa. She wore a gown of white gossamer, her curly dark hair filled with star-like ivory flowers. As she outstretched her hand, the fabric of her dress disintegrated into tiny fireflies. Nico found himself breathless in her magic.

"This is death?" Nico asked.

"I'm not sure," Misa floated into the night air. Her gown shifted to the darkening blue of the night sky as black butterfly wings emerged from her back.

"Wait! Where are you going?"

Misa reappeared beside him, her face decorated with a dotted pattern of sapphire gemstones.

"I'm still here," she giggled, "Will you fly after me?"

Nico took a few steps, unsure of what to do.

"I don't think I can."

Misa turned around.

"Try," she commanded.

Nico jumped, but couldn't fly. He tried to visualize his clothing changing, but it remained the same blue jacket he had always favored.

"Is it because I was a dreamspinner and you weren't? You can't control this realm?" Misa asked. The jewels and celestial dress vanished. She was her normal self, wearing a scarlet tunic and plain brown breeches.

She took his hand. It was as soft and warm as it had been when she was alive.

"How did you get here?" Misa asked.

"I drank fangberry poison."

"You took your own life?" Misa held up his hand, staring at it. The smile on her face slowly faded.

"I had to, Misa! I attacked a mage of Castle Nova. If the others had found me, they would have read my mind. Teren would be dead if they saw my memories!"

"How much poison did you drink?"

113

"A lot," Nico replied.

"Listen to me," Misa let his hand drop. "You don't belong here. It's only a matter of time before you leave the dream realm, and I have no idea what happens if you fade. Others have passed through. They don't stay."

Nico's joy was replaced with terror.

"But I killed a mage."

"Mages won't read your mind without consent, that's why your mother got herself into trouble. You have a chance, if you can run back home before the mages find you, you can go to earth. Jessi will save you."

"But, what if I can't?"

"Nico, if you die, my brother will never be the same."

"He already isn't."

"Try to wake up, you have a body and a chance. I don't."

Misa took a step back.

"I'm going to force you to wake up like I used to. When I do, take all of your energy and fight to live."

"But...I drank *poison*. I can't just will that away!"

"Please, Nico, stop arguing with me."

"I'm unconscious."

"Shut up and try!"

Nico awoke in agony, crushed by the weight of his own body. He opened his mouth to breathe, but no air flowed. Paralyzed, his lungs were two dead weights.

Nico continued to try to draw in air until he could finally give a small gasp. Minute amounts of oxygen trickled into his lungs as he thrashed on the ground. The amounts grew deeper with each breath as he expanded the capacity of his lungs. His vision returned, blurry and wild.

Aching back, he rolled onto his side, seeking relief. His cheek sunk into something unpleasantly warm and wet. If he were not so focused on breathing he would have gagged at the foul stench.

He continued to breathe, afraid to let his subconscious take over as he focused on each inhalation. It wasn't long before the exhaustion overtook him and he slowly trusted his body to do its job.

Reaching up to his face, he touched the foul liquid. He looked at his fingertips, realizing he was in a pool of his own bloody vomit.

Had Misa actually saved him? Or was it his own body expelling enough of the poison?

Shivering violently, the young man looked up. Shining overhead, the twin moons Kiuskia and Kilati illuminated the darkness of the forest.

CHAPTER 11

The rains of spring gave way to the height of summer in the castle as days ticked by.

Teren withdrew from daily events, dispatching orders through Savina, speaking to few of the castlefolk. He didn't tell anyone what had occurred. By an unspoken agreement, Jessica likewise remained silent. People asked her if she knew what was wrong with Teren, but she just shrugged. She began avoiding the castlefolk as well, spending her time cleaning and renovating the tower aviary.

Some castlefolk felt the twitch of the mark, but brushed it off with a moment of sadness and a prayer to the goddess. They didn't know who had died.

Jessica refused to cry. It was her single defense. As long as she didn't cry or let herself feel sadness, she could hope Teren sensed the wrong person.

On earth, the hot days of summer turned to the sweet crispness of fall. For the first time in a long while, Jessica preferred the simplicity of suburban life. It was easier to avoid Teren's abyss of melancholy if she stayed home on earth.

Early on Labor Day morning, Jessica found herself staring at forty-three pounds of packaged pork ribs. Laying out aluminum trays across the granite counter top, the teen unwrapped the cold meat. She seasoned the ribs as Ashlin worked on a fruit salad. It was painfully early, but there was a lot of work to be done before the picnic.

Carrie Anne was in the living room talking cheerfully on the phone. Their father was in the backyard hosing off the lawn furniture and scrubbing it to Carrie Anne's standards. Guests would arrive in the afternoon.

Jessica wondered if her parents ever hosted barbeques. Would her mother care if the plastic furniture was pristine? Jessica imagined not.

Ashlin sliced fruit for a salad, joyously hacking at the fat orange as if it were a tiny foe.

Jessica was amused.

"You're holding the knife wrong."

"Oh? You're a knife expert?"

"I have some experience," Jessica smiled, reaching over. "First of all, if you were using an overhand grip, you wouldn't keep your thumb on the butt of the knife like that. You can use both sides of the knife and strike someone bluntly if your thumb isn't in the way."

She adjusted her sister's fingers, recalling Wadjette doing the same for her.

"That's better."

Ashlin smiled, continuing to hack at the orange.

"Remember two years ago when I asked you to teach me how to fight? I still mean it."

Jessica regarded her sister carefully. The girl was thirteen, barely younger than Jessica when Misa arrived in her kitchen unannounced.

Jessica glanced into the living room. Carrie Anne was sitting on the couch, talking on her phone.

"Want to see a fun trick?" Jessica grinned.

"What trick?"

Jessica opened the silverware drawer and picked up three knives. She set three oranges on the countertop, propped against the tiled backsplash.

"Watch this."

With careful aim and a flick of her wrist, Jessica tossed the first knife across the kitchen. It neatly impaled the orange.

Jessica smiled and threw the next knife. Her aim was a little off, and it hit the ceramic, bouncing to the granite.

Luckily it didn't crack the tile.

"Third one I'll nail it."

"Can I try?"

"Just let me throw this last one and I'll show you." Jessica narrowed her eyes, remembering her early lessons in defense. She spent months being covered in bruises, and she hated every minute. Everything changed when Nico taught her how to think through her actions. Jessica still hated it, but she got better. The more she improved, the more she wanted to try.

Jessica flicked the last knife. It hit the orange, sending it flying off the counter and bouncing across the floor…to her father's feet. Stephen stood in the doorway, his shorts and t-shirt wet. Little bits of grass stuck to his sandals.

For a moment, he had a smile, but then he quickly masked it with a scowl.

"Do we need to waste fruit like this?"

"Dad, did you see what Jessi did?!" Ashlin was still impressed. "She's amazing!"

"You shouldn't try everything you see on the internet," he picked up the orange.

"It's fun Dad, you should try."

"No, Ashlin I thought you were helping your mother prepare?"

"I am helping, look!" Ashlin gestured to the giant bowl of strawberries and cantaloupe. "And then that watermelon there I'm going to turn into a pirate ship."

"You're making a pirate ship?" Stephen raised an eyebrow in amusement.

"Because a watermelon boat is lame, Dad, I'm thinking something more stylistically like a Spanish galleon," Ashlin smiled, "trust me."

"Well, can't wait to see it," Stephen kissed his youngest daughter on the forehead. "You'll make your mom happy no matter what you make. Just stop throwing knives."

"Okay," Ashlin turned back to her work.

"Jess, those ribs look good, just be careful not to use too much salt."

"Dad, I know. I do a lot of cooking at home."

It was a half lie. She never cooked at home, but castle chore rotations put her in the kitchens. The castle went through at least two burches and a dozen speckled necks a day.

Her father grabbed a roll of paper towels from beneath the sink and went back out to the garage.

"A pirate ship?" Jessica asked.

"Well, I had considered making a watermelon kraken but decided I needed to scale back," Ashlin grinned.

Carrie Anne walked into the kitchen.

"Oh Ashlin, be careful with that knife, you'll hurt yourself."

"I'm not gonna hurt myself. Mom, you should see what Jessi just did with the oranges."

Jessica held her tongue. If Carrie Anne thought a paring knife was dangerous, she probably would have an aneurysm just walking through the stable yard of Aurumice.

"It was nothing," Jessica shrugged. "Carrie Anne, I seasoned three racks with the Memphis dry rub. Then I did three with the garlic barbeque and then I was going to do the rest with the creole seasoning and mark those trays as spicy?"

"Oh perfect, Jessica, thank you so much for your help. It's so nice to have you around."

"I know," Jessica smiled, wrapping the meat in aluminum foil.

"Is your mother going to join us this afternoon?"

"I couldn't change her mind, sorry. I asked, I really did."

"Oh, I know," Carrie Anne pulled a pitcher of blackberry tea from the refrigerator. "It's my fault I think. Your father never wanted me to invite your mom to things, and I just went with it. And now that I started inviting her she always says no, or he says no. It's awkward and it isn't fair to you."

"I don't get those two, I just don't." Jessica neatly wrapped the edged of the foil around the ribs. The smell of cold pork and garlic was strong.

"Really, I never told you this, but there were so many times I asked him to invite her. I think your mother is a very nice woman. I have never had an ounce of any negativity towards her, but Stephen just puts up a brick wall."

Carrie Anne poured the tea into a tall glass.

Jessica glanced to her sister, the girl had moved on from the oranges and was plotting her design on the watermelon.

"What was he like when you met him?" Jessica asked suddenly. "If you don't mind me asking, because Mom won't tell me anything about my dad."

"He talked about you a lot, as if you were his whole world," Carrie Anne smiled. "I didn't think I would ever get entangled with another woman's husband. When I first met him, I thought he was no longer with your mother. Jessica, I truly did not know he was married."

"It's okay, Mom," Ashlin piped in. "We all break one of those Ten Commandments every once in a while."

"Oh, you hush up," Carrie Anne glared at the girl. "I swear, Ashlin, I don't know where this attitude has been coming from."

She turned back to Jessica.

"And Jessica, I take this very seriously, and this is why I think your mother is a very noble woman. I begged for her forgiveness, and she was so gracious. I know they were living apart at the time, but I felt immensely guilty. Your father was out of work, he was in a rough place."

"Where did you meet him?"

"Right at Eastridge Church, actually. He told me he had never been to a Baptist church before. So, I had to help him along in the service, and that seemed to make him very happy. I invited him to breakfast. I don't know what possessed me to, I hardly knew him. I was maybe twenty-two, he was older than me, but a perfect gentleman."

Carrie Anne leaned against the countertop, sipping the ice tea.

"He was probably the most cultured man I've ever met, and so brilliant. His view of the world was like nothing I had heard before. He really appreciated everything."

Jessica did some quick math. Her mother said her father walked out on them just after the castle fell under the energy field. Jessica was four and a half at the time. Ashlin was five years younger.

"Ashlin was born pretty quick, wasn't she?" Jessica said slowly. Finished with the meat, she washed her hands, avoiding eye contact.

Carrie Anne seemed uncomfortable.

"I didn't know he was still married, Jessi," Carrie Anne stated apologetically.

Ashlin stabbed the knife into the watermelon.

"This isn't new news. I'm in the wedding photos."

"But I'm not." Jessica pointed out. It never bothered her. Carrie Anne made certain that both girls had the same number of photos displayed throughout the house.

"I wanted you there, you would have made an adorable flower girl. I wanted you."

"But my mother said no?"

"They both said no. I asked them," Carrie Anne seemed so small and sad.

"Oh."

"He just can't find any forgiveness in his heart towards your mom, and I think it makes it hard on you. I pray he will someday."

The words compelled Jessica to set down the dish towel, cross the kitchen, and hug her step mother.

"Thank you for wanting me," she said. "I don't tell you that enough."

Carrie Anne brushed a strand of hair from Jessica's face.

"You are kind and brilliant young lady, and I am very happy to call you my daughter."

Jessica thought of her own mother, always walled up in her own pain, unable to see the hurt she caused all around.

"What if I had a secret, a secret that both my mother and father forbid me from ever telling? A secret I haven't told anyone, ever."

"Well, is this secret hurting someone?"

Ashlin set down her knife, suddenly the watermelon was not the most interesting thing in the room.

"What secret?" Ashlin asked.

"No," Jessica said. "Not really hurting anyone, like it's not illegal if that's what you're saying."

"And you want to tell me?" Carrie Anne asked.

"Yes," Jessica affirmed.

"Are you pregnant?"

"Oh no, no, no, no."

"Oh, well, it happens much easier than you think." Carrie Anne cautioned, nodding to Ashlin. "If you need any sort of preventative..."

"No, no, no!" Jessica held up her hands as Ashlin cringed. "We don't need to talk about sex, okay? I'm good! I got it, no problem!"

"Do you like girls, Jessi?" Ashlin asked.

"Yes, no, but nothing like that," Jessica laughed.

"How is that a yes and a no?"

"I've never been with anyone, how would I know what I really like? And some of my friends are bi," she said, referring to most of the Centernians.

"Is this a drug thing?" Carrie Anne asked.

"No, not drugs," Jessica glanced out the back window. Her father had left her line of sight. He would be angry if she told Carrie Anne and Ashlin. It didn't seem worth ruining the picnic and causing a stir before the guests arrived.

"Let me think about it more. Someday I'll tell you. I promise."

"Well whenever you're ready," Carrie Anne said, "I'm here, no matter what, I won't turn you away."

CHAPTER 12

The Sunday after the barbeque, Jessica climbed the stairs to her tower room in Aurumice, arms tired. She had spent all afternoon stringing lighting for the Fireflight Festival. It wasn't too crazy a display, just ten strands of Christmas lights hung from poles through the stable yard, but it made Kaity giddy with happiness. The leopard mage's happiness was infectious, though it made Jessica a little sad she would miss the event. The Fireflight Festival was a day-long celebration that started at nightfall one evening and stretched to sundown the next. She couldn't afford to miss class the second week of her senior year.

Jessica opened the door to her room and set her tool box on the desk. Settling into her scavenged wood chair, she sighed in contentment.

After a few weeks of work, the tower was starting to feel homey.

Wadjette and Penrik helped her board up the ceiling panels so that they no longer leaked. Once

that task was complete, Jessica had snaked wiring through the wall passages and drilled a hole in the thick floor. It was tedious work, but she finally was able to have a single power outlet in the room.

The aquarium floor was still filled with dusty, dried algae. The teen didn't have a bed, but instead had piled up a collection of cushions and thick blankets. Eventually she would scout out something more suitable, but she had other more interesting projects in mind.

Jessica opened up the manual for the radio she had just bought at a garage sale.

Radio was a technology she barely noticed at home. The castle was huge, the surrounding lands were vast, and the castlefolk were few in number relative to the distance they traveled. There were so many times radio communication would have saved the castlefolk from hardship.

Before she finished reading a single paragraph, a knock interrupted her.

The visitor didn't wait for her to acknowledge him.

"Hey there, sunshine," Jared said, hands in his pockets. "You going to the Fireflight Festival here or the city?"

"Neither, I have school tomorrow," Jessica replied. "Can you help me test these radios?"

"Sundown is nearly here."

"Jae, I know, I just finished setting up the lights."

"You did all that work decorating for my aunt and you're not even going to the festival?"

"Help me test this," Jessica held up the black handset. "I just bought this thing, I want to see how well it works."

"Only if you promise to go to the festival with me."

"Jared, I tried the hunt last year. I couldn't catch a single meep. Even the cubs did better than me."

"Ahhhhhh, so that's it. This has nothing to do with school."

The highlight of the Fireflight Festival was a hunt of speckled meeps through the darkness of the forest. Whoever captured the most was the duke of the festival.

To capture none was considered bad luck.

Jared settled into a chair.

"Come on Jess, it will be fun. At least go to the City with me and ditch Aurumice."

"Double nope."

Jared was quiet for a bit, gazing off into the distance. Jessica assumed he was spying on someone else. After a while, he focused back on the room.

"Why are you sleeping on potato sacks?" Jared pointed to her bed.

"No, no those are cushions I found on a couch that wasn't being used."

Jared looked at the wire she had running up the wall and out the skylight, and took note of the power outlet added to the smooth stucco.

"You had time for this but not bringing up a bed?"

"Yeah, I'll get to it. I haven't been sleeping here much."

"Because of your depressingly moody cousin?"

Jessica bristled. "Just leave him alone, he can be depressed and moody if he wants to be."

"That doesn't sound right," Jared pulled up a chair. "You know something."

"If Teren doesn't want to talk about it, then neither do I," Jessica replied. "You don't need to know everything that happens in this castle."

"Jess, I get the sense that this isn't just petty gossip. Something is seriously up with your cousin, and if you know, you should ask the rest of us for help."

"It can't be fixed, so just let it go," Jessica said, absentmindedly twisting a dial on the radio. "And if you're going to sit there and annoy me, you can help at the same time."

She placed the radio in his hand.

"You'll like this, it's another way to keep tabs on the castle."

"What's this thing?"

"A radio. Weren't you listening?"

"When you were talking radios, I thought you meant music. Is this an ugly brick from the 1980s? Why not use cell phones?"

"Because they would be harder to maintain, more expensive, full of proprietary software and it would take me years to figure it out."

"It doesn't have a screen. How do I know it's on?"

Jessica rotated the power dial, it clicked and a red LED illuminated.

"Very retro," Jared murmured.

"If you don't like my tech, you can build your own communications infrastructure."

"No, thank you. You can have this project. I like my job, and my hobbies. I will trade you. I'll help you do your testing if you come with me, and you can even be my partner for the meep hunt. The hunt starts just after sunset."

"Fine, but I need to leave in time for school in the morning."

"Deal."

Jessica turned her attention to the device on her desk. A foot in length and eight inches tall, the radio base station had an array of buttons and knobs. A coiled rubber cord connected to a microphone.

"So, that handset is already set to the correct channel. Can you just start moving and talking to me so I can figure out the range?"

"Ten-four," Jared spoke into the radio, walking away.

"You don't even know what that means."

"I watched enough tv as a kid," Jared descended the short staircase to the door and exited the room.

Jared was a funny enigma, so free to share some information, so secretive about others. He grew up as she did, on a diet of Sesame Street and Pop Tarts, but he never talked about his family.

"So how far should this reach?" Jared's voice came through the speakers.

"I'm not sure if there's anything that would cause interference," Jessica said. "I really don't know."

"How do you fix that?"

"Can you tell me where you are so I can track how far you go?"

"I'm in the hallway."

"Which hallway?"

"The one that leads to your door."

"If I figure it out, we set up repeaters, they make the signal go farther. And, theoretically, it should be easier to talk to someone outside than inside the castle, but I don't *know* know."

"Oh, so we could be talking for a while."

"Maybe. Where are you now?"

"At that big painting of the dragon dancing with the mermaids."

"Okay, keep going down that hallway."

"So how do you feel about Talon and your mom?" Jared asked.

"Why are we talking about my mom and Talon?"

"Because you refuse to talk about your super emo cousin."

Jessica sighed. Jared had to be obnoxious.

"I don't know," she replied. "Mom can do what she wants."

"Seems like an intense relationship to me. How about Talon as your second father?"

"Jared! If you're going to be an ass, I'm going home."

"I'm just making conversation. I'm supposed to talk—"

There was a burst of static.

"Where are you now?" Jessica was taking notes.

"By the statue of the bicorn drinking from the floating river with the dancing burches and otters with cute tails and phallic tortoises."

"How are they phallic? Don't answer that."

"If you look at the---"

Again, static broke up the signal. Jessica was dismayed. She knew there would be interference, she didn't realize how much.

"---Talon and your mom," Jared continued.

Jessica didn't want to know how he bridged the topics.

"I think they are good together," Jared's voice cracked through static, "and you should be nicer to Talon."

"How am I not nice to Talon?" Jessica asked.

"You know what I mean, you are just polite to him."

"Maybe if he didn't insult all the work I do."

"He didn't insult it, he just doesn't get it. He's scared of it, and there's a lot of that sort of thinking in the world. And the government fuels it, makes people scared of lightning."

"Oh, well, if Fentalon doesn't like electricity he shouldn't be with a lightning mage."

"See! That's the snark I was talking about."

"How about we not talk about Jessica's family, let's talk about Jared's family for a change. When's the last time you talked to your mom?"

The radio was silent.

"Did I finally strike a nerve?"

Silence.

"Jared?"

"Sorry, having trouble hearing you."

"What's your location?"

Jessica was greeted with a burst of static.

She sighed, more work to be done.

***

Twinkling colored lights were strung across the castleyard in a zig-zag pattern, creating a beautiful rainbow canopy. The strands were cheap Christmas lights, but they were different and unique to the castlefolk.

Over a hundred people gathered, holding nets of various shape and sizes. Jessica saw her mother, talking to Wadjette and watchfully surveying the crowd. Both wore full guard armor and did not look like they were participating in the hunt. Jessica was a little bit jealous of her mother. She fit in with the guard so easily.

Almost every bicorn in the castle was out, saddled and ready. Unlike their horse cousins, the fantastic beasts had impeccable night vision. They were much stronger and more agile, able to hunt in the forest without fear of breaking a leg. Omnivorous, the equines were fearless in the dark and more likely to engage than run away from a night predator.

On a podium, a large cage of brightly colored speckled meeps was on display. The fat little birds were known for their distinctive song and their ability to navigate the darkness. Nearby, an unusual black-tailed meadow dasher restlessly paced in the cage. He was a small dragon, about the size of a greyhound. Glistening, his red body appeared to be covered in oil to make his scales shine.

The meadowdasher was excited to hunt the meeps, sniffing the air in the direction of the other cage.

"I'll go get the bicorns, also you should smile," Jared poked her. "You're much too grumpy for this party."

"Last time I went to a party in the stableyard I puked in a bush and the castlefolk laughed at me."

"Jessica! You're going to miss it!" Penrik ran up to her. "We're almost out of cloaks."

Large barrels were set up by the grey barn. Jessica pulled out a rough piece of fabric. The stitching glowed in the darkness.

"I should have brought mine from Polaris, these are a little plain," Jared said, selecting a cloak out of the barrel. He pulled it over his head.

The cloak was short, designed to cover the wearer just past the elbows. It tied at the neck and had a hood. It was tradition to wear the cloak if you were participating in the hunt.

"Come on, we need to get the bicorns," Jared said, leading the way to the stables. Thankfully, Emberjade and Frostfire were already tied to a fence rail and saddled.

Emberjade was a pretty black mare, her mane and tail streaked with green, her muzzle speckled in red orange patches that traveled down her body. Bicorn naming tended to be literal, usually based on color or nature.

Frostfire seemed oddly calm. She got along well with Emberjade. Both mares were finicky, Frostfire was more aggressive, but Emberjade was known for lashing out viciously. Despite her obedience, the black mare was more dangerous than Frost.

Jessica took her bicorn's reins.

"Ready to fail again this year?" she said to the majestic beast.

"Come on, it will be fun," Jared said, leading Ember. "I'll help you catch one."

Temi ran by, wearing a little cloak.

"Even Temi will catch more than me, and she's probably not even riding tonight."

"Jared!" Kaity was following the fast-moving imp. "I thought Teren said you couldn't participate in the hunt."

"I have my partner, therefore I can play," Jared gestured to Jessica.

"Ah, I see the balance. Fair enough. Luck of the Goddess to you!" Kaity looked around and realized her daughter had already ran far ahead. She dashed after the child

"What's that supposed to mean? Why did Teren ban you?" Jessica led Frostfire behind Jared.

"He didn't ban me. I don't know what Kaity is talking about."

"Teren said Jared could only play if he had someone to slow him down," Savina filled in as she approached. "To counterbalance his demon-vision."

"He did not quite say it that way...."

"No, I believe he said you needed a handicap."

"Jared! What the hell!"

Jared cringed.

"Oh come on, Jess. Look at it this way, I'll make you better."

"And I make you worse, is that it?"

"No, no, no...."

"I am not here to start a lover's quarrel between you two," Savina interrupted. "I was actually here to talk about Teren."

"What about my cousin?" Jessica adjusted Frostfire's bridle.

"I was hoping one of you could try to get him to come out tonight," Savina said. "He is falling further into an abyss. Jessica I was hoping you could talk sense into him."

"There he is now, looks like he came out after all."

"Really?" Savina was surprised.

Teren climbed the podium, wearing a hunting cloak as well. He carried a Book of Aurora and a small silver horn.

"I'm surprised he's doing that reading instead of Kaity," Jared commented.

Teren was smiling as he set the items on a podium.

"Greetings people of Aurumice, honored guests, dear friends, I am happy to see you all gathered here for the Fireflight Festival. As is tradition, we will start the evening with a reading from the writings of the Goddess Aurora, but first, the release of the meeps."

Penrik hopped onto the stage, holding a large smoking incense burner. He stood in front of the crowd.

Teren approached the cage door, opposite the crowd, on the side of the forest.

Smelling the smoke, the meeps panicked. Teren swiftly opened the cage and flurry of fat birds flew out in a wild rainbow hurricane of feathers. The castlefolk cheered and the meadowdasher thrashed in his cage, eager to hunt the meeps.

Penrik took a little bow and hopped off the stage with the incense.

Teren returned to the holy book.

"Tonight I have selected a passage written in the Book of Gethseba, Chapter Six."

"Interesting," Savina murmured. "That passage has a dragon, but it's not one of the traditional readings for this."

Teren flipped open the book.

"In the spring of the yellow meadow, the fields had ceased to grow. The eggs did not hatch. Rivers froze in place. Time had stopped."

"Goddess Aurora was dismayed, so she sought out the answer. A powerful force had sought to rival her own and she feared the evil behind it. Goddess Aurora walked her lands, and searched, until she came upon a steep mountain in the land of darkness. On the precipice of the mountain was a dragon, lonely, for he was the last of his kind."

"The dragon was trying to turn back time, but time moves ever forward, and there is no return to what once was. Kindred spirits lost,

once untied from this world, are sent to the celestial rivers over which Aurora claims ultimate dominion."

Jessica understood why Teren selected the passage.
It was a funerary reading.

"The dragon demanded Aurora return his lost kin, but Aurora refused. Other dragons no longer had vessels, and to give them one would rob others of life. The source of the dragon's grief was his loneliness, so the goddess promised him a companion, someone to equal him in strength, and spirit, and wit. It was agreed, the dragon would release the flow of time and the goddess would give him a companion."

"Time was released, and the dragon turned to the Goddess, waiting to meet his new friend. The goddess said 'Your companion is a creature of this world, I promise you, if you search you will find your happiness. You will no longer suffer. I am giving you the gift of hope.' "

"Life returned to motion. The dragon had no choice but to move on, and so he searches the realms for his life companion, one who will not be taken to the celestial rivers."

Teren closed the book, pausing for a moment.
"Oh no, don't lose it Teren," Jessica whispered.
"These are the scribed words of the goddess," Teren ended, approaching the dragonette. Hissing, the red creature was riled and eager to escape. Teren pulled a metal rod out of the cage and a door fell open.
Launching itself into the sky, the meadowdasher gave a warrior's cry.
"The rules of tonight's game are simple...the pair with the most speckled meeps caught by sunrise wins the favor of the time dragon, and the right to make a wish to be heard in the span between time."
The castlefolk were ready to run into the woods after the beast. The meadowdasher could fly high, but the tasty speckled meeps were sure to keep him flying low enough to be caught.
"You want me to do this so you can make a wish?" Jessica asked Jared.

"No, I've got a bet going with Musian, riding on us catching more meeps than him and Jiberty."

"Oh, great."

Teren raised the horn to his lips, and blew one long trill note.

Jessica climbed onto Frostfire's back and they raced into the forest.

***

The fat little birds were deceptively difficult to catch.

Jessica held out her net and tried to snag one, but it kept jumping away just out of reach. She nudged Frostfire and leaned far out, but the pudgy yellow bird still hopped away.

Jared was much more agile on horseback, and Emberjade obeyed his commands with greater regard. He spotted a meep on a branch just out of reach. He signaled for Emberjade to stop. The mare remained motionless. Very carefully, Jared drew his feet up to crouch on the saddle. Without any hesitation, the young man stood to reach out and grab his third meep.

"How do you do that?" Jessica felt the sting of jealousy. "I could never stand on top of a saddle like you can."

Jared shrugged.

"I don't know," he said. "When you're a kid, you need to catch up to ailurian children, so it forces us to be more daring...or stupid, depending on how you look at it."

He settled back down into the saddle.

"I train a few times a week," Jessica lamented. "I'm always trying to do more, but it feels like I'll never catch up and be castlefolk."

"You are too hard on yourself. You just need to do your thing, and not care."

A fat blue meep landed on Frostfire's head. Jessica reached forward with two hands, but the bird slipped through her fingers and flew out of reach.

"This is not encouraging."

"It's early."

Jared blinked.

"There's a patch in the south meadow."

"Did you just cheat?"

"It's not cheating if it's my god given talent. Look, was I born with cat eyes and claws? No. Can I see well in the dark? No. So, the universe dealt me this nice little talent to balance that out. No problem."

Jared whickered to Emberjade. Tossing her head, the mare trotted forward into the darkness. Her twin horns gleamed wickedly in the light. Frostfire was quick to follow behind.

They soon came to an open meadow where the moons illuminated the beautiful grass.

Bo paced in the lunar glow. Strangely, a ridge of spikes had risen from its spine, something Jessica had not seen. The creature was fixated on the speckled meeps. Two dozen of the bright birds clustered around a brambleberry bush.

"That Fentalon's pet?" Jared said. "How did it get all the way out here?"

Jessica shrugged. She dismounted from Frostfire, grabbing her net.

"I have to be able to get at least one of those cheeping puff balls."

"What's that dog doing?" Jared asked. "Those spikes don't seem friendly."

"Jared, look at that little flock. They're so close," Jessica walked carefully.

Kaity and Temi entered the meadow. As soon as she saw the beast, Kaity grabbed her daughter by the shoulders.

"Jess, you should leave that bunch alone. I don't like the looks of Bo."

"I need to catch at least one meep," the teen replied, "and he's tame, right?"

The beast was eyeing the cluster of birds.

"Yeah, but I don't know anything about how it was trained. It's a Lazuli hunter, they're pretty vicious."

Jessica held up her net, walking very slowly towards the cheeping birds. As she passed Bo, she could smell the aroma of almonds. Drawing her forward, she found the smell to be intoxicating.

Jessica held her net ready, her confidence rising.

"GET AWAY!!!" Fentalon's voice bellowed from the far side of the meadow.

The creature startled, its spines stiffened, turning blue.

Without warning, the dog lunged at Jessica, its jaws snapping for her throat. Instinctively, she protected her neck with her arm. Simultaneously, she leaned back, reaching for the knife tucked in her boot.

As she pulled the weapon out from its sheath, the creature's crushing jaws seized her left forearm. Jessica howled from the pain, her right hand dropping the knife to the grass.

Jared ran forward, plunging his knife into the monster's chest, but its hide was incredibly thick, and all he could manage was a minor stab wound. The creature remained latched onto Jessica, its jaw grinding into her arm like a set of serrated knives.

Fentalon was next to reach the fray, drawing his sword. With decades of precision, he brought the lethal weapon down swiftly, chopping the creature in half at its torso. Entrails spilled onto the grass and a foul stench filled the night air.

"Get it off me!!!" Jessica screamed. "IT WON'T LET GO!!!"

Fentalon reached for the severed pet's mouth, trying to pry its jaws open, but the razor-like teeth cut into his fingers.

"Here, let me!" Kaity reached out with her telekinetic abilities. With a quick flick of her fingers, and the snapping of bone, the monster's jaws released.

And the situation became worse.

Jessica looked down at her arm. The deadly jaws had ground into her forearm, crushing it down to the bone and severing muscle tissue. Blood flowed from her radial artery like a tiny little hose.

She had just enough sense to clamp her right hand tightly over the wound before she fell to her knees. Her head swam. Someone quickly started wrapping her arm in a piece of fabric, trying to put pressure on the wound.

"Jessi, raise your arm above your head," Kaity ordered.

"That's not going to help her much," Fentalon said, "That girl needs a tourniquet."

"Like hell! I'm not losing my arm!" Jessica yelled at Fentalon. "If you hadn't shouted it wouldn't have startled!"

"You're too stupid to know not to approach a Lazuli hunter! Didn't you smell the pheromones? It was hunting the meeps and you got in the way! Bo is dead because of you!"

"How am I supposed to know it was going to lunge?!"

"You need a tourniquet stupid girl, you're going to die from blood loss!!!" he roared back at her.

"No, she's not. We're going home!" her mother was thankfully at her side. "Jared, come with me!"

"Okay, I got her."

Jessica felt Jared's strong arms, lifting her from the huddle of people. She clutched her wrapped arm to her chest as they ran to Emberjade. Jared lifted her onto the mare's back.

"Can you grab her neck with your good arm?" he asked.

"Yes," Jessica gritted her teeth, holding her arm close to her chest. She was grateful to be free of Fentalon, despite the dizzying pain. Jared climbed up behind her and they raced into the forest.

***

They bypassed calling an ambulance, and drove to the emergency room instead.

"Lily, your weapons," Jared warned as they got out of the Jeep.

Lily pulled off her armor and threw her guard arsenal into the front seat before running with Jared and Jessica to the emergency room entrance. With a quick glance at the amount of blood on Jessica's cloak, the staff immediately admitted her, peppering them with a slew of questions and a pile of forms.

Jared couldn't believe how quickly the evening had deteriorated. He ran his hands through his hair in panic. Jessica's wound was so bad, he wondered if her hand could be saved.

Eventually, they released Lily from questions and they were led to a waiting area.

"Take off your cloak," Lily murmured. "You look like you murdered a goat."

Jared glanced down, the fabric was darkened with blood. As he lifted the cloak, he realized his white shirt beneath was worse, stained in bright scarlet.

"I don't think that'll help," he said to Lily.

He glanced around the waiting room, filled with worried and sick faces. People were coughing, many of them looked a bit haggard.

"What happened to Jessi?"

Jared froze.

He recognized the voice of Ashlin, Jessica's little sister.

Glancing at Lily, it was clear the older woman was not happy.

"Ashlin, what are you doing here?" Lily asked.

"My mom passed out, we think as a side effect from her treatment," Ashlin explained, "…again."

"Where's your father?"

"In with my mom. What happened to Jessi? I saw you carry her in with all the blood."

"Dog bite," Lily responded. They had rehearsed an alibi in the car ride.

"Is she going to be okay?" Ashlin asked.

"I think so," Lily affirmed, lying through her teeth.

Jared took a seat on the mauve plastic chairs. He held his hands together, trying not to speak.

"Whose dog was it?"

They hadn't really thought through that part of the story.

"It was at a party," Lily said. "We were at a party."

"What kind of party?"

Lily panicked as she struggled with an answer.

"Birthday party," Jared said quickly. For someone who lied as much as Lily did, she really wasn't very good at it. "How is your mom doing? Jessi told me her cancer was kind of bad."

Jared asked the girl a series of questions, leading the topic from Carrie Anne to video games as he put on his most engaging charm. Lily was obviously in no state to answer questions from the thirteen-year-old.

The more he distracted Ashlin, the more he realized she was eager to talk. The girl was a lot like her sister, very bright and friendly. Ashlin used a slightly larger vocabulary. Jared could tell she was at the age where she was trying to be perceived as being mature.

He could also tell she was a bit lonely.

Lily took a seat across from them, looking downcast. The woman worried about her daughter all the time, but this time she looked *really* worried.

"How is your cloak glowing like that? Are those LEDS?"

Jared had completely forgotten the cloak from the hunt was unusual. The Luminescent stitching still glowed blue even in the fluorescent lights of the hospital.

"Sort of. Like the same stuff that's in glow sticks."

"Where'd you buy it? I'd love something like that."

"Online."

Stephen Ravenwolfe walked through the double doors. Jared's stomach dropped, knowing it would be impossible to divert the older man's attention. He was fairly certain if Lily could have run from the waiting room, she would have.

"Lily?"

"Stephen."

"What are you doing here?" the man was perplexed to see his ex-wife. Jared racked his brains for a way to distract the man.

"Jessi was bit by a dog," Ashlin explained, "and it really looked bad."

"A dog? Whose dog? Where?" Stephen asked. "Where was she bit?"

"Her arm," Lily explained. "We were at a party. I think she'll be okay, I think...I hope."

It was then Stephen's eyes locked onto Jared.

The blonde-haired boy swallowed, wishing he could melt into the floor.

"You again. What's your name?"

He stood, trying to muster his most respectful charm. He extended a hand. "My name is Jared Evansi, sir. It's nice to see you again."

Stephen's hand gripped Jared's tightly.

"Evansi? Where are you from?"

"Here," Jared replied. "I go to community college."

Stephen released his hand.

"So, you are my daughter's boyfriend?"

"Uh, no, sir. I am just her friend."

"You still don't think it's little odd for someone in college to be hanging out with a high school girl?"

"Well Jessica is very intelligent and mature"

"I don't like you and I don't want you around my daughter."

Jared caught Lily's glance behind Stephen's back. The woman's eyes were in complete panic. No matter what Jared said, he would have Stephen's ire.

But if he could keep it off Lily, it would be one less worry on the woman's mind.

"I can assure you sir, I am already attached to someone else and have no intentions towards your daughter. I just look out for her."

Stephen turned to his ex-wife.

"Lily, we need to talk, now. Outside."

A door opened.

"Lily Vance?" a nurse called out.

Jared silently thanked the Goddess.

Lily didn't respond to her ex-husband and walked up to the nurse.

"You can see your daughter, she's fine," the nurse said. "A few stitches."

Jared blinked, were they talking about the right girl?

Stephen insisted on following Lily. Jared slumped back in the chair, off the hook.

"What's the name of the shop you ordered your cloak?"

"I don't remember," he said. He looked at the fabric, if it wasn't stained in Jessica's blood he would have handed it to the girl right there.

Jared pondered how the bite could have warranted 'a few' stitches.

***

Jessica's head was throbbing. She felt numb as they stitched the gash on her arm, wondering if she dreamt the whole thing.

Her mother walked into the room.

Followed by her father.

And then a new sort of panic set in.

"Hi," she chirped.

"Hey," Stephen smiled, giving her a hug. "Your mom said you were bit by a dog."

"Yeah. You didn't need to come here, it was okay."

"Well, Carrie Anne had a dizzy spell. They're running more tests and they want to observe her for a while."

"Oh! Is she going to be okay?" Jessica's arm seemed minor in comparison.

"Yeah. I think so."

"I'd ask to see her, but I really would like to go home," Jessica told her father.

Jessica's mom hung back during the exchange, eyes distant.

There was a knock at the door and a nurse came in with discharge papers, a prescription for an antibiotic and information on caring for the wound. Jessica was in a daze as her parents led her back out into the waiting room.

Where Ashlin waited with Jared.

And she felt the night becoming even more bizarre.

They bid Ashlin and her father goodnight, walking out into the darkened parking lot. Shoving his hands in his pockets, Jared braced himself against the chilly wind. It was colder on earth than Centernia. Lily wrapped her arm around her daughter's shoulders, saying nothing.

It wasn't until they reached the old Jeep that Lily embraced her daughter.

"I'm so glad you're okay," the woman said. "You have no idea how worried I was, I thought we almost lost you."

Her mom must have been really worried, she *never* reacted so strongly.

"Mom…"

"I know, Jessi."

"Mom…."

"We will talk in the car."

Jared opened the passenger side-door and Jessica climbed into the cold car. He took the back seat behind her. Lily slid into the driver's side but didn't start the Jeep.

"Mom…"

"Jess, let me see your arm."

"It hurts."

"Can we turn on the heat? I'm freezing," Jared complained from the backseat.

"Jessica, I want to see your arm."

"It really hurts, and I'm sorry Fentalon had to kill his own pet. I didn't know and I'm really, really sorry!"

"Let me see that wound, *now*."

Trembling, the girl held out her arm. It was wrapped in a single neat bandage.

"Let me see," Jared peered forward.

"My arm was ripped and torn." Jessica stated. "And now it's not."

"The doctors are really that good here?" Jared asked.

Lily shook her head.

"Then what just happened?"

"How many stitches did they say?" Lily asked.

"I watched them. Twelve stitches. No broken bones. No missing chunks. Mom, that creature shredded the muscle. I *had* no feeling in my hand."

Jared grinned, a light of realization in his eyes.

"Ahhhh! I see it now! Holy Goddess! This is amazing!"

"Can you take the bandage off?" Lily asked.

"The nurse said…"

"Take it off."

Jessica unwrapped the bandage revealing twelve stitches in a little arch.

"I don't believe it," Lily grabbed her daughter's hand and pulled it close under the dim dome light. "Oh, Jessica, the Goddess has a sense of irony."

"This is amazing!" Jared was beaming. He reached around the seat, hugging Jessica in an awkward embrace that nearly strangled her. "I'm so happy for you! Welcome to the party!"

"Is healing a mage strength?" Jessica asked.

Lily smiled. "Yes, it is very much a mage strength."

"I did this?"

"Yes."

"You're not lying?"

"Jess, you did it, you really, really did, " Lily embraced her daughter again.

Two hugs from her mother, making it a banner night.

"How are you sure, mom? What if this is just some freak occurrence? Did that thing really bite me?"

"Jess, I've seen things, just trust me on this," Lily assured her daughter, almost laughing.

"You're a blood mage!" Jared shouted. "That is an amazing ability! Congrats, Jess, I'm so happy for you!"

"Blood mage?" Jessica winced at the term. "Healer sounds better. A blood mage sounds gross."

"He's right," her mother explained. "Generally, they are called blood mages because they can hurt as easily as they can heal."

"But I didn't do anything," Jessica said. "I didn't think about it."

"It's instinct at first, then frustration, then control," Jared explained giddily. "You'll get it."

Lily put her hand to her head as she collected her thoughts.

"Now listen carefully, when mage powers appear, they can be spectacular and abnormally strong. Do not assume this is any indication of what you can do. It takes a great deal of training and focus to do anything deliberately. Jared is right, this is on instinct. Do not go and do stupid things because you think you're invincible, do you understand me?"

"Your mom is really, really right about this one Jessica," Jared echoed. "It's like a cork on a bottle, a lot of fizz all at once, then just little bubbles. And we went through the Gate, that probably gave you a power boost, I'd almost be willing to bet that's when you healed yourself."

"So, what can I do?" Jessica was eager to learn.

Lily looked to Jared.

"What do you think?"

"Not much," he said. "Like maybe you can heal a papercut? But even if it's nothing right now, this is amazing. Aurumice could really use a blood mage because Otto is a really crappy doctor. Let's go back to the castle and celebrate!"

"Oh no," Lily held up a finger. "We keep this quiet. You stay on earth a few days. When you go back to Aurumice, you keep your arm bandaged, and you pretend it hurts and it's healing."

"But..."

"You don't tell anyone. Not even Teren, am I clear?"

"But..."

"Not a word, and you!" she turned her sights to Jared.

The boy retreated, hands up. "Don't worry, won't say a peep to anyone."

"You don't want to cause a stir, and I don't want to attract attention. Saurin Bane made me promise to bring you to Polaris Academy. You go there, you'll never graduate high school. You graduate, and then we talk about Polaris. Am I very clear?"

Jessica's disbelief slowly rose into elation.

She was a mage.

Things would never be the same.

CHAPTER 13

Nico traveled for days.

After awakening from his near-deadly sleep, his mind was a jumble. He fought to focus and read the stars. Misa's words pushed him forward, but the memory of the dead mage pushed him back.

Some days he would stop and lay in the grass, unable to get up as the weight of the world pulled him down.

At some point, he realized nuts and herbs were a poor substitute for real food. He fashioned a fishing pole from sticks and tried to make a line out of reeds but failed. His snare traps likewise failed. Finally, he relented, and hunted like a feral animal, stalking rodents to their little homes. Catching them with his claws and teeth, he snapped their necks then roasted their small bodies over the fire. His jacket and pants became tattered and torn, covered with mud and bloodstains from the small creatures. Beneath his clothing, his wounds from the Mines had ceased healing. Instead, they festered and bled.

On a cold morning, he came across a strange sight in a field.

The charred remains of a structure lay engulfed in weeds, overgrown protrusions of rusted metal and twisted scrap. There were many tall thin beams jutting out from the wreckage.

Looking closer, he realized it had likely never been a building, but a collection of broken down metal and garbage. Nico spotted some thin wire. Hoping to fashion a fishing line, he pulled the wire. Along with it came a rounded glass from the wreck, shaped like a cup with a riveted track.

He had seen the object in old photographs from his grandfather's childhood. It was an insulator from a power line, from the era when the land had technology. In the days before the attack from Graveer, the landscape had been dotted with utility poles.

Further inspection of the massive pile revealed more insulators, chunks of poles, old glass lights, and metal contraptions rusted beyond recognition.

It was a rusted graveyard of the bygone era of Madierna.

Salvaging the wire, much of it was rusted and brittle, but Nico found a few strands protected from the elements and still pliable. He braided it together, intrigued by the destroyed technology. He didn't often think about the time when his world embraced such marvels. He'd lived in his bubble in Aurumice, with a steady supply of new gadgets and parts coming through the Gate.

Nico's fingers pinched as bits of metal lodged in his skin, but he continued to make his fishing line.

Society's aversion was more than fear, it was law. To be caught in public with even a flashlight was a crime.

Nico stood, pleased with his fishing line attached to a sturdy stick. He created a barbed end then climbed off the metal graveyard.

Following the sound of the river, a foul stench assaulted his nose as he came upon another startling site. Bloated and decaying, a tiger-striped body lay in the grass. Dead for at least a week, the man was old and wrinkled, and dressed like a farmer. Little maggots were working their way out of his skin.

Nico bowed his head in respect, said a prayer to Goddess Aurora and then walked past the man. There was nothing he could do and nature would soon overtake the body. As he hurried past, a blue glimmer gave him pause.

A sapphire needlewasp hummed along the stranger's skin. Its shiny iridescent wings buzzed energetically in the sunlight. The creature was soon joined by three more.

Nico cringed.

Though the insects were common in the mines, it was the first time he had seen one out in the wild. He had no doubt the tiger's body was bursting with the demon insect larvae.

Nico continued on his path, pushing the sight out of his mind. He traveled through the forest with his new fishing pole, focusing on the sound of the river.

The dead man far behind, Nico forged through the unfamiliar forest. Stumbling his way to the shore, Nico breathed a sigh of relief. He had come upon a wide river emptying into a large lake. The water glistened in the afternoon sun. Herons cried and swooped down to gather fish.

Nico set to work, foraging for a fat wriggling grub. He impaled it on his fishing wire and climbed over to the water's edge, casting the line.

Nico silently waited, enjoying the warmth of the sun.

Alone in the woods, he noticed activity far across the lake. Miles away he could see a boat, moving along, heading for shore. The village was the first sign of civilization he had seen in weeks.

The line tugged and he carefully pulled a small silvery fish from the water.

With trembling hands, he pulled the metal hook from its mouth. Hunger overtaking him he bit into the wriggling creature. The skin was unpleasant but the raw flesh satisfying.

Staring across the lake, the jagged outline of the Mooncrest Mountains punctuated the skyline.

It was the first landmark he recognized since escaping to the unfamiliar shores.

Home was north-west.

***

Jessica walked down the noisy halls of Autumn Valley High School. The tiled walls reflected the fluorescent lights as the sound of lockers slamming reverberated through the air.

The warning bell rang as Jessica arrived at the classroom. She was required to attend an info session on college applications during her study hall. Entering the room, she scanned for a friendly face to sit next to. Loud teens packed the room. There was only one seat, next to a girl with blue and green stripes through her spiraled hair

Felicia Lee Jones.

Jessica's former best friend.

She clenched her left hand, taking solace in her newly healed arm. It was still bandaged and a bit sore, but it was stronger. Perhaps it was a sign of new beginnings.

Jessica walked to the back of the room, sitting down, she greeted her old friend.

"Hey."

Lee looked up from her sketchbook.

"Hi," she gave a little smile.

Jessica glanced over at the drawing. It was a beautiful illustration of a tree. It reminded her of the things her cousin Teren liked to draw in his very rare moments of free time.

"Your drawing is very nice," Jessica said.

"It's for my portfolio. I need one to apply for art school," Lee explained. She sounded friendly, but not the happy bubbly Lee that Jessica remembered.

Jessica glanced around the room. The teacher still hadn't arrived and the other seniors talked.

"What happened to your arm?" Lee asked.

"I was bit by David Bowie."

"You were *what?*"

"It was the dog's name. It was pretty bad bite, but it's almost healed," Jessica smiled.

The final bell rang but the teens continued to talk.

"Hey," Jessica turned to Lee. "I know it's been a long time, but I was wondering if you'd like to hang out this weekend?"

Lee shook her head.

"Sorry, but this portfolio is too important to me. If I don't have a good portfolio, I will never get a scholarship, and then I'm just going to AVCC, and I can't stand to be in this town anymore."

Lee sounded more determined than ever before, but she had a weariness in her eyes.

"I wish you luck," Jessica encouraged.

They had been best friends since middle school, but over two years ago they had gotten into an argument. Jessica could barely remember what the fight really was about. Teren had been hiding from Centernia and found safe haven with Lee. When Jessica had gone to retrieve him, her friend had demanded to know what was going on.

A lot was going on.

A lot of very bad things.

And Jessica couldn't think of even a half-baked lie to tell her friend, so she said nothing.

Lee couldn't forgive her.

"I miss hanging out," Jessica said suddenly. "What would it take to convince you that I'm sorry?"

Lee smiled.

"Jessica, we've had this conversation before. You and your cousin are nothing but a string of broken promises. How many times did you stand me up? How many times did you ignore me? It's the same story over and over again with you. It's like you don't exist outside of this high school. Teren's unbelievably rude, and not the type of person I want to be around. I was dumb, and I'm not falling for it again so don't even suggest it."

"Teren aside. What about me?"

"We're friends, I'm talking to you, right? I just don't really want to make plans just for you to cancel them with a dozen excuses."

"Okay," Jessica acknowledged. "I get that."

Jessica's phone buzzed in her pocket. The teacher still not arrived, she took it out and glanced at the text message.

```
Dad
Would you like to have pizza with me
afterschool today?
```

Jessica frowned at the odd message, but her mother had said to stay away from Centernia for a few more days. Jessica really had little else to do.

```
Jessica
Sure

Dad
I'll pick you up from school
```

Jessica slid the phone in her pocket as the instructor finally walked into the classroom with a cup of coffee and a stack of college pamphlets. Jessica was thoroughly tired of the bright shiny magazines. They promised fun and adventure and a future, but the price tag was so high.

Jessica looked down at her arm, feeling the unfairness of the situation. She needed to study at Polaris Academy if she wanted to be a blood mage, not go to an earth college

But without college, she had no hope of a paycheck big enough to protect the house.

"Do you want to hang out at lunch?" Lee interrupted her thoughts. "I'll be working in the art room. I can forge you a pass. The art teachers never care."

Jessica nodded, flexing her left hand in hope.

***

A car honked in the traffic circle at dismissal. Stephen's black Mercedes pulled around an errant minivan. Jessica had texted her mother to tell her about dinner. Lily appeared unconcerned at the strange message and replied that she was working late, so it was a good plan.

It was still a little odd.

"Have a good day at school?" her father asked as she climbed into the passenger seat. Stephen's cars were always new and smelled clean.

"Yeah, it was pretty good."

For once, her answer wasn't a half-hearted lie. Her lunch with Lee had been really nice. Lee spent most of the time working on a painting, but still talked as Jessica ate. Little had changed in Lee's life. She still lived with her mother and brother in a trailer. Now she had a part-time job working retail at the mall. Jessica didn't know why she had been so distant for so long.

"That's good," Stephen replied.

"Yes, though your text was a surprise. Is everything okay?"

"Yes, everything's fine, Carrie Anne is doing good today, her strength is back, going to her book club tonight. I just thought you and I hadn't done this in a long time, it was overdue."

Jessica was still wary that there was something her father wasn't telling her.

"How's your arm?" her dad asked. "That's a big bandage."

"It's nothing," Jessica shrugged. She peeled at the taped edges and revealed the small thin mark.

"Oh, that's good, looks like it healed no problem," Stephen commented.

"Yeah."

"Santoro's Pizza?"

"Dad, you haven't brought me to Santoro's since I was thirteen."

"You don't like it?" her father's face fell.

"No, it's still my favorite pizza place ever."

"Good, then that's where we're going."

***

They walked into the small Italian shop, the old-fashioned bell ringing as the door closed behind them. Fresh baking pizza filled the air with a sweet basil, garlic and tomato perfume. The walls were darkened wood paneling, decorated with old framed newspaper articles, Pepsi posters, and cardboard Halloween decorations. The linoleum floor was clean, but scuffed and broken in places.

Jessica and her father ordered four slices and two glass-bottled root beers, then sat at a tall table in the corner of the tiny pizza shop. Jessica eyed a glass case filled with pastries like the cream-filled cannolis and chocolate pastaciotti pies. Rainbow Neopolitan cookies were piled high.

She thought of Jared, he would have enjoyed lunch.

As Jessica chatted with her father, she started to feel relaxed.

"Jess, you know you mean to the world to me, right?" Stephen asked.

"Uh, yes..."

"Well, I don't tell you that enough. I feel like I'm a jerk to you, and I don't mean to be. I'm trying to be a good father, but hell, they don't give you any guidebooks."

"Dad, I know," Jessica sipped her root beer. She had the sense the conversation was about to turn awkward, but she also got the impression her dad was trying really hard to be sincere.

"Do you feel like you had a good childhood?"

Jessica was perplexed by the question. Two years ago, she had screamed at her father, asking him why he wasn't around more. She had made it very clear that she hadn't.

"When you were a kid, Carrie Anne and I tried to take you places. Remember we went to the beach every summer, and the amusement park, and the zoo? Remember we took you to Disney for spring break, and then there was the trip to Yosemite? We tried to bring you with us as much as possible, whenever your mother let us. She said no, a lot, and I didn't want to pressure her."

"Dad, I get that things were a little strange."

"And when you got older we just let you have your space because that's what you wanted."

"Yeah," Jessica bit into the greasy pizza. It was good, really good. She hoped the conversation wouldn't make it taste bad. She had positive mental associations with the pizza place.

"I don't know what happened between us, and I'm sorry. I'm sorry for offending you, for not listening, for being a tyrant and not your friend."

Jessica glanced awkwardly out the window. It really was a week of new beginnings.

"Dad, you're my dad. You're not supposed to be my friend. And I get that my mom is difficult, oh God, I know, she's crazy sometimes."

"I just feel like I never told you these things," Stephen continued. "When you were tiny, I took care of you. Your mom wasn't around much. Jessica, I want you to know that I was there for you. Your first steps, your first word, everything. I didn't want to leave you and I tried to be in your life as much as your mother let me."

Jessica didn't know what to say. She had never thought much about who raised her, her memories were so hazy.

"I brought you here today for a reason."

Jessica inhaled sharply. "What are you going to say this time? Ban me from something, tell me not to do something, what?"

"No, the opposite." Stephen handed her an envelope. "I was planning on giving you this for graduation, but seeing your arm the other night made me worry. I thought you may like this now instead."

It looked official, and had a bank imprint in the return address.

Jessica opened the envelope. She carefully unfolded the printed paper. It was a statement for a bank account

And the sum of money was more than the cost of a house.

Jessica was confused.

"What's this?" she asked.

"That is your college fund."

"My *what*?"

"My gift to you. You can go to any college, in the United States, Europe. Wherever, Jessi. Anywhere you want to go. College in Hawaii? Sure. Italy? Go for it. No boundaries, I just want you to chase your dreams."

Jessica felt embarrassed, like she didn't deserve the account.

"Dad, this is crazy. I can't take your money."

"It's your money."

"But for college, it's my money?"

"Jessica, you are so smart. Your science fair project last year was amazing."

"Water filtration?" Jessica smiled. "Yeah, I was proud of that one."

It was also necessary. A nasty bacterium had made its way into the water supply of Aurumice. If she hadn't devised a solution, dying of dysentery would have been more than an old Oregon Trail joke.

"Exactly! It was so well researched, so well done."

"But, it was nothing. My science grade is mediocre, all my grades are mediocre."

"I get that high school can be boring, maybe you just need two years at a smaller-name college before you move on to something bigger." Stephen reached out, clasping his daughter's hand.

"Whatever you want, I just want you to use your skills and intelligence and chase all the adventure in the world."

Jessica didn't doubt her father's sincerity. It was an amazing gift, she never thought she would be able to afford college, let alone *any* college. Looking down at her left arm, she realized the terrible irony. In the span of two days, she had gained the ability to go both Polaris Academy and any earth university that would admit her.

"Now, I know most applications are due in about two months, but, if you want to visit any schools, you let me know. I can take time off, we can fly out to wherever. Whatever your heart desires."

That tipped the scales.

"Dad, I appreciate your sincerity, I appreciate your gift, don't take this the wrong way, but I know what you're trying to do here."

"Oh?"

"You want me to stay here, and not stay there, the other *there*."

"I want you to think through your choices, Jessica." Stephen's voice lowered. "I admit, after seeing Jared in your mother's house, I panicked. I panicked and I realized I was losing my little girl. And I've got this fear now that you're going to walk into that Gate, and never come back."

"Dad, that's not true."

"Oh really? What do we know about the magic portal? How do we know they won't just close without warning?" Stephen leaned forward. "Jessica, this is the real world. That other place, it's just a dreamland."

Jessica clenched her left fist. If it was a dreamland, then it certainly still hurt.

"Dad…"

"Look, I really want to fix things between us. I'm leaving the door open. I want you to trust me again. Hey, even your boyfriend, he can come for dinner. I would like to apologize for all the questions I asked him the other night."

Jessica chuckled in spite of herself. Jared enjoyed recounting every detail of his nerve-wracking conversation with Stephen.

"Jae is very much not my boyfriend."

"Well, whoever, I would like to talk to him again."

Jessica sat back, reconsidering her father.

"You know, if you want, I could bring you to the other place."

"Nah, Jess, thank you, but I just can't."

Jessica leaned forward.

"You told me you had been there once, you never said anything else and mom has her lips sealed. What happened?"

Stephen glanced around. The other diners were absorbed in their lives.

"I don't remember much," he said. "It was a jumble, it was terrifying crossing the Gate. And when I got there, there was a crazy woman in my head. It was terrible."

"It's not like that now. That was Elina, she died a long time ago. Centernia is really nice. I think if you just followed me once, you would understand."

"I don't think your mom wants me around. Even if your mom did want me around again, how would that look to Carrie Anne?"

"Oh, I think Mom is pretty distracted right now."

"Oh?"

"Yeah, she's been seeing someone. Sort of."

Stephen sat back.

"From where?"

Jessica grabbed her root beer. Her father seemed disappointed?

"I'll give you three guesses, but you already know that answer."

"This guy have a name?"

"None you've ever heard of."

"Do you like him?"

"I barely know him at all, but, everyone else says he's a pretty nice guy. And he's my friend's dad."

Stephen seemed uncomfortable with that answer.

"Dad, are you jealous that Mom is dating again?"

"No." he sat back, taking a deep breath. "Nope. It's okay, it's good, really good. I want her to be happy. And Jessica, whatever you chose to do, it's okay. College is fine, whenever you're ready. You tell me when, I'll write the tuition check. And just know that I'm here for you, you're my daughter, and nothing changes that. I mean it, we are starting over. I don't want to lose you, just promise me you won't vanish forever, and I'll be okay."

"Dad, I'm not leaving you," Jessica could see, her father was a very scared hurt man. Carrie Anne's illness was weighing on him heavily. His life was spinning out of control, and he needed some reassurance.

He was a kind father, and Jessica knew her mother stood in his way.

"Look at me," Jessica said. "Dad, I'm not going anywhere, at least not far. Thank you for this gift, and I know, this thing with Carrie Anne is difficult, it's difficult for you and Ashlin, and I am here."

***

Stephen dropped Jessica off and she walked up the cracked driveway.

It truly had been a day of new beginnings.

As Jessica entered her house, it felt empty. Brushing the feelings aside, she flexed her left arm. Something about it still felt a little tight and odd. She ignored it as she focused on her homework.

Lily arrived home shortly after Jessica. She was relieved to have someone to fill the silence. Her mother was strangely all smiles as she kicked off her heels.

"Jess, how's your arm?"

"Fine, a little sore but definitely not mauled and useless."

"And dinner with your dad?"

"Nice," Jessica said. The bank statement was in her bookbag, but she wasn't sure what to tell her mother. The woman ran up the stairs.

Shortly after, her mother quickly came down, wearing boots, riding pants, and a traditional asymmetrical Aurumician tunic. The red garment had an elegant series of tear drop cutouts through the upper portion, revealing a little more cleavage than her mother usually displayed.

"Can you stay here for a bit?" Jessica pleaded. "If I can't go to Aurumice, it's going to be quiet."

"You have homework to focus on. Graduation, remember?"

"Homework isn't very talkative."

"Jess…"

"Is Fentalon mad at me because he had to kill Bo?"

"I think you owe him some words of apology and a thank you for saving your life, but I think he is far more concerned about your arm."

"When I go back, I'll say something. Are you sure you couldn't stay home tonight?"

"Can you call one of your friends and talk?"

Jessica shrugged. "I had lunch today with Lee, it was really nice, and I want to talk to her, but not come across as suddenly clingy. Even though I'm a bad friend."

"What about your sister? She's always been your friend, and she could use someone right now. Why don't you text her?"

"Mom, she's like five years younger than me, and we're not really friends."

"That's funny, because I'm sure five years didn't stop Teren or Nico from being your friend, or Misa for that matter, and she was six years older than you."

"It gets weird with Ashlin. I can't tell anyone the most important thing in my life. What sort of friendship is that?" Jessica looked down. "It's the same thing with Lee. I can't tell her why I kept getting pulled away, and I can't tell her why my cousin is so strange. Nothing. Just nothing. How the hell did you ever have friends? How did you even meet Dad with all the crazy Centernian stuff in your life?"

Lily sat down at the table.

"I had your aunt, and I guess I forget that," she folded her hands. "She and I were best friends."

Jessica nodded, her mom very rarely talked about her deceased sister. She knew more about Aunt Beatrix from everyone else in the castle.

"Think I can ever fix things with Lee?"

"Sorry Jess, it's hard to fix a broken friendship. When Elina drove a rift between me and your aunt, it was bad. Really bad, it was like she stuck a wedge between us and no matter what I tried to do I could not get through to your aunt, and it was the most frustrating feeling in the entire world."

"Mom, do you think... "

A knock at the cellar door interrupted Jessica.

"That's weird," the teen stated.

Jared never knocked.

"Come in," Lily called out.

The door opened, and a white haired young man poked his face in.

"Hello, we just came to see how you were doing."

"Oh," Jessica sat up. "Good."

Teren opened the door, wearing a purple jacket lined in silver. Jared followed behind him, wearing jeans and an attractive black tunic. The blond boy held a bouquet of crimson blood flowers in a crystal vase. Each tiny blossom had luminescent stripes running through its delicate petals.

"Jared said you were fine, but I did not believe him."

Jessica held out her arm for her cousin's inspection. She had switched the wrapping to a smaller one

Teren appeared perplexed.

He took her arm carefully, his smooth white hands gently running across the bandage. He touched her palm, analyzing very carefully. Jared set the flowers on the table, smiling.

"Brought these to wish you a quick recovery."

Jessica laughed.

"Blood flowers? They are *very* pretty Jared!"

"Yes Jared, blood flowers," Lily glared.

"I can order Chinese if you want to stay," Jessica was hopeful her evening would not be empty. "We could watch a movie."

Like normal friends, she thought.

"We could stay a bit," Teren still analyzed her hand. He squeezed her arm gingerly, his eyes carefully watching Jessica's face.

Her cousin dug his sharp nail into her palm without warning.

"Ouch!" Jessica jerked her hand away. "What the hell, Teren?!"

"You weren't reacting with pain. I wanted to see if you still had feeling in your hand."

Jessica sucked at the tiny wound.

"Yes, I do!"

Teren turned to Lily. Then he looked at Jared, smirking, gesturing to the bouquet. Jessica's cousin chuckled softly. Jared beamed, clasping the vase very happily. Teren's chuckle burst into full-fledged laughter, a sound Jessica rarely heard.

He pointed at Jared.

"Oh, you bastard, you are good."

"I don't know what you're talking about." Jared gave a broad smile.

Lily glared at him again.

"I kept to my promise, Lady Vance, I said not a single word."

"May I see your arm?" Teren asked Jessica. The girl unwrapped the loose bandage, displaying the neat little stitches.

"My cousin, finally a mage!" he held out his arms, and Jessica stood to embrace him. "A blood mage, that is so wonderful for you, wonderful for Aurumice. We have never had a blood mage! Oh, this is perfect, too perfect!"

Teren was truly happy, hugging her tightly. Through the corner of her eye, Jessica could see her mother's worried expression.

CHAPTER 14

Jessica finally returned to Centernia, her arm wrapped in a heavy bandage. The wrap was annoying, but she would deal with it to be allowed to return.

She was giddy to uncover what she could do with her new-found healing abilities.

Unfortunately, she needed to be hurt in order to be healed.

Jessica ascended the stairs to her atrium room. Sitting at her desk, Jessica lit a candle and waved a small knife blade over the flame. After some time, she balanced the handle of the knife on the top of a cup, waiting for the blade to cool.

Picking up the knife, she winced and sliced a little one inch cut on her forearm.

She hoped the rest of her education wouldn't be so painful.

A thin line of crimson appeared.

Jessica stared, trying to will the cut back together.

She watched it as the minutes on the nightflight wall clock ticked.

The cut would not heal.

It slowly coagulated of its own accord.

She sliced at the wound again, making it a little longer. Still, the cut would not heal. Eventually, it clotted with little miracle or magic.

Jessica was frustrated, realizing she had a poor understanding of mage powers. Abandoning the knife, she sought out Kaity Cosette. She checked the woman's offices, then the dining room, then went out to the stable yard. People kindly asked about her arm. Word had spread pretty quickly and each tale got more exaggerated as she went on.

Finally, Jessica found the leopard mage in stableyard with her daughter. Bicorns grazed nearby in a little herd. Moontower was amongst them. Jessica rarely saw the tall, dark blue beast. He had belonged to Nico, but shied away from people in his master's absence.

"Jessica, you're well!" Kaity hugged her. "How is your hand?"

"Better, thanks to the doctors. I should have full use."

"Miraculous, the work of Earth. It's such a shame the Mage Consortium at Nova is not more open to working with Earth. We could benefit so much!"

Temi was running around, playing with white flowers.

"Temi, you look like a little bride."

"An Earth bride maybe, not an Aurumician bride," Kaity remarked.

"How are they different?" Jessica climbed up onto a low stone wall.

"You've never seen one?" Kaity was incredulous. "Oh Jessi, it's a beautiful ceremony.

We wear a multitude of colors for our weddings. Brides don't carry flowers, they carry a chalice."

Temi grew tired of her bouquet, and instead found a stick to fight with. She handed Jessica a stick of equal size and took on an adorable fencing pose.

Jessica smiled and humored the child, engaging in a mock sword fight.

"That sounds…interesting." Jessica parried. She wanted to ask about mage strengths, but Kaity continued to talk.

"They do a blood binding, and it ties you together, forever, in the magic of Aurora. It's much like the castlemarks connecting us to Aurumice. I bet if earth had this magic, your people would never have invented that terrible practice of divorce."

"But married couples still argue here," Jessica pointed out. "So it's not like magic makes everything perfect."

Temi abandoned the sword fight and leapt up at Jessica, climbing onto her back like a little monkey. The child was getting heavier and nearly knocked her off balance. Temi pulled at Jessica's hair, holding the stick at her neck as if she was going to slice the girl's throat. The cub squealed in delight.

Kaity continued to talk as Jessica extricated herself from the wild child.

"It makes everything better."

"I wish I was a mage," Jessica said. "What's it like when a mage strength shows up at first? How do you know?"

"Why do you ask?" Kaity inquired, pulling the giggling Temi from Jessica's back.

"Just curious."

Kaity grabbed Jessica's wrist and smirked.

"What?" Jessica tried to feign ignorance.

"Jess, I saw your arm. It should have taken months before you would have the strength to lift Temi. You're not in pain."

"Good drugs?"

Kaity shook her head.

"Other people may think earth doctors are demi gods, I do not. You should never have regained full motion in your hand, and not certainly after a week."

Jessica glanced aside. She valued Kaity's friendship, and she didn't want to lie to the woman.

"Your mom told you not to say anything, didn't she? Especially not to official mage of the Consortium, right? Afraid we're going to take you away to Polaris Academy?" Kaity rolled her eyes.

Jessica didn't know how to respond.

"I get it," Kaity said. "I won't tell Corwin. But Jessica, you need to realize two things. One, mage strengths are wild. Many mages have the ability to create an opposing force to their talent, and a first manifestation might not even be the direction your strengths will flow."

"Huh?"

"Okay, your mother. Weather witch…lightning and freezing. Acceleration and deceleration of particles. Lightning is easy for her, it's the primary way her magic wants to go. Frost, is difficult and painful for her. You healed, but it doesn't mean healing will be the way your magic wants to go. You may find it easier to rip apart flesh than knit it together."

Jessica grimaced at the thought.

"Yes, it's important to get that," Kaity cautioned. "I know your mom wants to keep you safe, and I know Teren wants to keep you home, but you owe it to *this* world to learn how to heal people. You need to go to Polaris Academy. Think how Aurumice would have been different if we had a blood mage. So many people wouldn't have died, your Aunt Trixie, your cousin Misa, Nico's little sister, his father, the list goes on."

Jessica nodded.

"Is the only place to learn to be a mage Polaris Academy?"

"Yes, well, the Holy Circus what they call high priests, and most of them are mages. They never get very advanced and Polaris recruits them. Auroriates don't really know how to train mages well."

"So there is only one Polaris Academy? And that's just in Katanzarko? What if I don't want to leave Aurumice?"

"Jess, think about it for a while. And don't worry, I will keep your secret until you graduate high school."

"Thank you."

Kaity reached out and hugged Jessica tightly.

"Congratulations, and you know I will always be your confidante, and also, once we can tell the 'folk, I am throwing you the grandest celebratory dinner."

Jessica nodded, relieved Kaity was not upset.

"Kait, I do have one question. Can a blood mage heal cancer?"

"I have no idea what the limits of the strength are, but I would be surprised if they couldn't find a way."

***

Teren waited in the humid offices of the Trabalis city elder, Vex Chezidian. It was a monthly ritual Teren loathed, but as long as Aurumice was under the jurisdiction of Trabalis, Teren had to appear and pay the castle fines.

Wadjette and three guards waited with him. It was really unnecessary, he could ward off thieves without much difficulty, but no one needed to know that.

He tapped his fingers on the leather arm of the chair, looking around the room. The walls were white, covered with a stucco. Support beams of the room were inlaid with stones. The windows were small, but decorated in stained glass, depicting scenes on the River White. Teren was dismayed that there didn't appear to be any mechanism to open them, accounting for the stuffy heat of the chamber.

Vexllel Chezidian finally entered the room. He was a tall bearded man, ailurian in ancestry, his skin striped like a tiger.

Chezidian was followed by an assistant, a woman who was mostly ailurian as well, though she had two small caprasian horns. Behind her walked a panther-faced man with bushy eyebrows and a tail with a slight crook to it.

"My apologies for keeping you waiting," Chezidian said. "You remember Magistrate Denniton from the treasury?"

"Ah, yes, and Magistrate Chezidian, it was no bother waiting. Your time is most important. I greet you Magistrate Denniton," Teren replied smoothly, greeting the man with a formal bow.

Chezidian took his time to shuffle through is papers and organize his desk. Teren knew it was a show, the man could care less about wasting Teren's time.

"How are things in the castle?"

"Reasonably well," Teren replied. "I have our payment for this moon cycle."

Wadjette produced a large wooden chest, the length of a forearm and a handbreadth in high. She set it on Vex's desk and unlocked it, revealing a neatly stacked array of coins.

"Ah, good, if you could move it to that table so that Denniton can account for it."

"Of course, magistrate," Wadjette replied with an acknowledging bow. She closed the box and carried to a nearby table. The guard followed her to observe the counting of the coins.

"We are certainly moving towards the repayment of that debt," Chezidian stated.

It was a farce. Interest on the debt stacked faster than they could pay it down.

"And now I have another matter I wished to discuss in private before bringing you to a formal hearing."

Teren's stomach dropped like a stone. Out of the corner of his eye, he saw Wadjette's ears swivel in Chezidian's direction. A formal hearing was never good. It always meant Trabalis was to make some show of force over Aurumice, determined to squash the castle further.

It was maddening.

There was a time when Aurumice protected Trabalis, allowing the city to flourish. Now Trabalis did nothing but drain the castle.

"We have discussed the electricity of the castle before, but now it has come to the point where we can no longer ignore this violation of the law. I heard of your garish rainbow display during the Fire Flight Festival."

Teren could hear his cousin laughing in the back of his mind. It was a few strings of Christmas lights.

"With all respect sir," Teren said. "We use glowstones outside. We know the law forbids use of electricity outside of a private residence."

"You have lights that can be seen a great distance away. The people talk. Your balls and parties, though really quite lovely, are a flagrant and grandiose insult to Trabalis. I have reports that these were not ordinary glowstones, as glowstones don't blink. Do you have an explanation for that?"

Teren's mind raced, annoyed that his powers had little effect on Vex Chezidian.

"I have turned my back for quite some time," Chezidian continued, "but the problem is now the people of Trabalis are getting more inspired. Since the destruction of the energy field, we have had more instances of illegal electricity usage than I can count."

He gestured to a large stack of papers and sat back.

"This is unacceptable. These are people who think that because the Castle Aurumice can piss on the law, they can do so without consequence. There must be consequences!"

"But the law forbids the use of electricity outside of a private residence, our lights are inside the castle."

"Well we know that's a half truth."

"We are converting the exterior lamps to gas, it is a process," Teren said, dodging around the topic of the Fire Flight lights. "We will cease using electric lights until the gas conversion is complete."

It was a lie to buy him more time.

"You must understand the essence of the law." Chezidian lectured. "It was written that way over a hundred years ago, to prevent people from being arrested for little trinkets and baubles that they may still have possessed since the war with Graveer. But lately we have seen more experimentation, and this is dangerous."

Don't argue, don't argue, don't argue....

"With all respect sir, what are the cases of fire caused by lanterns and candle? I imagine quite high. Electric lights burn safely."

"People can't be trusted to have wires running through their homes. It's dangerous. As a child, I saw my schoolmates electrocuted when they found an old power generator . It's frightening, like the power of lightning. People cannot harness that strength."

Teren's annoyance continued to bubble and blister. Conversations with Vex Chezidian were particularly frustrating because he couldn't sway the man's emotions. He could sense them, and nudge them, but they were very stalwart. A handful people were resistant to the powers of the Sinari naturally, likely Chezidian had an ancestor who had been given the Mark of Corvalian. The effects to block a psychic mage lingered in his bloodstream.

"So, what is your proposal?" Teren asked.

"I want the power shut down. People cannot see your flagrant show."

Teren could not contain his annoyance any longer.

"You know there was once a time, forgotten now, Trabalis was a bustling city with a renowned theatre district? Shopping was unparalleled and rich with our trade goods, and the streets lined with electric lights. We have photographs in the castle that document this beautiful history, I would be happy to show them to you! And Graveer wiped it out from the public mind, burned your books, made the world forget that Trabalis was an amazing little city. The shore on the River White was lit with a rainbow of lights that made people talk about our city from the Bay of Figasha to the Therissina Islands! Would it be so terrible to bring Trabalis back to those days? We can make it happen, I have people in the castle with this knowledge. Why hide in darkness?"

Teren hoped he could convince Vex Chezidian with his impassioned speech, but his words fell to deaf ears.

"Trabalis was a prosperous city, until some hot-headed idiotic Aurumician mages threw a forcefield across our only trade route and suffocated our economy for a decade! That's *my* problem. And as for your books and photographs, I recall there are also laws on record for the destruction of any material that would inspire people to take on the folly of electricity."

Settling against the back of his chair, Teren relented. As long as Magistrate Chezidian held power over Trabalis, there was no way he could win the argument.

"As it stands, we are fining you until the power is gone and your water-generator or whatever it is you hide in your basement is dismantled."

"We can turn off the power, but dismantling the generator will be a long and dangerous process."

"I could also ask you to remove all the electrical lines from your castle, that would also be costly."

"Castle Aurumice is a private residence," Teren repeated. "By the letter of the law, we are not in violation."

"The *essence* of the law says otherwise. If you want to argue, I will gladly have the soldiers of Trabalis take your castle, toss out all your people, back to the streets. I don't fear your handful of mages, we have Castle Nova behind us. And the law on electricity stems from *their* books, not just ours. Do you want to fight with a real mage army?"

Teren finally gave up the argument.

"You make yourself perfectly clear. We will comply with the law."

***

"You want me to do what?!"

Jessica was *not* happy.

After dinner, the leaders Aurumice had gathered. Each aspect of the castle had an appointed representative who spoke on matters that would impact everyone. From the kitchens, to the stables, to the fields, from the cellars to the guards. Roughly twenty castlefolk gathered as the kitchens bustled with the sounds of cleaning and washing dishes.

"Shut it down, just temporarily, so we can have the Trabalis daywatch traipsing through the hallways with their muddy boots. Then a soon as they're gone, we'll turn it all back on, and just make sure no exterior rooms have lights."

"Can't you just tell them to go screw themselves?"

Teren glared at his cousin. The girl sat backwards in a chair, wearing jeans underneath a Centernian tunic. Her attitude was not helping.

"If I could tell off the council of Trabalis and Vex Chezidian, do you think Nico would have ever gone to Briken?!"

"I know you can't Teren! But come on, they take our money all the time. Any profit we seem to get they just take. It sucks."

"We need to comply with the law," Fentalon pointed out. "They are right to tell us to stop this dangerous way of doing things. You don't need these lights. A glowstone is fine, a lantern is perfectly serviceable."

"What the hell! I'm busting my tail trying to put together a radio system. Do you know how badly we suck at communication? You have no idea how amazing it would be to have something so simple! It would save time, and stress, and lives. I can do it! I've had this plan in place for a while, I'm not moving backwards."

"At some point, yes, you can build whatever you wish, just now is not that point," Teren stated. "Now we cannot afford to argue with the Council of Trabalis!"

"Yes, we can!" Jessica protested. "Why do you think Chezidian said people have been doing experiments with electricity? Because we inspired them! Because it's the natural order of things! You people live in the frickin' middle ages and you don't need to!"

"Jessica, please I know you and your mother come from a world that is a bit different from ours, but you must respect our ways," Fentalon argued.

"I'm castlefolk same as you," Jessica pointed out. "You can't see the mark on my back, but it's there. What you're arguing is one way of Aurumice, but mine is the other. There were a lot of wires running through these walls long before I showed up."

"The stables would be functional without our electric lights," Savina stated. "Though, torches are dangerous. It would limit what we could do at night."

"And the kitchens couldn't function," Jessica said. "Where's Cookie? Why isn't he out here?"

She jumped out of her chair and ran into the kitchens.

"I am torn on this one," Alba said. She was an old white cat and a castle elder. "The gardens in the courtyard do not need electricity. But the power has been a part of Aurumice as long as I can remember. It has never done us harm, and has done much good."

"Candles and lamps lead to fires," Kaity pointed out.

"That is not true," Fentalon argued. "The fire in the East Hallway was caused by bad wiring. And the worst fire this castle faced had nothing to do with candles! It was a child mage with no training!"

Teren didn't appreciate the reference to Nico, but Fentalon had a point.

"We have a lot of glowstones," Eve pointed out. "Really, an amazing amount. They aren't very bright, but they're serviceable. We are mostly ailurians, no offense to those of your who have sapien or caprasian eyes, but I would say glowstones are fine. The children of the castle don't need electricity, and quite honestly, I would prefer not needing to worry about the errant cub poking into one of those ghastly outports or outlets or whatever you call the holes in the walls."

"Even as a caprasian," Dr. Onyxgrove added. "I can get by with glowstones."

"Teren, let me try to re-negotiate this," Kaity interjected.

"You are not shutting down my freezer!" Cookie burst from the kitchen, Jessica behind him. "We need the freezer! And I am not working under glowstones and those smelly gas torches!"

"I understand you are frustrated..." Teren began.

"It's stupidity and foolishness!"

"Gestheban," Fentalon interrupted, referring to Cookie by his real name, "electricity is dangerous, and unpredictable and unnecessary!"

"That is not true!" Jessica argued. "It's more predictable than mage power. It's science, it follows rules. And I told you, this castle needs a communication system that's better than a bunch of bells. And there's more, I can add a water pump, and better heaters, and it would be amazing to maybe have some fun, like movies and projectors, and that's a whole different thing, but radio!"

"We have done well with bells," Eve pointed out.

"Jessica does raise a good point," Wadjette said. "She showed me what she was working on, it would be useful to the guard to talk a distance instantly. Father, you must see the practical application."

"What was the reason Castle Nova banned electricity in the first place? Because the old generation became too reliant. It made us weak."

"It didn't make you weak, it was Graveer and a god damn EMP that did that! And going forward, we're weaker than we were," Jessica argued.

"Let me at least try to talk to the Council of Trabalis," Kaity pleaded.

"I really do not want a public spectacle," Teren stated. "Chezidian made it clear, this was our calm option."

"Teren, I will not let you do this!" Cookie argued.

"I understand that you are upset, but Trabalis is going to level another fine at us, and we are already in more debt than we can handle right now," Teren tried to be diplomatic. He didn't want to sway Cookie's emotions, he hoped he could get the man to reason.

"Why should Vex Chezidian tell us what to do when Trabalis does nothing for us?!" Cookie disputed. "They cast us to Rockwood, stripped us of our rights, where was our apology for that? So many castlefolk died because of the arrogance of Trabalis' little dictator and I will *not* forget that! Nico should not be tortured in the Mines of Briken right now! Labor camp my tail end!"

Cookie's face turned scarlet. "Nico's work in the mines does nothing. He is there as an example, Teren! They are torturing him to make you, to make all of us, scared!"

Cookie's words were true. Teren sensed the general opinion of the castlefolk begin to shift. Those who were once complacent seemed a bit more defiant. The swirl of emotions made his head ache, and he did not like Nico's name constantly being evoked in the argument. He did not need to think of his lost friend.

"Gestheban, we need to work with the law," Fentalon argued.

"You weren't there!" Cookie was now shouting, "You ran elsewhere while the castlefolk suffered! If we give Trabalis this, then what else will they take? What if they want the crops before they reach the kitchens? What if they want us to labor for them in the city? What if they decide the castlefolk would make for excellent indentured servants to pay the debt? You're the captain of the guard, you're supposed to protect us!"

"Let us bring this to a vote," Teren said. "It is the way things are done. But let me stress, whatever we decide today is *not* permanent. Vex Chezidian is Chief Magistrate of Trabalis, but at some point, he will not be, and then we have a new chance to negotiate. Aurumice embraces the electricity, it is part of the fibers of this castle and it is *not* an abomination."

They conducted a vote by standing, those who opposed turning off the power sat. Jessica, Cookie, and Kaity sat firmly, everyone else stood. Savina hesitated, but ultimately remained standing. Wadjette had no vote as her father spoke for the guard. Teren leaned against the table, his vote would not have swayed the outcome.

He was disappointed, but he saw no other choice.

"Well, the castle has spoken."

"The castle has not spoken," Kaity crossed her arms. "Something this big needs a full vote, from everyone. I demand it! And for the record, Nico would have been against it, and *Misa would have never just let Chezidian have his way!*"

Kaity knew how to slice into the most painful nerve.

"We will take this temporary measure," Teren said, barely able to restrain his fury. Why did Kaity always try to undermine him in the worst arguments?

"We will prevent Aurumice from incurring any more fines, and then we will have a full vote. Jess, let's talk about a way to shut some circuits, maybe we can hide the freezer with a shelf or something, but the lights need to go off.

Jessica crossed her arms.

"I disagree, give Kaity a chance to talk to Trabalis, and until she does, you can't force me to turn it off."

"Yes, he can," Fentalon interjected. "We voted, and if you want to disagree, and put this castle in harm's way by garnering the ire of Trabalis, then you can pay consequences for your choices!"

Teren cringed as he sensed Jessica's fury.

"Jessica, stop!" Teren held out a hand before his cousin could speak. Whatever she was going to say would only pour gas onto the fire. He used a tiny bit of influence to quell her fury. He hated himself for doing so, but she and Fentalon were already a powder keg.

"We will talk," he said. "I am closing this meeting."

***

169

Jessica left Aurumice calm, but by the time she was back home, she was furious again. Thinking back, she realized her cousin had used his powers to silence her.

And that made her even angrier.

She tried to focus on homework, but the words ran together on the page. Her weekend would be full spending time with her father's family and she would have little time to work. When the the clock displayed 2am, she realized there was no way she could keep her eyes open.

On her dresser, she had a box full of used radio equipment. She had hoped to have a working test up and running before Christmas. Now it seemed impossible.

She left her room, hoping to find her mom home. As she walked into the darkened bedroom, she remembered years before how Misa made a terrible mess searching for the Shadow Sphere. Her cousin was crazy, and high as a kitewing, but she didn't give up on her hopes to save the castle.

Lily's bed was empty, and the sight made Jessica sick. She *hated* the idea of her mother sleeping with Fentalon. She kicked the door, denting the cheap wood and damaging the sheetrock behind the door handle.

A scream formed in her mouth, but she held it back with clenched teeth as she returned to her bedroom. Throwing herself on her bed, Franklin, the little stuffed chick, fell to the floor. The bird had been a gift from her cousin to convince Jessica to return to Aurumice.

Jessica grabbed the cherished stuffed creature and threw it against the wall. It struck with a very unsatisfying *thuff*.

She wouldn't even have a chance to confront her mother in the morning. She was leaving at 6am for a long drive and a college visit with her father's family.

Jessica sat back down on the bed, thinking of the bank account. She had been so happy to find her blood mage powers, but maybe college was her Brightpath. If Castle Aurumice wanted to be insanely stupid, then the castlefolk could wallow in the middle ages without her.

***

Morning sunlight filtered bright through autumn tree canopies. The upstate New York campus was idyllic and calm, far from the disagreement in Aurumice. Jessica was still irritated, trying to think of a new strategy.

Carrie Anne and Ashlin accompanied them as they toured the technical campus on the mid-October day. It was a pretty little school with modern brick buildings, winding paths, and neatly maintained landscaping. Students walked in a sleepy stupor or zipped by on skateboard.

The classroom facilities were extensive and the equipment in the labs made Jessica's head spin. The residence halls reminded Jessica of Castle Aurumice. Each little room had the distinct personality of its inhabitants.

Carrie Anne seemed a little slower than usual, but smiled as she walked. Her stepmother wore a bright magenta scarf over her thinning hair and a little brown sunhat. On her neck, she displayed the jade necklace Jessica had given her from Aurumice.

"Jessi, I am impressed with this school," Carrie Anne bubbled. "This is so exciting!"

"It's really nice."

The leaves crunched beneath their feet. Jessica sipped her warm, sweet mocha latte.

"So much nicer than the college I went to!" Carrie Anne continued. "Oh Jessi, I want you to go away to school! You will have so much fun! It's like a whole different world!"

"I know. This campus is nice."

"Reminds me of my days at school," Stephen smiled. "Those were the best days."

"Tell us stories about your wild days, Dad," Ashlin gave their father a gentle shove.

"Oh, far too many stories to tell. We did the dumbest things. We drank until we were stupid, we pulled the most ridiculous pranks. Once we got this beautiful old car, and we drove it into a dining hall without a scratch and then..." his voice trailed, catching his wife's glare.

"It was irresponsible and stupid and we were lucky no one got hurt...badly...too often," he snickered.

"Come on, tell us more," Ashlin pleaded.

"We rode around 'til dawn, all the time. Days were endless, and we never slept. I don't know how we ever learned anything."

"You had a motorcycle back then, right?"

"I had a motorcycle. It was black, you should have seen it. God, I miss that thing like you wouldn't believe. But that was a different time, a different wilder life."

Stephen absentmindedly ran his tongue over his front teeth. They were false, his real ones lost in a college lacrosse game.

"Mom, I want a motorcycle." Ashlin said.

"Oh Ashlin, you are going to be the death of me," Carrie Anne rolled her eyes.

The family walked down a cement stairwell, passing bleary eyed freshmen who barely gave them a grunt as he walked by in flip-flops.

"Dad, you got your tattoos in college?"

Stephen had two tattoos, one on each forearm. On his right was an electric guitar, a snake woven around it. On his left was a cross and a Dia del los Muertos skull. When Jessica was a child, the skull frightened her, so her dad often wore long sleeve shirts to cover them up.

"Mom, what are you going to do if Jessi gets a tattoo in college?"

"They are so tacky. Why would you do something like that?"

"My mom has a tattoo." Jessica pointed out.

And I had one too, until she burned it off.

"Oh, I mean no offense to your mom…"

"Dad, do *you* regret your tattoos?" Ashlin pressed. "They look really cool. Makes you a much more awesome dad."

"It was probably the most stupid decision I made in my entire life," he said earnestly, "but I was young, and I didn't think about the consequences I would live with."

"Dad, they don't look bad!"

"Well, I need to be careful in business meetings. Some clients may be offended."

"Well then they're boring stupid clients."

"Ash, corporate America doesn't work that way," Stephen sighed. "I need to be respectable."

"I don't ever want to work in the business world. I want to do something so much cooler. Space exploration would be awesome, or maybe I'll be an artist."

"My friend Felicia is going to art school," Jessica said.

"You don't talk about her much," Ashlin commented.

"We're both pretty busy."

Carrie Anne stumbled on the stairs, and Stephen was quick to catch her.

"Are you alright?"

"I'm fine," Carrie Anne smiled. "I just tripped. Okay? Nothing at all, I tripped, Stephen."

Jessica became transfixed by her father's panicked expression.

"Are you sure? Do you want to rest? Do you need anything?"

"I tripped! Look, the stairs are uneven. I tripped, don't worry."

Stephen's eyes were so sad. It was as if in that moment of falling, he was losing her forever.

And he was.

No idyllic college visit, no quaint family outing, would change that fact.

I can't go here.

Jessica almost said the words aloud.

What was she doing considering college?

She was a blood mage, the time to act was now.

She needed to be some place far more important.

And if the castlefolk didn't accept her ways, then it was time to move on to Polaris Academy to save Carrie Anne.

***

It was late Sunday afternoon before Jessica had a chance to speak to her mother.

"Missed you Friday night," Lily commented. "I heard you got into an argument with Talon."

Her mother was in the equipment shed, cleaning the chest plate of a sparring suit. The smell of the oil-based cleanser was sharp in the air.

"It was more than me arguing, it was me and Kaity and Cookie. Fentalon was way off base."

"I also heard that you were defiant towards your cousin in front of everyone."

"Mom, you know we can't listen to Trabalis!"

"Jessica, it's complicated, and I know, you're just mad that you can't do your projects.

You'll get a chance. Just not right now."

"And what am I supposed to do in the meantime? If Aurumice has no electricity, what's my job here?"

"Focus on high school and college," Lily set down the cleaning rag and selected a sword from the rack. She held it up to the light, examining the blade.

"Mom, I can't go to an American college!"

"Jess, let me relax on my Sunday, I don't want to hear it."

"I refuse to go to college."

"Oh really? Why?"

"I need to go to Polaris Academy and I can't wait any longer. With *Lord* Fentalon's determination that the castle doesn't need electricity and we should kiss the tail of Chezidian, then there's nothing for me to do here."

"You will graduate high school and that is the end of the discussion. Focus on that, Jess, and just come and here and do barn chores." Lily held up the metal chest plate to the sunlight streaming in the window.

"No. I'm a blood mage, I am a healer, and Carrie Anne is dying of cancer! I might be the only one who can save her."

"Oh Jessi, it's a very noble and sweet thought, but blood mage powers just do not work that way."

"You don't know that," Jessica almost told her mother about Kaity's opinion, but thought better.

"I was friends with a blood mage. I am pretty familiar with their strengths."

"But you aren't one, how do you really know?"

"Jessi, please, just let it go."

"Mom, she's getting weaker, the chemo is kicking her butt. She's going to die and it's going to break Dad's heart, which, I know you don't care about."

"Watch your tone with me," Lily glared.

"No, I won't. You don't care. You're being selfish. You can't stand to see Dad happy. You've always hated Carrie Anne!"

"Now that is not true," Lily glared. "I always had pity for the woman. She was a clueless little wallflower who got herself into trouble."

"Yeah, and you know what? For a clueless little wallflower, she has always been nice to me, which is more than I can say for your stupid arrogant boyfriend. Carrie Anne loves me, and she loves Ashlin. And did you ever stop to consider once that I don't want to lose my stepmother? She's a better mother than you have been!"

Lily slapped Jessica across the face.

The girl was stunned. Her hand went to her reddened cheek. Her pride smarted more than her skin.

"I have given my life for Aurumice, don't you dare call me selfish! Let me make one thing clear. I have my reasons, and you are my child, you are not entitled to know why I make my choices. I am very sorry Carrie Anne has cancer, but you will not be able to save her, so give up. Your Uncle Justen had a cancer in his lungs and no blood mage was able to help him."

Jessica had run out of arguments. She left the shed, slamming the door behind her. So lost in her fury, she collided with Penrik.

"Jess, I was just looking for you! You're up next on the field. You're not even dressed to play ribbons."

"What?! With this arm?" Jessica held up the bandage.

"Fentalon said you should still practice. That we always need to be prepared to fight."

"I don't care, I need to find Jared."

"Why?" the younger man was confused. "Is something wrong?"

"I'm not doing what Fentalon says. He can't tell me to fight and he can't tell me how to keep the castle running."

"For what it's worth, I heard about the argument with Council of Trabalis and the electricity and I think you're right. And I think they should let everyone vote, and they will. Chezidian won't win."

"Thanks," Jessica replied.

"Come on, spar with me," Penrik encouraged. "I'll put in the least effort possible."

Jessica finally relented. She had no reason to be angry with Penrik. She grabbed a set of armor and strapped on the leathery plates. It was difficult to slide the armor over the bandage, making her more annoyed.

Reluctantly, she followed Penrik to the bench by the side of the field. Jessica considered a staff, then realized she would need two hands. She picked a wooden sword instead, not her favorite weapon.

She sat on a wooden bench. As she pondered in silence, she became grateful Penrik had interrupted her escape.

She would not overreact.

She would act as if nothing was unusual.

And then leave.

Her mother would never strike her again.

On the field, Alba sparred in a game of ribbons against Perlin. The white cat was the oldest member of the castle, but still, she still fought hard.

Jessica watched them fight as she wondered how long it would take to travel to Polaris. Was it worth waiting for a school holiday? Should she just leave that night?

Across the field, Fentalon came outside and sat on a bench.

Lily walked across the field and sat next to Fentalon.

`Jessica bit her lower lip.

"It's nice to see your mom with Talon. It makes Wadjette happy," Penrik said.

"He was the one who wants me to cut the power to the castle."

"Oh, he's just stuck in the old ways. Your cousin is behind you, and so is Kaity, so you can't lose. Everyone knows they always can convince the castle."

"But you weren't there Pen, Teren was arguing *against* me."

"Just because he doesn't want the castlefolk to think he's unfair," Penrik replied.

The match ended. Fentalon gestured to Jessica, indicating it was her turn.

"Let's get this spar over with." Jessica stood to take the field, Wadjette walked out.

"I'm sparring against Pen," Jessica said to her friend. "I don't want to spar with you."

"Yeah," Penrik said. "Talon, I claimed this round!"

"Wadjette will be a better match," Fentalon said. "She'll be more cautious with Jessica's bad arm."

Who asked your opinion?!

"Oh, forget it then, if my arm's so bad I'm leaving," Jessica glared. "I don't need to play this stupid game."

So much for pretending everything was okay, she was still furious.

"Jess, just spar with Wadjette," Lily said.

"Father," Wadjette argued, "If she does not want to play..."

"Wadjette, it's just as important as a leader to teach the castlefolk that they can fight when not at their best. Jessi has one bad arm, but she also has one good one."

Wadjette's face fell, she did not like disappointing her father. She took opening position in the center.

"But I wanted to spar with Penrik," Jessica argued.

"I think Wadjette would be a better opponent," Fentalon argued. "Pen lacks control, you could be hurt worse. Jessica, in the castle, you can argue all you want with me. But here, the sparring field belongs to the guard."

Jessica's blood boiled. She really, *really* wanted to hit something. If Wadjette wanted to fight her, then she would get her fight.

Jessica walked to the equipment rack to take her ribbons. She slipped on a helmet and attached a few heavier pieces of armor. She picked up the purple ribbons and clipped them into their designated spaces. They were attached to her head, chest, and thigh. As she attached each, she vowed to convince Jared to take her to Polaris.

Trudging back out to the center of the field with her staff, she faced Wadjette.

"You will be fine, " the panther girl encouraged. "I will be cautious of your arm."

Talon whistled the start of the match. They took ten steps, bowed, and began.

Wadjette assumed the offensive, but Jessica deflected. The wood clacked. Jessica's wrist on her uninjured arm bent back too far in her defense. It smarted and she swore.

Wadjette dove at her again, and Jessica rolled to avoid the attack. She tried to grab at Wadjette's leg ribbon but was too slow.

She rolled into a defensive position. Wadjette slapped her staff square across Jessica's back. The pain was sharp and as Jessica lost her concentration Wadjette grabbed her leg ribbon.

Fentalon whistled the end of the round. When they played in matches, the combatants reset after each ribbon grab.

"Bloody goddess that sucked," Jessica grimaced, clutching her backside. She hoped her healing powers would start to work quickly.

The game resumed.

Wadjette did not relent, causing Jessica to defend weakly. She got in a good punch to Jessica's gut, knocking the wind from the teen's lungs.

Jessica gasped, doubling over, Wadjette grabbed her head ribbon.

Talon signaled again, ending the round.

"I hope you're having fun," Jessica staggered backwards.

"I'm being cautious of your wrist."

"But not the rest of me!"

Wadjette turned around to resume her position, but Jessica lashed out with her staff, striking Wadjette in the back of the knee.

The girl stumbled, caught off guard.

"That was an illegal move!" Fentalon bellowed. "The round hadn't started!"

Jessica realized she had hit Wadjette a little too hard when the pantheress couldn't stand up straight. The girl limped a few paces, then stumbled to the ground.

Fentalon and Lily ran out onto the field.

"Of all the disrespectful things I have seen, that was low and inexcusable!" Fentalon shouted, overreacting.

"Father, I am fine," Wadjette stood slowly. "I will handle this."

"You are shameful child," Fentalon continued to lecture Jessica. "That is not how the 'folk act! First you disrespect your cousins' wishes and now this? Kaity and Teren's lack of control is shameful and breeding insolence, and isn't the way of Aurumice!"

Jessica recalled Jiberty's words weeks before.

Fentalon would bring the old ways back to the castle.

Jessica exploded, swearing in a string of darkly vulgar Centernian curses before launching into her verbal attack.

"I am not a child, so stop talking to me as if I were one! Second of all, you had no right forcing me to fight Wadjette. You're an ass, and I wish you would go back to wherever you came from! I don't care if you think I'm shameful, because despite the fact you're going at it with my mother, you are not my father!

"Maybe if you had a father you would have more respect," Fentalon countered.

"What the hell!" Jessica shouted. "Look, I have a father, I have always had a father! I had dinner with him last night!"

Her voice echoed across the field and she couldn't stop the words from tumbling out.

"I'm so sick of this bullshit! I'm tired of hiding who I am and the rest of my family! I am tired of lying to the rest of my family about you! My dad is very real, and doesn't live here, he's on earth re-married to someone else, but he raised me very well thank you!"

Fentalon turned to Lily.

"I thought you didn't know who her father was," he was puzzled.

Lily was stunned.

Jessica's anger boiled over.

"I am so tired of this," she continued, "she had a *husband.* I was born *in* wedlock! In my world, we have ex-husbands. We have this practice called divorce. It means anyone can toss their vows aside as soon as they're bored with their partner. It means your spouse doesn't need to die for you to be rid of them. So, while you're giving me life advice Fentalon, let me give you some. If you don't want your stupid heart broken, then don't sleep with my mother!"

Jessica flung the sword and stomped off the field. As she walked, she realized the small gathering had gone silent.

All eyes were on her.

CHAPTER 15

Jessica searched for Jared. When she couldn't find the older boy, she retreated to her private quarters. By the time she emerged from the tower and went down for dinner, she realized something was terribly different.

Word had spread through the entire castle like poison. As Jessica entered the dining room, the chatter turned to whispers. No one made eye contact or spoke to her.

Taking a small loaf of bread, she hurriedly left the dinner. She searched for Teren and found him on the balcony over the courtyard. Her cousin was drinking wine instead of eating.

"I am too disgusted to speak to you," he stated curtly. "We warned you again and again about talking about your parents. You crossed a hallowed line, and it will take a long while to untangle this."

"Maybe people shouldn't be so uptight about divorce."

"You're not going to change the way an entire society thinks. If you have a child with someone and you're married, nothing can undo that. Nothing *should* undo that."

"But what if he's a terrible person?"

"If he's so terrible, he, or she, goes to jail. Your father is not terrible."

"But…"

"And that aside, what possessed you to curse out Fentalon on the sparring field, and to attack Wadjette!? Jessica, why Wadjette?!"

Teren's eyes zeroed in on her. Jessica cringed, feeling the sting of his fury. She really had gone too far.

"I…"

"Go on," he crossed his arms.

"I was angry at my mom, she slapped me."

"Because?"

"She won't listen to me about Polaris Academy."

Teren threw his head back in frustration.

"Jessica, I have so many serious problems, and you go and create this mire!"

"But I want to go to Polaris to help Carrie Anne!"

"Polaris Academy is a joke and den of murderous liars!"

"I don't care, I need to learn! Teren, listen to me! I'm sorry! I didn't mean to make the castlefolk angry. Help me!"

"No, figure out this mess yourself," Teren left her alone on the balcony.

***

"Now what am I holding?" little Pepper asked. The red-haired cub was at Jared's left and Temi was at his right.

"Two grey rocks and……."

Jared drew out his 'guess' for dramatic effect, though it wasn't a guess. He plainly saw the collection of objects through her eyes as Pepper had collected them along the forest edge.

"…a feather."

Pepper jumped up and down. Temi mimicked the older girl's excitement.

"You got it right!" she bounced.

The five-year-old still insisted Jared was guessing no matter how many times he explained his mage strength to her.

Jared was returning from a hike through the woods with the his aunt, uncle, and the castle children. Eve La'Roch waited for them on the grassy knoll just beyond the outdoor smokers.

"Temi this is a feather." Pepper took it from Jared and made a waving gesture with her hand. "Feather!"

Temi mimicked the movement. Pepper was trying to teach the girl their own sign-language. It was a wonderful gesture, but a bit disorganized and erratic at times.

"Let's guess another!"

"Pepper, I think Corwin is about to start his last story before dinner."

The other children had gathered a distance away under a green blossom tree, as Corwin prepared to tell his last lesson for the evening.

"Okay, but we'll play again, right?" Pepper insisted.

"Yes, Pepper," Jared fought hard not to roll his eyes.

Pepper grabbed Temi's hand and pointed to the other children gathering around Corwin. The two ran off.

The breeze brought the aroma of smoking meat and Jared's mind turned to dinner. They had missed it by a bit, but he was optimistic they had set aside something tasty.

Kaity sat on a fence rail as an irritated Eve La'Roch approached.

"I am disgusted with Jessi beyond belief."

Jared's ears perked up. He had intended to make a quick exit, instead, he pretended to watch the Corwin's lesson as he listened.

"I wasn't there, but the whole castle is talking and my brother is mortified! That girl attacked my niece on the sparring field…"

"Attacked?" Kaity questioned. "*Jessica* attacked Wadjette?"

"They weren't even in a spar! Jessi attacked Wadjette with a sword, then started shouting at my brother. Called him all sort of horrible names, and then worst of all, you'll never believe what she said."

"What?"

"Her father is alive, and lives in the other world! Broke their marriage vows, it's disgusting! Lily is just trash," Eve shook her head.

"That's terrible…" Kaity said.

"Did you know?" Eve accused.

Jared didn't want to turn to look, instead he jumped into Kaity's eyes. Going between the two he could see their mouths and make out any words lost to the distance.

"Did I know what?" Kaity asked.

"Did you know? That Jessi has a father? You know more about the other world."

"Well, I have crossed the Gate a handful of times, but I would hardly call myself an expert."

"But did you know about it, Kaity?" Eve was insistent.

Jared's aunt took a deep breath.

"No," Kaity replied. Jared bristled, he knew Kaity was lying.

Eve crossed her arms, "Can't believe Lily. What woman does that? What parents just break their home in half? I would give anything to have my husband back. I can't imagine just giving up on him!"

"I know. I would never leave Corwin. As much as we disagree, it would destroy Temi."

"So, this world they come from. Why bother to even have marriage? You're better off with bastard children with a mother's love and rule. To have their father take a second wife, then force the children obey by her new rules. I would never want another mother raising my child, and to watch it? That's torture."

"I know," Kaity nodded.

Jared could tell Kaity was trying to draw herself out of the conversation as Eve continued to rant.

"I can never look at her the same way again, her or her daughter, and Wadjette's leg is in terrible shape. Jessi should be punished severely!"

"I'm sure Jessi will be minding the dung larvae for a very long time."

"Better than trying to burn down the castle with her dangerous hobbies," Eve said.

Jared waited for Kaity to say something diplomatic and soften Eve's anger.

His aunt only nodded.

"It goes to show you what happens if you split a marriage," Eve continued. "You break the child and she becomes an ungrateful hellsprite."

Jared couldn't handle Eve's toxicity.

Against his better judgement, he approached the conversation.

"Ladies, I gotta step in here," he said.

"Jared…" Kaity glared in warning. Jared didn't forget that his aunt was barely a few years older than him, and couldn't see the careless poison of Eve's words.

"Eve, I can't believe Jessi would attack Wadjette. That's not like her…"

"This was a private conversation. Why do you always spy on us? It's rude."

"Yeah, well thanks to my spying, Perlin didn't lose her life to a sting lizard, Musian didn't die under a fallen tree, Pepper wasn't lost in that snowstorm, and I recall you ran into trouble once with a thrasher bear.

183

And, just to be clear, I was now listening with my ears from about fifteen paces away."

"It's still rude!"

"Let's take a step back. All I want to clarify is that Jessi is not a hell sprite or a brat."

"You go look at my niece's knee and tell me that girl isn't disrespectful!" Eve yelled.

"I'm sure it's exaggerated. Jess just had her arm torn open by that jack dog, how could she best Wadjette in a fight?"

"It was an illegal move and furthermore, you're not even castlefolk, you have no part in this."

"Come on Eve, you're going to hold a little tattoo against me? Vina just got her mark, but no one gave her hell before she got it."

"Savina was raised with the castlefolk, and suffered on the streets with the rest of us. You are an outsider, and you will always be one."

Jared's defense of Jessica was lost into the petty argument with Eve.

Jared finally retreated, muttering under his breath and taking a quick glance into the castle. He looked through Jessica's eyes and saw the glass floor of the tower aviary.

***

"What the hell did you do?!"

Jessica jumped to her feet, startled by Jared opening the door to her room.

"You need to take me to Polaris!" she yelped. "Please, I'll do anything!"

"I have never heard so much gossip flying around this castle, which says a lot. I just argued with Eve La'Roch, and lost, miserably. How did you hurt Wadjette?"

"Teren won't even help me. I got into a fight with my mom, and then I was going to spar with Penrik, but Fentalon made me spar with Wadjette, and I got mad, and I hit her outside of the round. I shouldn't have Jared! I shouldn't have, and I'm sorry…"

"And then you got mad at Fentalon and called him every name in the book and then told everyone about your dad?!"

"Jared, I need to go to Polaris. I need to learn how to heal and save Carrie Anne. You're the only one who can take me."

Jared sat in a wooden chair, resting his head in his hands.

"The castlefolk are really getting on my nerves, but I just can't do what you're asking me to."

"Yes, you can," Jessica knelt at his side. "I'm a blood mage. I can save people, you know that. And it doesn't do me any good, sitting here, worrying about college! I'm not going! I want to go to Polaris!"

"And what does your mother say?"

"She hit me," Jessica snapped. "Before the spar even began! She didn't like what I said about Carrie Anne, so she slapped me."

Jared heaved a sigh.

"You Vance girls are going to be the death of me."

"Jared, please. I don't belong here. I need to go to Polaris and you're the only one who can bring me."

"I doubt it's going to really solve all your problems, but, fine, get me a piece of paper."

"Paper?"

"Yes, paper, please," he replied.

Jessica handed him a notebook and a pen. He jotted down a few notes then passed the book back to the teen.

"This looks like a grocery list."

"It's important, you'll see. Get me every item on that list, and pack your things. We'll leave before I change my mind."

"Really? You'll take me?!"

"Yes! Now hurry before common sense catches up with me!"

CHAPTER 16

"What is that?!" Jessica was astounded.

She stood beside Jared at the train tracks.

Jessica had fulfilled his list as quickly as she could, returning home and walking to the convenience store. She had avoided her mother for the rest of the evening. After Lily left for work the next morning, instead of catching the bus, Jessica went to Centernia. They bribed Penrik to take them in to the city on a cart.

Now they waited at the train station, and Jessica was astounded. The train was short, but where the engine should have been was an enormous beast.

At first the teen thought it was a triceratops, but as she got closer she realized it had shaggy fur upon its neck ridge and a face that was like a wolf. It had three horns and a very short stubby tail.

The size of the beast was breath-taking, larger than an elephant and built of pure muscle. Its hide was tough and armor-plated.

"My dear Jessica, you are looking at a northern mammoth baelaena."

"It's unbelievable. *That's* what pulls the train?"

Jared gestured to the stairs.

"After you?"

Jessica was delighted to discover that the interior was much like an old-time train from a western film. The seats were cushioned in red pillows, the entire walls trimmed in wood. They took their spots and Jessica stared out the window.

Rumbling, the train trundled through the landscape, soon leaving the city behind. The terrain grew rockier the further they traveled from Trabalis. Every so often, the baelaena would let out a thunderous rumble as it pounded the earth. The lumbering car rocked and rumbled so much Jessica was sure it would come off the track.

Jared watched Jessica in amusement, nestled in his long coat and wide-brimmed hat. His legs stretched to the seats across from them.

"I don't understand why you think this is so grand. You've flown in a plane."

"But I've never seen the world beyond Trabalis!" Jessica said. "Except once, at night, and I couldn't see much of anything."

"It's trees, and farms, and mountains and dirt. It *isn't* much of anything."

"That's not true," Jessica grinned. "There's places like Yellow Valley and Daconite, and the Starlight Desert and the Swamps of Kalimoor and the province of Trinion and the islands of Therissina. I've studied the maps and I want to see it all!"

"Before or after your mother kills you?"

"I don't care what she has to say. She sided with Fentalon. I'm through with her."

"But you struck Wadjette behind the knee. I would have yelled at you too."

"I don't want to talk about it," Jessica fidgeted with her bandage and slowly peeled it off. The skin was healed well enough and she no longer needed to hide.

"What happens when we get to Polaris?"

"I'll see what I can set up with the mage council. They like blood mages."

"Is there tuition? Or room and board?" The thought had not occurred to Jessica.

"Nah, just a lifetime of servitude," he smirked, "but most people like it. Service days, practicing your craft, but that's a long ways out for you."

"I can't wait."

"Just so you're not surprised, I am thinking I may leave Aurumice after this adventure. I suspect Teren and your mother and my uncle and aunt will not want me around anymore."

"Oh," Jessica hadn't thought of the consequences for Jared. "Maybe they'll get over it."

"After the things Eve La'Roch said, not sure I want to be around castlefolk much." Jared continued.

"What did she say?"

"Just garbage about me spying on people."

"But you do."

"I keep people out of trouble, Jess, I see a lot that I never talk about too. I let people keep their secrets."

"I know you do."

"I saw the day in the tower with your cousin."

"You did?"

Jared nodded.

"I was hoping you would just be up front and tell me," Jared continued. "Let's be honest, there's a very short list of people who would make Teren cry like that. All of those people I know are still alive, except for one."

Jessica sat back. "He thinks Nico's dead."

"Damn," Jared glanced away. "I'm sorry, Jess. I always hoped he would come back."

"Yeah, me too," she replied, staring out at the landscape.

They traveled for the day and through the night. At every station, their baelaena would be swapped for a different beast. Each one had a different pace and rhythm. The train trundled across bridges and Jessica felt her ears pop from an elevation change. Beautiful rock formations reflected the light in different ways. Every once in a while, they passed an interesting sculpture.

"Here it is," Jared grinned widely, "Look out the window now!"

As they rounded a corner, the trees broke for a spectacular view of the ocean. Ahead, a range of mountains pierced the sky. As they got closer, Jessica realized they were magnificent architectural formations twisted and pulled from the rocks.

"It's a little city!"

She blinked.

"It's a big city! Out of the rocks?"

"Yes. A very, very long time ago, mage sculptors built the entire city from the mountains. Rock shapers they call them."

"I don't remember any of this last time I was here."

"You were pretty exhausted and out of it, I imagine."

The last time Jessica had traveled to Castle Nova, she had done so by a hidden Gate. She had briefly been inside one building, but then they took nightflights in the dark to return back to Aurumice.

"Which is Castle Nova?"

"That little one made from the multicolored rock."

"That's not little, Jared!"

"It is comparatively."

"So, what's Polaris Academy?"

"It's that blue chunk over there. Nova is just where the Consortium of Mages sits, they're a separate entity from the school."

"What's the whole thing called?"

"Katanzarko City."

***

Once they arrived inside the city, Jared hailed a small carriage pulled by a pair of unassuming dappled grey horses. The carriage was small and could probably hold four people. Its sides were black and bore a nightflight signet.

"These carriages bring you to Polaris Academy, and you don't need to pay for them," Jared explained.

Jessica climbed into the carriage, settling into the velvety blue seat. The bench was hard and the coach smelled musty. As they traveled through the city, Jessica forgot about Aurumice and Earth as her eyes glued to the windows.

Katanzarko had an ambiance like none she had ever seen before.

The first thing Jessica noticed were the strange flag poles, spaced like street lamps. Each had intricate metal designs at the top. Webs of shimmering gossamer were woven in between the openings like lace.

"What are those flags for?"

"What flags?"

"The things on poles."

"Oh, you will love this," Jared leaned over. "That is bioluminescent webbing, made from the crestgoats. Lightspinners harvest the thread when crestgoats build nests, then make those designs, and they glow for almost a year every nightfall."

"That's amazing!"

"Ah, there's one now. See the man in the blue and white uniform? Those are the lightweavers, he's probably going to replace the threads over there."

The man wore a white uniform with long coat tails and large black goggles.

"The bioluminescent stuff can get pretty nasty if you're exposed to too much. Glasses protect his eyes," Jared explained.

"Are the lightweavers mages?"

"No, not everyone here is a mage. A lightspinner is a pretty respectable city profession. In Katanzarko, almost everything is run through Polaris Academy or Castle Nova, to a ridiculous degree of bureaucracy. But, it makes for a pretty city."

They left the lightweaver far behind. Indeed, every building they passed appeared clean and bright. Many of the buildings were covered in mosaic tile, others were constructed from woven rock formations that appeared to have sprouted from the ground.

"You'll like the next part," Jared said.

Crossing a bridge and rounding a corner, they came to the top of a hill. Down below, the city continued to spread. At its center was a great green tree, its limbs stretching to the sky, its base hundreds of feet in diameter.

"What is…?"

"That is the same sort of magic that made Aurumice. That tree is called Garner's Hope. People live in it. It's one of the oldest structures in Katanzarko."

"Aurumice looks so different. Aurumice looks like a castle, but that is a giant tree! It's as big as a city block!"

"Yeah, I said it's different. Magic formed and feeds that, pretty self-sustainable. Maybe every hundred years a new mage with a green thumb maintains it. I think it helps keep the air clean, but makes for some nasty problems of you have pollen allergies."

"Who lives in there?"

"Just people. City workers. My friend Macedon is from Garner's Hope. His mom is a lightweaver."

"What does your friend do?"

"Oh, you'll meet him later," Jared smiled. "He works for Polaris Academy."

"A mage?" Jessica was intrigued. The little carriage turned down another street. The buildings were farther spread apart and they started to approach a new set of buildings made from blue bricks.

"Well, Mace is barely a mage. He's a glow bug, and his powers aren't strong enough to do more than just make things glow...a tiny, tiny bit. He didn't qualify for field work so he's part of the grounds keeping at Polaris."

Looking out the window, Jessica's heart filled with hope.

"Jess, I knew you would love this place, this is where you belong. I mean, Aurumice is beautiful in its own right, but this is where our kind live."

"This place pales the castle," Jessica felt saddened. "I used to think Aurumice was the most beautiful structure I had ever seen. Guess everything changes."

"Well, don't forget your mom is still probably going to kill us both."

"I don't know why she's kept me from this place," Jessica turned to the window. "It's like Aurumice to me, I feel the draw."

The carriage continued to approach the blue bricked buildings.

"That up ahead, that's our destination, Polaris Academy."

Jessica was enamored. Polaris sprawled with immaculately maintained landscape, blooming flowers and sculpted shrubbery bordering every walkway. Following the cobblestone path, they traveled to a section with whimsical little cottages that reminded Jessica of mushroom houses.

"This is our stop," Jared said.

The carriage came to a halt. Jared opened the door and extended a hand to Jessica.

"Oh my God, these are adorable!"

"Housing for mage families and faculty," he said, grabbing their packs from the back of the carriage. He thanked the driver and the vehicle drove off.

"I live with my aunt and uncle," Jared explained, leading her up a little hill to a small tan cottage with a rounded blue roof.

"Is this where you grew up?"

"Nope, my family lives more in the city," Jared explained, unlocking the front door.

The cabin's interior was quaint, even though the furniture coated in dust. Copious amounts of books crammed bookshelves, taking up a large amount of the wallspace. Cozy and warm, the front room had an overstuffed green couch and a fireplace.

"Will I get to meet your family?"

Jared dropped his packs and grimaced.

"Jess, I may have glossed over a few minor details that might be worth discussing. You know how I said I helped your cousin Misa? Back when she needed to get the knowledge to open the Gate to your house? It was pretty much tantamount to grand larceny. I got in an epic amount of trouble for that. Saurin Bane and my uncle pretty much saved my rear, and I think the only reason my uncle helped at all is because Kaity forced him to. I helped the castlefolk, so Saurin Bane and Kaity helped me."

"But Saurin Bane isn't castlefolk."

Jessica had met the old mage once. He had been her mother's mentor and helped Jessica the day she dangerously used a fractured Shadow Sphere to Gate jump to Polaris.

"Saurin Bane actually is castlefolk. There's a rumor he got in an argument with Nico's grandfather? And that's why he sticks to the mages. Don't ask him about it, he won't talk."

Jared drew the curtains, opening a window and letting in the fresh air.

"My family sort of hates me, in fact, they haven't talked to me since I was put on super serious we-are-about-to-expel-you-and-jail-you probation. I can't go home, so Kaity and Corwin have been helping me out. I'm not allowed to have dorm housing anymore. I'm restricted in the classes I can take, I'm banned from the library, and Castle Nova. It's pretty bad, and I haven't been doing much to fix it, just sort of hanging out in Aurumice until I figure it out."

Jessica wasn't sure what to say to her friend.

"Aww Jess, don't look so sad about it. Aurumice was great, and I help things there. Maybe someday things will be forgiven and I'll officially join the castlefolk, though Teren might not be so happy with me once he reads the note I left him. Put it all behind you! We've got plans for tonight, and I promise it will be unforgettable!"

***

Penrik entered the dining room, holding a tan envelope.

He handed it to Teren.

"Jared said I was supposed to give this to you this afternoon, and not a minute before."

"Really?" Teren's eyes narrowed as he took the envelope. "If you are involved in one of his pranks, I may hold you responsible for the contents of this letter."

"Hey!" Penrik held up his hands innocently. "I gave them a ride into Trabalis. I have no idea what they're doing."

Teren opened the letter, glanced at it quickly, and growled in frustration.

Penrik cringed.

"Bad?"

"You had better pray this letter is a joke. Have you seen Kaity Cosette?"

"Yeah, out in the stableyard."

***

Kaity Cosette stood in the pasture, removing Cloudspark's tack. Temi ran around, playing in the dirt. They had just come back from an afternoon ride. Kaity was proud, Temi had good balance and was fearless of the bicorns.

Teren approached, looking unhappy. It always hurt Kaity's heart to see Teren upset. She remembered when he had been a carefree boy.

But that was a very, very long time ago.

"What's wrong?" Kaity asked, placing Cloudspark's saddle on the fence.

Teren held up a letter.

"This," he handed it to her.

She opened it.

"I can't read American English," she glared.

"It is from your nephew. Jessi convinced him to take her to Polaris. She thinks the castlefolk hate her."

"She should never have struck Wadjette and she should never have opened her mouth!" Kaity defended.

"You're not surprised she's going to Polaris," Teren stated.

"No, I'm not. You think I'm so daft I couldn't figure out that Jessi's arm healed? She's where she needs to be, Teren."

"Regardless, what can we do right now?"

"How long ago did they leave?"

"Penrik said Jared gave him the note yesterday morning."

"Then they've made it to Katanzarko City by now. We've already missed the last train, you could take a bicorn but you'd probably burn them out trying to get there. If Jared already told Polaris, then there is nothing we can do. The mages will not let her go easily."

Teren gripped his forehead.

"Stupid, stupid girl."

"Honestly, you believe she's stupid?" Kaity's blood boiled. With every passing day, she did not understand Teren's way of seeing the world.

"Teren, if she was just castlefolk, she would have gone already! A blood mage is not a strength to be squandered! I know her earth schooling is important, but really, is it? She's never going to live there, she will choose to stay with us."

"She still has a choice to make."

"Jessi has talked to you about it, hasn't she? Every conversation she's ever had with me, it's the same. She wants to be here. Granted, now she knows the sting of the 'folk, but they'll get over it as soon as someone else does something foolish."

"This is still not good."

"Jess will be fine," Kaity reassured, picking the brambles from Cloudspark's mane. "She's following who she really is. I know you're not a mage and can't understand this, but the call is strong. To deny it would be like having legs and never trying to walk."

"She should have waited, and I blame that stupid far-seer for this."

"Well you can blame me too," Kaity said. "I told her she should go to Polaris. She's hoping for a way to help Carrie Anne."

"I need to bring this note to Lily now. Would you like to accompany me since you put the idea of Polaris in Jessica's head?"

"No thank you, I would prefer to live."

Teren did not like her response. He kicked a bucket then walked back to the castle.

***

Jessica and Jared spent the afternoon in the cottage. Jared left briefly to send a note with a courier, but soon returned to reclining on the couch.

Jessica looked out the windows and occasionally flipped through books, eager to begin exploration.

"We were stuck on a train for almost a day, how are you still tired?"

"I didn't sleep well," Jared mumbled from beneath his hat. "We have a busy night ahead of us, you should sleep too."

"Where are we going?"

"We picked the best night of the month to arrive in Polaris," he replied.

"Oh?" Jessica was curious.

"You'll see."

As evening fell, Jared woke up from his sleepy stupor. Jessica was so bored she was ready to start climbing the walls.

"Wear jeans, take your bag with you, with all those supplies I made you buy," Jared advised.

Jessica obliged, curious what Jared planned to do with cookies and soda.

Her curiosity was soon forgotten and replaced with delight as they left the cottage. Polaris Academy was an absolutely picturesque campus, like a fairy tale village. Far in the distance, Jessica could see Castle Nova, its sides reflecting the last rays of the sun.

Jessica and Jared arrived at a cluster of stone buildings arranged around a courtyard. Inside, vendors sold a variety of foods, warming the air with the smell of woodsmoke and herbs. They briefly stopped at a little cart with smoked meats. Jared paid the vendor and they munched on grilled burch and carboni sticks that reminded Jessica of French Fries.

"What do you think?"

"Not as good as Aurumice, it's a little dry, but still good," she said. Jessica was enthralled as she watched students pass by.

"Are these all mages?" she asked, wondering if she would catch a glimpse of their unique powers.

"Mostly," Jared replied. He was less talkative than usual, and Jessica got the impression he did not want to be overheard by passersby.

Shortly after eating, they left the populated paths and walked through areas that seemed less trodden, far from the cottages and the academic buildings. The foliage was overgrown and wild.

"This is creepy," Jessica commented.

"How is it different from the woods of Aurumice?"

"Everything in Aurumice is a little overgrown and old, everything here is so perfect this feels wrong."

"Jess, you are about to see the best-kept secret in all of Nova, perhaps even in all of Centernia."

"Really?" She raised an eyebrow.

"Yes."

"Better than the nightflights of the Holy Circus?"

"Better."

The blonde boy grinned.

Night had completely fallen as the elevation changed and became rockier. Jared approached a thick green bush. He pulled back the branches, revealing a little opening in the hillside, about four feet high and three feet wide.

"After you, my dear."

"It's dark."

"It's a cave. For someone who blindly follows strangers into bad situations, I take offense that you're questioning me now."

Jessica glared.

"I would follow Misa again in a heartbeat, and you know it," she stepped into the darkness.

"Yeah, I know, I would too," he murmured, taking her hand and leading her forward.

They didn't travel far. Reaching out ahead of her, Jessica felt a wooden wall.

"Hold on a sec, need to open the door," Jared said. She could hear him fumbling with keys. The door clicked and he pushed it open. Beyond was a hallway illuminated by glowstones set into dirt walls.

"Cozy," Jessica commented.

Jared chuckled softly.

Walking through a series of twists and turns, Jessica was careful to memorize each passage. In recent years, she had learned to rely on her own sense of direction. A murmur of talking let her know they were close to their destination.

They came to a hallway and a single door. In front of the door was a wooden desk, three chairs and two people. One was a very tall young woman, mostly sapien except for her cat ears. She wore a glitzy red mini skirt, tall boots and an orange bolero jacket. Her makeup was very American in style, a bit generously applied around her eyes with shimmery purple eyeshadow. Jessica had instant admiration and jealousy.

The other stranger was in his forties. He seemed to be pure sapien, wearing a brown sweatshirt and jeans. He was built like a football player and had a sincere smile.

"Jared!" The older man greeted. "Where the hell have you been hiding?"

Smiling, the young man embraced the two strangers.

"What can I say, Tino, I've been busy."

"Is it true you're hiding up in that cursed castle?" the woman asked. Her voice was rich, slightly deeper than Jessica was expecting.

"I wouldn't say cursed," Jared defended. "I would call it….quaint in an archaic sort of way."

"Who's this?" the woman asked, leaning forward. Her eyelashes were so long.

"She's a pureborn. Jess, this is Santino and Leaf, two of my old friends."

"Really pureborn?" Leaf hopped off the desk. She towered over Jessica in her black heels. "Where you from, girl?"

"Jess, you can tell him the truth," Jared ordered.

Him?

"Autumn Valley, Pennsylvania," she told Leaf.

"Really? What color is a jack o' lantern?"

"Orange?"

"Dorothy traveled where?"

"Dorothy? Like *Wizard of Oz* Dorothy? Kansas, I mean Oz. She's from Kansas, went to Oz, wanted to go home."

"And who is the first emperor of America?"

"America doesn't have an emperor, we have a president."

"She passes the test. Welcome to the Club Underground," Tino grinned. "You tell anyone we exist, we kill you."

"He doesn't really mean that," Jared waved away the threat. "You are gonna love it. If there is any place in Centernia you would belong, it's this very spot."

"I didn't hear of anyone new being admitted into the academy," Leaf said. "What's your name?"

"Jessica Vance."

"Holy Jesus, did you just say Vance?" Tino sat up.

Jared grinned.

"This is Trixie's niece."

"I cannot believe it," Tino clapped and howled. "Your aunt practically built the Club Underground."

Jessica smiled, though she was getting tired of people knowing more about her family than she did.

"I brought goods for you. Jess, give me your bag."

Jessica slipped out of her book bag. Jared handed it to the man.

"All fresh," Jared assured, "so don't tick around on price. You can match the expiration dates to the earth calendar."

"So, it's true?" Tino unzipped the book bag. He took out each package of candy and cookies. "It's true? Aurumice has a Gate, and it's open?"

"I wouldn't spread such rumors," Jared warned.

"Jared, no one's a fool. Everyone knows you're banned from the Gates forever."

Jared shrugged.

Tino's voice lowered.

"More people are going on the banned list, you know that? The council is getting jumpy, doling out that punishment left and right. When rumor of Aurumice came here, people started talking again. The old ones want to crush that little Castle, take it over. The young ones want to tell the council to screw off. People want to go to Aurumice, but they've banned that too. No one is getting stationed out anywhere near Trabalis."

"Well, the Council is holding the Consortium on a leash that's too tight. They're going to find someday that earthbred mages don't like being told what to do." Jared's voice edged with anger. "Anyways, payment please?"

Tino pulled a key from beneath his shirt and unlocked a drawer in the desk. The older man pulled out several large heavy pouches of coin and counted carefully. Jessica's eyes grew wide.

It was enough to buy a horse and *almost* enough for a bicorn.

Jared grinned and took the pile greedily and secured them under his jacket. Tino pulled the bag off the table. Jessica never expected the value of store-bought cookies and soda to be so high.

"Wait, did you just sell my book bag too?"

"You'll get another one."

"Jared!"

"Alright, alright."

"Then give me the money."

"You owed me the cookies. That was payment for my escort. I paid for the train, and your dinner, and you have a lot to buy in the next few weeks. Consider me your walking bank."

"Why didn't you tell me about this?"

"I had to show you first."

"What was all that talk about the Council and the Consortium?"

"The Consortium is Polaris Academy, the Council is Castle Nova. I don't want to talk politics tonight, shall we proceed?" Jared gestured forward.

Leaf unlocked the door. The thumping of heavy bass came through. It came from speakers, *big* speakers.

When the door swung open, Jessica was astounded by the cavern beyond.

Colors and lights assaulted her eyes. It was as if all of American pop culture had thrown up in a technicolor subterranean dance hall.

Jessica walked into the techno wonderland, a grin plastered to her face.

It was a club, a *real* club, set into a massive cavern. Electric lights were strung from every surface, and people danced on a huge dance floor below. The walls of the cavern were covered with the most eclectic collection of items from earth. Everything from old record covers to toys, giant road signs, movie posters and even cooking utensils. It reminded Jessica of the toy closet Aunt Beatrix had kept hidden in Castle Aurumice.

"Are they playing Madonna?" Jessica asked.

"Only earth music is played here."

A metal balcony circled the upper level of the dance hall. Jessica walked to the railing and stared down at the beautiful chaos.

"Jared, is that a car in the middle of the dance floor?!"

On a platform in the center of the dancers sat a bright blue classic car.

"1957 Chevy Bel Air," Jared grinned.

"How the hell did you know that?! I didn't know, and I'm from America."

"Best thing is, it was your aunt who brought it here. Jess, she was legend. You think Misa was crazy? Beatrix Vance was impulsive, and nuts, and just did incredible things, and probably should have died a hundred times…before she actually did…I mean…that's what they say."

"How did she get a car in here? How did she get a car through the Gate? And why does everyone else know this and its news to me?"

"Your mom forbid me from saying anything about the Club Underground."

"And you listened to her?"

Jared shrugged.

"I needed the Gate, Jess, I had to bargain with her. But you're here now. Let me point out a few things." Jared leaned on the railing and gestured down at the dancers.

"They are mostly bred mages. They're like me, usually an earth parent and a Centernian parent, raised on both sides but mostly here. Some have just Centernian parents and some are orphans."

"So, you're saying everyone down in that crowd is tied to earth, and they know it?"

"They celebrate it, but the Council controls the Gate, so people can't just go back and forth. The Club Underground was built in secret, as a place to hoard and celebrate everything Earth."

"Wait, earthborn can't go home?"

"I know what you're thinking. I'm telling you now, don't get Aurumice involved. Not now, maybe someday, but stay dodgy on that one," Jared's words were grave and Jessica had no desire to cross him. She turned to look at the crowd below, they were all very sapien. Some people had markings and features Jessica could identify as ailurian or caprasian. No one was like Wadjette or Savina. Everyone in the room could pass for human with a little bit of makeup or a hat or a tucked tail.

"This is where you belong. Not in Aurumice, not back in Pennsylvania. These people are all like you, caught somewhere between Earth and Centernia. Want to go down?" he grinned.

"Yes!"

He grabbed her hand and they ran down the staircase. Everywhere she looked, Jessica saw another strange sight – traffic lights, hub caps, plastic furniture, and posters of ABBA. Upon further inspection, she realized there were little rooms that branched from the main dance floor. Some served food, others were sitting areas around televisions playing movies. A pool table and a jukebox in one section were set up in another alcove like a bar. They checked their coats in a little coatroom and Jessica realized Jared was wearing a t-shirt and jeans.

Everything was amazingly normal and twice as fantastic because she was in Centernia.

"Where's the electricity coming from?"

Jared shrugged.

"That's the big secret. But rumor has it that the power came back around the time your aunt and mom were here."

Jessica grinned.

"I bet I know how."

"Normally you can't have electricity on display like this, but it's the Club Underground, so it's already forbidden."

Jessica's eyes traveled up the walls of the cavern. In the center of the room was a disco ball, spinning colored squares across the room.

"Would you like to dance?"

"Dance?"

"Yes, come on Jessica Ravenwolfe, dance with me."

Jessica laughed, delighted he used her real name. No one here would care that she was from a divorced home.

Jared pulled her out onto the floor. Strangers greeted him, and welcomed her. They called him trouble, and rogue, and a host of friendly insults. Jared had a reputation for sure.

The dance style was a cross between earth and Centernian. Some steps were elaborate, like many of the popular dances Jessica had been taught in Aurumice, but some of the moves were uniquely from earth.

And Jessica loved it.

Jared was a very good dancer, and she wondered why she had never noticed before. The boy had always been attractive, but she wrote him off with his arrogance. She feared he would never be interested in a girl like her.

Tonight, he wasn't keeping any distance. He picked up on the vibe of the dance floor.

Jessica laughed, arms wrapped around Jared. He was right. This was where she belonged.

"Hey, you!" a flash of bright teal hair cut in, tackling Jared. The stranger's face was smooth and human-like, but she had cat eyes and a fanged smile that reminded Jessica of Misa. Shimmering, the teen's eyeshadow and lips were as bright blue as her hair.

"Paisley!" Jared greeted.

"Is it true?" the loud girl put her hands on her hips. "Does the cursed castle have another Gate?"

Jared innocently blinked.

"You, where you from?!" Paisley asked, pointing to Jessica. The girl was intoxicated.

"Pennsylvania." Jessica replied.

"Jessica, this is Zapaisley Maeve Sarkisian, we call her Paisley Mae. She's a good friend of mine."

"Oh, my sweet crystal of Juniper, you're from the other Gate, aren't you?"

Jared put an arm around Jessica.

"Now Jess, you don't need to answer that."

"Come on you ass, everyone knows it!" Paisley Mae slapped Jared's shoulder. She turned to Jessica.

"Let me buy you a drink."

"You get her drunk, don't think she's going to bring you to earth."

Paisley Mae slipped an arm around Jessica's waist, pulling her away from Jared.

"Who said earth was my goal?" Paisley Mae's breath was heavy with beer. "There aren't many red-haired sapiens around."

Jessica was confused by the stranger but felt welcomed. Paisley Mae was very pretty, little butterflies tattooed next to her right eye in a cascade down the side of her face. Her bright teal blue hair was mesmerizing and soft. If Jessica had known the girl a little bit better, she would have been compelled to pet it.

Paisley Mae led her towards the bar. Jared trailed behind, amused. The raised bar was made of a beautiful red wood. Beneath a glass top, the surface contained an overwhelming amount magazine clippings from Earth.

Jared leaned past Paisley Mae and paid for the drinks. He handed a bottle to Jessica and one to Paisley Mae.

"It's not real," he said. "They rebottle it."

Jessica popped the cap. She tentatively took a drink.

"Jae, this is real beer!"

"Yes, I know, I didn't say it wasn't beer. It's not from earth, they brew it here, and rebottle it. Also, don't lose the bottle, I paid a deposit on it."

Paisley Mae took a large swig, then belched.

"Is it true they still won't let you at the Gate ever, ever?" she asked.

"Life ban generally means life ban." Jared took a drink. He leaned against the bar.

"So, was she worth it?" Paisley Mae asked.

Jared's expression saddened.

"Was who worth it?" Jessica carefully held the beer bottle. She took a tiny sip, not wanting to be out of place.

"The girl, with the curly black hair, the one you had a thing for. The one who was here some years back."

"Misa was worth it," Jared said affirmatively. "That girl was brilliant, and an amazing dreamspinner, and she sacrificed herself to save a lot of people. So yeah, I would do it again. I would say screw the council, screw all those dumb shmucks. Yeah, she was worth it."

Paisley Mae laughed, slapping his shoulder.

"You're going to lead us to revolution, boy? Screw it, and lead us all to your Castle Aurumice. Free the Gates, free the earth born!"

Paisley Mae was really, really drunk.

"We're going to change things around here," Jared nodded. "Trust me."

Jessica was very confused how quickly Jared went from 'don't talk about the Gate' to revolution.

"I'm so glad you're back!" Paisley Mae threw herself at Jared, giggling.

"I missed it. So tell me, what gossip am I behind on?" The music shifted to an old Celine Dion pop ballad.

"Oh, so much! Lady Starmina is pregnant with Juntil's child, which is bad news because she was supposed to be stationed in the Therissina islands, but he going to the northern mountains." Paisley Mae paused. "What else? My uncle was kicked off the council for almost dying out on a mission, because he was stoned on elven weed and completely drunk at the time."

"Again?"

"Oh! Lord Fallo embezzled over a hundred thousand bits from the scholar's fund and they sent him to prison. They were going to send him to the Mines of Briken, but Lady Lightsong intervened."

Jared shuddered.

"No one deserves to go to that hell pit, not even Lord Fallo. Any other news?"

"I did my first merge this afternoon. It was me and Larabeth. We combined our powers to make fire water. Though it was really just fire floating on one of her barriers, but it was still amazing."

"You know only psychic mages can do true merges."

"You're just jealous you're not still in classes," Paisley Mae hopped onto a bar stool.

"Do you have any other real news?"

"They found an airship and they're hiding it behind Castle Nova! No one's supposed to go near it. Want to go check it out, oh you with the wonderfully useful eyes?"

"Sure," Jared smiled. Of course, he could learn about the ship without even setting foot near it, but Paisley Mae was more concerned with adventure than knowledge.

The teal-haired girl squealed in delight and hugged him.

"I am so happy you're back! I'm gonna go find the others and tell them you're here."

She turned away, and gave Jessica's rear a friendly slap.

"Welcome to the club, princess. I'm serious too, we'll talk, later."

Paisley Mae tripped her way back to the dance floor.

"And I am never seeing the deposit on that bottle." Jared sighed. "But, hey, that's what friends are for."

"Jae! Jae Evansi, you rotten, maggoted slug in a ditch!"

If Jared's smile could get any bigger, it would have broken his face.

A young man approached, long black hair and dark eyes. He wore jeans and a white button down shirt, slightly unbuttoned. His pure smooth skin was tattooed with small elegant stripes at the corners of his eyes.

He was quite possibly the most attractive man Jessica had ever seen.

"Mace!" Jared embraced his friend with a ferocity Jessica did not expect. What happened next surprised her more.

Mace kissed Jared. It wasn't a platonic kiss by any stretch of the imagination. Jared was hot to begin with, Mace was even hotter. Blinking in awe, Jessica watched the nuclear explosion of male beauty.

Jared pulled away laughing, and took a large swig of the beer.

"Jess, this is my truest friend, the only person I ever regretted leaving back at Polaris. Macedon Thames."

"*Friend?*" Jessica questioned, taking Mace's hand.

"Yeah," Mace replied with a wink, "friend."

Jessica laughed.

"You're the Aurumician girl?" Mace asked. "The one from Pennsylvania? Jared has told me all about you, it's very nice to finally meet you!"

Mace was sincere, and Jessica instantly liked him.

"I wish I could say the same, I mean…" Jessica struggled with words. "Not that you're not important or…"

"It's okay," Mace shook his head. "I know it's tough being all the way out in Trabalis. We sort of agreed to just do our own thing for a while, but when Jared comes back, he's mine."

Jared smirked.

"Would you like to dance?" Mace asked, turning to Jessica.

"Wait, me?" Jessica was surprised he asked her instead of Jared.

"Yes, you, first time in the Club Underground. I love to dance."

"That would be amazing because you are really, really beautiful." As soon as the words popped out, Jessica clasped her mouth.

Mace laughed.

"Also, her first beer has taken out her filter in about two minutes apparently." Jared was amused.

"That's not physically possible," Jessica argued playfully. She was feeling good, and it wasn't the beer. She loved the Club Underground, surrounded by Earth. Aurumice and high school was a distant memory.

"Go, dance with him, have fun, Jess. You never have fun, you're never free. Go!"

Mace pulled her out onto the wild dance floor to a night that didn't end.

CHAPTER 17

They partied until the sun peaked over the horizon and then caroused in song back to the cottage. Jared let Jessica into the little house, then stumbled away with Mace. Jessica was too exhausted to ask any questions, and didn't really want to know. Exhausted, she looked for a place to sleep. She felt awkward taking any of the three little bedrooms, especially since Kaity and Corwin didn't know they were there.

Rummaging around, Jessica found a spare blanket and nestled into the small green couch in the living room.

Sometime later she was roused by the door opening and the sounds of buzzing insects. Jared poked his head in, his hair disheveled.

"You hungry?"

"Hungry?" Jessica tried to process his words.

"We gotta meet people for breakfast."

"Breakfast?"

"Yes, breakfast," Jared entered the cottage and proceeded to the little washroom. Jessica looked around for a clock. There was one small gryphon timepiece on the wall.

It was well past noon.

Jared emerged from the washroom, drying his face on a towel, his hair neater.

"You have a good night?" Jessica asked.

"My night hasn't ended, but come on, breakfast."

Jessica grinned and grabbed her pack, pushing past Jared to use the washroom.

"Can I wear jeans here?" she asked.

"Uh, better not. Go classic Trabalisan, pants, scarf, boots, you know, nice."

After getting ready, Jared brought Jessica to a little cozy café in the same courtyard they had dined the previous night. Other students walked about in a sleepy stupor.

They sat at a table covered with a lace tablecloth. A vase with a large blue flower was positioned in the center of the table.

Pouring tea, a server greeted them with a smile. Jessica was delighted to watch as the deep brown liquid swirled around in mid-air, as if it came through a thin invisible tube. It moved like a cork-screw, then crisscrossed, until it made contact with the cup.

Jessica's mouth was agape.

The waiter seemed not to notice, poured Jared's tea, and left the table.

"Was he a water mage?" Jessica pointed discretely to the waiter.

"Oh no, I think he's just a glow bug. I don't remember his name. He was a circus priest before Polaris recruited him, but he never got very far in his mage training."

"Then how does he do that trick with the tea?"

"It's the teapot that's been affected by a barrier mage. Like the same type of mage who built the forcefield, the pot permanently does that every time liquid is poured."

Jessica examined her tea carefully.

"The barrier field is on the pot," Jared reassured, "not the tea. Don't worry, you're not going to drink mage energy."

"Good morning, sunshine!" a trill voice crooned, taking the chair next to Jared. It was Paisley Mae. A little less drunk, but still intensely exuberant.

Or maybe she was still drunk.

"So, Jared, when you coming back to stay?" Paisley Mae asked.

"I am not sure yet, it depends what Jessica would like to do. She is a newly discovered blood mage."

"Oh! That's exciting. High demand too, and that can be pretty kinky."

Jared was about to take a sip of his tea, but snapped his mouth shut. Paisley Mae seemed to be in a vulgarity league of her own.

"Pais, sex is not the first thing I associated with a blood mage. You know, they have that whole saving people from death thing."

"But they can control nerve endings when they get really, really, good at their abilities, both pain and pleasure. Totally a useful power."

"Jess, words come out Paisley Mae's mouth, but you can just pretend they never happened."

"Jared is a prude with no imagination," Paisley Mae quipped, taking Jared's teacup.

"And blood mages typically cannot influence nerves," Jared continued. "That's a prickly mage."

"If the blood mage is *really* good they can manipulate nerves."

"But that's a different body system," Jared argued. "It's called blood mage for a reason, blood mages move blood."

"But if you move blood, you can flex muscle strands, and you can make them hit nerves!"

"I don't think you know what you're talking about," Jared argued.

"I'm the one who's still in classes. Besides, a blood mage can do lots of other things to the body," Paisley Mae pointed out. "They can make things flex and get hard. That I know must be true."

"Okay, yes, probably," Jared agreed, "but still low on the priority list of skills for a blood mage."

"It wouldn't be difficult to learn, I would imagine. Oh, though it would be bad if you made things explode. It would be awful, guts everywhere. That would kill a romantic evening."

Jessica sipped her tea slowly, very amused by the girl.

"So, what's your ability?" she asked.

"Fire mage!" Paisley Mae announced. She snapped her fingers and the blossom on the centerpiece burst into flames. She plucked the stem, turned it upside down, extinguishing it in the vase.

"Amazing! Jared, didn't tell me!"

"Ah, but I did. I told you I knew plenty of fire mages, and they had perfectly healthy relationships with people. Pais just isn't one of them."

Paisley Mae slapped Jared on the shoulder.

The server arrived and took their breakfast order.

"So, what's it like?" Jessica asked the girl. "How long did it take you to control your power?"

"Oh, I think I manifested when I was maybe five years old? That was funny, I set a library on fire."

"A library?"

"Okay, not really funny. But it was a small room in a small library."
Jared's hand went to his forehead.

"She singlehandedly destroyed the Archives of Valetina. And yet,
they ban *me* from the libraries."

"Yeah, well. But to answer your question, maybe a few months?
They were quick to keep me under control."

"Did you have problems with like…going all flame ball and your
clothing burning off?" Jessica would have never been so forward with a
stranger, but Paisley Mae seemed different.

"Um, no." Paisley Mae was confused. "If my clothing burned, then I
would have been in it. Fire mage does not mean flame retardant."

"That's weird, the one fire mage I know is."

"Oh, who do you know?"

Jessica looked to Jared, her eyes asking permission. Jared shrugged,
continuing to sip his tea.

"His name is Nicoveren, he's from Aurumice."

"Ooooooh, fire mage in Aurumice? That's exciting. I should visit
your castle someday if I'm allowed to, I'd like to meet him."

"He's not there anymore. But his clothing would burn away, and he
would be like a human torch."

"How does he do that? What base does he use to not burn his hair?"

"What do you mean, base?"

"Like how does he get the fire going?"

"I don't know, just midair?"

"He's gotta be doing some trick, maybe a flammable gas. You can't
make a flame without an energy source, it would just burn out. Might be
magic, but it still obeys the laws of physics."

Jared winced.

"Not quite sure that's true."

"I don't know how he does it, but he is different. His flames are
blue."

"Blue?" Paisley Mae sat back, "That's a really hot flame…you need
a pretty strong source to make a blue flame. How does he keep his hair
from burning? I have that problem a lot, this is a wig."

"But he….it…." Jessica's voice faltered, "but it looks like it's from thin air."

"That's not fire, girl."

"But it burns…I know it burns. He kissed me, and he lost control, and that's how I got this scar." Jessica gestured to the faint line on her lip.

"Ah, I knew you liked to have fun!" Paisley Mae was visibly amused.

"No, no, no, it was very much an accident," Jessica clarified.

"Interesting…very, very interesting," Paisley Mae sipped her tea. Jessica looked to Jared, worried she had said too much.

"Well if he's not a fire mage, then what is he?" Jared finally asked.

"Did you not pass Mage Types One?"

"I might have…forgotten…to go to class," Jared said. "Because it was a lame basic course. And the professor was boring, and we all know mage types."

"Then what is your friend?"

"I don't know, Pais, that's why I'm asking you!" Jared said. "It's a *was*, because he's probably dead."

Jessica glared at Jared.

"What?" he said. "I don't want to talk about Nico this morning. We've gotta get going soon, it'll be a long day."

"Good afternoon," Mace approached the little table.

Jared's annoyance vanished and the conversation about Nico was quickly forgotten.

***

Jared led Jessica into a pristine building with tall vaulted ceilings and echoing white marble floors. Everyone they passed wore a uniform or robes. Jessica felt compelled to stand a little straighter, not speak, and not glance about too much. Never in her time in Centernia had she visited a place so formal and grandiose.

After brunch they changed clothing, Jared opting for the simple grey uniform of the mages. Jessica was given clothing by Paisley Mae, a blue tunic and bolero jacket, a blue skirt and sandals with laces that tied up her calves. Paisley Mae also insisted on fixing Jessica's hair, braiding half of it with a simple blue ribbon, allowing the rest to hang down her back.

Now Jessica was very grateful to the girl, all of the attire she had packed would have left her woefully underdressed and shabby.

The duo arrived at a small room with glass benches and ornate miniature trees.

"Wait here a moment," Jared said, disappearing through a set of white doors. Jessica sat down carefully on the smooth bench.

A few minutes later he returned.

"Saurin Bane will talk to us, he's exactly who we want."

He gestured for her to follow. They walked down a hallway, passed another series of doors.

One caught her eye, in Madiernian text, the door plate read:

Tigard Sarkisian

She grabbed Jared's arm, pulling him close.

"Tigard Sarkisian," she whispered.

"What about it?"

"It was on the scroll that Misa left. He's got something to do with Aurumice."

"Jess, it's a really common last name, huge family. You had breakfast with a Sarkisian if you were paying attention."

"Wait, what?"

"You apparently were not listening last night, and we can talk about this later."

Jessica closed her mouth, sensing her friend's annoyance.

They entered an office. Milky white, the floor was so immaculate Jessica wondered if her sandals were too dirty.

The room was large, ten feet wide and twenty feet long. It had a small sitting area with green plush chairs and a dark mahogany desk. White walls gleamed and windows stretched from floor to ceiling. Planters were positioned by the windows, displaying unusually shaped foliage that crooked at right angles, forming squares. Beyond the unblemished glass, the landscape was rocky, the views breathtaking.

"Hello Jared, hello Jessica," Saurin Bane greeted them. He was a tall greying mage, wearing blue robes like a wizard.

212

Saurin gestured to a small set of grey upholstered chairs gathered around an interesting table. The furniture seemed to have grown out of the marble.

"Lord Bane, if Jessica is safe with you, I am returning to the cottages. Would you like me to return at a certain time?"

"No, I will escort her back to the cottages, enjoy your afternoon."

Jessica was suddenly frightened and she didn't know quite why. Jared gave a little bow, and placed a reassuring hand on her shoulder.

"Don't worry, you'll be fine, and you won't leave my sight," Jared tipped his hat and left Jessica with the old mage.

"Please, be seated. Lady Carmelina Lightsong will be here shortly."

Jessica took a seat on a chair, reassuring herself that Jared would be watching everything through her eyes. Her mouth dry with anxiety, the ramifications of her choices started bubbling up in her mind.

This was it, this was real.

"Why is your mother not with you?" Saurin asked.

"She was busy, unfortunately."

"She does not know you are here."

It was a statement and not a question.

"Oh, she knows I'm here…by now."

"Do you understand the impact of today?" Saurin asked. "If you are tested by Carmelina, and you are indeed a blood mage as Jared assumes, you will be invited to stay here at Polaris Academy. I use the word invite loosely, it is not an offer that can be declined easily."

"Am I allowed to visit home?"

"Oh, yes, certainly."

"Okay, sir, there is one thing that motivated me to come here. Someone really important to me is sick. I need to be able to help her."

"You will be expected to live here, not Aurumice, for the time being. You will need to gain permission, as Kaity did, to live there again."

"Yes, I know, I just need to know if I can visit Aurumice."

"Of course, we're not monsters."

"I heard other mages can't go to Aurumice."

"Well, it's your home, it's a bit different for you."

"How often can I go home to visit?"

"Oh, holidays, breaks, that sort of thing. If your mentors grant you permission, any time really, but your studies come first. Jessica, you must understand, if you are a blood mage, you will become important to a great many people. Your skills will save lives, so you must understand how gravely important your education will be."

"Well, there's really no turning back at this point, is there?" Jessica asked.

"Well, look at this way. If you are a blood mage and you stay in Aurumice your talents will go to waste. No one there can teach you. If you stay here, you can learn how to heal. Thousands will benefit from your skills, and you can find solace in knowing you were fulfilling a destiny you are truly born into."

Saurin's words were reassuring.

The door opened and an old woman entered, cat ears and human face. Her skin was a dark brown flecked with light honey-colored spots. Upon her shoulders, she donned a bold short cape that reminded Jessica of the blue feathers of a peacock.

"Jessica, this is Lady Carmelina Lightsong."

Jessica nervously stood out of respect.

Carmelina said nothing, reaching out.

"Your hands, girl, I have a busy afternoon."

Jessica placed her hands into the old woman's palms, feeling a strange tingle. It was similar to the sensation of a foot falling asleep just before it hit the painful part.

"Mage reverberation," Carmelina was delighted. "You are without a doubt a blood mage. This is good for Polaris, our numbers are few! Please, sit. Tell me, how did you know what you were?"

Carmelina's demeanor had completely changed. The little woman was more of a kind grandmother than an intimidating mage. Her busy schedule seemed forgotten.

"I healed faster than I should, impossibly fast," Jessica smiled. "I was bit by a lazuli hunter, and instead of losing my arm, it was restored."

"Ah, very classic emergence, but don't tangle with beasts any time soon. That was a burst of manifestation power, you'll find your strength little more than a trickle now. Don't do anything foolish!" Carmelina stood. "We will get you quarters and have you starting class tomorrow."

Her words startled Jessica.

Things had suddenly become very real.

"What is your name? Lord Bane gave me very little in the way of details."

"Jessica Ra…Vance," she almost tripped on her last name. The castlefolk knew her as Jessica Vance.

"Ra...Vance..Vance…I know that name. Beatrix's daughter?"

"No, Beatrix was my aunt. My mother is Lily."

Carmelina's demeanor changed. She sat back and glared at Saurin.

"Where were you born?"

Jessica panicked, looking to Saurin for guidance. He gave her a small nod. The older mage was as calm as ever.

"Pennsylvania."

"That's a land across the Gate. You came through Aurumice, didn't you?"

"Yes."

"Ugh, what a horrid muck. Jessica, I will teach you what you need to know, but know this: you are part of Polaris now. We do things with discipline, and honor. A blood mage is a wonderful gift. You will hold the lives of thousands in your hands. We respect the magic, not use it for our own gains. Aurumice is a blight on the landscape of Centernia."

"Carmelina, no need to talk politics on Jessica's first day here," Saurin Bane interjected. "This is a time for celebration, you can have your debates later."

"I find little to debate, *Lord* Bane," Carmelina replied. "Someday the Council will see reason and take proper control of that castle. Leaving a Gate node in the hands of idiots is foolish."

The nervous feeling returned to Jessica's gut.

"That has nothing to do with the fact you have a new apprentice, one who will undoubtedly reduce your work load." Saurin tried to sell the blood mage.

"This is true," Carmelina inclined her head. "Tell me girl, were you raised in Aurumice or Pennsylvania?"

"Mostly Pennsylvania."

"Your father, he is earthborn or from Centernia?"

"Oh, he's very human."

"Mage like your mother?"

"No, he's just normal."

"May I have your hand again, dear?"

Jessica extended her hand. Carmelina held out a needle and stabbed her quickly, but she felt no pain from the pinprick. Blood welled up from the tiny wound.

The crimson drop floated through the air. Carmelina eyed it carefully, then extended her index finger. Jessica's blood fell upon her finger tip.

Carmelina rubbed it between her fingers.

"Oh, you tried to lie to me! No. No. Absolutely not! Aurumice and cursed blood? I do not care how much we need another healer! I won't deal with this family again! NO!"

"She needs to learn somewhere," Saurin stated calmly.

"Not here. Go back to Pennsylvania, or I have a right mind to call a binder mage to mark you as a criminal as well!"

"Lina, you are being irrational," Saurin held up a hand.

"What did I do wrong?" Jessica panicked, hoping Jared could see through her eyes. "What's wrong with my blood? Why am I a criminal?"

"Savartos Sarkisian is an embarrassment and an insult to Polaris. He lied to me! Your father is the most foul blood mage I have ever taught. I would not ever give my knowledge to anyone of his family!"

Jessica stood.

"My father is Stephen Ravenwolfe, and he is from earth."

"Ravenwolfe? Ravenwolfe!" Carmelina laughed. "Leave Polaris or I will have the guards escort you out. If your father still lives, tell him to rot in hell. You are not worth my time. And as for you, Saurin Bane, I..."

"Carmelina, she is not her father," Saurin argued. "She doesn't even know who he truly is. You need to teach her, because we need more blood mages. I will take this to the Consortium and if I need to, all the way to a Council meeting!"

"Argue all you want, you cannot force me to teach her a damn thing!"

Carmelina gathered her skirts and left the room.

The door slammed with an echo that reverberated across the walls like fading ghosts.

Jessica was stunned.

"What's wrong with me?"

"I can assure you, nothing."

Jessica stood.

"I want to find Jared. This is not what I was told."

"In time, you need to hear me first. Jared can't help you, he doesn't know anything either."

"Are you going to tell me my father isn't really my father?"

"Oh, I suspect your father is your father," Saurin said. "Here, let us walk back to the cottages."

Jessica was grateful to leave the building. Before they left the room, Saurin took a volume from a bookshelf and slid it into a small leather bag, slinging it over his shoulder.

Jessica followed Saurin down a staircase into a courtyard with mermaid fountains. Tiny dragonettes with translucent fairy-wings flitted over the ponds in a graceful dance. Had Jessica not been so nervous, she would have enjoyed walking through the garden.

They rounded a corner and came to a familiar path. Jessica relaxed a little as they turned in the direction of the cottages. It was still a long walk.

"So, your father. He has marks, tattoos, on his left and right forearms, correct?"

"But my father isn't from here," Jessica argued, "and his tats aren't even Centernian. He has a skull and a cross and a guitar."

"I suspect they obscure something more."

As a group of students approached, Saurin took a different path, avoiding them.

"Stephen Ravenwolfe you said his name is?"

"Yes," Jessica replied, irritated. Where was Jared? Surely he saw what had happened!

"That is funny," Saurin Bane was amused and maddeningly calm.

The path led to a small garden behind high walls.

"Your father's real name *is* Savartos Sarkisian. He is, was, a blood mage of Polaris. I had always suspected this, but Carmelina certainly confirmed it."

"This is very difficult for me to believe," Jessica said. "You don't know my father."

"Your father is a brilliant strategic man. He is allergic to strawberries, plays chess and hates thunderstorms. Ravenwolfe, by the way, was his gryphon."

Jessica's father did hate thunderstorms, was to allergic strawberries, and loved chess.

"He wears false teeth," Saurin Bane continued. "He got them knocked out in a fight in his youth."

"Why would he lie to me?"

"It's a rather unpleasant story, normally I would respect his secrets, but you need to know. Your father is a convict. Some time ago he wounded another student. He said it was an accident, but then the girl died. When the psychic mages asked to scan his mind, he admitted to murder."

Saurin took a seat on a bench, and gestured for Jessica to sit beside him. He removed the book from his satchel.

"We once had yearbooks, when they allowed us electric power for the presses. Now they don't, the old idiots."

He flipped to a page and set the book open.

Jessica grabbed the volume from his hands.

It was true.

All true.

The photo was eerie. Her father had his arm lazily draped on her mother's shoulders as they sat in a gazebo. Aunt Beatrix grinned, a smile that was identical to Misa's. Justen sat close, holding his tiny infant daughter.

Jessica's heart tore in two, as she wanted to cry out at the people in the photograph. They didn't know what would happen. How did they go from such great friends to a tragedy? *How could her parents lie so blatantly to her, again?!*

Chills running through her spine, she flipped through the pages of the yearbook. It seemed a universe away.

"Jessica, you belong here. Forgive Carmelina, she really took your father's fall as her fault. Once she thinks on it, she will change her mind. Believe me, I have known her a long time. Just, please, be patient, and give me a little time. When I get this settled out I will send for you. Go back to the cottages."

Jessica did not find his words reassuring, but she stood and thanked him.

"I would keep this quiet from your friends," Saurin advised. "Use caution in revealing your parentage and your true name. Many people do not remember that time so fondly."

Jessica reluctantly handed the book back to the old mage.

"I must talk to Carmelina before she overreacts. Can I trust you to find your way back from here?"

"Yes, I can. Thank you? I think? I'm sorry, I really didn't think this is how today would go."

"Not your fault. Go to your friends, I will send for you."

***

Jessica returned to the cottage. She took a few wrong turns, meandered past a bicorn field, found the library, asked for directions, got lost again, and finally made it to the little faculty village an hour later.

She was exhausted, thirsty, and utterly confused.

Jessica knocked on the door of Kaity and Corwin's cottage, furious Jared had not come to find her.

No response.

She opened the door.

And froze.

Jared and Mace, in all their beautiful muscular glory, were completely naked, on the sofa and were...

"You've got to be kidding me," Jessica squeaked. "Jared, I need to talk to you, right now!"

She pulled the door closed, wide-eyed.

Her day could not get any stranger.

Taking a few steps down, she sat on the sidewalk amidst the pretty rainbow of flowers.

The door behind her opened, Mace stepped out, wearing pants and little else.

Her gaze did not go unnoticed.

"Beautiful, I know, right?" he smiled gesturing to his chest. "Stripes like these are typical in the Starsiville bloodline."

Jessica blushed.

"I'm sorry I walked in on you…"

"Ah, don't be embarrassed girl," Mace waved his hand. "This happens all the time in Polaris."

"That is Kaity and Corwin's living room," Jessica pointed out.

Mace shrugged.

"These cottages are passed from mage to mage, they're owned by Polaris right down to most of the furniture. I would bet that living room has seen a lot."

"Mace, really it doesn't make it any better."

The door opened behind them. Jared was thankfully wearing more clothing than Mace.

"So, what did you need to tell me right this instant?" Jared asked, leaning heavily on the doorframe. He sipped liquor directly from a glass bottle.

"Sorry I interrupted you, but it's a big deal.

"Of course, it's a big deal. They test you, then sit you down for like hours of lecture and paperwork, and then there's a written test that takes forever for class placement. Then someone takes you to eat a fancy dinner, it's like this whirlwind initiation. I wasn't expecting to see you until long after sunset."

"Well things didn't go as planned."

"What do you mean 'didn't go as planned'?"

"They don't want me. I failed."

"How can you 'fail'? That's impossible."

"Things got weird."

"Why?"

"I…." Jessica hesitated. Yes, Saurin Bane advised her to keep the knowledge to herself, but she had been through hell and back with Jared.

"We'll talk later."

"That's vague, Jessi," Jared took another sip.

"How much have you had to drink?"

Mace sighed.

"Told you you shouldn't drink so quickly."

"Leave or you will be trapped."

The words were whispered into Jessica's ear and she jumped, trying to find the source of the voice.

"Did you hear that?"

"Hear what?" Mace asked.

"Leave, the council will detain you."

Jessica looked around wildly, trying to find the source of the voice.

"Someone's whispering in my ear! It's in my head! It's in my ear!"

"What did they say?" Jared asked.

"Leave, the council will trap me!"

"A far-speaker," Mace said.

"Oh damn, we need to go," Jared panicked, "Mace, can you tidy up the cottage?"

"No problem."

"Who is talking in my ear?!" Jessica was frightened.

"I don't know, but whoever it is, I'm betting Saurin Bane is behind the message. Get your bag, we are running to the train, now!"

"Are you…"

"Jess, if a farspeaker tells you to run, you run."

CHAPTER 18

In a mad dash, Jared and Jessica made it to the station. They boarded the train, and took their seats far from the other passengers. The mammoth baeleana bellowed and the train trundled out of the station.

At first Jessica felt relief, but then she realized they were returning to Aurumice.

She felt like crying.

"Want to tell me what actually happened back there?" Jared asked gently.

Jessica remained silent.

"I'm just going to find out."

"Why weren't you watching out for me?"

"I was busy, and I thought you would be fine."

"Jared, I could have used you there," Jessica said. "It's crazy."

Jessica leaned closer, whispering.

"They told me my father is a mage."

The teen recounted the events of the afternoon. When she finished, Jared sat back.

"Savartos Sarkisian is your dad? I am beginning to think your family actually is cursed."

"Jared, it's not funny."

"I know it's not funny. You know what's even less funny? The fact that we're going right back to your mom and Teren. First Misa gets me banned from Polaris, now you're getting me banned from Aurumice. Your mom obviously didn't want you to know that your dad isn't your dad."

"But he is. He changed his name."

"Really?" Jared raised an eyebrow. "Now that's interesting."

"So you know of my father?"

"Jess, they make us memorize the history of every mage who's committed an act against Nova in the past two hundred years. They don't tolerate any screw-ups. This is bad."

"But it's not my fault!"

"Yes, it is. You should have listened to your mom. Just forget it. I don't even want to talk to you."

Jared put on his hat and refused to look at her. They travelled in silence for several hours.

Looking out the dirty glass, Jessica watched as the train passed through little towns late through the afternoon. The countryside had lost its wonder. She felt ill with the rickety motion of the train and the foul stench coming from the mammoth baelaena.

Jared napped for a while.

It was nearing the end of the day as he woke up.

"Jess, I didn't mean to snap at you. It's not your fault."

"It's okay," Jessica replied. "I was thinking, if I can't go home and I can't stay at Polaris, is there any place else to find a blood mage to teach me?"

"I don't know about teaching you, the only other healers I know are in the Holy Circus." Jared fished through his bag.

"Really?" Jessica sat up.

"Yeah, Polaris tries to down-play it, but there are real mages in the circus. I think they may have blood mages, but they don't call them mages, because then Polaris would get pissed. They're just called mystic priests and priestesses, or just mystics."

"Can we ask them? If we're already in trouble, why go back to Aurumice?"

"I don't know how the Circus feels about things since Castle Aurumice let Nico be taken to Briken."

"But the Auroriates preach the love of the goddess. It's a thing they're supposed to do. Can we find Amberynn and ask her?"

Jared pulled a small flask from his bag. He took a long drink.

"Well?" Jessica pressed.

Jared took another drink.

"Jared!"

"I'm pondering how much angrier your family will be with me if I bring you to the Holy Circus. Is anger exponential? Is it just the same? Is it possible for them to get angrier? If Teren is going to kick me out of Aurumice, it may as well be spectacular, right?"

"So, we'll do it?"

"Yes, I suppose."

Jared sat up, looking out the window. He watched the landscape for a while.

"Well?"

"I think that's the Little Mountain of Fayeby. If I'm right, in one stop we'll get off at the Yellow Valley and the Village of Daconite. There's a central temple of the Auroriates. From there we contact Amberynn a lot faster than if we go to one of the temples in Trabalis."

"You're really going to help me with this?"

"Well, the situation is bad. This could either fix it or turn it into a worse monstrosity of a problem. I'm not in a hurry to go back to Aurumice, so if we are going to fail, may as well up the failure level!"

Jessica grinned.

"Let's go find the Holy Circus."

***

They arrived in the Yellow Valley as the sun was beginning to set. It was a riverside town, on the route of the River White. As they arrived in the station, Jessica instantly liked the lush greenery. The people of the Yellow Valley prioritized plant life with a religious fervor. Around every corner, vegetation grew up the sides of the buildings, obscuring much of the brick work. The ground was cobblestoned with mossy patches and tiny flowers like a lush carpet.

"I've been here a few times," Jared said. "The temple should be in the center of town."

"Why did you visit the Yellow Valley?"

"When I was a kid, we stopped here on the way to the Lake Festival in the north. It's a nice place to stop, really pretty. They call it Yellow Valley for the stones in the soil. A lot of it has been collected away, but if you dig, you can find these deposits of yellow glass."

They stopped at a street merchant to buy dinner. After paying, Jared asked the vendor where to find the Auroriates.

"Oh, you just missed them. Was quite a show."

"What do you mean? Was the circus in town?"

"A big show was here all week. They packed up in the morning, headed east."

"Do you know which troupe?"

The vendor shrugged. "They all look the same to me."

"We actually were just looking for the temple."

"A block up the street, left at livery."

Jared thanked the vendor again, and they continued on their way.

Auroriates preached their religion in two places— town temples, and the extravagant traveling circus.

"We should go east to catch the traveling troupe," Jessica encouraged.

"We're going to walk after the Holy Circus? Let's just go to the temple."

"Maybe we could catch a ride."

"Jess, you don't just walk up to the Holy Circus and ask to hitchhike. We need to get transportation. This trip is getting expensive. Have you considered having a little faith in the medicine of your world to help Carrie Anne?"

"You said the opposite an hour ago."

"That's 'til I realized how much coin I had left and how much lodging will cost for several days. You forget there's no credit cards around here."

"Asking the Holy Circus won't hurt, but Carrie Anne could die if I don't. You wouldn't understand," Jessica angrily took a bite of bread.

"You don't know me," Jared replied. "You don't know anything about me or my family, so don't think I don't understand."

"For being up in everyone's business all the time, you're not the sharing type."

"Maybe because there's no point in being miserable about a situation you can't change."

"Well I can change this," Jessica said, holding up her arm to remind him.

Eventually the two came to a small footbridge over the river. Jared paused to lean over the flower-covered rail and look down into the River White.

Jessica gazed out to the small crowd in the town square. There were few sapiens, mostly ailurians, occasionally the horned caprasians. Jessica was surprised to see a feline-like family with wings. The vesperians were a rare race.

As she watched the interesting winged family, her eyes latched onto an echo of the past.

Time stopped.

Standing like a beacon in the sea of shuffling people, Jessica saw a hooded figure. An odd sensation ran down her spine, as if staring into a dream. The stranger seemed sad and old. His worried eyes darting around as if he feared being hunted.

But he wasn't that old, he was worn by long toil in the mines.

Time hadn't actually stopped, but the world around Jessica was suddenly less relevant. Only she and the figure existed.

He saw her, but turned away, blending in the shuffle of the crowd.

"It's Nico!" Jessica grabbed Jared's shoulder excitedly.

"What?"

"Look past the bat family- "

"Vesperian, we call them vesperian. Jess, you can't talk like that in public, you sound racist."

"Look!"

"I don't see anyone," Jared shoved her away. "And if Teren thinks he's dead, then I believe him."

The hooded form was gone. Jessica's heart beat wildly. She ran across the bridge into the crowd. How could he have been there one moment and gone the next? Nico saw her, there was no doubt in her mind.

No, no, no...we can't lose him...

"It's impossible," Jared shook his head. "Jess, it wasn't him. Even if he wasn't dead, why would he be in the Yellow Valley?"

"Maybe he's with the Auroriate Circus."

"The Holy Circus instead of Aurumice? No."

"I don't care! Look for him, Jared."

"Now you want to run after a figment of your imagination?"

"I know it's him. My cousin doesn't know everything!"

Jared grabbed her by the shoulders.

"You're not hearing me. I get you're upset about Polaris, and Carrie Anne, and Talon sleeping with your mom, but Nico isn't coming back."

"Jaejaredo Remington Evansi, if you don't take two minutes to look for him, I will make your life even more miserable."

"I regret ever telling you my full name."

Jared sighed. He blinked, his eyes taking on a familiar far-off look. Jessica could swear sometimes when he used his powers his eyes flashed white. It was barely perceptible and you had to be staring right at him.

Jared's strength was fairly accurate. He couldn't locate a complete stranger, but when he looked through the eyes of someone he knew, he had a sense of their essence. Each person's vision was a slightly different color and sharpness.

The blonde-haired boy scrunched up his face in annoyance.

Jared blinked, holding up a finger.

"You're right! East, near a temple."

Jared didn't apologize, but instead bolted. Jessica ran after him.

"Further east," Jared shouted. "Now I see a little purple candy cart!"

Jessica was always impressed by Jared's skills. The man had practiced long enough that he had the ability to determine cardinal directions based on cast shadows. He was an excellent tracker.

"Nico just won't stop moving," Jared gritted his teeth. "Jess, remember, we don't really know what's going on. Be on guard!"

And so, they began their hunt.

***

Exhilaration slowed into pure exhaustion.

Yellow Valley was a small town, a fifth of the size of Trabalis. Jessica was sure she had seen every corner of it as darkness fell. They lost Nico more times than Jessica could count, but always picked up the trail. The man never seemed to rest.

Luckily Nico stayed on foot, otherwise Jessica was sure they would have lost him completely. She was exhausted, but refused to give up.

Jared had a grim determination on his face as his eyes became reddened and dry.

"I don't understand him at all," Jared lamented. "He makes no sense. It's like he knows we're following him."

As they rounded a corner, Jessica froze.

A group of mages in uniform gathered on bicorns.

Jared grabbed Jessica, pulling her behind a hedge.

"This is not good. They've got a psychic with them. I went to class with her, she's a Finder."

"Are they going to arrest me?" Jessica asked.

"Probably going to escort us back," Jared grimaced. "Damnit, I hope Saurin Bane sorts this out."

"What do we do?"

"Lucky for us she's a weak tracker, if we put some distance between us and her, we might get away."

"But Nico…"

"Gonna still look for him, don't worry, we'll take a longer way around. Follow me."

Jared bolted in the opposite direction.

Jessica ran after him. The blonde boy seemed more determined than ever as he zig-zagged through the streets. Eventually they were on the outskirts of town again, near the docks of the River White.

"Man, never had to watch two moving people in two directions at once," Jared leaned against a fence post, his face red. "But the mages are pretty easy for me to far-see. They're a distance away."

"What if we lose Nico?" Jessica asked.

"We won't," he replied, "unless he sleeps, and I am determined to stay awake longer."

"Thank you."

"For what?" Jared was bewildered.

"For not giving up."

"I'd be bored without you," Jared blinked rapidly, trying to ward away the exhaustion. "He's moving again! Tavern with a red door!"

Jessica glanced around. A red-doored tavern was forty yards away. She pointed, and they resumed their chase.

"This way!" Jared picked up speed and turned down an alley.

Finally, they had their quarry cornered.

Jessica felt a lump in her throat, fearing Nico would vanish.

Standing in the shadows, Nico hunched over, cloaked in a mud-stained black mantle.

The man backed up, frightened like a feral dog. He looked wildly for an escape, but had picked the wrong alleyway. Crumbling and steep, the sides were too high to climb.

"Stay away from me," Nico growled. His voice was rough and cold, *but it was still his voice!*

"No, not until you tell us why you're running," Jessica stepped forward. Jared reached out, cautioning her to keep distant.

"Stay away," Nico warned again.

"Jess, be careful. We don't know what's going on here."

It was not the reunion she had hoped for, but Jessica didn't care. Tentatively, she took a few steps forward. Long before Jared, Nico had been her best friend, welcoming her to the castle and teaching her their ways.

"Nico, please, what happened?"

He didn't reply, hunched over.

"Nicoveren?"

Without warning, Nico lunged forward, shoving her backwards against the stucco wall.

One of his hands pressed tight at her waist, the other firmly gripped around her neck, his dirty clawed hands digging deep into her skin. In the dim light of the alley, she could see his terrifying face, pock marked and covered with welts and pus-filled wounds. His teeth were darkened, his fangs sharp as his lips drew back in a snarl, his gums black. His left eye was strange, not able to open fully. His right eye, blue and beautiful, narrowed in anger.

They were locked in place for barely a moment when Jessica's training surfaced. She shifted her weight, kicking forward and knocking him off balance.

"What is wrong with you?!" she shouted.

"I told you to go!"

"Look, Nico, I know Briken messed you up," Jared held up his hands. "I saw it, I saw it through your eyes. I was there. Teren and I were never very far, okay? You gotta stop running, please, come back home and we'll figure this out."

Nico tried to make a dash from the alleyway but Jared was quick. Tackling the dark man, he pulled him down to the ground. To Jessica's surprised Nico fought back viciously. Jared was nimble and fit, but Nico had brute strength on his side. As they fought, Jessica analyzed his movements as Wadjette had taught her. He was favoring his left side, as if his back were injured. She grabbed a scrap of wood, wielding it like a club.

"Stop fighting us!" Jessica warned.

Nico didn't heed her words, and she dashed back into the fray, striking bluntly at his weak side. He yelped and crumpled to the dirt. Jessica felt awful.

Jared pinned him to the ground. The dark man wouldn't admit defeat, and struck back at Jared until he was free.

"You are in danger!" Nico growled at him.

"Danger?" Jared laughed. "Do you know what Teren would do to me if I let you go? He is the last cat on this planet that I want to piss off."

Nico climbed to his feet. He drew a knife.

"Awww, maggot sucker, seriously, Nico!" Blood dripped from Jared's nose. "We can't go down this path."

"Nico, what are you doing?" Jessica never imagined Nico to have become so violent.

"Come on," Jared held a hand out. "You know knives are a bad idea. Don't want to bring this up, but you remember how things went when Corwin brought a knife to the party. Put it away."

Nico snarled, his arm twitching strangely.

He leapt at Jared, shoving the knife into his shoulder blade. Blood flowed from the wound, staining Jared's dark shirt.

"WHAT THE HELL!?!" Jared screamed, stumbling backwards. "Of all the rotten, you son of a bitch, stupid prince of maggot suckin' Aurumice! AURORA DAMN YOU!!!"

Jared clenched his teeth, letting out an even more colorfully repulsive string of curses.

Nico sprinted away.

"That wasn't a mortal wound," Jessica stated.

"We can't let him go," Jared cried through the pain. "Teren will kill us. Keep after him! I'll be behind you!"

Nico still in her sights, Jessica ran. She was fully aware her choice was stupid, but she also knew if Nico was crazed enough to attack, then something worse was after him.

He needed their help, and they would not abandon him.

Nico's limp slowed him down, and Jessica was able to keep an even pace

Lanterns on the street lit the way. Nico had the advantage. His ailurian vision was better suited to the night. Jessica was too human to be very keen in the darkness.

The air grew foggy as Jessica approached the docks of the River White. Soft waves sloshed in the shadows and the cobbles transitioned to wooden decking. Diffused by the fog and spread farther apart, the lanterns cast little useful light. Nico became harder and harder to see as the fog grew thicker.

Finally, Jessica could go no further. She had come to the water's edge and had no idea which path Nico had taken.

"Why are you doing this!?" she shouted into the empty dusk. "Nico!"

Her voice echoed across the water.

"Please! Come back! Don't leave us!"

No reply.

How could they come so close to getting him back only to lose him again? Her insides ached.

"Nico!" she called out again. "For the memory of Misa, please, answer me!"

It was the last thing she could think to say to turn his heart. It stung Jessica to invoke the name of their long-perished friend.

She knew Nico would do anything for Misa.

There was no reply. Jessica looked around. She had lost Jared and was alone on a strange dock in a strange city in a strange land. The exhilaration of the chase had kept her moving forward. Now that she had stopped, the absurdity hit her.

And the fear.

From the mists of the long dock, Nico's silhouette approached.

Jessica said nothing, holding her knife at the ready.

He spoke first.

"You are not safe here."

"If you don't explain what the hell is going on, I'm going to go ballistic."

Finally he relented.

"Hurry, follow me."

Nico led her back towards the Daconite, up a muddy embankment, to a small shed.

Every warning bell in Jessica's mind was screaming at her, but she was determined to find out what was wrong with Nico. He was the one who taught her how to rewire a lamp, ride a bicorn, and fight. She taught him algebra and earth history. The past had to count for something.

This is stupid, this is stupid, this is stupid...

But she followed. If he really wanted to hurt her, nothing would stop him. Yes, she could fight back, but Nico's true mage abilities were deadly.

He could incinerate her to a crisp.

They traveled around crates and storage sheds.

"Hurry, I'm being hunted," Nico warned.

"By who?"

He did not reply.

Jessica prayed Jared would catch up soon.

They arrived at a shed. Nico unbolted the door, releasing the stench of dung and rotten fish. Inside was a grey bicorn mare with a white muzzle. The creature had a pair of clipped jagged black horns.

"We need to get you back to Jared before they see me with you."

"Speaking of whom, we left him behind, *with a stab wound.*"

"I panicked, I thought it would deter you from following," Nico replied. "He shouldn't have any permanent damage."

"My mistake, I apparently woke up in an alternate universe where stabbing your friends is okay," Jessica was exasperated. "You vanish from Briken without a trace. You're free and you don't come home!? And who is hunting you that Jared and I and frickin' Castle Aurumice couldn't handle?!"

"How did you find me?" Nico hoisted the saddle onto the old bicorn.

"Answer my questions first."

"Fine, you want the truth?" Nico turned to her angrily. "I shot a mage, and I probably killed him, so now they're trying to arrest me! I thought I had evaded them, but then it was my folly to steal this stupid old mare. They alerted the mages outside of Yellow Valley and now they're on my tail."

Jessica was stunned.

"Okay, that's quite... a problem."

"Did Jared track me here?" Nico asked.

"It was an accident, actually. I was looking for the Holy Circus, were you with them?"

"No."

The saddle slipped from Nico's hands.

"You're hurt."

"It's nothing," he hoisted the saddle back up, hunched over. "Why do you want to find the Circus?"

"Carrie Anne is sick, and she needs a healer. The mages won't teach me, I was hoping the Holy Circus would. Will you ask your Aunt Amberynn for me?"

"I don't talk to the Auroriates and they can't 'teach' you anything your earth medicine can't do."

"Nico, I'm a blood mage."

He stopped fumbling with the saddle straps.

"You're a *what?*"

"Yeah, you've missed some things in Briken. Also, there is a chance those mages are looking for me, not you."

"What did you do?"

"Long story, not as interesting as yours. Let's run back to Aurumice and sort this out." Jessica pushed him gently to finish saddling the mare. As she touched Nico's hand, she noticed the missing fingers.

He pulled away, trying to hide his hands.

"Jess, if a mage hunting party is after us and they go to the castle, what do you think will happen to your cousin?!"

"Maybe we can make it across the Gate before they catch up. Hide in my mom's house."

"Too risky. I want you to take this mare and ride away, let's split up."

"No."

"Why are you so stubborn?!"

"Can this mare carry both of us? Let's run for Aurumice."

Nico was so agitated, Jessica wasn't sure if the man was going to strangle her or burst into tears. She thought it more likely the latter.

"Nico, for the love of the goddess, *let's get Jared and go home!*"

"Those mages are after me, and if you stay you're courting death," he finally stated, climbing onto the mare's back.

He extended a hand to Jessica.

She took his hand.

"It's my choice."

CHAPTER 19

Racing into the fog, the bicorn's hooves beat against the dry earth. Nico urged the bicorn further and further from the town center. Jessica wondered if it was even possible for Jared to find them.

"I want to get out of the city first. They'll have a harder time in the forest, and then we'll circle back to look for Jared."

As they tore through the darkness, Jessica's stupidity bubbled up in her mind.

Nico killed a mage and he stabbed Jared.

If the mages caught her with Nico, that wouldn't help her chances of convincing Carmelina to accept her.

Unless she sold him out.

What the hell was she thinking?!

The bicorn raced across uneven terrain. What had started as an exhilarating adventure had become a terrifying run.

Jessica weighed out her options.

She could ask him to stop, and then hide in the woods, make her way back to town. Jared would surely find her by daybreak if the mages didn't find her first.

If Jared was okay.

She glanced back behind them. Fog had begun to roll further in across the land, causing Jessica to shiver.

Far in the distance, she could make out the dark forms moving in their direction.

"Nico, I think they found us."

Her companion reined the grey mare, turning to look at the approaching bicorns.

"Damnit!"

He growled, rounding the grey mare and kicking her harshly. The beast bounded forward.

The terrain beneath them turned from soft earth to gravel. Trees became more sparse to their left. As they raced uphill, Jessica realized they were bordering the steep embankment of the river. A foul, cold, humid stench permeated the air. Twenty feet below, the water sloshed in the darkness. Jessica wondered if it was worth the risk as she eyed the uncomfortably close edge. Nico didn't notice, so caught by fear.

Again, Jessica looked back. The bicorns were gaining, about a city block away.

She didn't know which made her more nervous, the river's edge or their pursuants.

Without warning, the grey bicorn lost her footing, pitching them down the embankment.

Time slowed with disorienting flurry.

As Jessica screamed aloud her mind raced.

We're falling...we're falling into the river...and my family doesn't know where we are!

Jessica felt the weight of the bicorn on top of her as they rolled. Stone jabbed her back. Pain suffocated the girl as her ribs cracked. They tumbled through grass and stone. The bicorn brayed in agony.

Stupid...stupid...stupid...I don't want to die!

Water slammed into Jessica's face like an icy hammer. The forced sucked them into the raging cold waters of the River White. Nico grabbed her arm, and they fought against the current. Battering them like dolls, the river pulled them down and up in a dizzying frenzy. Jessica inhaled water and coughed violently as they bobbed out of the waves only to be sucked back down again.

Nico snagged a passing log, Jessica reached for the wood, trying to twist her aching limbs around the snarled broken branches. She pulled her head above water just enough to take a deep breath. Her mind clear, they swirled with the darkness of the river.

She wanted to scream but had no energy to waste on shouting.

Please Aurora, let the mages find us, please God, please anyone! Don't let us drown!

Jessica had no sense of time as they continued to be thrown by the river.

Eventually, the wild current ceased, and the log gently bobbed. She still gripped on, afraid to look around and slip into the water. Soon, her legs caught the tendrils of river plants and she could see a shore line. When the log could move no more, she fought her way to the beach. Desperate, she climbed up the grassy slick shore in the moonlight and collapsed onto a rock.

***

Jessica awoke on the shore. Every fiber of her body ached, but she was alive.

Dawn was breaking on the horizon.

She realized she had crawled to shore alone, abandoning Nico and the log.

Climbing to her feet, her sides burned. The teen screamed Nico's name. No reply. She cried out for Jared, but feared she was miles away and outside of his range. As Jessica shouted, pain intensified through her chest and she found it difficult to breathe.

In the dim light of dawn, she saw Nico, his body bobbing oddly amongst the rocks.

"No, no, no!"

Sloshing through the water, she ran to his side. He was unconscious, blood staining his forehead. Despite the growing pain in her chest, she pulled him onto the rocky shore.

Listening carefully, Jessica watched his chest rise and fall. He was alive, but did not look right.

"I wish I could heal you. I don't know how."

She pushed his hair from his eyes.

"Please, please wake up."

He did not stir.

Looking up to the sky, she begged the universe for help.

She took a deep breath, closing her eyes, and let Wadjette's training come back to her. Lost, injured, first priority was to stop Nico's bleeding.

Jessica pulled off her thin jacket and tore off a bit of the lining to form a bandage. As she did so, pain jabbed into her side. She pulled up her shirt and instantly felt sick and weak.

Her stomach was the icky purple of an internal hemorrhage.

She was in trouble.

A dragon-shaped shadow passed overhead, casting darkness across the earth.

Jessica turned her eyes to the sky.

"Goddess Aurora, thank God!" Jessica stood.

Jessica shouted at the top of her lungs, trying to get the rider's attention. The featherwing was joined by two more, but none of them paid her any mind. It was clear the dragon riders did not see her.

Jessica leaned down.

"Nico, I don't know if you hear me, but that's either the Holy Circus or mages, and either way, I'm going to find them."

She tied the bandage around his forehead. It was pathetically weak and likely riddled with bacteria from the river.

They both were going to die without help.

Studying the high cliffs around her, Jessica tried to lock in on landmarks. She would need to leave Nico, it was her only chance. The featherwings had flown a distance, but descended down near a distinct rock formation about a mile away.

Taking one more glance to make sure Nico was securely away from the water's edge, Jessica began to make her way to the featherwings, begging the goddess that she would be able to find them.

She kept pursuit as the sun began to rise.

The ache on her insides bit at her side, but she could not rest. Each step became even more excruciating than the last and she had to stop to catch her breath.

Jessica's stomach churned and she vomited stomach acid and blood onto the dark earth.

"No, no I can't stop," she hobbled along.

"Auroriates!" she shouted into the forest, "Auroriates! If you are there! I need your help! Please!"

If she stopped, they were both dead.

She continued to push onwards, climbing out of the riverbed up to the forest.

Finally, in the distance, she spotted the familiar colorful tents.

Jessica's heart pounded in joy, giving her a surge of adrenaline to fight her failing body. The crippling pain radiated into her back and legs, but the tents gave her enough energy to press on.

They were her only chance.

Jessica stumbled through the forest, vomiting blood again. Her entire body shook violently and she was certain she was running a fever and on the edge of shock.

The teen argued with herself.

"Stopping is death, can't stop."

Using a log, the teen climbed to her feet, and pressed onwards. Clutching her stomach, she hobbled to a clearing. A violent gust of wind slammed Jessica to the ground. A gryphon flew overhead and landed in front of her, flanked by two featherwings that landed a distance away.

She gazed up at the majestic beast. The creature was red-gold. A mane of soft feathers surrounded its head and cuffed its feet and wrists. Silken feathery wings folded neatly at its side.

Climbing to her elbows in the tall grass, Jessica cried out.

"I need your help!"

Covered in green dragon-skin armor, the rider wore the iconic mask of the Holy Circus.

"I was traveling with Nicoveren Aristo Verdian," Jessica continued, "son of Malachi and nephew of Amberynn! He's wounded terribly."

The words took all of Jessica's energy and she fought to catch her breath before she spoke again.

"Please, I'm bleeding inside! We fell into the river. Please, please, help us!"

Pulling off her mask, the rider revealed a leopard-face.

"This isn't Amberynn's troupe," said the stranger, "but I would give my right eye before I turn my back on castlefolk."

***

Jared's shoulder seared with pain as he stumbled through the lush streets of the Yellow Valley.

"Goddess damn you to hell stupid Aurumice prince bastard...."

Shivering with fever, he continued to grumble to himself,

He passed a woman with black hair and coal dark eyes.

"Girl, which way to the Air Sprint Courier?"

"Train station," she said.

Oh, that made sense. Fever was getting to him already.

Jared shuffled to the station. Every bench he passed seemed very inviting. He longed to sit and nap but doubted he would wake up very soon.

By the time he reached the knotty wooden door of the Air Sprint, he could barely stand. He stumbled in and leaned heavily on the counter.

"I need to send a message."

The attendant was a portly little ailurian, his red fur greying.

"You need a doctor. We can't help you."

"No, I need to send a message," Jared threw his coin pouch on the desk. "Now."

"Okay, okay."

Meadowdashers rattled in their cages. The small dragons were the fastest couriers in Centernia, but they weren't cheap.

"Where is the destination?"

"Trabalis. More than Trabalis, Castle Aurumice. I need the message to go to Trabalis and have a courier run to the castle."

"The cursed castle?" the man scoffed.

"Yes, the bloody cursed castle! I don't have time for this. I need to send a message."

"Better not lose a dragonette to that bad luck."

"You know who I am?" Jared growled. His patience was gone. The young man pulled out his small boot knife and stabbed it into the desk's smooth lacquered surface. Papers flew up in the air and a bottle of ink fell to the floor.

A nightflight symbol was cast into the knife's blue stone handle. Jared very rarely used the knife, but the message was clear.

"I am a Mage of Polaris, raised in the halls of Castle Nova. I am a far-seer, of the Evansi family, and if you don't help me there will be hell to pay."

"My apologies," the man stammered, "Lord Mage, sir."

He handed Jared the special paper.

Jared scrawled the note, opting for American English. On the outside label, he wrote Teren's name, his hand shaking.

"You need me to call for a doctor or something?" the man at the counter asked.

"I need a drink, and a doctor, and a time machine, to erase every stupid decision I have ever made. You know what happens when you go out of your way for people who don't appreciate you? You get kicked out of your home, treated like the butt of every joke, and stabbed in a back alley by the one man everyone seems to love." Jared threw the pen across the desk. He barely counted out a handful of coins, leaving a generous tip, and shoved the pile across the counter.

"How long is that letter going to take?"

"About three days' flight and some time for the courier. Though there's storms in the area, it may be delayed. Dragonettes don't fly in the rain."

"I could ride to Trabalis in a third that time! Air sprint my ass!"

"With respect, Lord Mage, with that shoulder you don't look like you should be riding anywhere."

"Right. Which way to a doctor? Or a tavern? I don't even care at this point."

CHAPTER 20

Stephen Ravenwolfe sat at the kitchen table in the tiny Vance kitchen.

Waiting.

Tick, tick, tick...

5:50pm.

He had hoped he would find his daughter, but it was obvious the girl hadn't been home.

Stephen tapped his fingers on the kitchen table. He hadn't bothered to change after work and still wore slacks.

The front door finally opened and Lily took three steps in.

Stephen looked up at his ex-wife, knowing what she was thinking. She was debating on running, but knew he would still find her.

"You broke into my home," she stated, closing the door slowly.

"You were not returning my calls," Stephen defended.

"I had nothing new to say."

"I don't believe you have no idea where Jessi is."

"If I did, would it make a difference? You're not going through the Gate."

Stephen slammed his hand on the table.

"She is my daughter, too! She missed dinner, and that worried Carrie Anne and then the high school called us. She hasn't been to school for an entire week!?"

Lily rolled her eyes, she had completely forgotten to call the school back with a silly excuse.

"I am worried sick, Carrie Anne is so upset she wants to go to the police and I am using lie after lie to stop her from wasting their time! I came here to find her, where is she?"

Lily crossed her arms.

"She's in Centernia, you know that."

He stood.

"Why do you think you have the right to do this to me? Haven't you tortured me enough? How many times do you want me to say that I am sorry?"

Lily looked down, setting her purse on the side table.

"I don't need to hear it. This has nothing to do with my sister."

"Then why do you need to torment me?"

"You think I'm not worried too!" she shouted. "Jessi ran away from me!"

"Maybe you gave her reason too, she apparently doesn't like this new lover of yours. Who are you sleeping with?"

"None of your damn business!"

Stephen cringed, maybe his words were accusatory, but his patience was gone. He was losing sleep, dreaming of all the horrors of Centernia, convinced Jessica was dead and Lily was completely denying it.

Stephen sighed, trying to find calm. Lily never backed down from an argument, so fueling the fire would do him no good.

"I apologize," he stated, taking a few steps towards her.

"Lily, please, hear me," Stephen whispered, "I am actually really, really worried this time. Where is she?"

Lily crossed her arms.

"She went to Polaris."

"Why?" Stephen questioned.

"I don't know. She's young, she's dumb, and we screwed up as parents, lots of reasons."

"Would you explain?" Stephen asked. He was fighting to remain calm, but screaming at Lily in voicemails had produced no results. Now that he saw her face he knew she was just as worried about their daughter.

"I will make some tea," Lily reconciled. "It's a long story, if you have the stomach to hear it."

Stephen knew he was difficult to deal with. For years, he had buried away every part of him that was Centernian. He told Lily repeatedly he didn't want to know anything of the world.

And she respected that wish.

But his life was hitting a point where his past kept creeping back, and as much as he wanted to lay waste to the world Savartos Sarkisian knew, he just couldn't.

He sat quietly as Lily set water to boil. For a brief instant, he felt a glimpse of his old life in the tiny house. He remembered Jessica as a toddler taking her first steps across the linoleum floor. It seemed like time had passed in an instant.

Lily sat at the table across from him. It was the same beat-up dinette they had found at a garage sale. He spent an afternoon repairing one of the chair legs. Those were the days he had time to stop and think, he had no job, just endless days to look after tiny Jessica.

"I miss her," Stephen said quietly, thinking of his little daughter. In those days, it was so easy to keep her safe, despite the fact every moment she was determined to scale furniture and eat paper.

For a while, Lily said nothing.

The clock ticked.

Finally, she spoke.

"If you must know, I was seeing Talon La'Roch, which is what I think caused some of this."

"Talon..." the name rattled around in Stephen's brain. "The guardsman...Fentalon... Malachi's friend?"

"Yes, now he leads the guard of Aurumice. His wife has long past. He returned, and one thing led to another rather quickly, and I don't think Jessi was happy with this. She got mad, and I think with Wadjette around she felt a little jealous."

"Wadjette is...?"

"Talon's daughter, she's exactly Jessi's age. She's an excellent fighter, and she put together the guard of Aurumice by herself. Jess got upset the other day and hit Wadjette in an illegal move in Ribbons, Talon got angry, and Jess shouted that I was divorced. Didn't go over too well."

"But our marriage was never blessed by the Auroriates. It's unsealed, and even if it was, I'm technically a criminal, so you would have been freed of it."

"Doesn't matter Stephen, not to the castlefolk, not the way Jessi said it. I mean our closest friends always knew, and they didn't care. The rest, like Talon, they're a bit more Centernian. They don't get it."

Stephen watched his ex-wife's face carefully. He knew she must have faced humiliation from the castlefolk.

There was one part of the story he still didn't quite understand.

"Why would Jessi hurt this girl? It doesn't sound like her."

"I don't know, years of losing, she was just mad, mad at Talon because she's been told to shut down the power to the castle."

"What's she got to do with the castle power?"

"Everything, Stephen. That girl single-handedly keeps that archaic electrical system running, and she's really good at it, but I don't think the castlefolk tell her thanks enough. Then when she couldn't handle the 'folk being jerks, she had Jared take her to Nova. She also had it in her head that she could help Carrie Anne, no matter how many times I told her it wouldn't do any good!"

"How could Nova possibly help Carrie Anne?" Stephen was very puzzled.

Lily rested her head on her knuckles.

"Your daughter is a blood mage."

A strange sensation of disbelief and pride flowed through Stephen's veins.

"That's impossible. That's like lightning striking twice in the same place."

"I didn't believe it either, until…"

"The dog bite. She healed herself that night?"

"Yes."

"I wondered what was up. The way Ashlin talked it sounded much, much worse."

"It was, she nearly lost her arm to a Lazuli hunter."

Stephen grimaced, the scaly dogs were hellish little monsters.

The tea kettle whistled and Lily stood to prepare the tea.

"I blame myself, Jessica does not know things like common Centernians do. It's like not knowing that if you pet a cat's belly you'll get a handful of claw."

"A Lazuli hunter is a lot more dangerous than a house cat."

"Exactly. We know that, she doesn't."

Lily brought two cups to the table. Despite the dismalness, there was something strangely reassuring talking to the woman about Centernia.

Stephen had kept it hidden so long, it was therapeutic to recall the strange land he had called home.

"Can you go back to the beginning?"

"Which beginning?" Lily asked.

"The start of this mess."

"Pretty much when Misa came through the Gate three years ago," Lily explained, "you really have time?"

Stephen shrugged.

"Go ahead."

Lily recounted everything, from the day Misa came through the Gate, seeking their daughter. She told Stephen about Misa's pursuit of the shadow sphere, of destroying the forcefield. She talked about their daughter's friendship with Nico. She spoke of the tenuous days when the Holy Circus came to Aurumice, bringing Malachi and discontent, and the taxes of Trabalis.

Stephen put on a second pot of tea. Even the white kettle with the blue flowers was the same. Lily hadn't updated a single thing since he left. He opened the pantry and found a box of chocolate chip cookies.

"Mind if I?"

Lily nodded.

Stephen returned to the table, opening the package.

"I never cared much for the Auroriates."

"Stephen, you were raised with the mages, not exactly a friendly group with the Holy Circus."

"They do things strangely." Stephen recalled the exotic performers in their unusual masks and secretive society. It was a den of spies and thieves, shrouded by the illusion of religion.

"And the mages don't always do things that are most kind." To his surprise, Lily reached out and touched the skull tattoo on his forearm.

It had been nearly twelve years since he felt her fingertips.

"You covered these up well," she ran her fingers along the faint blue lines in the design. The original mage marks had been sapphire, twisted into a knotted pattern. Stephen had been involuntarily tattooed with the mark of a mage criminal.

"It took me a while to find an artist who could cover them," Stephen stated. "But please, go on, I want to know more."

Lily continued her story, told her ex-husband about the Trabalis government sending Nico to the Mines of Briken. She skimmed through the craziness of the past year and discovery of their daughter's powers.

"Why are you here, Lily? Why haven't you gone to get her from Nova?

"You know it's too late. She wants to be there Stephen, and I don't blame her. She got it in her head that blood mages can cure cancer."

"But they can't."

"Yeah, you and I know that. Jessi wants to do good, and to help Aurumice. And really, she can. Any other Centernian parents would be overjoyed to say their daughter is a Blood Mage."

"She won't graduate high school."

"Guess that means she's part of this family."

Stephen wasn't certain how to reply. He wanted to be reassuring, but he couldn't formulate the words. He was exhausted, worried. Everything he knew was slipping away.

"You better call the school with an excuse."

"I will."

"This is going to upset Carrie Anne. She won't let up, she'll insist we look for Jessica."

"I know, can't exactly tell her the truth."

Stephen gave a half smile.

"Sometimes I just want to. Tell her everything, show her everything. But if I could cross the Gate, we wouldn't be in this predicament, would we?"

He stood.

"Thank you, I will go now." Stephen walked away.

Lily did not move from the table.

He opened the door of the house he once lived in, and stepped out into the cold night.

***

Teren drew the bow across the strings, filling the gilt lounge with a mournfully sweet melody. The curtains billowed with the warmth.

Savina sat by at her desk, flipping through pages of notes, charting the lineage of the bicorns. Their numbers were growing, it was good to see such progress. She also calculated how many they could afford to sell to bring in more revenue to Aurumice.

And that killed her inside.

A soft knock at the door roused her from the calculations.

Corwin entered.

He was a quiet sullen man, Savina felt bad for him.

"You look concerned," Teren stated.

"Yes, I am," Corwin carried in a pile of books.

"About Jessica's absence?"

"Honestly, that does not worry me much. Polaris is the best place for her," Corwin said. "And I do not wish to get into your family's affairs, this is more pressing."

Teren tucked the violin under his arm.

"What?"

"Needlewasps."

Teren seemed puzzled.

"What about them?"

"There are already reports from the north that this decade's infestation is worse than predicted," Corwin stated. "It is so bad that Polaris Academy has requested that I provide them with research on the topic."

Teren raised an eyebrow.

"I hope that does not involve giving them books from the libraries of Aurumice."

"Oh no, no, no, I am just collecting the information I find for a report."

"Just a bunch of bugs," Savina rolled her eyes, "And people looking to make a quick coin off of their mists and incense."

"I wish that were the case, but this is a very unique situation, more of a *swarm* of needlewasps than the typical small groups. I have received information through Polaris from mages stationed in the north. This cycle has been behaving frighteningly different. Your standard common needlewasp migrates from the mouth of the Blackturn River down to the

Bonifur forest where it feeds, mates, then the females travel back north. It lays its eggs in larger insects and grubs. It's a ground parasite."

Corwin set a book in front of Teren.

"This is quite a different creature," he explained. "Much deadlier to people."

Teren gestured for him to continue. Savina sat back, Corwin always seemed to dance around before he got to his point. He was boring to listen to.

"They used to be rare. Now, we have hardly seen any common needlewasps, it's as if the frost needlewasps have overtaken the smaller cousins. These are not ground parasites. They prefer to inject their eggs into larger mammals, including people, and they can carry deadly bacteria. Just one egg injection under the skin if left untreated will bring Puce fever."

That got Savina's attention.

Teren looked at the book.

"What threat will they actually pose to Aurumice?" he asked. Savina peered over Teren's shoulder at the old book. The pages were covered with detailed illustrations of the tiny creatures and ghastly drawings of people covered in boils and pustules. She shuddered.

"I really don't know," Corwin said. "They appear to be following the same pattern as needlewasps, making me think they have cross-bred. A swarm can be impressive in size, perhaps as large as a house."

"That sounds like an exaggerated tale. There can't be a swarm that big."

"It has happened," Corwin cautioned. "I am not saying we should panic, I am saying we should have a plan. We need to double up our food stores, seal cracks in the exterior walls, which would certainly help with winter drafts, just little things…"

Teren heaved a visible sigh and Savina cringed again. These were things she knew Teren wanted to have done, but it seemed like there was never enough hours in the day.

"I appreciate your concern, I will see what we can do…"

"You don't believe me, do you?"

"No, Corwin, I do believe you think this is a threat, but you have a tendency to overreact." Teren stopped himself. "Sorry, worded that poorly. If you could do more research—"

Another knock at the door interrupted him.

Wadjette entered the room, carrying a stack of messages. It was unusual for the pantheress to bring the mail.

"Sorry for my intrusion. This came by special courier," she said. "It's addressed to you and it looks urgent."

"Is it from Jessica?" Savina asked.

Teren took the message tube from Wadjette. Corwin collected his books.

"I hope it is," the warrior said. "We need her."

"Aye," Savina agreed, "freezer broke again. Cookie said we lost a lot."

"I thought I told her to shut down the kitchens."

Savina glanced away.

"She turned them back on before she left."

"I will be going," Corwin said, "There is more I need to discuss, Teren."

"Of course," Teren replied, focused on the message. Corwin left the room with his eyes downcast.

"Remind me to talk to him again later," Teren said to Savina, as he struggled to untie the rope on the message.

"You're doing that wrong," Savina said, taking the tube from him. "There's a pattern to the way you open these things, haven't you learned that by now?"

"I really hope Jessica returns home," Wadjette lamented. "I miss her. I don't care what she did on the sparring field. She was angry. All fighters get angry. And I truly do not care that her father is around somewhere, she can't control that."

"I honestly don't care much either," Savina said, handing the tube back to Teren. "Perhaps I also should not have gossiped behind her back."

Teren opened the tube.

"Vina, you always say terrible things to Jess. It's the cornerstone of your friendship."

"This time was bad."

"Teren," Wadjette said, "would it be alright if I took leave and traveled to the mage city? I feel like I should tell Jessica that she should come home."

"Well, if that damn sight mage brought her to Polaris then she's gone for years. I didn't mention this to you two because it seemed not prudent, but Jessica's gifts appeared. She's a blood mage."

"Oh, my goodness," Wadjette smiled, "that's how Bo didn't destroy her arm, isn't it?"

"Blood mage," Savina repeated. "That little imp is a healer?! Aurumice has a healer?!"

"No, thanks to that stupid son of a bitch, the mages have Jessica now," Teren said. "Probably will come back for holiday leave, and when she finishes her schooling with them, they will send her elsewhere. So no, Aurumice will not have their own blood mage. And we can all thank Jared for it."

He unrolled the message, walking away.

"Is that written in the script from the demon world?" Savina asked.

Teren took a few more steps away.

"It's not Jessi's handwriting. This is from Jae…"

He took a few more steps, his back to his friends.

"Teren, what is it?" Savina stood. She looked at Wadjette, the younger woman was just as concerned.

"Teren, what does it say?" Savina repeated. "Please, tell us."

"He's alive," Teren's voice shook. "He's alive. I was wrong, he's alive!"

His hand rubbed his eyes before he turned.

"Who? Nico?!" Savina asked.

Teren grinned, grabbing her by the waist and spinning her around. Savina was drawn to kiss him, and as her lips touched his she felt an outpouring of his beautiful, wild magic. Joy and elation surged into her body, echoing her own. Unable to breathe, her heart beat rapidly and she was lost in his happiness as he danced with her across the room.

He released his grasp on her gently, but she pounced on him again, taking another kiss. He held her at bay before she could take a third.

"Later, love," he whispered in her ear. "We have work to do."

Teren embraced Wadjette with a friendly hug. The guard captain laughed.

"It's true? Nico is alive? And we know where he is?"

"Yes! Yes! I am going to kill Jared, but first we're going to prepare him a banquet, and then I will kill him!"

***

Nico awoke slowly, eyes fighting to focus. He could see white walls, decorated in blue. Tiny wrinkles traveled across the uneven surface.

The walls weren't walls.

It was fabric.

He was in a tent.

Sweet incense filled the air with a familiar aroma.

He was home, a home from a long time ago.

Finally, his eyes focused and his full consciousness returned. Yes, he was in a tent of the Auroriates, the Holy Circus, and his father's family!

Nico sat up slowly, realizing he was not alone.

"Va grati'ora, va grati'ora."

Thanks to the goddess, thanks to the goddess

Nico was covered in blankets and little else in a sleeping palette of furs. Jessica slept on a mattress a few feet away, nestled in equally luxurious bedding.

"Don't worry. You're safe, boy."

It had been a long time since anyone had addressed Nico as if he were a child.

The woman wore a mask and was dressed as a typical Auroriate—boots, red pants, and an asymmetrical tunic that harkened to the goddess. Asymmetry was the hallmark of Holy Circus design.

Nico waited for the Auroriate to speak.

"Do you remember me?" she asked, closing the book in her hand.

He tried to recall the names of all the cousins he had met.

She removed the mask, revealing a face that was not of the Holy Circus, but castlefolk.

Sienna Cosette, Kaity Cosette's older sister.

He had not seen the woman in over thirteen years. He remembered little of her, other than she tended to live in the library, was obsessed with nightflights, and constantly irritated by Kaity.

"Sienna!? How did you find us?"

"Your girl there, she found us when you were a speck away from death."

Nico turned to look at Jessica. The young woman seemed pale, but peaceful.

"She was pretty bad off herself with broken ribs," Sienna continued, "but she was tough for being so sapien. We tended your wounds, but thought it best to keep you both sedated with redvice to give you a chance to heal."

Nico's left side began to tremor.

"You should rest," Sienna said. "Your nerves seem bad off."

"No, this won't go away," he said. "I was like this before."

"How did you escape the Mines of Briken?" Sienna asked.

Nico couldn't decide how much to reveal.

Sienna waited for him to elaborate. When he remained silent, she poured him a mug of tea. The cup was the distinct bright red dishware used by the Holy Circus.

"You've had a rough time, haven't you?" she said. "I can't imagine what it's like to lose your father and then be forced into that hell pit."

Sienna's words were sincere. She reached out and brushed strands of hair away from his eyes like a doting mother. Nico sipped the tea, debating what he could safely say.

"I did not escape," he finally stated. "I was sold, to whom I don't know."

"Slavery is outlawed in the continent," Sienna replied.

"Yes, but that didn't stop someone from buying me. I have no idea what I am now, escaped convict? Slave?"

"You are safe, that is what you are," Sienna said kindly. "You're amongst family now. Auroriates will always protect you."

Nico glanced over at Jessica.

"Is she hurt?" he asked.

"She is, but her injuries are healing."

"Thank you for your kindness," Nico said, sipping his tea slowly. The bitter sweet liquid was intoxicating. He had not tasted good Auroriate tea in a long while.

"Nicoveren, did your father tell you about me?"

Nico looked up at the leopard cattess, perplexed by her question.

Shaking his head slowly, he took another sip of the delicious tea. It was likely laced with an intoxicant to keep him relaxed and meditative.

"Even beyond the grave, he surprises me. Nico, I am a part of your family. I am your second-mother."

"When did you marry my father?!"

"After your mother passed to the Goddess. Thirteen years ago, when we escaped Trabalis and the Castle forcefield. I saved him and he saved me in turn, brought me to the Auroriates so I wouldn't be on the streets like everyone else. I am sorry you didn't know. He was afraid if Trabalis Council found out about me, I may be tangled in the tax debt of Aurumice. I thought he would have at least mentioned me to you."

Nico had many more questions, but kept silent.

"Your girl mentioned the mages, and little else before she passed out. Rest assured, we have moved and our scouts alerted. No mage is pursuing you."

"Whose caravan are we with?" Nico asked, "My Aunt Amberynn?"

"No, your Aunt Dahlia."

Dahlia was the eldest of his father's siblings. She was a fierce leader whom Nico admired a great deal.

"Please, if there is a spare bicorn, even a horse, let me take it and leave?"

"You aren't healed, and neither is she. Stay with us. You know we are masters at obscuring what does not want to be found." Sienna grinned.

"Yes, yes I know."

"You look weary," Sienna said. "Just give yourself time. I will leave you to sleep, but I will not be far. There's clothing for you in that chest. I selected some prayer books for you and a few other titles you may find interesting. If you need anything else, please let me know."

The leopardess left the tent.

Nico glanced over at Jessica, the girl was definitely asleep.

The Holy Circus was the last place he thought he'd find himself, let alone under the care of his second mother.

Second mother?

How?

Somehow it did not surprise him that it would be Sienna. His mother had never liked the young woman, now he understood why.

Nico slid out from beneath the covers, his legs collapsing under him. His body felt too sore to have been asleep for just a day and he wondered how long he had been slumbering. Swathed in a fur blanket, he climbed slowly to his feet and hobbled to the chest. He opened the heavy lid. Inside was clothing of the Holy Circus, and a white mask typically worn by an acolyte.

He picked up the mask, turning the beautifully crafted leather in his hands. The surface had tiny swirled lines and florals pressed into the leather.

Nico thought of his father in sorrow. He would have been happy to see his son amongst the circusfolk.

Nico put on the mask and looked in a small mirror hung from a thick piece of twine. The mask obscured his face, covering scars left from Briken.

CHAPTER 21

Jared had found a little inn when his body could take no more. The wound wasn't deep, but it was infected.

He curled up under the thin stiff blankets, wishing for a dose of amoxicillin, or penicillin, or any antibiotic that would stamp out the infection with just a few little pills.

The accommodations were sparsely decorated, wood floors, wood walls, and one small effigy of the goddess hung across from the bed. The poorly-painted art stared at him as if mocking his torture.

To pass the time, Jared let his mind's eye wander, jumping from person to person. He stretched his sight as far as he could, trying in vain to locate Jessica and Nico.

He ordered a bottle of the strongest alcohol from the meager bar. Over a wash basin he poured the dark liquid on the wound, trying to flush out the bacteria. His effort seemed futile, so he took a drink instead and staggered back to the bed.

Jared wondered if the castlefolk would be coming for him soon, optimistic that all would be forgiven because he'd found Nico. Staring up at the wooden ceiling, he decided that if he lived through the infection, he would ask the castlefolk to mark him so he could officially join their clan. Aurumice was more his home than any other place.

Jared drifted to sleep and was awoken by a pounding at the door. A quick glance through the eyes of the visitors revealed Lily, Kaity, Teren, and Savina. Mustering the last of his strength, he climbed out of bed and unbolted the latch.

A hand grasped his collar and a fist slammed squarely into his jaw.

"Give me one reason why I shouldn't kill you right now?!" Lily threatened. "You should have never taken Jessi to Polaris!"

"Stab wound, watch the stab wound!" Jared croaked, "The one caused by your stupid lord of Aurumice!"

"Where are they?!"

"I don't know!"

"How could you lose them?! You're a tracker!"

Lily's hand cracked with electrical energy.

"Lily please!"

"I told you to never bring her to Polaris!"

Lily shoved him against a wall, slamming the back of his head against the hard wood. A wave of dizziness spun over Jared. He fought to free himself from Lily's grasp. The other castlefolk stood behind her, but none made move to help him. Jared struggled and kicked.

"GET HER AWAY FROM ME!" he shouted.

"We promised Lily thirty seconds to beat you once we found you," Savina said. "It seemed fair."

Lily released her grasp and Jared crawled away, wedging himself between the bed and the wall.

"I am sorry! But you listen to me first before you kill me! Jess made me take her because none of you listened. She needs to cure Carrie Anne's cancer!"

"But she can't!" Lily argued. "If you had paid attention in your classes you would have known what blood mages can't do!"

"It doesn't matter, none of you listened to Jess! She doesn't give a damn about college, she cares about Aurumice, she cares about keeping the electricity on, and you took that from her! Now she's a damn blood mage and you won't let her be who she is! And who gives a rat's ass if she has a step-mom! All of you knew before, but you stood by as the castlefolk spat their poisoned words! *All of you turned your backs on Jess, all of you! And now I have a fever and I could be dying and I wish someone would get me a pill instead of punching me in the face!!!*"

He ripped away the makeshift bandage, exposing the oozing wound. The sight of the red and purple pus-filled infection caused the castlefolk to visibly grimace.

"Nico did that to you?" Teren asked.

"No, I was stabbed by a suckin' ghost. Yes! He stabbed me! Jess ran after him and then I lost sight of them. He was being hunted by someone."

"Why didn't you track him?"

"Stab wound. I lost a lot of blood..."

"But why did you get stabbed?" his Aunt Kaity asked

The question bewildered Jared. Her tone implied that he was the cause of his own wound.

He finally lost it.

"I don't know what's going on in his rotten head! I think he was trying to scare us off, but what does it matter anymore?! I don't care about you and your cursed castle and stupid castlefolk. From the day Misa walked into my room, it has been nothing but hell! Pure hell!" He paused and let lose a string of curses, then continued, unable to quell his bottled rage.

"You ruined my life and still, I served Aurumice! I gave a year of my life helping track Nico in the Mines of Briken. I spend my time babysitting Jessi!!! For once, I would like a thank you! Thank you, Jared! Thank you for saving everyone's asses. Thank you, Jared, for helping Misa get the key to open the Gate to Earth, even though you lost everything. Thank you, Jared, for giving your time, thank you Jared for finding Nico! I did what none of you could do, and you still treat me like trash! I gave everything and all you ever do is make pervert jokes about my mage strength. I'M DONE WITH YOU AND I HOPE YOUR CURSED CASTLE BURNS TO THE GROUND!!!"

By now, the tears were streaming down his face, as he felt betrayed and stupid. How could he ever think he could ever be one of the castlefolk?

Teren took a deep breath, kneeling beside Jared.

"I am sorry. Where did you see them last?"

Jared wanted to spat the word Sinari at Teren. The sound was stuck in his teeth. He fought with himself, so close to shouting the secret in front of his Aunt Kaity.

Instead, he answered the question.

"Six days ago, by the docks. She was chasing him, then I lost the trail. The last thing I saw was a grey bicorn, and that's all I know. I have been searching and scanning, but nothing.

Teren took Jared's hand.

"What did Nico say to you?"

"Nothing except to stay away. He's lost his mind."

"Lily and I will go to the docks, Kaity, find out what you can in town. Savina, take care of Jared."

Teren released Jared's hand, and he knew the Sinari had used his magic to quell his anger. He *wanted* to be angrier, but could not find the fury he craved. Instead, his head swam with fever.

The castlefolk dispersed, leaving as quickly as they had barged in. Savina gently helped Jared to the bed. Opened a pack, she pulled out medical supplies.

"I hate you all," Jared grumbled, burying his face in a pillow.

***

Jessica could not fight the veil of sleep. Her body was weak. The strangers woke her up long enough to eat. She asked about Nico, and they assured her he was doing well.

The girl's dreams were muddied with colors that appeared in ways she didn't expect. It was disconcerting and exhilarating at the same time. She stood at the edge of a cliff, overlooking a beautiful valley.

Misa sat next to her, draped in a wispy yellow gown. A little bird perched on her finger.

Candy-scented wind caught her cousin's curly hair. Misa looked out, amethyst eyes shining, lips pursed in a tight little smile.

"Are you real?" Jessica was enamored.

"You're dreaming and you know it," Misa replied. "And I think you're higher than a kitewing."

"No, that's not what I mean," Jessica clarified. "Are you in my mind only, or are you real? Like really you?"

"Didn't I just tell you that you're dreaming?"

"But you're pretty much the princess of dreams. You died in the magic of the Gate. You could be alive."

Misa scrunched up her face in disbelief.

"You know my body is wrapped in a sheet under a meter of dirt in the woods behind Aurumice?"

"I know," Jessica replied. She couldn't take her eyes off her cousin, studying the girl's pretty profile. Even if it was all a dream, she wanted to keep the memory of Misa alive in her mind's eye.

"So why are you here?"

"It's your dream, how am I supposed to know?"

"Damn, the Auroriates must have given me some really trippy drugs," Jessica held her head in her hands.

Misa laughed.

"Yeah, they always had the best stuff. Elven weed is nothing compared to smoking sirens."

"You know that's really not amusing," Jessica argued. "You died because you were high."

"Jess, I died because I tried to control a massive energy field a few kilometers in size…" she shrugged, "and then I tripped down a set of stairs."

"You could be less clumsy in your next life," Jessica replied, looking away. The valley below was filled with little houses.

"I wasn't clumsy. I fell deliberately."

"Why?" Jessica cried out.

"It sucked being trapped in a body that didn't listen to me," Misa pulled her knees up to her chin. "I was thinking of coming back next life as something not human. Really cool and graceful. Maybe a fish."

"A fish?"

"Can't trip down stairs if you're a fish."

"Can't get high either."

"Oh," Misa frowned. "The ocean might have some hallucinogenic anemones. Think I could lick it like a mushroom?"

"Why are you so weird?"

"Creativity is never appreciated," Misa began floating away.

"Wait! Will you stay here?" Jessica asked.

"I can't hold on to this place for long. Besides, I have other people to visit. I'm like the tooth fairy, except without the dental fetish."

The world grew dim. Jessica felt the cliff dematerialize beneath her and her eyes snapped open.

Looking up at the canvas of the tent, Jessica awoke, feeling ill and needing to use the restroom. It was the most awake she felt in a long time. She sat up groggily, the tent was empty and dark. The flap moved softly with a breeze, sunlight peeking in.

Jessica climbed out of bed, chest aching. She found herself dressed in a very thin sheath. Looking around she found a little single-strapped tan tunic, pants, and soft boots on a chair nearby. They looked to be her size and she slipped them on quickly.

Jessica peered out of the tent. Her eyes painfully adjusted to the sunlight.

The tent was in the middle of the most massive Auroriate encampment she had ever seen. Creatures and circusfolk were everywhere, in a never-ending sea of bright colored tents.

A green-haired girl walked by, her face covered by a simple white mask. It was the tradition of the circusfolk to wear masks in public, to make them equal servants in the eyes of the goddess.

"Excuse me," Jessica called out.

"Yes?" the woman said.

"Is there a privy tent nearby? Or a bathhouse? Or is this a 'use the woods' kinda place?"

"We are only staying one more day so there are no privy huts, you can use the woods that way, and there's a nice little river just over that ridge."

"Thanks!" Jessica hurried towards the grove of trees, though her legs were sore and tight.

She was glad Castle Aurumice had actual indoor toilets, though they were little more that holes in the floor. The woods weren't all that terrible once she got over the idea.

Jessica found a secluded little knot of trees, then went in search of the little river. As the green-haired girl had said, there was a stream not far. Jessica washed up then walked back to camp. The air was overly humid and the afternoon buzzed with insects.

She made her way back to the overwhelming and delightfully garish camp. Jessica felt out of place amongst the performers going about their daily routines.

The Holy Circus spread the word of the Goddess by traveling from town to town, enriching the work of the temples. Rigorously trained, the religious performers gave spectacular shows with their unique menagerie of beasts, telling the stories of Aurora. They were a remarkable religion with a truly loyal following.

The circusfolk seemed to pay her no mind in their juggling and acrobatic practice. Someone practiced a jaunty tune on a trumpet nearby.

Jessica knew circusfolk were secretive. When they had camped in Aurumice, they tended to stick to the woods. The castlefolk invited them into the castle, but the circus did not reciprocate. Jessica had never been so far into the center of a Holy Circus camp.

"Hey! You're awake!"

Jessica looked down. A little boy grinned up at her, wearing a dark blue tunic. His hair was raven black, his eyes a startling blue, his face striped on the sides. He was like a miniature Nico. The child had to be a cousin, perhaps six years old.

And he was adorable.

"You're Jessica!" the boy continued.

"Yes, I'm Jessica. Who are you?"

"Reese!"

"Nice to meet you, Reese."

Eagerly, the little boy reached out and took Jessica's hand.

"A big litter of gryphons were born yesterday. Do you want to see them?"

The child didn't wait for a reply and led Jessica through the maze of tents. Her muscles protested, but it felt good to break through the sleepiness.

"Reese, I really need to find Nico…I was with him…do you know if he's here? Or there was a leopardess who said she would help me. Do you know any leopardess?"

"My mum's got spots of a leopard and I think Nico is near the gryphon nest."

The child clutched Jessica's hand so tightly, she began to lose circulation. A stray painted burch wandered into their path and she almost tripped over its hard tortoise-like shell. It snorted, its little hippopotamus face wrinkled and green. Burches made for the most delicious stews, but the circusfolk liked to train them for clown shows.

Reese continued to drag Jessica further into the camp. She saw fire breathers and mechanical bats, majestic winged bicorns and giant snarl-tooth toads.

"I'm glad you brought my brother here," Reese said, sidestepping an errant goose. "I didn't think I'd ever meet him."

"What brother?"

"You brought Nico here."

"Nico is your *brother*?"

"Yes!"

They continued to run between garishly colored tents as Jessica tried to comprehend the child.

Nico had only one sibling, Zari, and she was long past.

"How old are you, Reese?" Jessica chose her words cautiously.

"Six."

It was *possible*. Malachi had died two years prior, and before that, he was with the Holy Circus.

"How do you know that you are Nico's brother?" Jessica asked. Reese led her towards an open area of the encampment.

The child stopped and looked at Jessica strangely. His eyes were startling blue, the same shade as Nico's, but so much wider and more innocent.

"My father and Nico's father was Malachi, and that makes us brothers. And our father went to Aurumice to save Nico from the Mines of Briken, and that's how he died."

Jessica felt a solid lump in her throat, knowing the whole story was darker and more complicated.

Reese was thankfully unemotional over his father. They came to a nest of fabric and fresh smelling hay, nestled under twisted trees.

Jessica marveled at the great creature who sat serenely in the shade.

It was a gryphon.

Jessica had only seen one up close when the circus visited Aurumice, but it was younger and smaller. This beast was an adult. It stood taller than a horse, its golden fur soft and gleaming.

Reese stepped forward, fearless of the huge beast with the pointed beak and lion's paws.

"Hi, Zastrugi, we just came to say hi to your chicklets."

The way Reese said *chicklet* melted Jessica's heart. The hay beneath Zastrugi stirred, one by one, four downy fluff balls emerged. Three were gold like their mother, one was silvery blue.

They were about the size of small house cats, but had enormous paws, soft feathers, tiny wings, big bright eyes and little beaks. Their lion tails wriggled around as they nested in a tight little warm pile of fuzziness.

Reese picked up the blue chicklet.

"Zastrugi is my mother's favorite gryphon and Aunt Dahlia said I get first pick of this litter, and this one is going to be mine."

Jessica's attention was drawn past the chicklet to a figure that sat across the gryphon's nest. The man was dressed in a hood, vacant eyes cast downward.

"Nico?"

"My mother said my brother is sick and we shouldn't bother him until he feels better."

Jessica ignored the child.

"Nico? Are you okay?" she walked around the edge of the gryphon's nest.

Nico looked up, his expression strange and distant.

She sat down next to him.

"Hello," he said, arm trembling.

"Are you okay?" she asked. "What's wrong with your arm?"

"Old injury."

Jessica tried to make sense of the recent past. She did remember sleeping, she remembered waking to eat a sweet porridge, and drifting off.

"You want to hold one?" Reese asked Jessica, lifting up a golden gryphon baby.

Jessica looked down at the child. The creature in his arms extended a fluffy paw and gave a little yawn.

"Am I allowed to hold it?" she asked Nico, wary of animals since her encounter with Bo.

"You just can't keep it," Reese told her. "There aren't many left, but this one is going to be mine."

"Do people hunt them?"

"No, overbreeding and a virus. The Holy Circus is one of the few holders of gryphons left on the continent," Nico explained, carefully taking the chicklet from Reese and setting it in Jessica's arms. The creature had the softest fur Jessica had ever touched. She immediately wanted to run away and snuggle with the creature forever.

"Oh, you are so cute you'd break the internet," she squeaked, carefully cradling the baby gryphon.

She had heard that gryphons were smarter than bicorns, and smarter than any dragon. By the time they reach adulthood, they had the intelligence level of a human child.

A leopardess approached, dressed in lavender and scarlet and carrying a book. She wore small diamond-shaped gems high on her cheeks just below the corners of her eyes. It was a very pretty piercing, but Jessica imagined it must have hurt.

"Jessica, you are awake and well I see!"

"It's you!" Jessica exclaimed. "You were the one I met in the forest! You saved us. Thank you so much, Nico and I would have died if it wasn't for you!"

The white leopardess seemed pleased.

"I could never turn my back on castlefolk," she said, large blue eyes glimmering. "We have met before, but you were too young to remember. I am Sienna Cosette, you know my little sister, Kaity, and I see you have met my youngest son, Reese."

"Yes, I…"

It took a moment for the words to hit Jessica's brain.

Youngest?

Nico had more siblings?

Sienna was Nico's step-mother?

And a lot younger than Malachi.

A lot.

And she was Kaity Cosette's sister?

How the hell did that even happen?

The little gryphon wiggled in Jessica's arms, reaching up and anchoring her back to reality. She felt a little dizzy.

Think, think, and say something, not stupid!

"I know," Sienna said. "Nico told me that Malachi didn't mention me or our children, so we must be a surprise. He didn't know what would happen with Trabalis law and the taxes and the Mines of Briken. He wanted to keep us all out of harm's way."

Jessica's brain wanted to shut down immediately.

"I am sorry for your loss," Jessica said quietly. She *hated* offering condolences because words could never, ever truly reflect the sorrow of death.

"Thank you," Sienna replied.

"You look faint," Nico commented to Jessica.

"Yeah, I don't feel too good. Maybe I need to eat."

"Stew will be brought to the tent soon. We should go."

Nico gently pulled the gryphon chicklet from her arms.

"Yeah," Jessica agreed. "Stew sounds good."

"I am very happy to meet you," Sienna reached out, clasping Jessica's arm. "You are welcome in Dahlia's camp as family, please know that. I promise, I regard all of Malachi's children as my own, especially castlefolk. That welcome extends to you."

"Thank you," was all Jessica could say, not quite understanding Sienna's words.

***

Nico led Jessica back through the dizzying and garish circus. He worried she still had internal bleeding and hurried her along, keeping his head down beneath the cloaked hood.

As he had predicted, the Auroriates had left a small pot of stew on the tiny table inside the tent. Jessica took a seat on the bed as Nico ladled the warm liquid into bowls and handed one to her. The aroma of the stew was very earthy. Small chopped roots floated in a thin broth.

"You have a lot to explain," Jessica's hands quivered.

"Eat," he said, bracing himself for her barrage of questions. Trembling, the pale girl took the bowl. He ladled a little for himself and leaned on the bench opposite her.

Jessica ate a few bites then spoke.

"Where are we? What happened to you? What happened with the mages?"

"How do you feel?" he countered.

"I think I just needed to sit, but my chest still hurts. How did you escape the Mines?"

"I wouldn't call it an escape," he muttered, bringing the spoon to his lips. The broth was well seasoned, herby with just enough salt. After the hell of Briken, food would be a treasure he would never take for granted.

He ate in silence.

"Why aren't you answering my questions?" her voice lowered. "Are we not safe to talk here?"

"No, this camp is safe," Nico replied. "I was taken from the Mines, by slavers. I have no idea who they were. Jess, it was bad, I really do not want to talk about it."

The storm on the airship coiled through his mind and he shivered involuntarily.

"Why didn't you send word to us?"

He struggled with a response. She stared, waiting for an answer. Her concern was sincere, and he knew he should have been compelled to hug her, to tell her everything. Instead, it felt as if a wall had risen between them, leaving him chained on one side.

"Things got messy," Nico replied. "I had a bad run-in with mages. I couldn't go back without endangering the castle, so I was hiding around Yellow Valley until I figured it out."

"Yellow Valley! Jared!" Jessica jumped to her feet. "You stabbed him. We left him back there! We have to go back for him! Why the hell did you stab Jared?!"

Jessica lost her balance and braced herself on a tent support. Nico stood and helped her back to the edge of the bed.

"Easy, you've probably got redvice still in your system and that soup also has relaxing herbs in it."

"They drugged me?" Jessica stuttered.

"Jessi, you were hurt badly. Your body needed to rest."

"Where are we?"

"Twelve days south east of the Yellow Valley."

"How have I been sleeping for so long? We're two weeks from Aurumice?! My mother is going to kill me! Did you send them word?"

"No."

"Why did you stab Jared?!"

"Stop asking me questions," he shamefully turned away.

Nico cringed, his mind muddled. He honestly didn't know why he hurt Jared. Why was he acting so stupidly? Why was everything so difficult?

"Nico, I really need your help," Jessica ignored his plea for silence. "I need to learn how to be a blood mage. Can we find a mystic in the Holy Circus to teach me? Polaris won't accept me. Funny story, really, apparently my dad is actually a mage and he was expelled for killing another mage. And now they don't want me."

Not a story he was expecting, but Jessica's family was always a bit odd.

"What can your powers do?"

"Not much....yet."

Jessica slowly reached out for him, gently lowering his hood. He endured her gaze as she stared at his damaged eye and scarred face.

"I know they tortured you," she whispered. "I can help you, I can help so many others. I just need to find someone to teach me."

Her words gave him a sliver of hope.

"You need to rest," he finally replied. "We'll talk more later."

Nico stood, pulling the shroud over his head, he left her alone.

CHAPTER 22

The next day, Jessica awoke in the strange tent. Her chest still ached, but she knew not to move too quickly.

More alert, she was able to take better stock of her surroundings. Tan and blue, the tent was about eight feet high and ten feet around. The space was crowded with a trunk, a tiny table, two chairs and two sleeping palettes. She noticed that Nico's bed had been pushed further away from hers.

Jessica vaguely recalled Nico sleeping in the tent, but he was nowhere to be found. A few breakfast rolls had been set on the table with a warm pot of tea and a piece of cooked fish.

She helped herself to the food. An embroidered red tunic had been laid out on the trunk, clearly for her. After eating, she readied herself for the day.

By the time she was dressed, Nico had returned. He wore a deep blue cloak and a white Auroriate acolyte mask.

"You look better," he commented, then he paused. "You still have my necklace."

Jessica placed her hand to the talisman.

"Yeah, I always wear it, like a replacement for the castlemark my mom burned off

my shoulder."

She also wanted to tell him that it reminded her of him everyday, but was too scared to hear his response.

"Ready to meet my Aunt Dahlia? She's the one who can help you find a Mystic Healer."

***

Jessica seemed more alert, and that made Nico feel at ease. The night before she had seemed unstable and he didn't know if it was her injuries or the pain killers.

As they walked between the tents, he noticed tiny details that he did not see before. Jessica walked with a confidence in her step, a little lighter, a bit more Centernian. She had taken the time to style her hair in braids, much like Kaity would have done.

He didn't know why, but he found the necklace concerning. He had given it to her on impulse, it felt right at the time, but he hoped she didn't get the wrong idea.

Though he wasn't sure what the right idea was.

Rounding a corner, they passed a small green nightflight with laughing cubs climbing upon her back. Nico was reminded of the first time his father's family visited the castle. It was his happiest and earliest memory. He recalled standing in front of the majestic beast, his father reassuring him that nightflights only ate children seasoned with onion. Nico believed Malachi for a very long time, staying far from onions when the circus visited.

They approached a tent was not remarkably different from the other circusfolk tents. Stitched together with a stiff fabric, it was dyed with gryphon patterns. The tent flaps were closed, but a green cord hung along the side. Nico gently pulled the rope and heard the soft tinkling of melodic bells inside the tent.

After a moment, a strong old hand pulled the tent flap aside.

Aunt Dahlia greeted them, leaning on her staff. She was very ailurian, her ears round, her nose formed into a snout. Her grey hair was entwined into a circlet around her head like a crown. The old woman wore a death choker at her neck as a symbol of mourning. A rose-shaped stone was woven into the fibers and Nico wondered if she wore it for his father. He had never gotten the chance to mourn properly, the guards of Briken would have ripped the mourning choker from his neck.

"I have been expecting you both, please come in."

Nico had not been inside Aunt Dahlia's tent before. She had many fine pieces of carved furniture. The floor was lined with elegant purple woven rugs, laid upon sturdy wooden planks to prevent any rain from seeping in. Each panel of the tent was decorated with the stories of the goddess, painstakingly drawn in brown ink across every surface.

A network of gold lanterns hung across the top of the tent like a spider's web, but in each lantern, instead of a flame, was a glowstone. In the center of the tent, on a pedestal, was the largest white glowstone Nico had ever seen. It was very rare to find a colorless crystal, but it did not surprise him to see one in Dahlia's tent.

Nico removed his mask out of respect and introduced Jessica. Giving her most elegant bow, the teen placed her hands together and splayed her fingers. As the girl rose, her hand went to her lower chest and he knew her ribs were still damaged.

"Please, sit," Aunt Dahlia said, gesturing with her staff to a pair of reed chairs arranged opposite a large wooden desk. Several skulls and stones were arranged on the desk's surface was well as an array of rainbow candles, statues, and a painted portrait of Dahlia's long-deceased wife, Khalalee.

Aunt Dahlia's tent was crowded with an opulent number of artifacts and items. Nico imagined the move from campsite to campsite was a chore, but was certain no one would protest. The graying woman was one of the high elders, ranking higher than his Aunt Amberynn. Aunt Dahlia was the eldest of all his circusfolk aunts and uncles.

"Candy?" Aunt Dahlia asked, gesturing to a bowl. Her eyes were glazed white with cataracts

and Nico wondered how she could see anything.

Jessica politely took a wrapped red piece and put it in her pocket.

"Aunt Dahlia, we are very grateful to the Auroriates for tending to our injuries. Your kindness is without bounds," Nico said, making certain he was polite. Dahlia was his aunt, but her status was very high.

"Nicoveren, we will always welcome you home."

"We are here this morning because I have another favor to ask of you," he said. "Jessica is looking for a healer, one who is a teacher. She's a blood mage, but Polaris Academy is not the right place for her."

"Ah, the Goddess has led you to us, child," Aunt Dahlia grinned. Her fanged teeth had yellowed with age. "We don't have a healer with us, but I will send word through the Circus and find you a teacher."

"Really?" Jessica leaned forward. "I would be so appreciative! Thank you! Thank you for your hospitality and saving our lives, and thank you for this."

Aunt Dahlia sat back.

"In the meantime, would you like to begin the training of an acolyte? If you're with Nico, you certainly would be welcome here."

"Uh," Jessica stuttered, struggling for a proper response. She looked to him for guidance.

"Please, make no decision now," Aunt Dahlia suggested. "Train as initiates, learn what you can. If Nico regards you as family, then you are welcome here."

Jessica made no move to correct Dahlia.

Nico thanked her silently a thousand times over for saying nothing. He knew what his Aunt was implying. If Jessica had denied it, she would not have been permitted to stay so easily.

"If you would like to, you should train here," Nico encouraged.

"Yes, I can be an acolyte, I can do that," Jessica agreed. "If that means I can learn from an Auroriate healer, then yes."

"Ah, the Goddess is so good, bringing you both to us," Aunt Dahlia opened a desk drawer and pulled out a white mask. Like Nico's, it was elegant and white, its surface had subtle decoration pressed into the leather. She handed the mask to Jessica. "Here, you shall have many masks with us, but this is your first."

"Thank you," Jessica accepted the gift with delight.

"Aunt Dahlia, I may not be able to stay long," Nico warned. "My situation may put the Circus in danger."

The old woman smirked, standing with the aid of her staff. A yellow crystal had been embedded into its knobby handle, and Nico suspected it was far more than decorative.

"Child, the Auroriates fear no one."

"Aunt Dahlia, with great respect to you, you must understand my situation is grave. I say this in confidence. I was bought from the Mines of Briken, not freed. Slavers took me on an airship, but we were intercepted by mages. I was forced to fight and I killed one of them. If I stay, the mages will no doubt come looking for me.'"

"Airship? How interesting. Regardless, we can hide you," Aunt Dahlia selected a mask from a shelf. The old woman seemed unsurprised by his words.

"But I killed a mage," Nico repeated.

"The short-sighted idiots in Katanzarko pretend they have authority over this land. If you were forced to fight them, then they were too foolish to see you were a victim. By the laws of Aurora, if you truly are sorry for killing this mage, the holy mother will forgive you."

"But Aunt Dahlia, the holy mother may forgive me, but the mages still will search for me. I need to leave, but will the Circus help Jessica in my absence?"

"Your aura is obscured, like dust caked onto glass. It will do you no good to wander the world without the blessings of the goddess. Like your father, take sanctuary with us. We will help you forge a new identity, and stay away from the ire of the mages."

Nico thought about it a moment. Aunt Dahlia's words were forceful, and she was very experienced and wise. If the mages came crashing through camp, he had at least done all he could to warn her.

Finally, he agreed. Aunt Dahlia seemed pleased.

"Then it is settled. I will advise Sienna to guide you, as is fitting since she is your second-mother. We are happy to have you, and I know your mage skills will be a welcome gift to the circus."

"It's gone," Nico corrected his Aunt abruptly.

"Gone?"

"My fire magic is gone."

"What?!" Jessica could not contain her disbelief. "That's not possible! Is it? I thought being a mage was forever."

"I agree, in all my years I have never heard of a mage ceasing to be one. I know the Mark of Corvalian to block the powers of the psychic, but other than that, nothing can stop a mage."

Aunt Dahlia held up her staff, peering through the crystal.

"This is impossible. In all my years, I have never known any mage or Auroriate to lose their abilities, save for crossing the Gate into the unholy dimension."

Jessica cringed ever so slightly at the mention of her home.

"This is an enigma, and we will help you unravel it as well."

***

After their meeting with Dahlia, they had a brief lunch. Jessica took the time to write a note to her mother, but carefully left out their exact location. She did not want to risk her family dragging her home before she could meet the Auroriate healer.

Sienna approached by the cook fire. The leopardess always seemed to have a happy spring in her step, much like her sister Kaity.

"We will start with candle making, but first you should understand the ways of the camp," Sienna explained.

"I think I would like to go rest instead," Nico excused himself abruptly and left the two women alone.

Jessica found Nico's behavior concerning.

After he left, Sienna crossed her arms.

"They hurt him pretty badly in the Mines, didn't they?" she asked.

"He hasn't said much, but I assume it was awful."

"I've seen it before. You leave a prison, but the prison never leaves you."

"Think the Auroriates can help him?" Jessica inquired.

"We are the people of miracles," Sienna smiled. "Now, come on, you have a tour."

Jessica tried to put Nico out of her mind as she became determined to quickly learn the ways of the Auroriates. The camp was bustling with excitement and energy at all hours. Overwhelmingly large, the troupe was made up of two hundred people, greater than the halls of Aurumice.

Unlike Aunt Amberynn's troupe, which seemed to be a mix of races, Dahlia's was dominantly ailurian, though many wore their masks on a daily basis so it was difficult to really discern.

"We arrange the tents according to the tear of the goddess," Sienna explained. Jessica was familiar with the symbol, it looked much like a normal teardrop, but the origin curved slightly inward.

"The tents of the leaders are always to the north, the beasts of the earth are kept to the east, beasts of the sky to the west. South is everyone else. It seems disjointed from down here but if you were in the air you would seat how we arrange the tents."

"Do you get to fly a lot?" Jessica asked.

Sienna grinned.

"Best part of joining the Holy Circus. I was so obsessed with nightflights as a cub, and I came here; I ride every day with the patrols, and my acts all have flying beasts. It's like a dream. I would have never been able to do that back in the Castle."

"Do you like living in a tent and wagon?" Jessica asked. "I mean, in comparison to Aurumice."

"At first I thought the constant noise was annoying," Sienna said, "but I got used to it. I like Auroriate life, it's easier than living with the castlefolk. Only thing I miss is the libraries of Aurumice, but when you travel you can find different books in different cities."

An Auroriate in a blue mask and shiny blue dragon skin approached Jessica.

"Welcome to the realm of the goddess, stranger," she grinned, offering Jessica a rose. Before Jessica could accept the flower, the woman in blue snapped her fingers. Flames engulfed the blossom, reminding Jessica of Nico's father, Malachi.

"Have you heard the Psalm of the Hydrali?"

Jessica shook her head.

Sienna crossed her arms, smiling wryly.

"It is written in the Book of Fandeer, that across the Lake of Snakerock, north of the Blackturn River was a half-swan man and a wise turtle." Extending her arms, the stranger grinned. Impressive fabric wings unfolded on a sturdy armature.

"This man lived the folly of sloth…"

As the performer told the story, she moved carefully like a dancer. The tale was a metaphor similar to the cricket and the grasshopper, but longer and with more characters. The half-swan man foolishly believed no harm was likely to come to him, and did not prepare for the coming autumn storms. Of course, the wise slow turtle did prepare and was the savior of the swan-man. Jessica found the story difficult to follow with additional characters, but somehow mesmerizing at the same time. The swan-man survived the storm, rescued another, and found love.

A second pair of arms extended behind the stranger, creating a second pair of wings. As the story concluded, a second figure materialized from the cloak. The second performer was of similar height but had a masculine build.

Both bowed.

"Well, how was that?" the female inquired. "Do we get to use the oscuro cloaks on the street? And maybe then the gill masks if we perform it in the big show?"

"Your transition was a little weak," Sienna said. "I could see Kristo when you were talking about the frost giant."

"Hunter, I told you that you lean too much to the left!"

The other performer, presumably Kristo was irritated.

"If you weren't so slow we wouldn't have that problem."

"We're never going to get to do anything fun on the street or in the real show! You're a lousy brother and a lousy partner. Reese could do better!"

Sienna cleared her throat.

"Oh, right, hi," she said to Jessica. "I'm Hunter, it's nice to see you awake."

"Jessica, I know you have met Reese, these are my other two children, Hunter and Kristofori."

"Please to make your acquaintance," Jessica said. She brought her hands together and splayed her fingers in the traditional sign of greeting.

Sienna cleared her throat again.

Kristofori took off his mask, revealing a grey white face with unusual pale leopard marks. He elbowed his sister.

"What? She's not circus folk," Hunter balked.

"Yeah, but she's with our brother," Kristofori argued.

Hunter removed her dragon mask.

There was no doubt the girl was Malachi's daughter. Her face was striped in black. She even had similar piercings on her ears and lips. It was more than the markings and piercings that reminded Jessica of Nico's father. Her eyes had the same arrogance and confidence.

"Sorry," Hunter said. "Glad to see you lived. You were hurt pretty badly, like a horse sat on you."

"I don't think that's far from the truth," Jessica replied. "I think a bicorn rolled over on top of me."

"Why didn't you jump out of its way?"

"Because it was on the edge of a river cliff."

Hunter was incredulous. Jessica wanted to tell the young teen that they were fleeing from mages, but thought it unwise.

"Will you two help prepare for tonight's performance? I'm sure there are costumes to be mended."

Hunter let out an audible sigh.

"Shall we continue our tour, Jessica?" Sienna asked.

"Oh, you dropped this," Hunter said, tossing an object at Jessica. It was the red candy the teen had placed in her pocket after meeting Dahlia.

"Hunter!" Sienna was even more irritated. "That's not how Blessings of the Goddess is supposed to play out."

"Sorry," Hunter shrugged. "I was going to use it for another trick and then I forgot."

Jessica wondered when she had lost the candy.

Kristofori leaned forward.

"You know she took that out of your pocket, right?" the boy said.

Jessica wasn't sure what to make out of the comment.

"You two, you have chores elsewhere," Sienna glared at her children. "Go clean the gryphon pens!"

Hunter rolled her eyes, putting her mask back on. Her brother followed.

***

Nico lay on the bed, quietly trying to read the prayer book. He found reading to be a challenge. Headaches would come on quickly and he wanted to sleep in the soft comfort of the blankets.

The tent flap opened without any announcement. It was Jessica.

"Sienna wanted me to tell you there's a performance tonight if you want to watch." Jessica paused, "And also, I met Hunter and Kristofori."

Nico nodded.

"How are you feeling?" the young woman sat on the edge of her bed.

"Okay," he replied, though he was never really okay. An inescapable weight rested on his back, the Mines twisted with memories of Zia and the airship.

"Your sister looks so much like your dad," Jessica commented. "Did you know you had a step mom?"

"Second mother, a Kilati mother. Step-parents don't exist here."

"Yes, yes, yes, divorce is a banned taboo," Jessica seemed strangely irritated at his words. "Apparently, you just cheat on each other instead."

"My father did not..." Nico inhaled deeply. Yes, he had heard enough rumors to know that his parents secretly kept their relationship open, but they were fiercely loyal to each other. No midnight dalliance would change the fact that they were bonded forever.

"Sienna has got to be like your age," Jessica continued.

"Sienna is almost a decade older than me." Nico said, "So she in her early twenties when the castle fell under the forcefield."

"That age gap though is still kinda...sketchy..."

"You of all people are not to judge my family!" Nico blood boiled. "Your parents ended their marriage out of convenience! Then they built this little hell around you, called it a step family, and went on as if it normal for a child to have two sets of parents! Jessica, it may be your culture, but it's an abomination. I have no doubt my parents loved each other until the last breath they each breathed. They did not just abandon each other because they found it too difficult!"

"Okay, okay, point taken," Jessica held up her hands in defeat. "I get it, earth people suck at marriage, got it! I've heard it enough!"

"You are *not* to judge my parents."

His words were colder than he intended.

"I don't understand you," Jessica scowled. "Why are you so angry all of a sudden?"

"I want to be left in peace," he retorted.

"But you've been locked away for so long, and all you want to do now is hide in a tent?!"

Jessica sighed. "Look, I shouldn't have gotten snappy. The castlefolk found out about my parents being divorced and they pretty much stopped talking to me. That's part of why I left Aurumice. Then I get to Polaris and they don't admit me because of my dad. I'm sick of people judging me for my parents."

Nico heard the girl's words, but didn't really care. He rolled over, his back to her.

He had not intended to get so angry, but something about the conversation stirred a hornet's nest in his heart. He had no reason to dislike Sienna and her children, but yet a part of him did. And he hated himself for it.

"Nico?"

It seemed pointless to talk anymore.

He craved peace.

Though he didn't know where to find it.

CHAPTER 23

The tavern was loud and too warm at midday.

Teren's eyes wandered around the room, watching the patrons go about their daily business. After splitting up with Jared, they had traveled south of the Yellow Valley, moving east towards Fire Grace Lake.

"I do wish Jessica had finished her radio project," Teren stated. "I feel like we are incredibly inefficient with our search." The young man was exhausted. He spent every waking moment trying to stretch his senses to find his cousin and Nico.

"Maybe I should go to Polaris and beg for a finder mage, and you should go back to Aurumice," Lily said.

"I am beginning to think that may be a viable plan."

Finder mages were exceptionally good at locating other mages, able to detect their unique energy signature.

Of course, a finder mage would spell death for Teren if their paths were to cross.

"When do you need to go back to Pennsylvania?"

"I think I've gotten myself into trouble already."

"Your job?"

Lily sipped the cup of mead. The older blonde woman was dejected.

"Pretty sure they fired me by now, but we have savings this time. If I can find a similar job in a month we should make the mortgage payment."

"Lily, maybe you should go back."

"I trust you and Jared and the others will search to the ends of the earth, but I'm her mother, you expect me to just go home as if nothing were wrong?" Lily asked.

The door to the tavern opened, letting in sunlight and a welcome breeze. Fentalon stepped through, shrouded in a heavy brown cloak. He scanned the crowd and made his way over to their table.

"That's odd, we were supposed to meet you in two days?" Teren said.

"I know, glad I found you," Fentalon was breathless. "A letter came to the post box in Red Rustle. I can't read a word of it but the address. It went to Aurumice, but Alba forwarded it on."

He pulled it out of his pocket and set it on the table.

Teren opened it. Inside the leather tube was a rolled scroll. The scroll was wrapped in ribbon with a word scrawled across it.

Teren held it up.

It was Teren's name, written in the English alphabet.

"It's Jessi," Lily leaned forward.

Teren opened the letter.

We are safe with friends.
Don't worry about us.
Blessings of the goddess.
;-)
Jess

He handed it to Lily, letting her read it in silence.

"What does it say? What does it mean?" Fentalon asked.

"It's the language of my home," Lily explained.

"She's safe, but it doesn't say where," Teren explained. "And what's this odd punctuation at the signature line?"

"It's a winking face," Lily explained.

"Ah," Teren pondered a moment. "Ah, I see. Clever! You see the message here?"

"Yeah, yeah I do. If I understand this right, she's with the Holy Circus," Lily told Fentalon. "We need to find them, we need to contact Amberynn."

"But if she doesn't want to be found, she won't be found," Teren stated. "She could have spelled out her location."

"You think it's a lie? What if she's in trouble?"

"It's written in English, so that's a good sign," Teren reassured. "Let's go back to the castle and have Corwin read the note and see if there is anything underlying. From there we can contact Aunt Amberynn."

"But what if this is a distraction?" Lily persisted.

"Lily, please," Fentalon said. "We will find out."

His words were kind.

As frustrating as their situation was, it made it convenient for Teren to repair the damage Jessica had done to her mother's relationship with Fentalon. It didn't take much influence. Every time Lily expressed worry about her daughter, he allowed Fentalon to feel great compassion for the woman. In time, that compassion turned to support for her cause, and then support for her, and then Fentalon began to feel forgiveness.

It was a little wrong, but Teren knew at Fentalon's core he wanted to look away from Lily's odd past.

Away from Aurumice, there were no snickering of the castlefolk to squash.

Teren held up the letter again.

"Lily, think about the letter. You said yourself, there are very few people who can read this alphabet. If she was in trouble, she could have certainly spelled it out clearly. She isn't in trouble. She's safe."

Lily leaned forward, pressing her fingertips to her temples.

"But why the damn Circus?"

"It makes good sense," Fentalon said. "Nico would get them safe haven, and if that boy is in trouble, circusfolk will make it a priority to protect them."

"If she's safe, then she's acting stupid."

Teren hesitated, not sure what to say.

"We are better off returning to Aurumice, and reaching out to the Circus directly," Fentalon advised. "It would be foolish to run across the countryside looking for them. We just need to beg audience with one of the leaders, and they will tell us where to go."

Lily considered his offer.

Teren agonized for a moment, then made a decision.

Giving Lily the tiniest bit of trust and hope, centered on Fentalon.

Lily was exhausted buried under the weight of her responsibilities. The nudge was enough to convince her to believe them and agree to return home.

***

At nightfall, Jessica sat on a high bench in the tall circus tent in a crowd of at least a hundred people. They sat high up in the stands, a little distanced from the paying audience.

Sides aching ferociously, Jessica regretted walking around so much that afternoon. Her desire to see the Holy Circus perform overrode her pain. The teen rationalized that she could be just as sore sitting alone in the tent as sitting on the bench watching the show.

Nico accompanied her, sullen and angry. It was a very strange feeling. Never had he been cross with her before, and she didn't know how to take it.

Worse, he didn't seem to want to talk.

The lights dimmed as the musicians played. Music filled the tent with booming horns and percussion. The crowd cheered.

Jessica had seen the performance of the Holy Circus years ago. She was astounded that they could achieve so much without electricity. Their secrets were closely guarded. Most presumed it to be divine magic.

Aunt Dahlia greeted the crowd. She reminded Jessica of Aunt Amberynn, and would have easily mistaken the sisters for each other under the theatre lights and makeup.

A dozen pure white bicorns circled Aunt Dahlia, galloping obediently in intricate patterns.

"Frostfire would never be able to do that," Jessica commented to Nico. "She would just stop and leave to find a snack."

Nico did not reply.

"Are you really going to be mad at me all night?" Jessica asked.

"I am not angry at you," he replied.

"Then why are you quiet?"

Nico shrugged.

"I'm tired. Being here is strange, and I really prefer not to discuss my parents, especially with you."

Jessica could not comprehend why he wasn't just happy to be out of the Mines.

A fire ball disrupted their conversation, exploding through the tent. Jessica flinched until the fire turned into hundreds of pink butterflies, delighting the crowd.

"How do they do that?" Jessica was enamored. "These illusions are unreal."

"It's a secret," Nico smiled.

"Will I learn it?"

"It takes a very long time. The big tricks I don't even know. You need to pass acolyte training."

The idea delighted Jessica. Healing plus the ability to create illusions would be an amazing combination.

With a shimmering twinkle of bells, the lighting changed and the first act began. Every performance was tied to a story of the Goddess Aurora, and incorporating a moral lesson. Pageantry and showmanship kept the audience deeply engaged.

If church was like this, Jessica would never miss a Sunday service.

Jessica found herself clinging to the edge of her seat. Her lungs burned from her injuries, but the performance was too beautiful not to watch.

A singer upon the back of a small blue nightflight told the tale of the blue-bellied snail, roughly an allegory of the tortoise and the hare. Her dress was feathery orange and blue. As the woman sang, she seemed to pulse with a red-purple light, the same rhythm as a heartbeat.

The nightflight and his skilled rider twisted and turned tightly around the support posts, somehow not crashing and bringing down the tent.

As the story neared the end, the nightflight flew up to the apex of the tent. Below, a pool of blue water was revealed. The singer placed her hands over her mouth, then dived into the illuminated blue water.

Dancing under the water, the performer created waves and shadows that shifted with mesmerizing patterns.

Jessica missed the point of the water metaphor.

"How does she stay under water so long?" she whispered to Nico.

"That I can tell you," he replied. "It's a gill mask, she doesn't need breathe for hours."

"Amazing," Jessica was giddy, "can I try one of those at some point?"

Nico shrugged.

"Never used one. But Sienna looks like she knows what she's doing, so you can ask her."

"Wait, that's Sienna?" Jessica was astounded.

"Yeah, it's Sienna," Nico replied. "Her voice was not an obvious clue?"

"No, it really wasn't. That singing and flying amazing, this afternoon she just seemed plain and normal to me."

Sienna continued to swim, creating more intricate patterns in the water. It seemed like she used an oily ink that held together long enough to create striking lines.

"Jessi, don't be naïve, you know Auroriates are never what they seem," Nico replied.

"I am not naïve, and you're being a little obnoxious tonight."

"Well you're asking foolish questions."

"What is your problem? Just because you don't like your new mom, you can't dump all your grumpiness on me."

"I said I don't want to discuss my family," he whispered, glaring at her.

"Well, we're staying with them, so how can I ignore them?"

"Leave my father's choices in the past."

"If I knew it would make you this angry, I wouldn't have brought it up. You're in such a terrible mood!"

"Did you ever think for once that I did not want to be found?" Nico asked her abruptly.

His reply astounded her.

"I just thought—"

"Stop assuming anything, you are annoying."

Jessica bristled. "Well, if I'm so annoying, I'll be getting my own tent tonight. "

Nico shook his head.

"Not wise," he whispered. "You won't be allowed to travel with the circus unless they believe you are with me. You want to meet the mystic healer, then I'm your best chance."

Jessica continued to watch the show, not sure how to reply. The situation was nothing like she expected. In all her dreams, she envisioned Nico's return to be amazing, not miserable.

She resolved that she would wait it out until she met the healer, and then figure out her next move.

The surface of the pool crystalized as Sienna vanished into the darkness.

CHAPTER 24

Jazzy holiday music played over the mall speakers. If Ashlin heard a cover of *Jingle Bell Rock* one more time, she was quite sure she would bludgeon someone.

"Do you think Jessica would like this for Christmas?"

It was the seventeenth time Ashlin's mom had asked the question. She had begun counting after the third, or maybe it was the fourth time. The statement was shuffled in between 'would your dad like this?' and 'do you think so-and-so at church needs this?'.

No one had heard from Jessica in almost two months. A case worker from child protective services had been to their home, but there was no real follow up.

Lily had said that her daughter ran away with her cousins.

Carrie Anne wavered between assuming her step daughter was on an adventurous holiday and hysterical fits of worry.

"Do you think Jessica would like this scarf for Christmas?" Carrie Anne repeated, holding out the bluebird patterned scarf.

Ashlin shrugged. Her jacket was too warm. She was bored.

"Maybe the green?" her mother continued.

"I can tell you what I would like for Christmas."

"Oh Ash, I already bought your gifts."

"Okay, I don't know what Jessica would want for Christmas."

"But you talk to her."

"Barely before she left."

"I think the blue," Carrie Anne asserted, adding it to the small pile over her skeletal wrist.

"Here, Mom, let me carry those," Ashlin reached out and took the clothing.

"Oh, you're always so helpful," Carrie Anne smiled.

"Can we get tacos before we leave?"

"I need to find your father and see what he wants to do."

As they approached the register, Carrie Anne stopped at a display of silver earrings.

"Do you think Jessica would like the red or the blue to match the scarf?"

"She doesn't have pierced ears," Ashlin reminded. "Isn't that like the fifth gift you've picked out for her?"

"Oh, but they're mostly small," Carrie Anne selected a blue beaded bracelet instead.

They approached the register.

"What if Jessica doesn't come back...in time for Christmas?" Ashlin regretted the words as soon as they popped out of her mouth. It was no good to suggest the older teen was never returning, it would just make Carrie Anne more upset.

"Of course she'll come back! It's Christmas! Why would she miss Christmas?"

"But we don't know that. We don't know where she is."

"Well, Lily said she's off somewhere with her cousins."

"Skipping school for two months, and that's okay?"

"No, it's not okay," Carrie Anne snapped.

"Well, where is she? What if she's never coming back? This is not normal, and there's something really wrong with her mom."

"Ashlin, please do not talk about other people that way, it's rude."

"She's right though," the cashier interrupted. Behind the counter stood a high school girl with hair dyed black and red. Glittery snowflake temporary tattoos trailed from the corners of her eyes.

Carrie Anne paused, looking at the girl's nametag.

Felicia

"Mom, that's Lee, Jessi's friend."

"Sorry, I didn't mean to interrupt your conversation," Lee said, scanning the items carefully. "Is Jessi really missing?"

"Missing? No," Carrie Anne pulled her credit card from her meticulously organized wallet.

"We don't know where she is, and she hasn't called in two months, that's missing," Ashlin corrected.

"She's run away, and that's hard to say, but yes, she's run away," Carrie Anne explained.

"With her weird cousins?" Lee asked. "And your total is ninety-two thirty-six."

Lee gestured to the card reader.

"What do you know about her cousins?" Carrie Anne asked as her credit card was processed.

Ashlin was equally curious.

"Not much. Nico is nice, but he's just their friend. Teren is her cousin, he pretends to be a gentleman, but he's really rude."

"Do you know where he lives?"

"No, doesn't even have a cell phone, but Jared does."

"Who is Jared?" Carrie Anne said thoughtfully. "I remember that name."

"He's the one who was at the hospital," Ashlin said, "and at Halloween in the mall."

"Let me give you my number and maybe we can talk more when you're not working," Carrie Anne asked, flipping through her purse. Producing her hearts and puppies notepad, she scribbled down her number.

Lee took the piece of paper.

"I don't really think I'll be able to help you," she said. "I don't know Jessi anymore. I tried to be her friend, but she just has her own priorities."

"But anything you say might lead us to her," Carrie Anne encouraged. "Can I get Jared's number from you?"

"I don't have it," Lee replied, handing the bag to Carrie Anne. "Hope you find her. Have a nice holiday."

***

Sunset faded over the stable yard. The weather in Centernia had begun to chill with autumn's breath.

Teren sat on a rooftop perch, wrapped up in an old blanket. To his right was a decanter of spirits and a glass. Cradling his violin, he carefully plucked out a tune, lazily balancing the bow on his fingers. His feet propped up on the stone edge of the building as he relaxed into a heavy plush chair.

Below, he watched Penrik light the torches that now illuminated the stable yard. It was terribly inefficient and foolish. Teren hated running the castle without electricity.

His stomach was a little sour from the spirits, and he tried to remember if he had eaten an actual meal that day. No matter how much paperwork he trudged through, no matter how many problems he mediated, it never ended. The castle was always two inches away from crisis, whether it be Corwin's paranoia of needlewasps or little Temi lost in the woods.

A door opened behind him.

Teren did not need to turn to know it was his aunt.

Lily approached, then sat on the ledge overlooking the yard. They watched in silence as the herders and stable hands brought in the livestock for the night.

"Teren, am I a bad mother?" Lily asked.

Jessica had been gone two months. It had been confirmed that she was with the Holy Circus, and safe, but their Circus contacts refused to specify where. He prodded and poked, but it seemed as if every liaison they sent actually did not know the location of his cousin and Nico.

His powers were useless.

"Teren?" Lily repeated.

"What?" he asked, looking at his glass. The alcohol was too sugary and could have used ice cubes. He wished he had ice cubes. Why did he listen to Trabalis?

"It's Christmas Eve," Lily said. "And she's not home."

Teren's mother had loved Christmas with a fervent devotion, so he understood the significance. The date no doubt fueled Lily's worry.

"Am I a bad mother. I feel like a failure. Did I drive her away? Does she hate me?"

"You want me to answer that?" he replied, "Because you shouldn't ask someone like me a question you don't want the truthful answer to."

Lily's heart was heavy with despair. Teren felt shameful. He knew he didn't need to be so cold, not when his aunt was seeking comfort. It was rare she came to him for advice.

The woman was lost.

A gentle breeze brought the kiss of night and a sweet ballad of evening insects.

"I shouldn't have slept with Talon. She ran away with Jared out of revenge, and now that she found Nico, she's never coming back."

Teren huffed in amusement, taking a sip from his glass. The honey-colored liquid pleasantly warmed his throat. Maybe ice cubes were unwarranted.

"Aunt Lily, I think the drama with Talon was a convenient excuse for Jessica to run. She's been upset a long while, we should have listened to her more. She worries about Carrie Anne."

"But blood mages can't cure cancer…"

"I know that, you know that. But look at all of us who surround her. You freeze and fry things, Jared is an amazing spy, Corwin reads the past, Kaity moves things with her mind, we have these strengths we use that defy logic. Even Wadjette as Vice Captain of the guard, equal to Jessi's age, is impressive without a speck of magic. Jessica wants to earn her place."

"But she keeps the lights on! That freezer would have failed a half-dozen times without her!

"And then you have Talon questioning if she knows what she's doing, and the castlefolk scared of wires."

"You told her to shut down the electrical system!"

"It was easier than arguing with Trabalis."

"You could have stood by her."

"And so could you," Teren leaned forward. "You are her mother, you are the one who is supposed to help her. Jessi doesn't feel like anyone takes her seriously."

"She is important!"

"When is the last time you told her that?"

"But she knows!" Lily argued. "I don't need to tell her that I love her and she makes me proud."

"But you do need to *say those words*," Teren explained.

"What about you? Why don't you tell her?"

"I do, but your words mean more than mine."

Lily didn't reply. She silently wallowed in her sadness.

Teren set the glass down onto the stone. The last rays of autumn sunlight reflected in the crystalline cup.

"I think you've been a good influence," Lily said. "She listens more to you than she ever does me or her father."

"I'm her peer not her parent," Teren pointed out. "My apologies, you have the difficult job."

Lily rested her head in her hands.

"I am proud of her, I don't know why I don't say it, but I really am!"

"Because my grandparents never said it to you?" Teren suggested. It was rare he mentioned them.

Lily sighed, "We were never good enough. I tried so hard to make them happy, and your mom just gave up she ran in the opposite direction. I guess that's what Jessica is doing. But I'm afraid if I'm not strict, she'll think it's okay to do stupid things."

"Like run away from home and join the circus? Aunt Lily, when we do find her, you need to change your approach."

The door behind them opened.

Teren sighed.

So much for enjoying the sunset in peace.

"Hi, hope you don't mind my intrusion," Jared said. "Had something I needed to say to Lily, privately, and by privately, I mean I needed Teren as a buffer zone in case you got angry and went all thunder-god on me."

"I'm not mad at you anymore, Jared."

"Thanks, good, keep that in mind. Ooooh, is that a bottle of sweet flower brandy?"

"Yes, and no, you can't have any."

Jared walked over and took Teren's glass, adding more brandy to it and sitting on the stone wall that bordered the roof. After the argument in the Yellow Valley, Teren had brokered peace between Jared and Lily. Once his wound was bandaged and his fever mitigated, Jared was back to his amiable self.

"So, I told you both a half-truth as far as why we left Polaris."

Jared sipped Teren's brandy slowly.

"Do you want me to push you off the edge of the roof?" Teren asked.

"Hear me out, this is about to be a mind-blowing revelation, and this may be my last drink."

Lily crossed her arms.

"Go ahead, what do you need to tell me?"

"I should have said this before, but I was angry, but now I think you should know. Jess and I didn't *choose* to leave Polaris. We ran from a really angry Lady Carmelina Lightsong. She's the oldest blood mage in Polaris. And Lightsong was mad because she read Jessi's blood. Apparently, Jessi's dad was her former student, and that didn't end so well."

Lily's emotions shifted so quickly, Teren didn't doubt the truth in Jared's words.

The woman was angry and embarrassed.

Really angry.

Teren held a hand up.

"Don't!"

He dampened her anger.

Just a tiny bit.

Just enough to save Jared from getting punched again.

"Aunt Lily, please, do not kill the messenger," Teren said.

"You should never have brought her to Polaris!" Lily argued. "These are my private affairs, stay out of them!"

"I'm trying to explain what's going on in your daughter's head, Lily!" Jared pleaded. "She's upset, she's hiding, and I want her to come home instead of living out with those circus freaks!"

"No, you've made everything worse!" Lily stormed to the door.

"Maybe you should try explaining and apologizing, instead of being angry!"

"I should have sold the house, left the Gate, moved away!"

"Aunt Lily, please listen...we were just talking about this..." Teren pleaded.

"Jessi is not the one I'm angry with!"

Jared shrunk back in fear. "Why are you mad at me? I told you the truth!"

"I'm not angry at you either! I'm preventing myself from killing you!"

"Aunt Lily!"

"Just go to hell!" she slammed the door.

"See?" Jared gestured with his pilfered glass. "Why does she do this all the time? She makes all her own problems."

Teren took his glass back and sat down.

"You should just change her," Jared said. "Make her happy."

"Not right. I promised her I would never do that...much."

"She'd never know."

"No."

Teren cradled the neck of his violin, plucking out a ballad.

"So, I wonder if we know Jessi's father," he mused.

"Oh, we do," Jared grinned. "It's Stephen, but here he was Savartos Sarkisian."

That *did* surprise Teren.

The name also had a very familiar sound to it. He couldn't remember why, but that name was important.

"See, her parents lie to her. You can lie to Lily and change her emotions, balances the world, everyone is happy."

"But did they actually lie? I imagine Jessica never asked her father if he was a mage. If the question was not asked, then there was no lie."

"Interesting point. You know Jess isn't going to see it that way."

"Well that is her choice."

"You don't seem very surprised by any of this."

"I had no idea, honestly, but I do know my aunt has always struggled with truth. I think it has more to do with fear, and hurt, a lot of hurt. She would rather bury a truth than deal with the waves it may cause."

"You know, Lily as a person is okay. If I wasn't always caught between her and Jess I don't think I'd mind her so much."

Teren chose not to reply, watching the sun set over the stable yard.

"Speaking of hurt, you have been drinking quite a bit more as of late. It's not healthy."

"Hypocrite," Jared scoffed.

"I drink when I want to block out everyone's business. What's your problem?"

"Guess I am the same."

CHAPTER 25

Each day tumbled by as Jessica found a new normal. She avoided thinking about the earth calendar as the days ticked past Christmas and New Years.

As she waited patiently to meet the Auroriate healer, the teen immersed herself in the religion. She had difficulty reading the prayer books, they were written in Madiernian script and the language of the Auroriates. She asked Nico for help, but he seemed to have little interest in assisting her.

Nico was a stranger. He slept often and spent most of his time alone, reading in silence. When a formal prayer session was called, he was present, respectful, but as soon as his presence was not mandated, he was gone again.

"He's an old goat, isn't he?" Hunter remarked, carrying buckets of entrails out to the featherwing troughs. "I think he hates people."

Jessica shook her head. "He didn't used to be like this."

"I haven't seen him do much of anything since he got here."

"You know what depression is?" Jessica asked. "Is that a word your people use?"

"Sad?" Hunter asked.

"No, more than sad. It's a different kind of sad. It's a sad that stops people from getting out of bed in the morning. You think too much about the wrong things."

"When we got word that our father died, my mother hid in her tent for a week. He's sad for our father?"

Jessica nodded wordlessly, not wanting to tell Hunter the details of Nico's life. Jessica dumped her bucket into the feeding trough. Fish and intestines sloshed out.

A group of baby featherwings bounded to the feast, eager to eat. They were knee-height rounded little dragons, their wings soft and fluffy.

Typically the tiny beasts were fed by their own parents, but the Auroriates also brought them snacks to domesticate them. Of the featherwings, there was a particular grey one that Jessica liked.

She ran her hands along the creature's horns and scratched behind her ears. Unlike nightflights, featherwings had a few areas where their scales were thin enough that they could easily feel a human's nails. Closing her jewel-like eyes, the featherwing purred like a cat.

Though Jessica had not learned anything of healing, she had learned much of the Auroriates. Their creatures were most interesting. Featherwings were much like cats— aloof, intelligent, selective. Gryphons were like dogs— loyal, bouncy, energetic. Nightflights were very skittery, fierce, dangerous, but had impeccable memories. When trained well, the bat-winged lizards could carry out more complex commands than either featherwings or gryphons.

All three were amazing to ride above the treetops.

The featherwing rolled onto her back and took a playful nip at Jessica's finger. The razor-sharp
beak pierced the girl's skin. Jessica unceremoniously dropped the creature, who bounded away to join its brethren.

"You're really bad with animals," Hunter commented as Jessica sucked on the wound.

"You're a really bad Auroriate," Jessica examined the bite. It was small, only about a half inch.

Her back to Hunter, she stared at the wound, willing it to close.

Please, please, please, magic help me

Instead of healing, the wound grew to an inch in length. Purple blotches spread across the finger.

Startled, she pressed her thumb against the cut, hoping it would knit before Hunter noticed.

"Jessica! We are working on candle making," Sienna called out as she approached. "Can you find Nico?"

"Sure," Jessica held her hand casually out of Sienna's line of sight.

"I wouldn't waste your time, mother," Hunter remarked. "He'll never be a proper Auroriate."

"Hunter, that is rude of you."

"But he only goes to prayer gatherings."

"Healing takes time, daughter."

The word healing rattled around in Jessica's brain.

"He's not sick," Hunter scoffed. "He's just sad and lazy."

Sienna was at the edge of her patience.

"You will clean the impacted scent glands of the gryphons for the next season if you keep talking like that."

Hunter looked as if she was going to be sick.

"Sorry, very sorry," the teen apologized.

"Now, Jessica," Sienna smiled. "Please, tell Nico I would like to speak with him."

***

The unpleasant smell of hot wax filled the large yellow tent. Nico and Jessica joined the young acolytes, gathered around cauldrons of bright colored liquid. The wax-filled pots were all set into a bubbling water bath heated by a large coal oven.

Nico noted that the young circusfolk were very cat-like, tiger striped and spotted. Jessica was the only one in the tent with pale smooth skin and round human ears. Nico felt like they were intruding.

Jessica tried to make small talk, but Nico remained silent.

Sienna led the group, her hair bound up beneath a scarf.

"Making the holy relics is a common task among our people, it is a skill you must master before you are allow to street preach or perform on your own."

Sienna showed them the technique, a wick string was draped over a thin little plank, hanging on either side. A little weight was affixed to each base. The candle was dipped in wax, then in water to cool. Back into the wax, then into water. Over time, the hot wax formed a taper and eventually two long candles took shape on either side of the plank.

"As you work, you pray," Sienna explained. "Now, Nico, do you remember the Prayers of the Prophet Juniper?"

"Yeah, some of them," Nico nodded.

"And Jessica?"

Lines of worry creased on the girl's face.

"I read them, but I don't have them memorized."

297

"Do not stress. You clear your mind, you give thanks to the goddess. When all the candles are complete, they are blessed by a high elder, so they are still most holy."

Jessica nodded. Nico watched her face, the teen seemed very intent on learning the technique.

He had no desire to make candles. It was a waste of their time.

Sienna showed them again, and set them up with their own stations. The circusfolk youths worked diligently, murmuring. They dipped the candles in different colored pots, hands moving quickly as they built up dozens of colors on each waxy base. As the candles were still warm, they used special tools to carve away designs. Peeling the layers of color, patterned lines were revealed.

Nico was mesmerized in spite of himself. He had seen the elaborate candles of the circus, but had no idea how they were formed. Each candle was a slightly different variation of curves and curls, animals and symbols. They worked with a delicacy Nico envied, as he knew his hands had become clumsy. His monocular vision also didn't make things any easier.

"As soon as you have made your dozen, you may take leave for lunch," Sienna said to the youths.

One by one they finished, setting their stunning creations on a table with dozens of other bright candles. Sienna inspected each carefully and dismissed the youths.

Jessica and Nico were still working at the dip technique, trying to create layers of equal thickness with no bubbles and machine-like precision.

"I will stay and watch a bit," Sienna explained, crossing her arms.

Nico fixed the weight to the wick with wax, then draped the string.

"Nicoveren, I wish to speak to you. May I talk freely in front of Jessica?"

"Yes," Nico replied. He didn't like how Sienna used his full name and he disliked her politeness even more.

"I wanted talk to you more about your father and I."

Nico shrugged, rolling up his sleeves, exposing the deep scars.

"I believe my father was fortunate to find love a second time," Nico stated, hoping to stomp out the conversation as quickly as possible.

"I am grateful he brought me to the Auroriates," Sienna said. "And I miss him terribly."

You don't know what it's like to miss him, or be abandoned by him and still miss him every day.

Sienna pulled her candle out of the wax and picked up a knife, peeling away beautiful red petals, swirled with white and gold. Nico wanted to tell her to stop talking, but he remained silent. He didn't want to know the details.

"Your father traveled often, seeking a way to break the magic of the forcefield, but he always came back. And he never stopped talking about you, how he was determined to find you."

The words stung, but Nico said nothing, dipping his candle repeatedly in the orange wax.

"Nico, isn't that hot?!" Jessica warned.

Steaming, the wax had dripped onto his nerve-damaged hand, but he had hardly noticed. He wiped it away. A little welt formed on his skin.

Sienna placed a reassuring palm on his shoulder.

"I am sorry you suffered so badly in the mines of Briken. Your father was ready to take that sacrifice from you."

"It's past," Nico said tersely, shrugging her away.

"Is it true?" Sienna asked. "How he died?"

Ah, here was the question he waited for. It had taken Sienna two turns of the moon to bring it up.

"Is it true Corwin killed him with a knife? For no reason? That's what we were told."

Nico held the candles suspended in air. If he recalled, there was some history between Sienna and Corwin, but had had been too young to know the details nor care.

Jessica continued to move methodically, refusing to look up. Nico tried to formulate an answer.

"I'm sorry if this is difficult for you," Sienna said.

"Yes, Corwin did. I was there, we both were," he glanced at Jessica. "And he walks free?"

"I doubt Corwin's intent was to kill," Nico snapped. "My father had locked Kaity in the cellars."

"Well, my sister was always impulsive and arrogant."

Nico disagreed with Sienna, but chose his next words very carefully. He could not create riffs in the Circus.

"Sienna, I lost my father and my freedom, but I will not raise a hand against Corwin. My father was in the wrong for imprisoning Kaity, regardless of what he feared. Aurumice has its own rules. Corwin has my pardon."

Nico felt he had to defend Corwin, even though he wished the grey cat would fall off the face of the planet. He really did it for Kaity.

Sienna pondered this, cutting tiny birds into the sides of the red candle.

"You know my father often acted without thinking. He was paranoid around mages, and he never liked Kaity. Please, do not misunderstand me," Nico continued. "I respect you, as his Kilati wife."

"Good, that was really my biggest fear," Sienna gave a small smile, though she was clearly unhappy with his words. "I am glad the goddess brought you to us. I want Hunter, Kristo and Reese to hear what you have to say. You knew Malachi differently than they did. I want them to know, to not feel so distanced. They are castlefolk and maybe someday they may return."

Nico's skin prickled at the idea. He liked his siblings well enough, but he did not feel inclined to welcome them in Aurumice.

If he ever returned.

"Hunter, is all her father... very much of the Auroriates, and I suspect Dahlia wants her to lead someday. Kristofori, he is a quiet thinker, he is young but I can see him being scholarly, perhaps the sort who has trouble accepting all of the glory of the Goddess. He would like to see the castle. And Reese, oh he is into everything and anything."

"He is a very sweet boy," Jessica said softly, setting her third batch of candles to the side. She had a knack for dipping, all of hers were perfect. All of Nico's candles were misshaped and embarrassing.

"Reese is so excited to get to know you both. You are the first castlefolk my children have met, and I don't talk much about that part of me. But the mark on your back means you never really lose Aurumice, no matter how far away you are."

Sienna finished the large crimson candle. When it was done, it had spires, like the castle. The birds were actually winged bicorns, dancing between tigers. It was clear, the candle was in honor of their home.

Sienna leveled the base with a warm plate and dipped the candle in a shiny clear protective glaze. It was a masterful work of art.

"Jessica, may I gift this to you?" Sienna asked.

The girl nodded.

"I had also heard your mother tried to take the debt, and go to Briken in my husband's place. That makes me happy, and I am grateful for her."

It was a half-truth. Lily had indeed done so, partially out of guilt, but more so as a bargaining chip. At the time, they had assumed Malachi had imprisoned both Kaity and Teren, and she tried to free them both, not knowing that Teren had chosen to hide on the earth.

But it was a sacrifice nonetheless.

Jessica accepted the candle, grinning in delight.

"Shall we break for lunch?" Sienna asked.

Nico nodded. He wanted to say something else polite to Sienna, but couldn't move past his irritation. Sienna spoke so kindly, but he wished the ground would open and pull him into its depths.

CHAPTER 26

Teren and Fentalon walked down the east hallway. Fentalon spoke about the guard, giving a report on their latest progress. Teren nodded, but his mind was elsewhere.

"Today we commenced cleaning the chamber underneath the ballroom," Fentalon was saying. " I think it will make for a good training ground in the winter months."

Beneath the ballroom was a large chamber with a dirt floor. There was a time when it had been used for the storage of carts and wagons. In inclement weather, herds of livestock could be driven below ground for shelter.

"I have not been down there in some time, is it full?"

"No, on contrary, empty. It's been empty for years, but very muddy. We have some drainage issues."

As they walked, Teren drifted further into his own thoughts. It had been more than three months since Jessica had contacted them and the silence was troubling. Teren began to doubt this plan to let Jessica have space. He also not happy the Holy Circus seemed unwilling to assist them.

As they passed the library, Teren held up a finger.

"Ah, one moment. Corwin had wanted to speak with me and I should stop before I forget."

Teren open the door to the library.

The room was musky with the fragrance of ancient books. Teren and Fentalon walked in, passing by the small tree kept in a planter. It had once grown in the floor of the library itself, but Corwin had preserved a portion and tended it carefully in a pot.

The young castlefolk were gathered in a corner of the room. Eve La'Roch watching the children. Teren was curious what they gathered around. On the table was a metal box as big as a loaf of bread. One side was a glass window.

"Do they bite?" Aden leaned forward. The little black panther cub was intrigued.

Teren crossed his arms.

Did what bite?

"Not per say," Corwin said. "Needlewasps are parasites. They need a host for their young and prefer laying eggs in people. That is the true danger of these insects."

"Ewwwwww," Abrianna took a step back. Teren agreed with the panther child's repulsion. Frost needlewasps were disgusting, and he was not too pleased to have them in the castle.

"After the larvae emerge, they fall to the ground and burrow deep. They can stay in hibernation for years."

Fentalon walked forward, curious. The children greeted them both.

"Your timing is excellent," Corwin said. "I was just explaining the cubs about the fascinating evolution between the common and the frost needlewasp."

Fentalon peered at the little box with the small window.

"These shouldn't be kept in the castle," he stated. "One could trigger an outbreak of Puce fever."

"Actually, people are not carriers for Puce fever," Corwin informed him. "The bacteria only transmit through blood, not other means. So, the possibility of catching the fever from someone who has it is low."

Fentalon glanced up.

"And the person who catches the fever will be dead within a few days if not treated properly."

Teren could sense the argument brewing. Fentalon was fearful of the insects, Corwin seemed to regard them with no harm. Undoubtedly Fentalon would demand their removal.

"For the safety of the castle, they should be destroyed."

And there it was.

"I am studying them *for* the safety of the castle. They were delivered yesterday by a mage courier, at the request of Polaris Academy and the Consortium of Mages. We know little of this new breed of frost needlewasps."

"Polaris should study them, not you."

The insects in the box buzzed in anger.

"Children," Teren stated, hoping to cut through the argument. He didn't like living needlewasps, they made his skin crawl, but Corwin was very passionate about learning the nature of the little beasts.

"This is a lesson to be discussed," Teren continued. "If I may?" He looked to Eve for permission, the teacher nodded.

"This is a question that comes up often in Aurumice," Teren walked around the group. "Danger versus knowledge, risk versus potential strength. How can one decide what weighs out? We have an interesting quandary here. We know this box of frost needlewasps is dangerous, if one were to escape, it could prove deadly for any of us. If more than one escapes, we could have an infestation on our hands. But, as Corwin has stated, we know little of the frost wasps, but we know they grow in numbers in the north. How can we approach this?"

"By asking questions," said Abrianna.

"Yes, what questions?" Teren took control of the library, holding the children's attention.

"Who can get hurt?" Jiberty's tawny daughter Mareen said. "If a lot more people will be hurt if we don't know what the wild needlewasp will do."

"What other questions should we ask?" Teren continued.

The children peppered him with ideas.

"How quick do they sting?"

"What do they eat?"

"Are they fast?"

"How long do they live?"

"Does it hurt if they lay eggs in your skin?"

"How quick do you get Puce fever?"

"Can't we just kill them now?"

"Can't we put the box in a bigger box?" suggested Abrianna, "If the little box breaks, it won't go anywhere."

"Ahhhh, wise child," Teren said. "That, gentlemen, is our solution. If I recall correctly, in the west wing, in one of the upper floors there is a glass case that was used in the old days as an aquarium of sorts. It may be fitted to suit this purpose."

"This plan is still dangerous," Fentalon warned.

"Yes, but ignorance and fear are also dangerous." Teren pointed out. "Children, let's go beyond these little insects. What else could be dangerous but also good?"

"A knife."

"A sword."

"A crossbow."

"A nightflight."

"A sting lizard."

"How can a stinglizard be good?" Mareen balked. "They just hurt people."

"You can eat a stinglizard. Can't you? Guardsman Talon, isn't that true?" Pepper asked.

"If you cook it well," Fentalon replied.

"I wouldn't want to eat a stinglizard," Aden said. "They're gross."

"But, Pepper raised a point, they could be eaten. Is it wise to keep a stinglizard for its food? Probably not, there is not much to be gained and burch is much tastier. But what else is dangerous?"

"The white Lazuli hunter that bit Jessi," Mareen said.

Abrianna poked her. "You're being rude to my uncle. That was his pet that died."

"I didn't say anything bad, I just answered Gentleman Wynter's question," Mareen bristled. Her tan tail curled up in an irritated question mark.

"Abrianna, it's a truth, Mareen meant no disrespect, I assure you. But that is the point, the dog was dangerous. It did cause Jessica harm, but it was also a very loyal beast, and lived up to its name. It was an excellent hunter."

"The electricity is bad too," said Abrianna. "We're not supposed to touch it."

"Excellent," Teren was pleased the children had finally arrived at his point. "It is very dangerous, but it's kept in the wires, and it keeps our castle lit. Without it, we now must use candles, and gas lamps."

"But we've got glow stones," said Aden.

"But they fade and they're not very bright," Teren replied, "and glow stones cannot power the fridges which keep our food healthy. Jessica was working on a radio before she left, it will let us talk across the castle."

"Without being a mage?" Abrianna asked.

"Yes, without being a mage. Anyone can talk to anyone," Teren said.

"Aren't mages bad too?" Aden said. "Like not bad but dangerous."

"Ah," Teren had not considered that point, but it was valid. "That is a great question for castlefolk to ask, as there have always been mages in Aurumice. They are powerful, some when they are young are dangerous. What should we do with mages? Aden, if your sister woke up tomorrow morning with the power to unseat you from a bicorn just by asking it, how would you feel?"

"Uh, I think it would be neat, because then she could talk to Seadancer, and tell her to run faster."

"But what if your sister was angry at you?" Teren asked. "What if you broke her favorite fishing pole? What if she was so angry she told Seadancer to pitch you into the bramble, and you broke your arm?"

"I'd be mad."

"What if she didn't mean it?" Teren asked. "What if she meant it for an instant but then was sorry?"

"She should be punished, and told not to talk to animals anymore," Aden replied affirmatively. He glared at his sister.

"Now, what if she apologized? She learns, and when she grows up, she has the ability to call all the wolves and foxes and wildcats of the forest to her command, and uses them to protect us?"

Teren hadn't intended for the metaphor to take that direction, but it did. He recalled the morning his mother did just that, called all the beasts of the forest to protect them from Naja Dashier. For a moment, he was brought back to that day, watching the trees shake as the creatures came running to their aid.

"I think it would be good if she could get the animals to help us!" Aden affirmed.

"Consider these possibilities children, when you face this choice," Teren said.

***

The night was still. Jessica breathed in and out uneasily, her ribs still ached in the evenings. Burrowing in her bed, she luxuriated in the blankets. The air outside the tent was frigid as they had made their way high into the mountains past Grey Point. Earlier that evening, she and Nico had begun to learn street-preaching. Bundled up, Sienna had led them to the night markets of Bandaturk. Telling stories of the goddess, they collected coin and sold candles. The crowd was eager to pay, delighted that the Circus had made its way to their frigid town. Jessica enjoyed speaking to the crowd, hidden beneath her mask, but Nico had remained silent for most of the adventure.

Exhausted and freezing, they returned to camp. Nico immediately fell asleep, but Jessica tossed and turned in the cold. She suspected one of the hot beverages she had enjoyed was heavily caffeinated. Had it not been so cold, she would have gone for a walk.

Jessica peered out from her blanket, planning to look for a book.

Instead, she was startled to see a light.

Across the tent, Nico was *glowing*.

Jessica blinked, wondering if one of the drinks was a hallucinogenic. No, she was alert, and he was definitely glowing.

When Nico's mage powers appeared in the past, they had been blue, but this color was different. It was purple and a hue she just could not find a word for. The color was maddening as her mind tried to arrive at a description. It wasn't purple, it wasn't red, it wasn't blue.

It was a color that had no name.

Jessica watched the waves pulse, in, out, like a steady heartbeat. The light cast no heat nor sparks. It was pleasant to observe, calming. Jessica found her own breathing moving in rhythm to the light.

She debated waking Nico, but the warmth of the blankets around her quickly challenged that thought. He might light the tent on fire, but the strangeness of the glow somehow convinced Jessica otherwise.

As suddenly as it had begun, the pulse vanished without a trace, bringing the darkness back to the tent. She stayed awake for a few minutes more, then sleep overtook her.

***

Nico huddled in the corner of his Briken cell.

The door was open, but the hall was empty. He was too paralyzed to move, fearful that the guards would accuse him of trying to escape.

A familiar whinny caught his attention. Moontower, the blue bicorn, stood in the hallway, waiting for him.

The sight of the beast brought Nico to his feet. He had to get Moontower out of the prison. The beautiful creature could be put to work at the hands of the labor camp.

"Tower, you shouldn't have come here," Nico tried to pull the bicorn through the darkness of the caves. Every step was through a quick-sand mire of coal dust.

Relentless, needlewasps swarmed Moontower, first tangling in the beast's mane and then coating his skin. Nico tried to beat the terrible insects away, but he was too late. Chunks of bicorn flesh came off in his hands, blood mixing with the needlewasps as the insects coated his own arms. The hunks of flesh and muscle continued to fall off his old friend until nothing was left but bone and needlewasps.

Nico's heart broke for his old companion.

Another whinny caught Nico's attention, Frostfire. The feisty mare ran away, her red tail behind her like a flag.

Nico abandoned Moontower's remains to catch the fiery bicorn. He crossed through a doorway, into a room with giant vats of caustic chemicals, bubbling with bright colors. Blue-green smoke permeated the air.

Prison guards waited for Nico across the walkway.

Seeing no chance for escape, Nico fell to his knees, begging forgiveness, hoping the guards would not find Frostfire.

Past the guards, Misa sat upon Frostfire's back, sword in hand. Jessica stood on the ground with a crossbow.

Zia Casimirio walked into the hellscape, wielding an ax, flanked by an armored gryphon with blood-red eyes. The woman was furious and had his friends in her sights.

"No!" Nico shouted. "No!"

His voice faded.

Screaming, no sound came from his mouth no matter how much he tried.

The bridge beneath his feet broke apart.

Something bound his arms.

"I'm here," Jessica's voice cut through the dream as the details of the tent seeped back into his eyes. He continued to fight and thrash when he realized he wasn't moving at all. He sat up, inhaling deeply. Lungs protesting, he coughed and gagged, throwing up black phlegm onto the rug.

"You were screaming," Jessica said, grabbing a mug. Nico tried to take the cup, but his hand trembled violently. She held it steady at his lips, wrapping one arm around his shoulders. It took a few moments, but he was finally able to down the lukewarm tea. He finished then handed the cup back to his friend.

Shamefully, he buried his face in his hands. Jessica said nothing, keeping one solid arm around his heaving shoulders. Her touch was both comforting and revolting. He wanted to rest in her arms, but hated himself.

Jessica said nothing in the cold. She patiently sat, holding him as his self-loathing emerged as tears. He buried his face in her shirt and she wrapped her other arm around him. No questions, no promises, she just held him until he stopped shaking.

Finally, he stood, hastily wiped the puddle of vomit with a dirtied shirt, and left the tent.

***

In the morning, Jessica gave no mention of the glow or his sleep terrors. She asked him how he was feeling. He mumbled a half-hearted okay. Pulling up the hood of his cloak, he walked away into the frosty camp with a prayer book tucked under his hand.

This became his new pattern. If he got out of bed, he barely ate, hid under his cloak, and went off into the surrounding forest.

Nico was losing himself further.

CHAPTER 27

The circus traveled from the mountains down to the valley. Jessica grew restless and worried that it was taking far too long to meet the Auroriate healer. She was completely annoyed with her roommate, and hoped she could have her own quarters soon. If she proved herself to the Mystic Healer, she could drop the charade of her relationship with Nico. Jessica was surprised circusfolk bought into the lie because they hardly went anywhere together. She imagined everyone was too busy with their own affairs to actually care.

After lunch, she decided to stop in Aunt Dahlia's tent. She did not speak to the woman very often. Pulling the green rope, the chimes inside the tent played their welcoming chord.

"Enter!" Dahlia's voice called through the canvas.

Jessica stepped into the warm, opulent tent. Dahlia was alone, her eyes closed, legs crossed in meditation.

"Welcome child, how are you finding your studies?" Aunt Dahlia asked, eyes remaining closed.

"Good," Jessica said, "I am learning so much now. It's very nice, different from what I learned with the castlefolk."

"Excellent, we are happy to have you with us."

"I came here because I was wondering when we would be crossing paths with the healer?"

Aunt Dahlia opened her white eyes.

"Ah, the healer is in Strabs Valley, with the troupe of my cousin Dalendile. From what I understand, they had to divert their path to avoid the needlewasp swarms that seem to have become more prevalent as of late. I will let you know as soon as we will be near."

"Is there a way I might be able to just go to them instead of waiting?"

"It's quite a distance now. Not safe for you to travel on your own, and you have obligations this afternoon. We are presiding over a wedding and I would like you to stand in the honor guard."

Dahlia pivoted conversations so smoothly, Jessica wasn't sure how to politely press more about the healer.

"We are traveling out to the town of Red Clay, for a wedding of the magistrate's daughter," Dahlia continued, "and I think you are ready for such an honor."

"I'm not sure…"

Dahlia opened a wooden box and produced a white mask decorated with diamonds and scales.

"Here, you deserve to wear this! You have been studying so much, Jessica, the goddess rewards. And believe me child, the banquet that follows has the most decadent desserts." Dahlia winked.

"Alright…"

"I will tell Sienna to bring you with her this afternoon instead of your usual lesson. You deserve this honor."

***

Jessica found herself on the back of an ostrich-like Plookory bird, wearing robes and the white mask. She was mildly irritated that Aunt Dahlia dismissed her request to go find the mystic healer, but did not want to insult the woman.

The bird hopped suddenly. Jessica fought to sit up straight in the uncomfortable decorated saddle. The Plookory were docile and needed little direction, but their gait was very jaunty. She wished Nico had joined them. Even in his grumpiness, it would have been nice to not be the newest circusfolk in attendance.

They arrived at the temple of the moon sisters in the town of Red Clay. North of Greypoint, the little village was nestled in a valley of massive evergreens. Many of the buildings were made of finely crafted brick that reminded Jessica of a quaint German village. The land was covered in a fine mist and the air was humid but pleasant with the fragrance of the trees.

One of the Auroriates minded the giant birds. Jessica remained silent, falling in line behind the other bird-riders. The temple was a massive brick and stone structure.

Long benches filled the space, packed with guests in elegant attire.

Jessica took her place as instructed, standing amongst the eight in red and black robes, in the far back of the temple. She didn't need to say or do anything, just stand like a guardian.

It was nice being an Auroriate.

The real procession began, relatively demure by the circus' standards. A small entourage of twelve performers danced in, performing a processional melody in brass and percussion. They were followed by Sienna. Wearing a bird-like mask, she took her place at the dais.

"I welcome you all today to the union of Mikael and Gwenna, under the protection Goddess Aurora."

With fanfare, the bride and groom entered together.

The groom was a white-robed ailuro with horns, his long fur a creamy coffee-brown. The bride was a red with ears like a lynx. She wore a robe of a wild colors. The ceremony was long and full of prayers. Jessica found it difficult to stand still, but was determined not to fidget. She envied the Auroriates who seemed to have no trouble remaining as rigid as statues.

Jessica's mind began to wander, as she tried to imagine what the wedding had been like for her Aunt Trixie and Uncle Justen. He was an Auroriate, and she was Christian. Did they honor her religion at all? Did she pretend to be Auroriate? These were thoughts that had never crossed Jessica's mind.

Jessica pushed the musings aside, they only made her fidget more. She straightened her back, thankful the mask covered her lips.

Then the back of her hand started to tickle.

A tiny insect was crawling on it.

Clenching her fist, Jessica tried to obscure her hand beneath the sleeve of her robe.

Stop itching.

A large crystal bottle was revealed by Sienna. An audible gasp of awe rippled through the audience.

The vessel itself looked like an elegant wine decanter, rounded at its base with a long neck, nearly a foot tall. Inside, a black liquid swirled with tiny specks of iridescent light. Even from the back of the room, it was mesmerizing, like a swirling nebula of black rainbow.

"I present the blood of Aurora, most sacred of all holy objects," Sienna told the onlookers. "This blessed ambrosia is the binding of love, the true moment of marriage."

A quartet of strings began playing. With the music as a distraction, Jessica reached up to her itchy nose. She glanced at her finger to see an insect with an iridescent shell, much like the pretty needlewasp Teren had brought her months before. Jessica flicked the tiny critter away and focused her attention back on the altar.

As the music played, Sienna took a careful step away from the vessel and drew a very sharp knife from her belt. One of the Auroriate attendants stepped forward with a small glass bowl, a moon attendant walked forward with a wooden bowl of equal size.

Jessica was intrigued.

Both the bride and groom presented their hands. Sienna cut a deep wound into each of their palms as the couple tried not to flinch. Carefully, the blood was collected into the bowls. It seemed like a lot of blood. The bridal couple pulsed in a red-purple hue, as did the bowl. Jessica's heart raced and she felt tingles across her chest.

Attendants carried the blood to the large vessel of black rainbows. Chimes rang as the blood was poured in and instantly glowed. The chemicals turned molten humming liquid. The blend was poured into two chalices.

"If you wish to be bonded forever, in true marriage, please drink. Be warned, this is a magic that may never be undone. Only death may divide you, and even then, may you never take another in this ceremony. As children of the Goddess, we sign our hearts to eternity. The magic will reflect the strength of your own, you may become aware of each other in ways you have not imagined."

As the couple drank from the chalices, Jessica was astounded and ashamed for embarrassing her mother. She had no idea a Centernian wedding was a sacred affair of magic.

***

After the ceremony, they were invited for a feast of decadent barbequed meats, crisp vegetables and desserts rich with fresh sweet cream. Jessica had been told Red Clay was known for its stubby Carmine cows, producers of the richest milk in Madeirna. She severely underestimated indulgent their desserts could be. After a dalvanian mousse and two pieces of a cinnamon pie Jessica found herself wrapped in a blanket of food coma, forgetting the ceremony.

The Auroriates stayed until the sun began to set, and they returned to the ostrich-like mounts.

Traveling through the town in silence, Jessica admired the architecture of the neat brick buildings. As the houses thinned, Sienna came up beside Jessica. Her bird was the leader, proudly wearing a spiked helmet and trailing saddle blanket.

"What did you think of the wedding?"

"It was beautiful, and magical, and the food was amazing."

"You belong with us Jess, you fit in so well with the ways of the goddess."

"Thank you," Jessica gazed into the distance. Living amongst the circusfolk was the calmest, most purposeful span of months Jessica had ever experienced. Inhaling deeply, she thanked the goddess.

As Jessica opened her eyes and gazed out onto the horizon, she noticed an odd grey cloud settling in at the distance. At first, she thought it was smoke, but it didn't billow and rise.

Other circusfolk noticed as well, and they reined their birds.

"Sienna, what's that?"

The leopardess stared out, her expression puzzled.

Fear rippled through the group as they consulted and repeated one phrase: *swarm*.

"We need to run!" Sienna kicked her mount.

Peace shattered, the procession raced towards camp. Jessica gripped the jaunty creature as it ran over the rough terrain. She soon was no longer steering as her bird followed the others. She was grateful for the mask that protected her face from the dust.

The pace quickened and the birds ahead of her started a wild bounding hop like a kangaroo. Her bird followed the flock and Jessica gritted her teeth, grabbing for the creature's neck. Gripping with her legs she fought to hold on.

By the time they arrived at camp, word had already reached the other Auroriates. People rushed to pack up supplies, bolting them into tents and wagons. Circusfolk ran around her, packing up and not caring for much else. Fear rippled through the camp.

Nightflights and featherwings filled the sky as every flying beast was saddled and ridden.

Jessica searched for Nico, running to the place they had raised their tent.

It was gone.

Jessica frantically searched for Nico, fearful he had left her behind.

***

Nico hunted for Jessica, worried she was still at the village of Red Clay. He had never heard of needlewasps swarming, but didn't doubt the scouts of the Circus.

Dashing between two carts, he spotted her.

"What the hell is going on?!" she shouted.

"A swarm! They think it's Needlewasps! Follow me, we need to catch a cart."

As they ran, Nico was reminded of the night years prior when they fled a deadly storm with Misa and Teren.

"Where are our things?!"

"Already packed!"

They duo ran to a large wooden cart with solid sides. The driver box was sealed up in a canvas cover, fitted with a glass top.

Kristofori was in the cart with other Auroriates Nico had never spoken to.

As they settled into their seats, one of the Auroriates opened a wooden panel and signaled to the driver to move. The cart lurched and Nico braced himself against the side wall.

"What will the swarm do?" Jessica asked.

"Needlewasps, but not the normal kind, the blue kind. Little buggish bastards," Nico explained. "They lay their eggs in living things, and they give people puce fever."

"Ugh, that sounds terrible."

"I have never seen them outside the Mines of Briken. I had no idea they had spread."

"This first time I have seen them," Kristofori added. "In the last two years we have heard of three big nests, but this is the first time I've heard of a swarm."

"It was as big as a house," Jessica said, "I saw it on the horizon."

"I hate needlewasps," Nico shuddered, trying to quell the suffocation of the Mines. He clenched his fist, feeling powerless.

For the first time in a very long while, he wished he could touch the magic. The Auroriates had no way to fend off a swarm, but his incinerating powers would be enough to destroy the insects.

He opened his palm, so fearful he tried recklessly to release the energy from his hands.

Nothing happened.

The goddess had a sense of irony. She took the powers he had cursed, and now he needed them back.

"If we are evacuating, what about the town of Red Clay?" Jessica asked. "That wedding banquet was supposed to continue to party outside all night."

An uncomfortable silence fell over the wagon.

"We sent a warning scout to the town," Kristofori said, "people are smart, and they will keep inside."

"We should pray to the goddess to protect those of the town," one of the Auroriates suggested. "Holy goddess, mother of all, protect Red Clay..."

And so they recited a somber string of prayers as the wagon sped away.

CHAPTER 28

Kaity furiously pounded on Teren's door.

Teren opened the door, rubbing the sleep out of his eyes. He hadn't been sleeping well and tried to catch afternoon naps.

"What's wrong?" He sensed the maelstrom of her anger.

"What's wrong? Fentalon is what's wrong! You said Corwin could keep studying the needlewasps, and now he's getting in the way again. He destroyed Corwin's work and he's got the castle all riled up as if Corwin was the demon!"

"Well, you have just as much power as I do," Teren yawned. "Tell them to stop."

"No!" she growled. "It's so much more than that. They don't listen to me, they don't believe me. They agree to my face and I *know* they're snickering behind my back."

Teren leaned heavily against the doorframe, a headache forming between his eyebrows. Kaity

was red-faced, her hair tousled, and she was not going away until he did something.

"Kaity, you were raised in this castle the same as I. You know castlefolk gossip, it's their way. They don't mean any harm."

"But it's harmful to Corwin! Everything goes back to that bastard Malachi, even dead he tortures me! Corwin should be regarded as a scholar, not an old dog to be kicked."

"Then maybe he should go back to a place where he will be regarded as such," Teren quipped.

He regretted the words as soon as they left his mouth. Kaity's emotions skyrocketed and Teren was thrown backwards, tumbling onto the wooden floor. She stormed in, the door slamming behind her.

"You aren't hearing me either!"

Teren glared at his old friend. His inclination was to dampen her emotions, but he knew they had been festering so long it would be as wise as corking a bottle of lit fireworks.

"Fentalon destroyed Corwin's work. We need to know about those frost wasps before they pose a threat to Aurumice!"

"Kaity! It's a bunch of dangerous nasty bugs that have no place in this castle."

"Get up and help me mitigate this argument. Castlefolk are not supposed to destroy the belongings of others, that's our rules!"

"Fine, fine, I will get involved," he climbed to his feet. "But it looks bad that you need to call me to help you. The 'folk need to respect you."

"Talon gets more respect than me, and I'm not about to remind people that I can crush them with one thought! Do you want me to remind them?!"

"But you have no problem reminding me. My tailbone is going to hurt for a month."

"You'll live," she opened the door and shoved him out into the hallway.

Kaity did have a point. Though they tried to lead in equal measure, the castlefolk regarded Teren with greater authority. He had no doubt his powers created his imbalance, and Kaity had no idea.

The leopardess led him to the library. Teren could sense the turmoil before entering the room.

"Worthless maggot! Should go back to Polaris where you belong and stay out of our castle!"

Teren's blood chilled as he saw the open needlewasp box. Jiberty was red-faced, yelling at Corwin. Fentalon stood by calmly. Jared stood between Jiberty and his uncle. A group of a half dozen castlefolk gathered around Fentalon.

The group went silent as Teren entered the library.

"Of course, you all shut up to listen to him," Kaity bristled.

"What happened?" Teren asked, resisting the urge to force the entire room to run in terror. He really, really wanted to return to his nap.

"Fentalon deliberately destroyed Corwin's work!" Kaity argued.

"I am protecting the castle!" Fentalon huffed. "I found two of those bugs in the dining room."

"That was impossible!" Corwin argued, "I had twenty-three and they were all here until you squashed them all!"

"Were you that certain…."

"You act without thinking!"

"Me? I act without thinking?" Fentalon was stunned. "Were you the one who killed Malachi in cold blood?"

"He had my wife prisoner!"

"You didn't know that."

"We have argued this over and over again," Teren lost his patience. "Corwin has pardon. Nico pardoned him, he was the one who had the most to lose and suffered the most. You all need to respect his words."

"How long before the mage turns on one of us?" Jiberty argued. "We've never housed a murderer in Aurumice!"

"Jiberty, that's not true," Fentalon pointed out.

"Not anyone who's taken the life of castlefolk!" Jiberty argued.

"Also not true!" Kaity argued. "Why do none of you care about what Malachi did to me?"

"He was wrong, but he didn't deserve to die!" Jiberty said. "We lost Nico because of this idiot! I want to know why you—"

"STOP THIS BICKERING!" Teren bellowed.

Everyone in the room cringed.

It was very rare that he raised his voice.

"Now the heart of the matter…the wasps."

Fentalon spoke up.

"We were all in the dining room. The children were playing, and Pepper caught one of those little bastards. Temi was right there too, either child could have been stung! Then we found another one buzzing next to the curtains…"

Teren focused intently on Fentalon, trying to discern if he sincerely spoke the truth.

"I believe that these creatures are dangerous," Fentalon turned to Corwin. "That's why I came here and demanded that you destroy them. You're the one who got angry with me."

"You came in here, startling me, and the insect I was looking at took flight. You fail to understand these are more than just normal needlewasps! They have a magical signature that is different than anything I have ever past-read, it's like they don't belong here. I have more research to do! Polaris Academy is counting on me!"

"You work for Aurumice, not Polaris! You are castlefolk or you leave!" Fentalon snapped.

"Stop, stop, stop," Teren interrupted. "You had the door open, you were in a trance, Fentalon startled you, the bugs got loose, and Fentalon squashed them?"

"One got loose," Corwin corrected, "and then he squashed them all like a mad cabomum!"

Teren addressed Fentalon.

"You were worried about the children and that's why you came in here?" Teren repeated.

"I worry for all the castle! None of those bugs should be loose!"

Teren did not doubt the sincerity of Fentalon's words, nor did he doubt Corwin.

"Why does this library have any electricity at all?" Fentalon continued, gesturing to a lamp. "It was supposed to have been shut down. You defy our rules. Teren said no power, you have to respect that! And if you can't follow our rules, then you don't stay!"

"How dare you say that to my husband!" Kaity crossed her arms. "You come in here with your followers, bully my husband and destroy his work! I should destroy the sparring fields."

Kaity made a menacing fist and the shelves around them began to vibrate. The castlefolk startled and Teren worried for the nearby bookshelves.

"Kaity! I believe that Talon was worried, and with good cause." The vibration ceased.

"Well I don't! You didn't even ask Jared what he saw!"

Jared seemed uncomfortable being pulled into the argument.

"I wasn't actually watching," he confessed. "I don't know what happened."

"Kaity, let's discuss this privately later. Clearly the insects are already dead so there is nothing immediately to decide. Now if you excuse me."

Teren brushed past Kaity, feeling her ire as he walked away. She would wait, or he would lose the last of his patience.

"We are not done discussing this, Teren!" she stormed after him into the hallway. Teren rolled his eyes. They were like two parents fighting in front of children, both would lose their credibility as leaders.

The leopardess grabbed his shoulder.

He dampened her fury a tiny bit.

Kaity pushed open the door to a small sitting room, and gestured for him to enter. It was his least favorite of all the sitting rooms throughout the castle. The stuffy space was devoid of windows. The furniture was depressing, covered in a hideous pattern of poorly stitched sea creatures.

"Why do you believe Fentalon over Corwin?" she demanded as she closed the door.

Under her anger, she was hurt.

He sighed, knowing he couldn't tell one of his oldest friends the truth.

"It's very logical Kaity. If Fentalon found needlewasps in the dining room, in front of anyone, his concern would be justified. I am also concerned."

"But they're just taking this as another excuse to kick down Corwin," the proud woman was on the verge of tears. "Teren, I can't take much more of this. No one respects him, no one talks to him, and it's all because of that stupid dead bastard."

"Many of them liked Malachi, and those who didn't were not happy Nico went to the Mines instead of him. I can't change this!"

"But I was imprisoned in cellars!"

"And that still did not make sense to me," Teren said. He didn't intend to walk down that path with Kaity, but she brought it up. "Did Malachi have cause imprison you?"

"No," Kaity's voice softened. "He was afraid of me because he hated mages. You would never understand what it's like to be feared for something you can't control!"

Teren focused on her emotions, detecting a strange shift.

Kaity was lying.

He was faced with an odd quandary, he could push her further and draw out the truth, or he could respect her privacy.

"Why would you ask me that question, Teren? Do you believe me?"

Any true friend would have said yes in an instant, and Teren cared deeply about his childhood companion.

"Is that really the reason Malachi locked you up?" he finally asked. If she had something to share, he preferred not to force her. "Did you threaten him, Kaity?"

"That's it, I'm done!" she threw her hands up. "For all I've given for Aurumice! We're leaving! We're going home to Polaris! I'm tired of worrying about money and politics and stupid castlefolk! Malachi poisoned me with redvice, do you ever think for a moment that that may be the reason Temi is deaf? Did you?!"

It was an idea that was whispered about, but redvice was generally regarded as a sedative, not a poison.

He made the mistake of hesitating a moment too long.

"Teren! Are you even listening to me?!"

The temptation to squash her anger was so strong. He could twist it to fear, to lust, to elation, any way he chose.

Instead, he walked away.

"We're leaving!" Kaity shouted. "We're leaving this forsaken castle! You will regret how little you've appreciated us!"

Teren paused at the door.

"If that is what you really desire, then I wish you the best, Kaity Cosette."

CHAPTER 29

Carrie Anne switched the calendar to February. The last of her hair had fallen away and she wrapped her head in a bright pink knitted cap. Delicately stitched, the border was adorned with little hearts for Valentine's Day. Ashlin watched her mother stare at the calendar, counting the days backwards to October. The woman shook her head, and left the room, hugging herself.

Ashlin tapped on the keyboard, a cold chill settled on her shoulders. She began searching for Felicia Lee's profile and to her surprise, uncovered it fairly easily

Sending a message request, Ashlin sat back and waited patiently until a window popped up.

```
Lee
Hello


Ashlin
Hi! Sorry to bother you, this is Jessica's
sister. I was wondering if you have any idea
how to find Jessica?


Lee
You still haven't heard from her?


Ashlin
Not since October. My mom's really upset over
```

```
her, she's not eating or sleeping right anymore,
or it's her cancer treatment. I don't know which
but it's not helping. Do you have any ideas how
to find Jessi?
```

For a long while, Lee did not respond. Ashlin was disappointed. She debated contacting Jessica's mother directly, but it felt like a worse idea than reaching out to her sister's former best friend.

```
Lee
(929) 249-0763
```

```
Lee
I don't know if that number even works but you
can try it. Jared gave it to me when we went
to a party a couple years ago
```

```
Lee
I hope you find your sister
```

Ashlin could not believe that she was able to get a number so easily. She looked to the living room and debated telling her mother. On one hand, Carrie Anne would be happy, but if the number didn't work, she would be crushed. Ashlin had to test it first.

Very carefully, she typed the number into her phone and sent a message.

Then, she waited.

***

The needlewasps forced Dahlia and her troupe to travel outside of their planned route. The landscape turned bitter cold as they rode north. Jessica watched out the window of the cart as they trundled through. She both liked and hated travel between camps. The teen saw so many sights she had never expected to see, but the days were long and boring.

Jessica tried to follow along on a map, but it was difficult. There were no mile markers and very few signposts. Sometimes there wasn't even much of a road. It was tiresome and she began to miss home, despite her previous idea to stay with the circus.

Two weeks after the needlewasps in Red Clay, she penned another letter to Aurumice.

Jessica wrote the note carefully, this time actually telling her family who they were with. They could decide if they would come visit her, or drag her away. She secretly hoped the latter. Their flight from the needlewasps had cast a shadow over her heart. They packed so quickly, she didn't honestly believe the village of Red Clay had been warned enough.

Jessica brought her letter to Aunt Dahlia.

"Could this be delivered to Aurumice?" Jessica asked.

"Of course, child," Dahlia replied. "You seem upset."

"I had some issues going on at home that I'm worried about. I have someone who is pretty sick," Jessica said. "She needs magic or a miracle, and if she gets worse, I want them to tell me."

"The circus is experts in both magic and miracles," Dahlia reminded her. "The goddess listens to those who open their hearts."

"Yeah, but it's a little more complicated than that. Can you send that letter for me?"

"Of course. How is Nico doing by your observations?"

Jessica hesitated.

"He's not the same as before Briken," Jessica looked down, "I'm worried."

Secretly, she hoped Teren would read the letter and come for them. Nico was not getting better and Jessica knew she was ill-equipped to help him. If Teren failed, she wondered if she could find him answers on Earth.

"I am taking the troupe on an unusual route," said Dahlia. "It will perhaps bring Nicoveren to confront what ails him."

"Oh?" Jessica was intrigued.

"You shall see. Trust me."

Jessica wasn't sure how to take Dahlia's tone, but she got the clear impression the woman wouldn't say much more. The teen returned to her tent. Nico was inside, sleeping, though it wasn't even the dinner hour yet. She longed to talk to him, to get caught up in hours of intellectual banter that they used to have.

Pulling a blanket over her shoulders, Jessica settled into her sleeping palette, wondering how she had gotten to this strange point. She didn't know where she was, traveling with a stranger, and his strange family, tossing high school away.

She pulled the blanket tighter around her. She wondered what Dahlia would say if she asked for a nightflight escort home. Or maybe she should ask Sienna instead. Conversations with Dahlia always seemed to redirect, no matter how much Jessica tried to keep them on course. Sienna was easier to talk to, but she was always busy.

"Nico?" Jessica had to try a new approach.

No reply.

"Nico?" she repeated.

He grumbled.

"Nico, are you awake?" she asked, slightly louder.

He opened his one eye, grimacing. The other was less puffy, but firmly closed.

"Now I am," he said. "I'm not hungry."

"No, I wasn't going to ask about dinner. I'm thinking about going back to Aurumice. Would you come with me?"

"No," he replied. "Let me sleep."

"Please, I want to go home, but I can't go alone."

"Why?" he said bitterly. "You're not a child, do what you want."

He turned over, facing the tent wall.

"But I don't want to go back without you," Jessica said. "And Teren will be angry with me if I show up without you."

"Teren will be dead if I go back, or have you forgotten?" he growled, turning over. "Let me sleep."

"It's been months, the mages haven't found you here. Maybe they stopped looking."

"I doubt the mages have given up, I think it's more likely Dahlia has evaded them. Do not underestimate the Circus, Jessica."

"What if you get the Mark of Corvalian like your father used to hide from the psychic mages? They would never find you and you wouldn't need to hide on earth."

Malachi hid for weeks in Castle Aurumice and slipped by Teren's detection with the tattoo. It seemed like a plausible option.

"Oh, of course, let me pop over to the next village marketplace and pick up some Corvalian stones!" Nico snapped. "Jess, you're so daft sometimes it's adorable! The stones are hidden in the north mountains, where Castle Nova can't find them and murder whoever is hiding them."

Jessica hopped to her feet, enraged.

"I'm trying to help you and you have to be an abominable ass! I wish you were still locked up in Briken!"

Jessica ran from the tent, feeling like an idiot for thinking he would ever get better and be the same Nico she knew.

***

Several days past.

Nico felt like pond sludge for arguing with Jessica, but the idea of going back to Aurumice chilled him. He didn't know why he snapped at her. All of his frustration seemed to manifest itself in her presence.

Maybe it was because he knew, unlike the Holy Circus, that she was the only one who wouldn't abandon him.

Nico wasn't very fond of staying with the circusfolk. As he watched Sienna with her little family, he realized how easily his father gave up on Aurumice and started over. Nico's resentment towards his father's second family grew with each turn of the wheel.

As they traveled, Nico lost track of his surroundings and felt little need to pay much attention. But as the air grew cold and dry, he had an odd feeling. He expected it to pass, but they traveled further north.

When they set up camp for the night, he stared at the stars, trying to run calculations in his mind.

He wasn't certain of their location, but it seemed to be uncomfortably close to Briken.

Clouds hazed over the night sky. Nico approached the lively central fire where the circusfolk gathered, something he had not done in months. His circus brethren laughed, practiced tricks and drank.

Nico became homesick for the old days of Aurumice as he listened to the din of people relaxing from a hard day's work.

Kristofori was at a bench sitting by himself reading, oblivious to the jugglers and musicians surrounding him. He squinted and hunched over in the firelight. As Nico approached, he was amused to note that it was not a prayer book or historical text. Instead, it was a book on steam power. Nico got the impression that his brother was not a typical Auroriate.

Kristofori looked up with a start, surprised to see Nico.

"Do you know where we are exactly?" Nico asked.

"Just south of the Spine Ridge Mountains."

"How far south?"

"Maybe a day's ride," Kristofori replied.

The Spine Ridge mountains were north of Briken. It was a small range. Nico was certain they were very close to the gritty mining town. The air would only get worse the closer they traveled.

"I need to talk to Aunt Dahlia, have you seen her?" Nico asked.

Kristofori gestured across the fire.

Nico sought out the old matriarch. He found his aunt deep in discussion with a small group of older women. Metallic fabric glinted in the firelight and she pointed out details in the tapestry.

"Aunt Dahlia, excuse me, if we may speak?"

"Ah, yes nephew?"

"May we speak privately?"

"Ah, walk with me," Aunt Dahlia said, excusing herself from her companions. As the woman took her staff, Nico noticed she limped badly.

"Why are we here?" he stated.

"For you, of course," Aunt Dahlia said. "And we were evading needlewasps."

"Well this is not the place you want to be to avoid needlewasps. I say this with the most respect, but Aunt Dahlia, truly is this wise? You know my history, this is a terrible place for me!"

"You're caught in your own head, son, you need to get out and rejoin the living."

"Aunt Dahlia, I do not like this. I implore you to turn the wagons west. It's not a healthy town, the air is poisoned."

"We will not stay long. The people of Briken deserve the touch of the goddess as much as anyone else."

"No, there's nothing there, just the miners and a handful of townsfolk!"

"Who have not been visited by the Holy Circus in far too many years. It would do well to brighten their spirits."

"Aunt Dahlia…"

The old woman continued to walk in silence until they stood under a gnarled tree, a short distance from the circusfolk. She learned on her staff, her milky eyes orange with the reflection of firelight.

"You know, every day I see my brother in you, but it saddens me because you're just a shadow. Malachi had never-ending energy, a thousand schemes and dreams, and would not let a day go by without talking to almost everyone. He did a lot of good for the circus. From what I gather from Jessica, you were once not much different."

"This is for you, Nico. I do not expect you to walk plain-faced into the Mines, that would be foolish. I want you to walk as an Auroriate, and see that you are not of this place. Their control over you is all in your mind!"

"Aunt Dahlia, it would be terribly dangerous to go to Briken!"

"Nicoveren, do you hear yourself? You are a powerful mage, born to both the leaders of Castle Aurumice and the Holy Circus, but you cower like a skittering tree rat."

"I am none of those things anymore," Nico argued.

"The world will always find ways to kick you down in its indifference, and it is your choice alone to stand again. Now, prepare, you will go out into the streets of Briken and give the word of the goddess."

"Aunt Dahlia! I am not a child! You cannot make me do this!"

"Then rot in your own head!" Dahlia snapped. "You sit around in misery, not part of circusfolk life. It's shameful that you do not embrace the healing of the goddess! Boy, you seem to have one aspect of your father, you're stubborn."

Aunt Dahlia abandoned him and returned to the central fires. Nico watched, helpless as she limped away.

***

When they arrived in Briken, Nico stayed in the tent.

Jessica thought it strange that Aunt Dahlia would take him back to this well of torture, but nothing else had worked.

Nico said nothing, instead sitting on his bed, prayer book in hand, staring in a daze. When he did doze, he seemed to be caught in restless sleep.

Jessica understood the torture of nightmares. Months after Traveling through the fracture Shadow Sphere to Polaris she had been plagued by dreams of the Gate. She could not escape the constant feeling that she was lost and suffocating, over and over again. She became upset at the visions and angry at herself for being unable to escape her own fear.

Sleeping in Aurumice usually brought more vivid dreams, but it also brought relief. Teren and Jared would be at her side, like vigilant guardian angels. When her nightmares had been their worst, they had held her in the darkness until the dreams had faded away.

Jessica realized she missed the two terribly. She second-guessed her choice in trying to help Nico on her own. No matter what she said or did, he seemed to stay distanced. She prayed Aunt Dahlia's Briken gamble would work.

When the time came for street-preaching, Nico refused to move.

Jessica was used to going out as an acolyte without Nico. She traveled with Sienna, Kristofori and Hunter to the street, dressed in their circusfolk masks, selling candles. They rode on olive ponies, the only bit of green in the dull landscape.

Most of the little buildings they passed were in grave disrepair. The entire town reminded Jessica of the streets of Rockwood. Most windows were boarded, and the rest were obscured by dust. Barely any people walked outside in the eerie grey world. There were no birds and few rodents. Jessica saw a lizards and needlewasps. Her skin crawled at the sight of the insects.

One was pretty, more than that was chilling.

For the first time, few townsfolk responded to their presence, unimpressed with the Circus. Jessica sold a handful of candles to grey-faced people who haggled heavily and gave them very little coin.

"This place is awful," Hunter murmured. "My throat hurts."

Sienna silenced her with a sound that sounded like a cross between a hiss and a keck.

"Well it's the truth," Hunter muttered from beneath her mask.

"Mother, why is the sky dark?" Kristofori asked.

"I don't know, son," Sienna said. "I imagine it comes from the Mines."

The leopardess gestured to the towering smokestacks in the distance.

They went into a tiny tavern. There was one barkeep and one patron, a grizzled looking old ailurian with bloodshot eyes.

"We bring the word of the Goddess!" Sienna began.

"Auroriates?" the patron croaked. "You run out of people to bother?"

Hunter did her fire rose trick, the same one she had shown Jessi.

"We are here to speak the goddess' love," she said smoothly, holding up the flaming rose.

The man dumped his cup on the rose, extinguishing the bloom.

"Stupid girl! Don't go sprouting fire, there's gas pockets everywhere! You could blow up the whole town!"

"Goddess has a way of cleansing the world," Hunter muttered.

"We bring hope and brightness!" Sienna interjected. "May I tell you a tale of the goddess?"

"There haven't been any Auroriates in this town since I was a boy," the barkeep said. He was a skeletal grey man with jagged ears. "What brings the Holy Circus to our door?"

"To serve," Sienna gave a little bow.

"You looking for a free drink?" the barkeeper accused.

"On contrary," Sienna produced a silver flask from beneath her robe. It was a bottle of sweet liquor.

She set it upon the worn bar.

"We give," she said, bowing.

The barkeeper eyed the bottle suspiciously, then tucked it behind the counter.

"Haven't had Auroriates here since before the Mines, back when we still had blue skies."

"Sir, is it the mining that makes the sky so dark?" Kristofori asked.

"Aye," the barkeep nodded. "When I was a boy this land was beautiful. Then the Mining Company came to the mountains and started digging. Our little village expanded and my grandfather built this tavern. Briken was nice. That's when the Holy Circus came, and oh what a show! I would never forget it."

The barkeep stared off in the distanced, lost in his memory.

"There were nightflights and gryphons, and dancers...."

"Sir, the Auroriates travel to many places, and many mines, why is this one so toxic?"

The barkeep shrugged.

"Curse of the goddess, likely. Punishment. Magistrate wanted cheap workers, and they turned Briken into a prison camp. Garbage dump, place for all the other towns to store their degenerates. Displaced all the miners, then they set up those furnaces. The fires never go out, spew their poison until you could no longer see sun up or sundown. They destroyed the town. People moved out, and the Mining Company didn't care, bastards."

"What are they mining?" Jessica asked.

"Pallas ore, hasn't got much use to most of us. They ship it up north to the arctic where they use it because catches fire easier when it freezes."

Jessica was puzzled. What an odd sounding material.

"Is there a place where we can buy some?"

Barkeep shook his head.

"Mining Company controls the ore, they pack it up and ship out every pebble."

Interesting. She would have to ask Corwin to look up information on pallas ore.

If she ever returned home.

"Would you like to hear the word of the goddess? Perhaps the Tale of the River Fox?" Hunter asked. She needed to redeem herself for her offhanded comment.

The barkeep nodded.

They performed the parable and stayed for two more. The bartender seemed appreciative.

"May want to head back to your camp before the rains come, they are more than a bit nasty. More punishment from the goddess."

They thanked him and returned to the dusty streets.

"Can we go to the Mines?" Jessica asked. Her curiosity had been peaked by the bartender's story.

"I don't see why not," Sienna replied. "They need the word of the goddess as much as anyone."

Jessica was both nervous and excited by her words.

As they traveled out of the town towards the Mines, Jessica's eyes scanned the rocky terrain. She searched for the little house the Aurumicians had camped out. Jessica's throat was sore and she felt bad for Savina, Jared and Teren. They had endured months of the awful town trying to help Nico.

Large smokestacks pumped dark soot in the air. Buildings were guarded with menacing looking fences. She narrowed her eyes, noticing a strange red-purple glow surrounding a small grey building.

Thinking of industrial sites on earth, she worried that they were inhaling too many deadly chemicals. There were no government regulations to prevent carcinogens from being pumped into the air.

"Sienna, perhaps we had best turn back. The air here is not good."

"We will be fine," Sienna said as they approached the main entrance to the Mines. Armed guards stood motionless.

Jessica could see the grey building more clearly. It had a blue door. The magenta glow flickered quickly like a strobe light and made Jessica feel ill.

"We come hailing the name of the goddess!" Sienna announced.

"All respect, Priestess, the Goddess has no place here. Go back to town."

"Sir, if we may preach our word. It is the way."

"No, leave. No one enters Briken."

Sienna continued to argue, but they would not admit her. Jessica could see a small group of workers in the distance, lifting heavy crates onto a cart. Their clothes were ragged, hanging off their thin bodies. Like a stone army, the workers' skin was the same dusty grey of the mines.

"Sienna…"

"Sir, we speak the love of the goddess, if we may preach her word here. Let me tell you a tale," Sienna said.

"Ma'am, you need to take shelter, the rains are coming."

"Sir, the goddess is the joy of the rain!"

"Oh, this isn't goddess love, this is the piss of the devil," the guard replied. "The rain is acidic, sit too long and it will turn your skin red, a few days out in it will blister the skin off a bicorn."

"Sienna," Jessica pleaded nervously. "We should turn back. The goddess preaches that wisdom only comes to those with open ears."

The stubborn leopardess finally heeded the guard's warning. They turned their mounts and walked back towards the town. Sienna was silent, a sign she was furious at being turned away.

As they re-entered the sad village, the rain came down. The air had a sharp smell, at first Jessica found it pleasant like gasoline, but it quickly became sickening. Her eyes became irritated as they rode back to camp, but she had no means to wipe away the foul rain.

Thick ash-filled clouds continued to blanket the sky.

When they made it back to the pens at camp, the Auroriates were trying desperately to cover the animals. In the muddy downpour, they erected tents usually reserved for performances, herding their creatures inside and out of the foul rain.

After her pony was secure, Jessica returned to the tent.

Nico was curled up in a corner of his bed, wrapped in a blanket. The man's eyes seemed sunken and dark. No doubt the memories of Briken were torturing his already fractured psyche.

"Are you okay?" he croaked.

Jessica coughed. "Yeah, happy to be out of that rain."

"You need to take off those clothes, throw them outside. They're not good anymore. We need to leave this place and get clear of the blackened clouds."

Jessica nodded, continuing to cough. She felt very strange, as if her senses had become dull.

Nico averted his eyes as she stripped out of the foul clothing. She followed his guidance, and tossed the pile of acid-soaked fabric outside the tent.

Jessica slipped into a soft tunic and pants, feeling a little better, but her hands were reddened and still had a faint odor. Her hair smelled worse.

"Hey, I'm dressed. Do we have any water?"

"No, we didn't refill the jugs."

Jessica was dismayed, worried about the strange rain in her hair and the burning in her throat. She settled onto her bed, crossing her arms. Coughing, she wished for some relief from the burning sensation.

Nico stood and walked over to the tent flap. The rain had let up and was little more than stray drops. He grabbed his cloak and pulled it over his head, going out into the grey darkness.

Jessica looked at her reddened and irritated skin. She closed her eyes slightly, hoping her blood mage magic would surface and relieve the burn. Desperate, she wished she could learn more about her gifts, and regretted not considering going home to ask her father. The worst he could have said was no.

As she sat, a buzzing startled her. An insect flew wildly and struck the top of the tent, searching for a way out. Jessica held her breath, keeping her eyes locked on the bug.

Eventually it landed on her blanket, its tiny legs walking across the fabric.

It was a fat shiny needlewasp.

Fear turned to fury as Jessica thought of the wedding at Red Clay. Staring at the insect, she wished to punish it. Suddenly, the insect burst from the inside, its blue hemolymph splattering a tiny stain across the blanket.

Jessica clutched her sides, her eyes stinging, disgusted by the bug guts. She gathered the blanket and threw it into a pile in the corner of the room, hating herself.

Briken was driving her mad.

She thought of Teren and felt even worse. She had begged him to take her to Briken and every time he said no.

Now she understood why.

Shame overcame her. How stupid had she been to ask Sienna to visit the Mines! It was like being a tourist at Auschwitz.

Briken was a rotten blight upon Centernia, and Aunt Dahlia was so wrong to lead them there.

When Nico returned, he was carrying a small satchel. Jessica wanted to immediately tell him she was sorry he suffered for so long, but instead she remained silent, watching him carefully. She likewise did not mention the bug, trying to make sense of the insect explosion.

Nico pulled off his cloak, wrapping it up and setting it outside the tent.

He walked over to the table and pulled out two cups. The satchel had two green bird eggs. Carefully, he cracked the shells, separating out the yolks from the whites. He handed her the cup of egg whites.

"Drink this."

"But what if it has salmonella?"

"Plookory eggs, they are known to be very basic. It should help neautralize the acid in your throat," Nico replied. His words were so logical. He seemed like his old self, rational and analytical. Few people in Centernia would speak of liquids in terms of ph levels, but Nico was not ordinary. He had spent his life devouring the literature of earth.

It was that fascination that had given rise to their friendship years ago.

Jessica eyed the drink and took it. It wasn't the tastiest thing she had ever had, but it soothed her burning throat. She asked herself again what she was doing with the circusfolk. She wanted to go home.

"Did it help?" Nico asked.

Jessica nodded, her eyes still stinging.

"I wish my healing powers would work. I really screwed up, coming out here instead of going home and figuring out how to get to Polaris."

"Do you want to go there instead of waiting for the circus healer? May be a better choice for you."

"I can't. Lady Lightsong won't teach me because my dad is a criminal, so unless someone convinces her otherwise, I'm stuck. Always stuck. Always someone telling me no, I shouldn't, I can't, because they know what's best for me."

"I don't see how those two are connected."

"They're not! Lady Lightsong has her reasons, but what I meant is it's just one more roadblock! Teren told me to shut off the power to

Aurumice. My mom told me not to go to Polaris. My dad lied about everything, and I'm sure when I ask him, he'll tell me it was to protect me. I just want to make progress with *one life path*, that's all. I want a Bright Path like Wadjette. Is that so wrong?"

"Which one?" Nico settled onto his bed with a history book.

"What?" Jessica was taken aback by his comment.

"What would you do?"

"No one has ever asked me that question before," Jessica replied, thinking carefully for a moment. She glanced in the direction of the needlewasp guts.

"I don't know."

"What about Pennsylvania?" he asked. "If I were you, that would be my choice but I've always been fascinated by your world."

Jessica stared down into the empty cup.

"Yeah, there's parts of home I like too. I would give anything now to order pizza and watch a movie on the couch."

She paused.

"Nico, what I want is to bring parts of Polaris to Aurumice. The mages, the teaching, but to be there with the castlefolk, and be free to go home on a Friday night."

"That's it?"

Again, Jessica looked into the empty cup, then glanced up.

"I would also like a family of my own, one that isn't broken. I'd like to be with someone who understands Centernia and Earth."

Nico shook his head.

"Not me, Jessi. I wish things were different. In another life, maybe, but never again."

Nico drew his eyes down to the pages of the book.

Jessica's heart beat wildly, astounded he suddenly said such a thing aloud. It was like a tiny crack in the wall with just a sliver of light.

She tried to think of a clever response, but instead just sat in silence.

The tempo of the rain increased again, beating against the roof of the tiny tent.

CHAPTER 30

```
Ashlin
Do you know where my sister is?
```

```
Jared
Sort of
```

```
Ashlin
What do you know? We're going crazy looking
for her! Please help!
```

```
Jared
I know she's safe and with friends but I don't
know where they are
```

```
Ashlin
What friends?
```

Jared stared at the phone, standing under a Pennsylvania streetlight on a frigid February evening. It had been months since he had bothered to turn it on. He had a pre-pay plan and luckily the account still had a balance.

He did not expect to find a message from Ashlin.

Jared struggled with an answer. Now that he knew about the girl's father, she suddenly became tangled in the same web as he.

Ashlin
Please help us. My mother is worried sick.

Jared regretted two things, not bringing a scarf, and turning on the phone. Shoving the device into his pocket he briskly walked, weighing his options carefully. He had gone to earth out of boredom, but Ashlin's message only brought him worry, not entertainment.

Jared could go to Stephen, and tell him all that they knew. The man was no longer a clueless human, he was a Nova mage, that made a difference.

He could go to Ashlin, and tell her the entire truth. Though the girl would appreciate the info, but her parents would likely be furious with him.

The third option was to search for Jessica and convince her to return. None of his choices were appealing.

***

After one night in Briken, the Holy Circus packed up. Once they were clear of the terrible air, they spent days scrubbing every surface of the foul rain and dust. The circusfolk muttered curses amongst holy words, irritated with Dahlia's choice to visit the mining town.

They travelled to the south east, hitting the expanse of land known as the Starlight Desert. The villages were far apart, but the desert dwellers were grateful to see the Holy Circus. In every town, they greeted the circusfolk with floral wreaths and beaded chains. The inhabitants wore elaborate head-dresses and lavish scarves, taking inspiration from the beautiful landscape that surrounded them.

Nico was intrigued by the breath-taking stone formations. The land was rich in differing minerals, changing the landscape from sapphire, to scarlet, to rocky jade green as they continued to travel from town to town.

The Starlight Desert took its name not from the sky above, but from the ground itself. The soil was teeming with glittering rocks and great glass pools from long-past volcanic activity. As a result, large swatches of the reflective landscape would mirror the night sky on clear nights.

Two weeks after their misadventure in Briken, Nico and Jessica sat by a small campfire. Kristofori had deliberately built the fire over a sunken patch of violet crystal earth. The light refracted and danced through the ground beneath their feet.

Nico was reminded of the cavern of the Azure Lake in Aurumice.

"What is it like living in the castle?" Kristofori asked. Reese was quietly sitting by, watching a gryphon chicklet play with a featherwing hatchling. The child was wrapped in a thick fluffy blanket despite the warmth in the air.

"Aurumice is a lot of crazy. It's big, there are a lot of people," Jessica explained. She was decorating a gill mask, painting small lines on the surface of the breathing device.

"Is it true you have electric lights?" the boy asked quickly.

"Yeah, it's true."

"How do you not get in trouble?"

"Oh, we do," Jessica said. "We very much do."

Nico looked over at his sister. Hunter sat by away from the group, sharpening knives. The song of scraping metal rang softly, melding with the crackle of the fire.

"How much trouble?"

"Like Teren is swearing about it every week trouble," Jessica explained, looking more closely at the gill mask. The teen seemed dismayed by her handiwork.

"That is your cousin?" Kristofori asked. "You said he leads the castle, but I thought Nico owned the castle."

Nico chose to not respond, letting Jessica speak.

"Well, it's complicated. When Nico was sent to Briken, he gave leadership to my cousin."

"And your cousin doesn't like Trabalis? How does the castle get in trouble for electricity?" the boy asked. He was more intrigued by the details of the technology than the odd political situation.

"They fine us," Jessica replied.

"In the old days, they didn't care so much," Nico remarked.

"Teren says he thinks it was your grandfather in the old days that kept a good relationship with the city. They tolerated your mom but after the forcefield they just aren't having any understanding. Chezidian demanded we turn off the power or be fined."

"That would be impossible," Nico crossed his arms.

"You and I know that, but Teren made me do it anyways. I shut a few of the main breakers."

"I just cannot believe Teren would concede to them."

"Really, Nico? We couldn't win the fight for you, you think we would win over a few lights?"

"I would think it would have gotten better since I left."

"Trabalis doesn't care for the haunted castle," Jessica stated as the fire popped and crackled.

"Really haunted? Real ghosts?" Reese piped up. The boy's eyes were red and glassy.

"No ghosts," Nico said. "No such thing."

"Reese, are you feeling okay?" Jessica's voice was full of worry.

"I'm just cold."

Jessica stood and placed the back of her hand to the little boy's forehead.

"You are burning up with fever, little one. Come on, let's go find your mum."

The boy didn't protest as she led him away.

"You going back to Aurumice someday?" Kristofori asked.

Nico shrugged.

"Could you take me with you if you go for a visit? I promise I won't do anything to Corwin Evansi."

"I suppose."

Hunter threw a knife against a petrified tree stump, followed by three more in a perfect circle.

Her message was clear.

She glanced over.

"What? Just practicing."

"I have forgiven Corwin, and I was there when our father died." Nico stated.

Hunter stood.

"I haven't forgiven that jack dog mage," she pulled the knives out of the stump. "And Kris, neither should you."

"But you heard what mom said, our father locked up our aunt. Corwin was trying to get her back."

"Kaity Cosette may be my aunt but I will never address her as such."

Hunter twirled the knife with elegant precision. She balanced the blade on her finger tip, making it dance back and forth.

"Father was frightened of the mage, I'm sure he had reason," Hunter continued. "Mages of Polaris can't be trusted. Father always said that."

Nico reflected on how Hunter spoke without thought for the people around her, she really was a shadow of Malachi. Nico's mother was a mage of Polaris, at least for a short while in her life. She didn't care much for the rules and chose to stay in Aurumice instead of serving Castle Nova.

"What if you wake up one day and find out your little brother is a mage?" Nico asked, "Could happen, your Aunt Kaity is a mage, and a pretty strong one, so it's somewhere in your bloodline."

"That's different," Hunter said. "Reese wouldn't go to Polaris. He's a true Auroriate."

"People change. Your mother was castlefolk, now she's here."

"Because she had to," Hunter threw the knife again. It struck the earth near Nico's feet.

Nico smirked. His little sister was trying to be threatening, but her tricks were an echo of Malachi. He would not pay mind to a paltry threat.

"The mages messed up the castle and no one could go home," Hunter said. "That's why you can't trust a mage. And I'm telling you, if I ever met him I wouldn't ask questions."

"Hunter, that is not the way of the goddess," Nico pointed out.

"Goddess protects her own. The goddess crumbles mountains and sends the roar of the sea to stop those who would hurt her children. Madiernian balance says one for one."

"But it's never one for one, and Madiernian balance is not written into any of the ancient texts of Aurora. Madiernian balance comes from the religion of the Kiuskia and Kilati. So, if you're telling me that's your way, than I would accept that, moon sister."

Hunter was taken aback. To call someone a moon sister was an insult amongst Auroriates.

"What, you think because I skip out on prayers and don't make candles that I'm not circusfolk?" Nico asked. "I know the ways of the goddess. I have read more books in her name than you will in your lifetime."

Kristofori smirked.

Hunter collected her knives, bristling from the insult.

"I'm just saying I would kill that mage if given a chance."

***

As the twin moons climbed into the night sky, Reese's fever also rose.

Sienna was beside herself with worry. A prayer circle was set up, and Dahlia herself watched over him, mixing a variety of medicines.

By morning, the little boy was barely responsive.

"This is bad, Nico," Jessica paced in their tent. "I wish I had antibiotics for him. Aurumice is how far by nightflight? A day if we took a really, really fast one?"

"And a day back," Nico murmured. He understood how Jessica felt, he desperately tried to think of a solution.

"With a fever that high, he's going to start having seizures," Jessica warned.

"Hey, you awake?" Hunter's voice came through the tent flap.

"Yes," Jessica pushed open the heavy fabric.

"My mother wants you to try your mage healer strength," Hunter said.

"Thought you couldn't trust a mage," Nico muttered. His sister glared.

"Hunter, how did you know about my abilities?"

"Circus people know many things, now go help my brother!"

"I do not know if that is the best idea," Nico interjected. "Jessi, the only person you have ever healed is yourself, right?"

"Yeah."

"And you haven't helped anyone since?"

"Yeah, I know. Maybe now is the time."

"I think this is unwise."

"I don't care what you think," Jessica said. "You barely interact with your own family. You sit around all day doing nothing but moping."

"You are just going to disappoint them," Nico cautioned, "or worse."

Jessica pulled on her boots and followed Hunter. Nico trailed behind. The girl was right, he did choose to wallow in loneliness, but she didn't understand the guilt upon his neck.

They entered Sienna's tent.

Reese clung tightly to a blanket, his little feet hanging out from the edge. His skin was pale.

Jessica sat down next to the bed.

"Please, Jessi, help him," Sienna pleaded. "This came on so fast. I can't lose him, I lost Malachi I can't lose Reese too."

Jessica held the little boy's hand, it burned with fever.

"This is the time to prove yourself, young priestess," Aunt Dahlia stated, leaning on her staff. "If you save him, that title is yours."

Jessica didn't know where to begin. She tried closing her eyes, praying and meditating. She felt nothing, saw nothing.

Minutes ticked by.

"Is it working?" Sienna asked.

"No, I don't know," Jessica stood quickly, bumping into a table. A clock fell and hit the ground with a clang.

"I'm sorry," she said, picking up the clock.

"It's broken?" Sienna asked, her eyes wide.

"I think, I'm so sorry. I will replace it."

"Oh no, no," Sienna looked ready to burst into tears.

"Sienna, can you give us a moment?" Nico said, "Maybe Jessi is overwhelmed with people."

"Okay, of course, of course," Sienna left the tent, crying as she ran out. Dahlia followed her younger sister-in-law.

"I'll buy her another," Jessica said. "Please don't tell me that was a priceless artifact."

Nico cocked his head.

"Jessica, that was more than a clock. It was bad luck. The Auroriates believe to break a clock is to spite the Time Dragon."

"I didn't know…"

"Focus, forget. It's superstition."

Jessica tried to calm herself.

"This isn't as easy as it looks," she said. "Nico, how did you used your mage strength?"

"I just did without thinking."

"But how? Please explain."

He sat beside her on the floor.

"It's very hard to explain. For me, it was like something was bottled inside. You know what soda is, right? That's a thing from where you're from?"

"Yes."

"Like when you shake a bottle of soda, and you see it fizzing up, and it's full, and you know if you let it out it will be like a gush. And you can't stop it. That's how I felt, all the time."

"But how did you actually free your power?"

"I didn't most of the time, because I knew it was dangerous. When I did, it was like this ripping feeling. Like if you tugged off a hangnail but went too deep."

Jessica grimaced.

"I did not like being a mage, and whatever happened to my powers, I'm grateful for it."

"This doesn't help."

Nico's voice lowered.

"When we were little, your cousin said it was like music. It was like listening to a song. Angry, beautiful, sweet, it had a rhythm and flow and he listened for it even though it wasn't his ears."

"Oh. What about Misa?"

"Touching. If someone was on the verge of sleep, she could feel their conscious relax. She would touch your hand, and the moment that energy dissipated enough, she could float right into your mind. But hers was like feeling. Like everyone had a coating outside them, and the coating thinned."

"This is interesting, but I don't know if this will help me," the teen lamented. "You're right."

"Just concentrate, try to think of him getting better," he said. "Jess, it's worth a try, because medicine and prayer aren't working."

"Why haven't they sent for the Circus healer?"

Nico cocked his head. It was a very, very good question.

"What? What is it?"

"I don't know. I imagine they did, but you're here now. Try and do something."

Reese began to moan, twitching.

They sat for a while longer, Jessica's shoulders dropping in despair. She rolled up her sleeves, revealing purple blotches.

"What's that?"

"I think my magic is backwards," Jessica whispered. "Every time I try to heal after that first time, this happens."

"Are you crazy?" Nico hissed. "You should not be doing this!"

"I want to help. Please don't tell Sienna," Jessica whispered, covering her arms.

"Stop trying to help before you hurt him."

"I should go home, and get him an antibiotic. It's all I can do."

A rustle outside the tent alerted them to Sienna's return. The worried mother poked her head into the tent.

"Any change?"

"I'm sorry," Jessica said. "I think I need to try something else. I need a nightflight, to go back to Aurumice."

Nico watched the little boy's foot twitch as he neared convulsions.

"Why Aurumice?"

Nico noticed the dark skin had a little spot on it.

And the spot seemed to be getting bigger. He peered closer.

"What is it?" Jessica asked.

"Get me a light," he lifted the little boy's foot. "I don't think you need to go back to the castle."

Jessica handed him a glowstone.

He looked close, seeing little necrotic track marks.

"I know how to help him."

"How?!" Sienna shouted.

"I need a knife," Nico explained. "A very, very sharp small knife, boiled until it's sterile. Tweezers as well. I also need the white glowstone from Dahlia's tent, a clean cloth, magnifying glass and a small jar."

Sienna ran from the tent to fetch the materials.

"What are you doing?" Jessica leaned close.

"I have a theory, but first I need to wash my hands."

Nico left the tent to find clean water and soap.

A short while later, Jessica held the magnifying glass as he used a delicate knife to slice a tiny little cut into the side of Reese's foot. The child was so sick he barely stirred.

As Nico cut into the flesh, black pus oozed out.

The knife sliced deeper.

A bright yellow dot appeared.

"What the hell is that?!" Jessica whispered.

"Thank you, Aurora," Nico murmured. "Thank you."

Nico cut into the foot further and created a flap of skin as large as a thumbnail. The flesh below was black, but eventually wriggling maggots appeared. The tiny insects squirmed out of the child's skin.

"Oh, my God what is that?!" Jessica grimaced.

Sienna was wide-eyed over Nico's shoulder as he plucked the yellow insects from the boy's flesh and placed them into the jar.

"This is needlewasp larvae," Nico explained. "Some of them carry Puce fever."

Nico continued to dig until he found bright red flesh.

After he finished the excavation, he poured a high-proof alcohol over it. He wrapped the wound in bandages.

"We need to check him over if he has any more, but I think he will be okay," Nico said.

"How did you know?" Sienna asked.

"The Mines of Briken were full of needlewasps. They lay their eggs in host. If you're lucky, it someplace you can reach. If you're unlucky, they get inside your ears, nose, that's bad."

Sienna blanched.

"The fever is a new thing," Nico continued, "when I was first imprisoned, no one caught it from the wasps, but by the time I left, it was more common. It's high fever, then the flesh around the egg site goes red, then puce, then necrotic from the inside out. Then the black veins start spreading. Reese barely has the black, and if we can get him to eat some grey speck mushrooms they have enough antibiotic properties that it will turn the tide back."

"Yes, yes of course!" Sienna cried, "Thank you, Nico, thank you so much!"

"Reese still has a road to travel, Sienna," he cautioned. Strangely though, as he spoke the words, he felt hope.

It had been years since he actually believed something would turn out okay.

He silently begged Aurora to not prove him wrong.

"If you weren't here, we wouldn't have known this! I've never seen Puce fever, I've never seen a needlewasp sting! I am so grateful the goddess brought you home to us!"

Nico reflected on this. Most people outside of the mines did not know about the danger. He would need to talk to Aunt Dahlia about spreading the word through the Auroriates, and to the people.

New illness traveled across the lands frequently, but something about the needlewasps did not set right with Nico. Maybe it was their prevalence in the Mines, but he couldn't shake the feeling there was something more sinister to the tiny insects.

***

They returned to their tent and slept late through the morning. When Jessica finally awoke, Nico was gone. His bed was neatly made, the blankets tucked.

She panicked, fearful for Reese.

Nico *always* slept later than her.

Jessica climbed out of bed and dug a pair of embroidered brown pants out of the wooden chest. She tossed on a yellow-green tunic and pulled her hair back into a ponytail. As she stepped out into the sunny afternoon of the Starlight Desert, she found she didn't have far to travel.

Nico was sitting on patch of pale desert grass. Spread out on a leather blanket were several books and array of tools. A mug of fragrant tea sat beside him with a half-eaten biscuit.

He had a small metal object in his hands.

Jessica watched in silence. Nico's hands shook as he held a flat-head screwdriver. Leaning in more closely, she realized it was the clock she had broken.

"Good morning," Jessica said.

"Afternoon," Nico corrected.

His tone was even. He was not happy, but not sad.

"How is Reese?"

"Much better," Nico nodded. "Much, much better, wanting to get out and about."

"That's wonderful!"

"Please, do me a one favor Jess. What you tried to do last night with healing, until you talk to the Holy Circus healer, just, please don't. You hurt yourself and could have done worse."

Jessica nodded, the bruises on her arms were fading but they still ached.

"I know, I was stupid."

"Your intent was admirable, you need to be careful," Nico set down the screwdriver. "Believe me, I've lived with a dangerous gift."

Jessica chose not to reply, instead she watched him. She wanted to ask more about his vanished power, but instead let him talk.

"This is difficult," he said finally. "It's difficult because my hands will not obey my mind no matter how many times I try to hold steady. The more I try the worse it gets! Briken destroyed my nerves!"

Nico swore.

"But you were able to do it last night with the knife," Jessica encouraged.

"I feel like the goddess was guiding me," he replied.

Jessica searched for the right words. In the past two months, she hadn't seen Nico work on any projects. She didn't want him to become frustrated.

"A table may help you," Jessica suggested. "Something to rest your elbow on? Those clockwork pieces seem very intricate, maybe if we can get that magnifying lens it would help as well."

"Yes, good ideas," Nico said. He set down the clock and the screwdriver. "This may take me a while. Would you mind if I set up a table inside the tent? I think it may rain later."

"Oh no, of course, go ahead."

***

Nico found a table, a magnifying lens on a stand, and more tools. He focused on the tiny clock. Jessica held her tongue, resisting the urge to offer to help him. She checked on Reese a few times, indeed, the boy was bright-eyed. By midday his fever was gone.

By nightfall, the clock was working again.

"Is it good luck to fix a clock?" Jessica grinned.

Nico shrugged.

"Thank you so much," Jessica said. "Hopefully Sienna won't be upset with me anymore."

"Sienna is grateful her son will live, I doubt the clock means anything."

"Can we bring it to her now?" Jessica asked. "But I don't want to carry it, in case I break it again."

"With my hands, you want me to carry it?"

"Fine," Jessica said, "but if I get double bad luck it's your fault."

They found Sienna with Reese. The boy was eating a stew brewed from his prescribed mushrooms. He hopped out of bed and tackled Nico.

"You saved me!" he shouted.

"Reese, stay in bed!" Sienna ordered. She noticed the clock in Jessica's hand and seemed puzzled.

"Nico fixed it," Jessica smiled. "I hope it's enough to wind back the bad luck. I'm very sorry again."

Sienna took the clock carefully.

"Oh, this is so wonderful."

Sienna set the clock on the table. Jessica took a measured step further away, afraid to break the clock again.

"You need to rest, child," Nico said, setting Reese back down on the bed. Jessica was reminded of Penrik, looking at Nico with those same eyes of admiration.

CHAPTER 31

Late one evening, Jared knocked on Teren's door. The man's emotions seemed different from his usual mix of joviality and masked brooding. Instead, there was an odd determination that Teren found intriguing.

He opened the door. Jared had a satchel over his shoulder.

"We have work to do, and you're going to help me," he proclaimed.

"What sort of work?"

"Grab your coat. We're heading to the Azure, and we will be there for a while."

Not sure what the mage had planned, Teren grabbed his long black jacket. The Azure Lake had a tendency to get chilly later in the year. He followed Jared down through the Castle, past the store rooms and wine cellars, through twisted dark passageways.

The tunnels under the Castle were largely uncharted and abandoned. It was rare anyone travelled beyond the food store rooms, past the ancient dungeon and crypts.

Teren followed Jared through clandestine dirt hallways until they came to yellow chamber with a massive machine. As big as the room, it whirred and growled as ancient gears turned. It was the fake power generator of Aurumice, used to obscure the fact the electricity came from the foundation itself. Teren continued to follow Jared past the machine, crawling through a small circular hatch to their destination— the glittering cavern of the Azure. Teren's breath caught in his throat.

It had been a long time since he stood on the shore of the placid lake. Phosphorescent plants grew on every surface and across the high rounded ceiling. Glow stones were embedded in the rock, giving the impression of a night sky.

Misa used to make up constellations and stories.

His heart ached, and he knew why he avoided this room. It was the most peaceful and secluded chamber in all of Castle Aurumice. Teren shook away the memories and masked them with sarcasm.

"If this is your plan to seduce me…" Teren began.

"No, this is more serious," Jared pulled a leather bound tome from his satchel. "Ashlin texted me, so I started following her family, and it's bad. Carrie Anne is not getting better. I don't know where the hell Jessi is, but I don't think she's okay, and we're stupid to pretend she is."

"What are you proposing?"

"We find her," Jared replied, flipping through the book. "How familiar are you with the basic mage-bond ritual?"

"I have never read mage texts," Teren said. "My powers are not generally covered in them, except to say I should die."

Jared handed him the book.

"A focus ritual, a chant. Jessi says the power of the wires is strange, especially down here. We know there is something to this lake. Misa said it once to me before, we're sitting on some sort of energy node."

Teren nodded. He also recalled his sister's ranting about the same idea. But she was an ephemeral mage and could sense things that he could not.

"You can feel when they are near, and I can see through their eyes. Together, if we combine our strengths and channel power from Aurumice, we may be able to cross the distance to find them."

"How? Seeing and feeling are two different things."

"Read the chapter in front of you. It talks about a far-listener and far-seer. Their powers are different but they magnify each other. The same as you and I. I'm just tossing the lake in there as a theoretical. If nothing else, no one will bother us down here."

Teren leaned against a rock, studying the book. Jared scouted a good spot where the moss was soft at the edge of the lake. The more Teren read, the more he understood the validity of Jared's point.

After a while, he closed the book.

"Alright, I am willing to try."

Jared sat in the moss bed, cross-legged. Teren carefully sat across from him, mirroring his pose.

"If this doesn't work, then we stand in the lake," Jared smirked, reaching for Teren's hands.

They both closed their eyes.

He sensed the swirl of the castlefolk around him. He pushed out further, touching the hearts of the nearby town. Some people were familiar to him, others were strangers. He stretched his mind as far as it would stretch, but he could go no further. His powers were remarkably ordinary.

Not wishing to break Jared's concentration, Teren continued to explore, but after a while he gave up.

"I sense nothing different."

"Neither do I," Jared said. "Try again."

Teren sighed, feeling the exercise to be pointless. He let his mind wander out into the castle. Again, he moved through the usual bustle of emotion, but found nothing unique. Eventually he settled on Jared's mind. His friend was feeling dejected.

Jared opened his eyes.

"Maybe I'm wrong and this is pointless."

"The book said it was possible, perhaps it just needs practice and meditation."

Teren reached for the book, reading the pages again. Jared lay back with a mournful sigh. He ran his hand along the water's edge.

"I think we are missing something," Teren said. "We're not connected so we're not focused together. Sit up, and concentrate on me."

Jared nodded, heeding Teren's request.

This time, Teren did not close his eyes, and neither did Jared.

"I see through your eyes," Jared said. "I look good today."

Teren smirked, sensing Jared's emotion. The comment was flippant, but his emotions were contradictory....fear....hope....worry...love...

Teren licked his dry lips.

"Show me what you see through your eyes," he commanded.

"How?"

"The book said the far-seer and far-listener were as one. I'm sure it would please you for that to mean physically, but they mean psychically. I will take your emotions. I'll push aside your fear, *you are determined. You will succeed.*"

"Yeah," Jared grinned, staring into Teren's eyes. "Yes, we can do this. I can do this."

Teren felt an odd sensation at the back of his eyeballs.

"You're doing something," he told Jared. "Keep doing it, make me see what you see."

Teren's vision vibrated, sending a wave of nausea rippling through his gut. He fought to control it.

"More."

The vision seemed to split, until he was seeing both himself and Jared at the same time. He realized he could see through Jared's eyes.

Without warning, his vision shifted completely. He saw through Vina's eyes as she walked down the hallway towards the dining room.

The woman was irritated.

"Whoa," Jared laughed. "She's angry at someone. This is the strangest feeling ever, I'm not angry, but I feel her anger!"

They jumped from castlefolk to castlefolk. Jared seemed to be steering. The effect was dizzying and Teren abruptly let go of Jared's hands, uncomfortable with the sensation.

"That was wild!" Jared grinned. "I've never felt anything like that in my entire life!"

"This is good," Teren was hopeful for the first time in months. "I just was feeling a little nauseous."

"Yeah, used to happen to me when I was a kid. Like spinning too much."

"Again?" Teren asked.

"Of course," Jared grabbed for his hands.

They locked their mage strengths much quicker, and jumped into the minds of the castlefolk. Their minds stretched further out, dancing through Trabalis.

"It's too wild, fixate on someone!" Teren warned.

"Who?"

"Think of anyone!"

"Who?"

"I don't know. Wadjette!"

Immediately, Teren saw the sparring field.

"Okay, we can do this. Let's start with Jessi. Think of Jessi."

They jumped through minds in Trabalis, past Rockwood, out to the southern roads. Green-lined streets filled Teren's vision.

"Yellow Valley," he said. "Do you normally stretch this far?"

Never did he think his powers could reach the lush little city of greenery.

"No," Jared's voice was in awe. "Usually I see a little ways around the castle, very rarely to Trabalis. Never to Yellow Valley."

Teren gripped Jared's hands tighter. Their minds continued to jump together. He didn't know how long they were locked in sync, but finally, Jared released his hands, falling back in exhaustion.

"I need a break."

"We're close!" Teren insisted.

"Yes, but my eyeballs are killing me."

"You will not give up now."

"I'm not giving up," Jared rubbed his eyes. "Give me a five minute break."

As Jared rested on the shore. Teren sat and thought, touching the rocky earth.

"Greenbriar, mother of the castle," he whispered. "Great grandmother Amethysta, hear me."

He closed his eyes. With his power, he reached down into the foundation, the same way he had connected with Jared. An eerie sensation crept up his spine and he got the feeling he and Jared were not the only two spirits in the underground cavern.

Teren allowed his mind to wander, though he could not see, he could feel with greater clarity. His castlemark began to tingle upon his shoulder.

"Jared, you were right to bring us down here. We can use the power of the castle to magnify our strength."

"How?" Jared asked.

"Touch the ground. Fixate on me, then focus on the foundation of Aurumice, invite in her essence."

"Okay," Jared seemed incredulous, but he took Teren's hands. "How do you know Aurumice is a woman?"

"She is, the castle was founded by Greenbriar, and Amethysta. She's the mother of the castle, the first mage here. All castlefolk know this. Are you helping me or not?"

"Okay, okay, I am."

"Focus on me first," Teren repeated, "then Aurumice."

Jared sat on the ground again, exhaling slowly. Teren connected with Jared, again he chose determination as a binding emotion.

"Reach into the foundation of the castle," Teren commanded.

As Teren followed his own advice, he was unprepared for the explosion of energy. Instead of channeling from mind to mind, they were pulled into the soil and the energy rivers that fed through the earth.

"It's too much," Jared gritted his teeth.

"Think of Jessi," Teren said. "Think of Nico. Focus on them."

As he spoke, his body tingled, his heart raced, and reality began to blur in a terribly familiar way.

"We hit the edge of a Gate!"

"This was your damn idea, focus on them!"

Teren shifted Jared's emotions, introducing love, determination and loyalty. He felt Jared's hands tighten around his.

Racing through the ground, their minds followed the veins of magic through the soil.

Until they slammed into their targets.

Teren could suddenly see the inside of a tent. It was Jessica's mind. She opened a tent flap, looking around.

They were still with the Holy Circus.

As she walked, Teren frantically tried to find a clue as to their location. The landscape was still fairly green with just a hint of fall. They continued to follow the girl around as she walked through the camp. It was fascinating, Teren had never seen the center of an Auroriate circus.

The girl walked into the forest, following a small river to a lake. The waters were very blue and pristine. Boats floated by in the distance at the edge of a small town, their sails striped in purple and yellow. Unique architecture dotted the landscape with short glowing spires.

"Watersglade," Jared said aloud. "Those boats have the mark of Quelyn Fishermen!"

"Are you certain?!"

"That town has a unique skyline, I know it, and see when she glances to the right? The steam? There's where they pull jahooli gas from the ground, it powers the city. It's Watersglade!"

Jared released Teren's hands and they both stood, breathless.

Behind Jared, on the opposite shore, his sister Misa was watching them intently.

"That was the single most amazing thing I've ever felt!" Jared exclaimed.

As Teren moved to point to the figure, she vanished. Teren shook it off as residual magic, taking in the enormity of their accomplishment.

"It was terrifying magic I've ever felt, but you were right!"

"To Watersglade?"

"Yes, to Watersglade."

***

Word spread quickly of the clock repair, and it seemed that everyone in the circus had a broken something that needed fixing. In the days that followed, a pile of odd mechanical projects arrived at their small tent.

It was something Nico found vastly more entertaining than prayers and candles.

When his hands grew too tired, or a malfunction too puzzling, Jessica was quick to help. She also found the work more interesting than acolyte training.

"What I wouldn't give for the internet," Jessica said, "and five minutes in a hardware store."

"And I should like two working eyes."

"It is looking better, almost normal from the outside."

"I've given up on it healing."

"You shouldn't. It may heal on its own, or I might be able to heal it some day. Just give me

time. I know it's not the same, but you'd be damn impressed by what I used to do fixing Aurumice when you were gone."

Nico studied Jessica's expression, her eyes were oddly sad.

"You still want to go home," he stated.

"No, and yes," she replied. "It's just today. If I did my calendar calculations right, it's my eighteenth birthday . It's also April which means it's been seven months. Nico, I'm not going to graduate high school."

"Oh," he replied. He knew such a statement was heavy on many levels. High school was a critical achievement in life, and for Jessica to pass it up, her parents would be furious. An eighteenth birthday was also a monument in her world, an event with much fanfare and freedom.

"You're not leaving the Circus though, are you?" she asked.

"No, this is my home now."

"Are you sure you don't want to try to find the Corvalian? We could just ask Sienna, maybe your father gave her a clue where to look."

"From what I understand he had to travel a long way to get that tattoo. I don't even know where to begin."

"Just ask Dahlia, or one of the other elders. Nico, your father was the type of person who wouldn't keep that to himself. He must have bragged to someone."

Nico did not reply.

Jessica shrugged and continued to focus on the project. Nico debated if it was worth seeking out the mark, but pushed the thoughts from his mind as he focused on the clockwork piece at hand. His finger rubbing along the metal edge, and he felt an unusual tingling sensation. Dismissing it, he unscrewed the mechanism and documented the pieces, his mind wandered again.

The absurdity of their strange existence struck Nico's suddenly. He was a fugitive, to hide amongst his father's family was logical. But Jessica was neither fugitive nor circusfolk. She was a mage who desperately needed training, and a girl of earth who had a life and family. Jessica waited so patiently to meet the mage healer of the Circus, Nico wondered if it was time to leave Dahlia and find the healer on their own.

If the Holy Circus healer even existed.

"What's this thing supposed to do?" Jessica said, picking up a mechanical bird.

"It's a clockwork bird, should have a key. It's part of the Wonders show."

Dahlia's troupe had an interesting collection of clockwork creatures and puppets. Some were large and powered by people who rode inside them. Others were small and displayed in a tent of wonders. Each creature was from a lesson of the goddess.

Nico reached over on the bench and selected a gold key with a green string.

"This I think went to that bird. Kristofori dropped it off last night. Just said it hasn't worked right in years."

Jessica took the key, looking for a corresponding socket. She carefully inserted it and twisted the key. The bird clicked.

When she released it, the bird began to chirp, its head bobbled and its eyes opened. One wing flapped smoothly and the other didn't move.

"That is amazing engineering. The sound quality is phenomenal, probably a little drum in there with the recording?" she asked. "I still can't get over how any of these mechanimals are handmade."

"I doubt some of them were," Nico said. "Most of these were made back when the Madiernan continent still had electricity. They had machine tooling."

"Well that explains a lot of this."

The bird's movements became jerkier, the other wing stopped flapping and the creature grinded to a halt.

"I think I'll work on this one next," she said.

"Are you really upset by your birthday?" Nico asked abruptly.

Jessica shrugged, and Nico resolved to find her a suitable replacement for a party.

He also decided it was time for them to travel to find the mystic healer on their own. They had waited far too long and he had been a miserable ass. He couldn't change the past few months, but maybe a gesture could serve as a small apology.

The duo spent the remainder of the afternoon working until the chime rang for prayers.

Jessica stood, placing the intricate parts in a box.

"I will see you at prayers?" Nico asked, hurrying. He wanted to find out more about the nearby town.

"Yeah," Jessica swore under her breath. She counted carefully. "I think I lost two screws."

The teen crawled on her hands and knees, searching. Nico took the opportunity to leave, thanking Aurora for the distraction.

***

Later in the evening, Nico was nervous as he approached the tent he shared with Jessica. He had achieved half of his goal, planning out an appropriate birthday surprise. The plans to leave the Dahlia to find the mystic healer he was still working on.

For the first time in years, he wore formal attire.

"I have something to show you," Nico approached Jessica, holding neatly folded fabric.

"What is it?" Jessica looked up from her work.

"Here, would you like to wear this?" he asked, holding out the fabric. "Sienna said it should be your fit."

Jessica took the garment, allowed it to unfold, revealing lavender dress of layered translucent fabric. The skirt was full, atypical for the clothing of the circusfolk.

"Wow, this looks like something extra-fancy. I mean everything the circusfolk wear is a different kind of pretty, but this…"

"I have jewelry too," he said, reaching into his pocket for strings of shiny beads.

"Okay," she said. "Where are we going? Does this have a mask to match?"

"No mask, you're not an Auroriate acolyte tonight. We're going into town," he explained, "to Watersglade."

"For…?"

"You will see."

"I'm really confused. This is so different."

"Give me a chance," he said, leaving the tent. He began to second guess his idea as frivolous.

Stupid, stupid, stupid

He argued with himself until Jessica emerged. Sienna was an excellent judge of fit, the lavender fabric wrapped around the girl's form perfectly.

"This way," Nico said, leading her to the edge of camp. A circus cart waited, hitched to a pair of dappled purple-grey bicorns. The cart was a little less garish than the typical ones used by the circus, but was covered like a proper coach. Kristofori sat in the box, flipping through a history book. Hunter sat beside her brother, juggling a set of fire pearls. The tiny little orbs caught the light and reflected it with an unusual brilliance. Neither circusfolk wore their masks or typical clothing. They looked like a pair of normal cubs from Trabalis.

Hunter caught most of the pearls in one seamless motion, but a few bounced away and she scrambled to get them from the base of the box.

She collected pearls and clambered to her feet.

"You both look nice," Kristofori complimented.

"Thank you," Jessica said. "Though I still don't know where I'm going."

"You'll like it," Hunter smirked. "But we need to leave before Reese escapes our mother. He was hopping mad that he couldn't come with us."

He had only asked Kristofori to tend the bicorns for the evening, but Hunter invited herself.

Nico opened the door and Jessica climbed into the coach. On the seat, Nico had left a cloak. He draped it around his shoulders, feeling secure under the hood.

It was the first night they had gone out into a city without the mask of the circusfolk. He silently hoped eyes would be on Jessica, and not pay as much attention to him.

"Is this for my birthday?" Jessica grinned.

He nodded as the carriage started moving.

"Circusfolk do not acknowledge birthdays, but Watersglade is a nice little town to have a night befitting of a birthday. It boasts some unique sights."

The jaunty wagon left the circusfolk camp and found the road to town. Nico glanced out the window. Somehow an awkward silence fell between them. Jessica kept her hands neatly folded together. She glanced to the left.

"I may need to figure out how to make a mold," Jessica said suddenly. "There's this piece inside the bird that snapped, I think. It's metal, and I have no way to solder it. Even if I had solder I don't think the joint would hold. But if I could make a mold, and we used the forge to do a pour, I may be able to recreate the piece."

"I'm sure the smith would help us," Nico said. "But how small a piece?"

"I'm sure I would need to grind down the final form," Jessica said. She went into detail explaining the piece and they argued about mold-making materials until they arrived at the entrance to Watersglade. A large sign of welcome was positioned over a bridge three carriages wide.

"Is that electricity?" Jessica sat up, noticing the lights in the distance

"No, it's jahooli gas." Nico explained, feeling warmth from her smile.

The buildings of Watersglade were characterized by poles of light built into the sides like swirled canes.

"It's only city in Madierna that has a gas system throughout the entire place," Nico explained. "It's regarded as the gem of the Gellius region."

"What if there's ever a fire?" Jessica asked.

"Do you always think of the worst thing first?" Hunter peered her head upside down through the window. Nico had almost forgotten about his sister.

"No. Things break, that's all," Jessica explained.

"You're a blusterbelsh," Hunter sighed.

"A what?"

"How do you not know what a blusterbelsh is?" Hunter asked. "Is Aurumice that backwards?"

"No, I'm the backwards one," Jessica smirked. "I'm not from Aurumice."

"You from the north?" Hunter asked, her face turning red.

"No."

"The Islands of Therissina?" she asked.

"No," Jessica replied.

"Then where?" Hunter slid through the open window, taking the bench seat across from Nico and Jessica.

"It's a puzzle, you can figure it out," Jessica smirked.

Nico shook his head, the game was a bad idea.

"Can we play Guess and Question?" Hunter asked.

"Sure."

"Can you see the ocean from your home town?"

"No."

"A lake?"

"No."

"A river?"

"Yes."

"Alright," Hunter sat back, thinking carefully.

The carriage came to a stop as the streets became more densely packed with people.

"Nico, I think this is far as I can get," Kristofori said. "I need to bring the carriage to the public yard."

"We will stay fairly close. We'll meet you there," Nico said.

He opened the door and Jessica climbed out.

Hunter leaned out of the carriage.

"Is it Lamby?" Hunter asked.

"No," Jessica replied.

Nico gave his sister an exaggerated wave goodbye and led Jessica through the streets of the little city. Sienna had given him a map earlier in the day and he studied the landmarks instead of attending prayers. He did not want to seem like a stranger to the city, that was the fastest way to garner a thief's attention.

Walking down stone streets, they soon came to a small lake, bordered on one side by public walkways. From the center of the water rose three towers.

"What's this?" Jessica asked. Couples in formal attire clustered around a small building bordered by statues of chimeras.

"This is the Hall of the King, it's Watersglade's most famous building. There's a celebration going on tonight," he explained. "They do one every full moon of Kiuskia. I am apologizing that it is not in your honor, but from what I understand, there is cake. Only place in Madierna you will find Jackinee cake. The frosting is made from Lingtang berries, which are only found growing on the beaches in Watersglade."

Jessica took his arm.

The couple walked into the small room, surrounded by party-goers in formal attire. Nico felt the suffocation of the crowd and began to panic, wanting to escape. What if there were mages of Nova at the event?

Jessica didn't release his arm. He fought down his fear, realizing he would look foolish to run from a crowd. Jessica either didn't notice or pretended not to notice as they followed the other attendees down a set of winding stairs.

"Underground?" Jessica was intrigued. "Someday I'll show you a place Jared showed me when we went to Katanzarko City."

"Jared has grown to be a good friend to you?" Nico asked.

"The best, I can count on him for anything."

"You like him? Romantically?"

"Oh no! Never! Kaity and I are pretty certain he has a thing for my cousin. Though I know he has a relationship with a guy in Polaris. I saw more of that than I ever wanted to see."

"Oh..." Nico wanted to ask more, but wasn't certain how to say it.

Descending deeper underground, they traveled down a dozen sets of stairs. Eventually they arrived in a gold and green hallway, lit by the gas lamp cylinders. Again, the panic and claustrophobia started to grip Nico. He could feel an excuse to run forming on his lips, but he moved forward. At last, they entered the main chamber.

Jessica was enthralled.

"It's amazing!"

The Hall of the King was an underwater marvel.

Spacious and bright, the room could hold a thousand people. The floor was filled with games of chance, tables of food and drinks.

A perfect dome of metal and glass separated the grand party from the lake above. The gas lights were aptly placed throughout the water so even at night the sea life was illuminated. Water dancers wearing gill masks swam outside the dome.

Jessica was delighted.

"Do you like games of chance?" Nico asked.

"I've never been to a casino before," Jessica said. "Nico, this is so amazing you have no idea. Back home, you need to be eighteen to gamble. What a perfect birthday gift!"

"Good. They have cake, that's what Sienna said, that the best bakeries in town typically showcase their goods at every moon dance."

"You know what this reminds me of?" Jessica said ascended a staircase to an elevated walkway. "It reminds me of the aquarium, maybe I should fill it and add fish."

"Aquarium?"

"In the tower room. Teren gave it to me. The aviary with the glass floor aquarium."

"Really? He unlocked that room for you?"

"Yeah."

"And what did he say?"

"Well, it was odd, because he was pretty sure you were dead." Jessica explained. "Couldn't stop crying."

"I hardly think I was the reason," Nico said. "That room was his mother's."

"Yeah, I knew that. All the animals had been there."

"That's where she died."

Jessica looked away from the glass and instead fixed her gaze on him. He instantly regretted his words.

"Why would he do that? Give that room to me?"

"Closure?" Nico shrugged. "Healing?"

"I wonder if it's haunted," Jessica mused.

"Ghosts are just stories," Nico replied. "We have magic, but no ghosts."

"I don't believe that," Jessica argued. "Because I've seen Misa in my dreams more than once since she died."

Nico wanted to tell her about his encounter, but knew it would stir up trouble he did not want to deal with.

Jessica became distracted by the games. He followed her explaining to her the rules of the dice and cards. They tried a few, losing horribly. The cake was as promised, spectacular in flavor, though the enjoyment was fleeting. The entire time, Nico felt a black cloud following him around. He feigned interest for her, but he felt like all eyes were upon him, any moment the mages would grab for him and rip him away.

In spite of his fear, he was acutely aware of Jessica's every movement. The girl would take his hand easily, no concern for the lack of fingers. She would lean against him ever so slightly.

Nico remembered the Halloween years before when he had followed Jessica and her friends around a Halloween-themed center of games and events. It was a strange echo. She was so different from the girl she was, but still the same.

"Dance with me," she said suddenly.

"Uh, no, dancing…"

"Oh, come on Nico, you can dance." Jessica encouraged. "Look, I'm never going to Prom, at least let me pretend to care about silly teenage things for one night."

He wanted to tell her not to think her customs silly, but she tugged on his arm and brought him to the dance floor.

"This is the Starflower Waltz, do you know the steps?" Nico asked.

"Jared taught me a lot," she replied. "Now are you leading or do I need to do that too?"

He relented as they joined the couples of the dancefloor in an elaborate series of twists and turns. His body seemed to remember the steps but his mind was running away. He felt terribly self-conscious and painfully aware he could only see part of the room.

The tempo slowed. She leaned close. Nico's hands vibrated from the core of his bones. It was a different sensation than the tremors, and the oddness only increased his anxiety. Something was wrong.

"Please," she encouraged. "Just be yourself again."

Jessica leaned closer.

Nico's heart raced and he dropped her hands.

Once he evaded her, the look of hurt broke his heart. He didn't know what else to do, so he ran from the dancefloor.

It was a foolish move.

She chased after him.

Embarrassed, he ran up the stairwell, pushing past people. He ran as fast as he could but his old injuries caught up. His back spasmed painfully as he ran out into the night. Nico ran past groups of people to an open park. The lavish Watersglade gardens were comprised of small islands, footbridges and decorative ponds.

Jessica caught up, grabbing his arm.

He wasn't going to escape her, so he stopped running. Eye downcast to the grass, he wanted to melt away into a puddle of black ichor and be washed away.

"What's wrong?!" she demanded.

"Everything."

"You make no sense to me. How is everything wrong?!"

"I don't know!" he cried out. "It's not you. I feel very strange, maybe my powers are coming back. And, my feelings are so…not where they should be."

"For me?"

"No," his hand went to his forehead. "About life."

For the first time, he put the sensation into words. It was the invisible force that drove him away from people, into the solitude of books and sleeping. It was the ever-present darkness that made him miserable.

And it was inside of himself.

"It's like the happiness is gone. I look toward the future, and nothing makes me excited. It's dread and this feeling that won't go away. The mages will get me, and I'll go back to prison. I am not free. I wish you could understand that, Jessi. This was stupid, this whole night was a mistake. I will never be able to change things."

A chilly night wind whispered through the park and Jessica folded her arms.

"But you're safe now. Everything we've been doing since the day you saved Reese. You were acting like yourself again! What was this? Tonight? What were you trying to say? This isn't a birthday party. It's a romantic night on the town. This is where we left off and this is what's been missing!"

Jessica reached into her pocket and pulled out his necklace of Aurumice.

"You gave this to me years ago, and I wore it every day you were gone! Not just because it made me feel like I had a castlemark, but it made me feel like you were still with me."

Nico could not stand to see the symbol of his home. He ripped the necklace from her hand and threw it in a pond.

It plinked with a tiny ripple and vanished beneath the surface of the water.

"Jessica, that life, that person, is dead! I had hoped that tonight would change things," Nico said. "I want to feel normal again. It's so maddening, because I know things are wrong. I shouldn't feel panic walking into a crowd, I shouldn't have nightmares every night. Even when the castle fell under the forcefield, it was nothing compared to this. I want to feel normal again!"

"You know how you just said that Teren gave me the atrium for closure, so he would heal?" her voice lowered and she fought back tears. "You're not letting yourself heal. Tell me what happened to you in the Mines and maybe it will free you. You think you were alone but you were never alone."

"I don't want to talk about the Mines," Nico turned and walked down the stony path. Jessica grabbed his hand, pulling him to a bench. They sat under a glade of white trees.

She took his hand in hers.

To his surprise, she pulled his hand to her lips and kissed the stubs of his destroyed finger. For a moment, he hoped her blood mage magic would surface and they would be healed. Instead all he felt was the lingering wetness of her kiss.

Jessica looked up, searching his face. In shame, he dodged her gaze.

"Did you *ever* have feelings for me?" she asked.

The question surprised him.

"Yes," he replied. "But I was doomed for the mines and you were young..."

"You gave me that necklace. What did it mean back then?"

"I...don't know.... I just wanted to give you something..."

"Why did you stop loving me?" she asked.

The question was strange.

His feelings for her had never truly vanished, but had greyed like all of his life.

"I forced myself to eat the cake tonight," he said suddenly.

Jessica crinkled her face, waiting for his explanation.

"I made myself eat the cake. I know it was good cake, the logical side of my brain said it was good cake. I felt nothing from it, no euphoria, no warm, happiness, all the little emotions that go with that first bite of a wonderful piece of cake. I have no appetite for any food. I ate it because I knew you would be sad and ask me why. So, I ate the cake, and pretended I liked it."

"Okay, so I'm cake," Jessica smiled at the absurdity of the metaphor, "but this is all of life for you?"

Nico nodded.

"But you are *not* cake," he insisted, "and I refuse to lie to you because it would be cruel."

He pulled his hand back.

Jessica withdrew to her side of the bench, pulling her knees to her chin. She pondered for a while and finally spoke.

"You know our friend can likely help you. He's quite good with emotions."

"No. It's dangerous."

"How?"

"Because, he tried to help my mother. He didn't know what he was doing, but his highs made the lows worse. If you are unable to sustain your happiness on your own, it simply won't work."

Jessica set her feet down on the ground.

"You'll heal," Jessica encouraged.

"I tried to kill myself once," he confessed. "But it didn't work, and some days I wish it had."

He leaned close resting his head on her shoulder. They sat for a few moments in silence until Nico stood.

"Sorry I ruined your birthday and threw the necklace."

"Nico, please believe me, it's not ruined," she said, wrapping her arm around his waist. Though he had not changed, he did feel a little more able to breathe.

***

They walked to the stable lot. It was a further walk than Nico had anticipated, and by the time they arrived his back ached so badly that he hobbled. Jessica did not comment though he was sure she noticed.

When they arrived, Kristofori was dozing, wrapped in a blanket in the box.

"Where's Hunter?" Nico asked.

Kristofori snorted awake, and looked around. He pointed.

The girl was leaving a shed that served warm drinks. She approached them.

"Some woman was looking for you."

"Woman?" Jessica asked.

"Not you, him," Hunter gestured to Nico.

"What did she look like?"

"Sapien-like," Hunter replied.

"My mom?" Jessica asked.

"No, younger, but older than you. Dark hair, dark eyes, weird blue marks. She actually had a pet gryphon following her around like a dog. I thought she was circusfolk, but no, she was weird."

"Oh no," Nico said. "We need to leave."

He couldn't believe his night could get any worse.

"She was a really odd burch," Hunter said. "Asked about you and then said not to say she was here. Rude."

Nico climbed into the box, taking the reins from Kristofori.

"We need to run!"

Jessica climbed into the carriage.

"But I just got my hot cider..." Hunter whined. "It's too full for bumps in the road."

"Now!"

"The halter straps are loose, you need to wait or the whole thing will rip off." Hunter warned her brother. Setting down the mug, she tightened the straps on the harness. "And calm yourself, she wasn't armed much as I can tell."

Hunter climbed into the box beside Nico.

"In fact, I knicked one of her knives because she annoyed me so much," Hunter displayed a small red-handled knife to Nico. A white X was painted on the side.

"It's sort of useless and dull."

"Hunter!" Kristofori's eyes were wide. "Mother told you to not steal!"

Nico snapped the reigns and the carriage lunged forward. Hunter spilled her cider on her cloak.

"Oh blood'ura," Hunter swore. "I wanted to drink that!"

Nico chose not to reply to his sister. Nico's hands trembled as he navigated the streets at a reckless speed.

***

When they arrived at camp, Nico abandoned the carriage and ran for his tent. Jessica and Hunter chased after him, leaving Kristofori to tend the bicorns.

"Nico, where are you going?!" Jessica shouted.

He turned.

"She bought me, she's going to try to bring me wherever she was going," he explained. "I don't know how she tracked me here, but I can't let her find me!"

"Well, I'm going with you," Jessica stated.

"No! Do not follow me! Either stay here, or go back to Aurumice."

"There is no one in Aurumice who can teach me how to heal…"

"Of course there is, you can talk to your father."

"No! He would be impossible! I'm going with you!"

"Nico, that woman was nothing!" Hunter interjected. "I'm certain even Kris would win in a fight against her!"

Nico dashed into the tent, grabbing a bag, trying to get his thoughts straight through the panic. The darkness overwhelmed him as he sat on the floor. His mind was sucked back to the strange jumble of existence between the mines and the Circus.

Unannounced, Aunt Dahlia entered the tent. The matriarch stood proudly, leaning on her staff. Hunter waited behind her.

"Leaving us?"

"Aunt Dahlia, I need to thank you for everything, but…"

"We need to talk. Come with me."

"There is a woman…"

"I know, you are safe here."

Nico glanced at Jessica.

"You don't understand!"

"Do not question me. Come, boy."

Nico relented and followed his Aunt Dahlia to her tent.

Inside, he sat on a woven stool, looking at the candles and not making eye contact with his aunt.

"Tell me what concerns you."

"It's very complicated. There is this woman who rescued me, and by the goddess, I was grateful even though she was a slaver. I escaped her when the mages attacked, but I fear she's found me again."

"Are you certain?"

"I have no doubt she approached Hunter and Kris in Watersglade."

"There is something that does not seem right," Aunt Dahlia said. "If you were truly grateful to this rescuer, why did you flee? You react as if she was a demon and not your savior."

Nico was quiet, then finally spoke.

"Aunt Dahlia, do you believe that the dead are truly gone and unreachable? That Aurora takes them to a land beyond?"

"There are tales of ghosts all across our books, you know that. It's the mages that try to pretend there are no spirits in the world. They claim superior knowledge."

"I think Misa is communicating with me"

"Misa, the dreamspinner mage? One of your castlefolk?"

Nico nodded. "She told me to flee, so I listened."

"Your friend, whether she be your spirit or inner voice is correct. Casimirio is no ally of yours."

Nico was astounded.

"You know her?"

"We hired her."

Nico was dumbfounded.

"To save me?"

"I say these words with the gravest of secrecy. If you tell anyone, we shall deny it, and outcast you. The implications that the Auroriates would hire a mercenary would be quite grave, but what had to be done was to be done. Casimirio could forge the proper documents, facilitate the payment, and get you out of that hell pit safely. She was supposed to deliver you to us before the mages intervened."

Nico crossed his arms.

He knew the reach of the Holy Circus was far, but was beginning to see there was much he did not know.

"Casimirio was supposed to meet us at Razim, west of the Starlight Desert, but I don't know what caused her to change her mind. Instead of handing you over, she stole a gryphon chicklet and ran. We had been hunting for her when the goddess delivered you to our camp."

"So you paid her for me, and she decided not to finish her side of the agreement? Aunt Dahlia, that makes no sense!"

"We assumed someone paid her more, perhaps your Aurumice."

"No. No way Aurumice could have afforded that. They're struggling to survive."

"The reason Casimirio changed her mind is irrelevant. She has betrayed the Holy Circus too many times. Stealing that gryphon directly from us is a grave offense. Be assured, if she comes near, she will be captured and dealt with," Aunt Dahlia crossed her arms. "I don't know why she's skulking around here, but she is an arrogant woman and likes to play deadly games. She has crossed the wrong people."

Dahlia gestured to her staff, the yellow crystal at its end glowed brightly.

"You are safe, please do not fear, nephew."

Nico reflected on her words as he sorted through the past few months.

"Thank you," he realized the staggering cost the Auroriates paid to free him.

"We want you to be a part of this family. We want you to stay with us, to perhaps even lead. You have gifts, you need to use them."

"I told you my power is gone."

"It will return. No mage has ever been stripped of their power. Whatever force has taken it from you, will be overcome. You will heal and it will return."

"Zia…"

"She will not cross into this camp, there are many protections and wards against her. Boy, trust me that you are safe."

"What if I leave?"

"Until I deal with Casimirio, we will assign you a guard."

"What about Jessica?"

"Likewise, she will be safe."

"Thank you."

"Rest easy, no one will ever take you from us," Aunt Dahlia reassured.

Nico thanked his aunt again. He stood to leave, and asked one more question.

"I am concerned that Jessi's skills are going to waste. If we do not cross paths with the healer soon, I want to take Jessi to her."

Aunt Dahlia nodded, but did not say anything.

Nico thought her response odd, but let it pass as he left the tent.

CHAPTER 32

Rosin pressed through the forest. The bicorn perked her ears, aware that something was ahead. The air was thick and damp with the coming rains.

Emberjade walked behind Rosin, content to follow the honey-colored mare.

"They're close," Jared said.

Teren closed his eyes, trusting Rosin to continue to walk the forest path. He reached out with his mind. A hundred emotions swirled in front of him like tiny melodies. Each one was distinct and unique and though he could not hear them with his ears, he could her them with his mind.

He allowed his sense to reach further, letting in the usual hum that he fought to keep quiet. Teren searched for one he recognized. Through the din, there it was… Jessica. She seemed content.

"She looks like she's okay," Jared said. "Is she okay?"

"I think so."

As Teren approached the camp, he was not surprised when a trio of Auroriates stopped him in the forest. The three wore green masks and rode pure black bicorns.

Teren smiled, extending a warm greeting.

"Hello! I am glad to see the ambassadors of the goddess!" He reined his bicorn and closed his senses. He did not need to be distracted by the emotions of the camp.

Teren bowed respectfully, Jared followed his lead.

"I am here to see my cousin. She is amongst your people. Her name is Jessica."

There was no need to lie to the circusfolk.

The Auroriate scouts warmly welcome and led them into their camp. Brilliant colors and abundant smells delighted Teren's senses. As a child, he reveled in the days when the circus came to visit. Walking through the camp brought a bitter sweet nostalgia.

Misa would have loved to be on the journey with him.

He waited patiently, looking around, trying to gauge the intent of the people surrounding him. He perceived no threat. Jared held Emberjade's reins tightly as he stood near. The young mage was much more apprehensive of circusfolk, watching the masked clerics warily.

Jessica appeared around a corner, dressed in the grey tunic and of an acolyte.

"You found me!" she hugged Teren tightly. He scooped her up, spinning her around. He leaned close to her ear.

"Are you in danger?" he whispered quickly.

He set her on the ground.

"Everything is okay," she said, "the circus has treated me very well, but I missed home."

Teren quelled the urge to yell at his cousin. She had a story to tell, and they did not want to ruffle

any circus feathers.

Jessica hugged Jared.

"I am so glad to see you! Your shoulder looks healed."

"Yes, thanks for abandoning me." Jared grumbled

"I'm sorry but once you hear my story you'll understand. When did you get my second letter?"

Jared glanced at Teren.

"We only received one."

"Then how did you find me?"

"Well that is also a story," Jared tapped her on the nose.

"Where's Nico?" Teren asked.

"Back in the tent, he was a little hesitant to come out, that's also a story. Follow me, and understand you're not allowed to walk anywhere unescorted. It's the rules of the camp."

"Have you gone all circusfolk on us?" Jared asked.

"Maybe," she replied, "but with good reason."

Jessica led them past practicing acrobats and wandering Plookory birds to a small tan and blue tent. As they approached, Teren senses were overwhelmed by the miserable emotions of their friend. It was as if Nico was forgotten in the bottom of a dark well, trapped in the throat of a serpent, life slowly bleeding out of him.

Teren had never sensed such abysmal misery.

Jessica drew back the flap and gestured.

Nico hunched over a workbench. He looked up slowly, eyes haunted.

"I apologize for not returning," Nico stood like a child trapped in a prison.

"No need to apologize," Teren embraced his old friend.

"Can you help me?" Nico whispered. "The darkness never leaves, it's killing me. Do you feel it?"

Tears streamed down Teren's face as he held Nico, nodding. The man's plea sliced into Teren's heart.

"Yes, yes, I'm so sorry you suffer. Of course, I will help you," he choked, kissing the side of Nico's face. "I thought for sure you were dead."

"I was."

"Thank the goddess you are alright," Teren said. "And yes, I will help you, just let me think how."

"I don't want to become like my mother," Nico lamented.

Teren withdrew, holding Nico's face in his hands, studying it intently. The right eye didn't open as much as the left, and a thin scar ran from his eyebrow to his cheekbone.

"Yes, and I refuse to make that mistake again, but I will do what I can."

Nico looked past Teren to Jared.

"Hello."

"Yeah, that stab wound healed up pretty nicely," Jared rotated his arm. "And yes, you are free to go ahead and apologize."

"I am sorry," Nico stated.

"You can apologize more," Jared looked encouragingly "Like, 'I am so sorry Jared for stabbing you and leaving you to bleed to death on the streets of the Yellow Valley.'"

"Yes, Jared, I am truly sorry, it was an act of desperation," Nico's voice was sincere and terribly sad. Jared actually cringed.

"Hey, it's okay. I get it, you have your reasons, though I am curious what they are."

"Sorry we don't have a much better place to sit and talk," Jessica said.

Teren looked to Jared.

"No eyes around here," he relaxed into a chair and placed his booted feet upon a chest.

"And I believe no curiosity is near," Teren added.

"I'll get some tea," Jessica said.

A short while later, they told their stories. Teren sat on the floor while Nico and Jessica sat atop their respective beds. They began at the race from the mages and told of the harrowing escape in the river. They talked of Sienna and her cubs, and their travels throughout the country side. When they spoke of the needlewasps, Teren grew very concerned. He explained Corwin's recent research, and his unfortunate leave from the castle. Nico was very troubled by the news.

"Jared, did you happen to hear anything of earth while I've been gone?" Jessica asked.

"Yeah, actually. I know you have a new life here, and you're waiting for that healer, but your sister reached out to me to find you. I followed your family for a bit, Carrie Anne doesn't look so great."

"Wait, how did Ashlin contact you?"

"She texted me."

"How?!"

"Lee gave her the number. Jess, your family was really grasping at straws to find you."

"But how did you find us?"

Jared grinned.

"A mage trick combining our gifts, it was pretty spectacular and I can explain more later, but really, Jess, you should go home."

"I want to Jared, but I won't learn…"

"Jess, blood mages can't heal cancer. Your mom said so, and I looked it up myself. It's almost impossible because cancer looks like the body. It's not an invading bacteria or a bone that's split."

"But…I want to try…"

"Jess, I don't think you're much of a healer anyways," Nico interrupted. "I think your gifts incline in the opposite direction."

"You don't know that," Jessica glared.

"Regardless, I think you should go home," Nico stated. "See if the mages may still take you."

"But the Holy Circus healer…"

"I think she's not worth waiting for," Nico was abrupt.

"Are you going home with us?" Jessica was concerned.

Teren sensed the shift in Nico's emotions. He was hiding something.

"I need to decide," his friend stated.

"Seriously?" Jared was incredulous.

"The mages are looking for me. It's too much danger and trouble to bring to the castle." Nico said. "Here, I wear a mask, I hide with people who move constantly. The circusfolk have already vowed to take that risk."

Jared shook his head.

"If that's how you really feel."

"I thank you both for coming out here," Nico said. "Please, stay a short while. Tonight is a bonfire dance, I will ask my aunt permission for you to attend."

"Of course, we would enjoy that," Teren nodded. He would take any excuse to stay if he could try to help his friend, and convince him to change his mind.

***

The heavy beat of drums echoed through the forest. The bonfires roared. Jessica sat beside her cousin, wearing a feathery red mask.

"You like being one of them?"

"It's been fun, but I'm ready to go home."

"Where's Nico?" Teren asked.

"He's coming to the fire, I hope."

"This is quite the sight," Teren commenting, sipping hot mead from a mug. "It amazes me that circusfolk can give so much time to perform and still have the energy to dance and sing for fun."

"The songs they're playing tonight are a bit bawdy," Jessica said, "and it's got a different style than the worship songs. You know I started playing violin again."

"Really? I didn't know you stopped."

"I stopped because you did."

"I never stopped playing violin," Teren said, "I just stopped playing around people. I still play."

379

"Oh, I just thought you stopped, but anyways, I've been teaching Hunter."

"His sister?"

"Yeah, she's been teaching me a few tricks too," she said, holding up his coin pouch.

Teren was confused for a moment until he recognized the purple ribbon.

"How did you?" he reached for his side, chuckling. "What a noble skill."

"It's for pocket blessings, it's just more fun in the reverse," Jessica explained. "And better than candle making."

"I can see Hunter is much like her father."

"Teren, seriously, I'm starting to understand Nico's father in a way I don't think I did before. I don't think he was so terrible."

"You misunderstand me, Jess, I never disliked his father. He had a very kind heart. He truly loved Elina and Nico. His downfall was that he was a man driven by passions and paranoia."

"Guys, hey, hey, I can hear my eyes," Jared stumbled over to them in a stupor, "And colors! I can hear colors through my eyes!"

"You ate the little red cookies, didn't you?" Jessica smirked.

"This amazing. I wonder if I can far hear rainbows," Jared sat down.

"How many did you eat?" Jessica asked.

"They were delicious," Jared replied. "I'm thirsty. Can I drink colors?"

"Here, I'll help you Jared," Jessica turned to Teren. "I'm going to go get some spring juice, do you want any?"

"The line looks long and I already have this mead."

"It's really good," Jessica pushed, "I'll get you one."

"Thank you, I haven't the energy to stand. You wouldn't think sitting on a bicorn for several days would be so tiring, but I am exhausted."

Teren watched his cousin walk away with Jared. He scanned the crowd, sensing the intentions around him. For the most part they were a benign soup of happy, jealous, wistful and amorous. There were a few odd blank spots. He imagined that a few of the circusfolk bore the Mark of Corvalian, rendering them immune to the effects of a psychic mage.

They were an elite group, likely the best warriors, hiding in a sea of preachers and clowns.

He wondered if Nico would join them soon and debated searching for his friend when a circusfolk woman sat next to him. Her face obscured by the white mask of an acolyte, she wore a grey tunic, black robes and a purple headscarf.

"Hello, stranger," she said. "I was watching you from across the fire. New to the circus?"

"Visiting my cousin," Teren replied.

"Travel far?"

"From the south," Teren took a sip of the ale.

"You've got an odd accent. I would say you're somewhere between Trabalis and Nova, but you've got that hint of Trinion in your voice."

"You travel quite far. Yes, I am from Trabalis, and my father was from the Trinion region, I seemed to have picked up some of his speech patterns."

He focused his attention more closely on the strange woman, trying to gauge if her intentions were amorous. Instead of a solid emotion, he encountered an odd swirling wall. It was like a symphony beginning to prepare for a concert, a hundred different melodies, each with skill and beauty, mashed together in a cacophony of sound.

He wondered if the circusfolk put hallucinogenic herbs in more than just the red cookies.

"Were you born circusfolk or did you join the circus by other means?" Teren asked.

"Circus took me in, years ago. Some of the kindest people to grace this planet."

"I am Teren," he said. "It is nice to meet you."

"Likewise."

"Do you have a name?"

"We are all the same in the eyes of the goddess," the stranger replied. "What should you like to call me?"

"An enigma, that's for certain," Teren said. "Would you like to dance?"

"Love to," the woman replied.

It was intriguing, not knowing what the stranger was thinking. Unlike the empty spots of Corvalian, this girl had emotions, buried in a strange hum. He probed at her mind, trying to find something that was her essence. He couldn't find it, and that was exciting. He didn't know if she really wanted to dance, or was simply being polite.

The woman smiled as he took one hand and rested the other on the small of her back.

As soon as their hands touched, Teren felt a strange tingling. It was a pleasant sensation that traveled through his entire body. She smiled, and he wondered if she too felt the connection. The sensation was exhilarating, causing his heart to beat quickly.

He led her across the dirt dance floor, swirling in the small group of circus folk by the light of the bonfire.

"Formally trained I see," the woman complimented.

"So are you. Where you from originally? Your accent is also interesting. I would say Katanzarko, maybe from the south, but there's something else there. I've heard it before."

"Yes, Katanzarko is correct."

The stranger smiled, and he tried to discern more of her features. Her chin was smooth, sapien-like. She wore dark blue lipstick, so dark it was almost black. He could see a few black strands of hair. Her eyes were as dark as coal with a hint of sapphire.

"You are a very good dancer," she beamed. "You have so much grace, I can follow your rhythm."

She laughed. Teren felt a sincerity in her tone, as if she was genuinely surprised. He also enjoyed holding her. She allowed him to direct her, her body easily following his lead. She knew the steps well.

"So, what does one do for fun in Trabalis?" she asked.

"Nothing too interesting. I play violin, and very rarely, I paint, and draw a bit."

"Artist? I like drawing," she said, "Don't get to do it much. What do you draw?"

"Oh, just little things here and there. Flowers mostly, bits of bone, a skull here, a goblet there."

"Echoes of things. I like to draw people. I find them very interesting."

"I find *you* quite interesting." The song ended. Teren was enthralled, but exhausted. He truly enjoyed dancing with the stranger.

"You look tired," she remarked as the music came to an end.

"It was a long journey to get here, but I think I'll be here at least a few days, perhaps we can chat more."

She led him towards a table of desserts. She selected a star-shaped ginger cookie, striped in a dark frosting.

"Winter star?" she said, offering him a cookie.

"One of my favorites," he replied. Well, truly his favorite was the type made with real chocolate, but the Centernian cookie was very close in flavor.

"Mine as well," the masked stranger said. "Why do you stare at me?"

"Sorry," Teren smiled sheepishly, biting the cookie. "I think I had something with a bit of elven weed earlier, so perhaps I am stoned."

"Yeah, actually me too, but for some reason it's just you."

Teren found her statement odd, but did not have time to dwell further as Jessica approached with Nico and Hunter. Teren still thought the girl's appearance frighteningly similar to Malachi's.

"Glad you could join us, friend," Teren said, "I was having a lovely dance with one of your brethren. Miss, what did you say your name was?"

The stranger hesitated to speak.

"Like all, just a daughter of the goddess," she replied.

Nico's expression told Teren everything.

His friend's emotions shifted to fear.

"That's an acolyte mask, but the markings are all wrong!" Hunter bristled and grabbed the stranger's mask. "You! You're the rude woman from the other night!!"

"I was just leaving," the stranger said.

"Who are you?!"

"It's the cursed witch!!!" Dahlia's voice boomed through the crowd. "Zia Casimirio! *SHA VAL DA NEE!* CURSED ONE!"

Hunter drew her knife. Zia pushed her way through the crowded dance floor as chaos erupted. She jumped onto a table as the crowd closed in.

"Oh, you don't want to do that," Zia argued. "I am a very powerful mage! You can't touch me!"

Teren sensed part of the crowd around them turned to fear.

But there was nothing to the girl that was frightening.

And then Teren understood the strange feelings.

"SHE IS SINARI!" Aunt Dahlia's voice echoed through the night. The old woman held out her staff. The orb crackled with yellow energy, catching the attention of the disjointed crowd. "She is an enemy of Aurora! She stole from us! She is poison!"

Zia jumped from table to table. It was clear she didn't have a strong grasp on the crowd. Zia was barely able to control a handful of people at a time.

In a mad attempt, she dove into the group, trying to make a clear run to the forest.

She would never make it alive.

Teren reached his senses out, amplifying the fear. Aurumice had made him a master of crowd control.

Reaching through the sea of emotion, twisting fear to hysteria.

Zia slipped into the forest. Teren felt a wave of relief.

***

The camp was a jumble of confusion.

Nico ran, not sure where to go. The woods were unsafe. He retreated to the tent, grabbing a pair of knives he hid in a corner. Not surprising, Jessica was right behind him.

He felt betrayed by his aunt. She had promise him sanctuary, but Zia had found him in the center of the Holy Circus! The weight of despair weighed heavily on his body as his heart raced. Curling into a ball, he wanted to stab the knife through his throat.

Jessica's hands touched him and he lashed out. She jerked back, just out of the path of the knives. He continued to shiver, mad with fear.

Another hand touched his arm, and he instantly felt a wash of peace.

Nico looked up. Teren knelt beside him, his eyes concerned.

"Can you drop the knives?" his friend asked.

Nico didn't realize how hard he had been clutching the weapons, hands white with tension. He set them on the ground.

"Can you make the darkness stay away?" Nico asked.

"I'll help you," Teren whispered. "I'll help you fight Zia."

"You know who she is?"

"Your aunt shouted her name, Zia Casimirio. She's the one who bought you, isn't she?"

Jessica sat by, watching curiously.

Nico clutched Teren, burying his face in his jacket.

"I loved her," he admitted through gritted teeth. "I killed for her even though Misa told me to stay away in my dreams! Misa warned me! Teren, your sister warned me!"

Teren held him, unwavering.

"My friend," Teren whispered in his ear, "I understand why your hurt is so great, it stretches beyond the Mines. Zia is a Sinari and she made a muck of your heart and she forced you to bend to her will."

Sinari…the word rattled around in Nico's brain.

Zia had poisoned his soul.

"Why didn't I see it?" Nico asked. "I should have known! Why didn't I know?"

"That's the curse, right? You wouldn't know."

"Misa knew."

"Or your subconscious recognized it, but your waking mind was too muddled by her magic to be rational."

"I miss Misa," Nico confessed. "I miss her and I miss my father and when I was with Zia all of that pain was gone. The world was right!"

"Listen to me," Teren's voice was soft. "What she did to you was wrong, and a lie, and it did more harm than good. Come home, and I will help you."

As they spoke, Jessica brought Nico water. He took it and drank greedily. When he finished, he tried to sort through his thoughts, feeling calmer. As he gave the cup back to Jessica, she grabbed his hand. Her touch was reassuring.

Before Jessica could speak, the rapt of a staff on the canvas wall announced the presence of his Aunt Dahlia.

"May I enter?"

"Yes," Nico replied.

As the woman stepped into the tent, Teren gave a bow out of respect.

"You must retrieve your mage companion," Aunt Dahlia commanded. "He is not permitted to wander without an escort, and especially not as high as a nightflight."

"I'm sorry, Aunt Dahlia," Jessica jumped to her feet. "In the commotion, we forgot about Jared…"

"No need to apologize, just make it right, child," the old woman said.

"Jessi, wait one moment," Nico said. "Aunt Dahlia, you have something else you would like to discuss?"

His aunt would have sent another of the circusfolk if she simply wanted Jared on a leash. Nico understood his aunt, she was fearful he would betray the secret of Zia's employment to the castlefolk.

"I am here to reassure you that we shall deal with that woman, and to apologize. Casimirio will not do that again, we will heighten our defenses."

"I understand," Nico nodded, taking a deep breath. "Aunt Dahlia, I have something to say while you are here. I do not question your sincerity and kindness, but I am concerned that Jessica's skills as a blood mage have been allowed to languor. Does this other healer even exist?"

Dahlia's expression told Nico everything he needed to know. As the old woman paused before responding, Nico gave her an out.

"I understand wisdom can be achieved by receiving the ways of the Goddess," he said.

Dahlia nodded.

"You are quite wise. Yes, I was hoping the ways of the goddess would give Jessica her own power."

"Wait," Jessica interrupted. "There are no mystic healers in the Circus? We've been waiting for *nothing?!*"

"Not nothing, you have learned much in meditation and focus and the ways of the goddess."

"But it's been months! I gave up high school!"

"You found peace."

"Like hell I found peace! What about my letter? Teren said he didn't get it!"

"I have no idea," the old woman replied. "I sent your letter."

Behind Aunt Dahlia, Teren shook his head a very tiny bit.

"Aunt Dahlia, with respect, it's been a very long evening. I would like to rest with my friends, and of course we will retrieve Jared."

Aunt Dahlia gave a bow.

"As you wish, nephew."

The woman left.

"Jess can you get Jared?" Nico said.

Jessica stared down dejectedly, playing with a gear on the desk.

"Jess?"

"She's a liar like the rest of them. I'm done. I'm leaving in the morning. I won't be with people who lie to me and I'm going to figure out how to go back to Polaris."

She abruptly left the tent.

Nico weighed his choices. He had no faith that the circus could keep him from Zia, and he feared her influence. But the mages were still hunting him.

"What?" Teren asked him. "What are you thinking?"

"I should just kill myself," Nico replied. "Because Zia or the mages will find me."

"You can go to earth."

"I'll still live in hiding," Nico said.

Teren reached for his hand, "I refuse to believe things are really hopeless."

"Now you sound like your sister," Nico stood and grabbed his cloak. "Glad one of us does."

Nico did not reply and left the tent.

CHAPTER 33

They left the Auroriates at dawn. Jessica thanked Sienna and Aunt Dahlia through a false smile and promised to return to acolyte training.

It was a lie, she was through with the Holy Circus.

Nico bid the castlefolk goodbye without emotion and returned to his tent.

The long journey back from Watersglade was somber. As they rode across the landscape, Jessica reflected upon all of her poor choices, in awe of her own stupidity. She had thrown away high school, didn't advance her powers, and lost time with Carrie Anne.

And she couldn't help Nico return home.

Stupid, stupid, stupid...

She hated herself.

After two days on the bicorns, they approached the edge of Trabalis. The air was crisp with the promise of the coming winter.

Teren reigned Rosin on a grassy knoll overlooking the city.

He glared.

"I am tired your never-ending emotional parade of self-loathing and anger. I want you to stop before we go home."

"Me or her?" Jared asked. Jessica sat behind him on Emberjade.

"Her!" Teren growled.

"But..." Jessica protested.

"I thought she was grumpy over leaving her boyfriend," Jared muttered.

"No," Teren said. "It's this cloud of pity and constant self-hatred, and this little tornado of fury that the world isn't fair. Jessica, you go home, we figure out how to move forward. You messed up. Move on."

"We shouldn't have left Nico behind, because you know he's not himself."

"It was his choice."

"We barely put up a fight!"

"If I forced him to do anything, it would break him. That's what that Sinari did to him, why he's such a mess. He needs to heal on his own."

"Well then leave me behind too, I don't want to go to Aurumice. Everyone will think I'm an idiot," Jessica said. "How can I face them after hiding with the Holy Circus? If we had brought back Nico, those months would have been worth it."

"They have shorter memories than you think, this all-powerful collective *them* you fear doesn't exist."

"Well that's odd," Jared interrupted their conversation. "Mages are on the move."

"Looking for Nico?" Jessica asked.

"I doubt it," Jared blinked. "Paisley is with them. She'd be too inexperienced for that sort of mission."

"How far away?"

"There," Jared pointed down the hill. "Nova has prohibited mage travel to Trabalis, so it's strange they would be so close."

In the distance, Jessica could make out ten mages in blue and brown, riding in a steady unhurried pace. The gifted warriors were headed in their direction.

"I want to talk to them," Jared said.

"And I prefer to keep my distance. Jessica, we will continue our discussion later. You're going home, or I will make you go home." Teren kicked Rosin and left the path, running through an open field. Rosin's coat gleamed like a ribbon of caramel candy as she vanished into the forest.

"I will make you go home," Jessica mockingly repeated. "I'll make you. Jerk. When I figure out my mage power, he won't be able to force me to do anything."

"How's that healing thing going?" Jared asked.

"Terribly," Jessica replied. "Thanks for asking."

Jared shrugged and urged Emberjade to continue onward. Eventually, they crossed the mages. In a sign of respect, Jared pulled Emberjade to the side of the road.

Svelte and well-groomed, the bicorns of the mages proudly paraded in the afternoon sun. Their manes were silken, bound in traditional battle braids. The uniforms of the mages were neatly pressed.

As Paisley Mae walked past, the girl's face erupted in a smile.

"Fancy seeing you in Trabalis," Jared called out.

"Hello! We're exterminating needlewasps on a mission from Nova," Paisley Mae explained, reigning her zebra-striped bicorn.

"Sounds like a lot of fun," Jared commented. "Want to stop by Aurumice when you're done with the bugs?"

Paisley's little bicorn tossed her head, unhappy, as the party continued on without her.

"I take my work with Nova seriously," Paisley Mae said quickly. "It's nice seeing you, Jared. Jessica, have a good afternoon."

"Right, haunted castle," Jared muttered as the parade of mages continued on.

Paisley Mae smiled and signaled to her bicorn. Whinnying, the little mare happily trotted away, eager to be with her brethren.

He waited until they were far out of earshot.

"I do miss them and feel sad for them at the same time."

"That was a weird conversation," Jessica said.

"It's Paisley's first mission. She doesn't want to screw up or look bad in front of the other mages. Talking to me would make her look bad. Jess, you sure you want to get Polaris to teach you?"

"Jared, don't worry, I would never stop talking to you."

"I don't know, maybe you should talk to your dad first to see if he can help you."

"I had considered it, but I have a feeling he won't be helpful."

"He may surprise you."

***

Nico regretted his decision as soon as his friends were out of sight. He spent the rest of the day in seclusion in his tent, miserable.

He thought it would seem foolish if he suddenly chased after them. He didn't know what he would do. He missed Jessica but didn't know if he would have the strength to tell her.

Instead, he chose to do nothing. By nightfall, boredom overwhelmed his misery and he left the tent. He wasn't certain what he was looking for.

Walking through the camp, he watched the circusfolk prepare for a midnight performance. In all the months with them, he had not been compelled to join in their acts. Their tricks were amusing enough, but they always seemed a little paltry. He imagined his ties to the mages had much to do with that perception.

Nico wandered into the large grey tent set up for rehearsal. A fire act trio was practicing, spinning rings of flame. His father had liked such tricks. Nico had never tried, the fire frightened him.

Ironic for a fire mage.

It took him a moment to realize that one of the performers was Hunter. The girl was proud to take on their father's legacy.

That bit gnawed at him.

In the months they spent with the circus, Nico had not truly mourned his father. Was he a terrible son? Or was his father a terrible man for abandoning his son and starting a new life? Every time a reminder bubbled up, he squashed it, but he was always surrounded by reminders, in the masks, in the tricks, in the words of the goddess. His father was everywhere.

And gone at the same time.

Nico clenched his fist, and as he did so, the odd sensation returned to the marrow of his bones. His hand vibrated from its core, as it had the night he danced with Jessica in Watersglade. He lifted it to see if it was actually trembling or it was simply his nerves hitting a new level of degeneration.

As he opened his palm, tiny beads of light dripped down his finger, racing along his wrist, and dissipating into the grass.

The sensation vanished.

His powers were returning.

Nico left the tent, his heart low.

He walked to the forest edge. Realizing Zia could be waiting for him, ready to control his mind, he stopped. The listless boredom turned to fear as he spiraled out of control.

Why had he not followed his friends?

Without warning, a spinning flaming hoop cut through his path. It struck a tree, scorching the bark before ricocheting and landing at Nico's feet. It burned the grass and fizzled out.

Nico glared at his younger sister.

"You could seriously kill someone."

Hunter retrieved the ring.

"You should try to do something fun for once instead of sitting around miserable. Now that your lover is gone, how about you act like circusfolk?"

"I have too much weighing on my mind for tricks."

"Don't worry about that Sinari, if she comes into camp again, I'm ready for her," Hunter smirked, drawing a wicked-looking serrated dagger. "Aunt Dahlia is offering a price for her head, and I'm determined to win it."

Nico chuckled in spite of himself.

"You think your will is stronger than a Sinari?"

"I think my blade is tougher than her skin," Hunter said. "And that's all that matters."

"Yes, until she makes you hate yourself so badly you put it to your own throat."

"She can't," Hunter affirmed.

"Yes, she can," Nico corrected.

"I may not be a mage like you," Hunter said, "However broken you may be. The goddess blessed me with one gift from father."

"What gift?" Nico asked.

Hunter turned around, pulling her hair up past her neck. She revealed a tattoo, shaped like an eye.

"Corvalian? How did you get that mark?" Nico asked.

Corvalian was a sect of ancient mage assassins, immune to psychic mages. Nico's father had taken the mark, not of malice, but to render himself undetectable by his wife's psychic surveillance.

"I was born with it," Hunter said.

"It's genetically transfered?" Nico was surprised. His father acquired the mark after his birth, so Nico wouldn't have possessed its power.

Every time he thought he understood the magic of the world, something odd happened.

"Did my father ever say anything about his mark?" Nico asked. He knew his father had journeyed, but that was all.

"A mage in the north. He liked to tell that story. Father tricked the mage into marking him with the stones."Hunter grinned. "And then he stole them from the stupid old mage. Perfect pocket blessings, leaving him with some dirty coal."

"He *stole* them?"

Jessica's suggestion had seemed far-fetched when Nico thought that he would need to seek out the last of the mage assassins, but now it was a possibility. He felt shameful for mocking his friend.

The Corvalian mark was his only chance at true freedom. Zia could never influence him, the mages would be unable to detect him, and even if they found him, his mind would never betray Teren!

"They're in the haunted castle," Hunter said. "He didn't say where, but he was angry they were locked in there."

The revelation was like a bomb.

And Nico felt like a fool. "No...no way. They can't possibly be in Aurumice. Too convenient."

Hunter shrugged. "Alright, where else would father hide them? He was married to your mother, he lived in that fancy castle. He wouldn't just go hide them in a burch pit out in the Starlight desert."

"If the marking stones are in Aurumice, then I have a chance after all. Hunter, this is my chance."

Hunter grinned.

"Take me with you," his sister pleaded. "I can help you!"

"No. You are not, because you want to murder castlefolk," Nico replied.

"I didn't say that!"

"You didn't need to."

"No, not fair, I give you this and you won't let me go to the castle!" "Hunter—"

"Father gave you everything, and left us with nothing! Not even a name to be spoken outside the circus!"

"Hunter, I need to deal with one problem at a time, please, do not give me new ones!"

CHAPTER 34

Jessica crossed through the basement Gate, landing in thin puddle of water. The basement was chilly and moldy.

As soon as they had arrived in Aurumice, Jared insisted she travel to earth to talk to her family. Wishing to avoid the castlefolk, it seemed like a good option.

She just wasn't sure what she would say to her father or Carrie Anne, or her mother.

Instead of worrying, she fixated on the little flood.

"That's not good." Jessica murmured, walking through the basement to find the source of the leak. She came to the hot water heater. Almost every towel they owned formed a circle around its base.

"Mom, seriously, you can't ignore this," she sighed, mentally adding up the cost of a new hot water heater. Not cheap. Jessica wondered if she could find the weak point in the rusty bottom and patch it. With what, she wasn't sure.

"Mom?" Jessica called out. "Mom are you home?"

She went upstairs.

Her house felt foreign and cold.

Really cold.

She glanced at the thermostat, it was set to 58. A pile of unopened letters sat on the table, a clear sign of delinquent bills past due.

Looking out the front window, there was no sign of the car in the driveway. Jessica searched through the house, finding her cell phone where she had left it, set on her nightstand. She plugged it in, grateful she still had service. It would have cost her mom more for breaking the contract and cancelling the phone.

Jessica
I'm home, and I'm sorry I made you worry.
Where are you?

Mom
JESSICA!!!!!!

Mom
Working a late shift, can't make it home until
after midnight

Jessica paused, her mother's old job was at an office, she wondered where the older woman was working now. Wherever it was, it likely didn't pay very well, which would explain the leaking hot water heater and the pile of bills.

Mom
Go back to Aurumice and I'll find you later.
Everything ok?

Jessica found the question odd. She had been gone for months, but she imagined her mother knew that Teren and Jared were going to the Circus to bring her back.

Jessica
Yes. Nico is still with the circus, but I'm
okay.

Mom
Good! I'll see you as soon as I can!!!

Feeling grimy and exhausted, Jessica walked upstairs. The teen was not looking forward to the prospect of a shower without hot water, but it was how she had been bathing for months. She showered quickly, at least it was better than river water. She felt cleaner than she had been in a long time.

Sliding into a pair of jeans, the teen realized she had lost weight with the circus. Auroriate food had been good, but not as good as Aurumice and Chinese takeout. As Jessica pulled a t-shirt over her head she remembered Jared's words and texted her dad. She knew if she waited too long, it would be worse.

Her father replied quickly, promising to pick her up as soon as he could for dinner.

Jessica waited by the front door. It appeared that there were new items in their little online business storeroom, a sign her mom was trying. The hot water heater gnawed at Jessica as she tried to figure out how to patch the leak.

Soon, she saw the familiar headlights of the Mercedes coming down the road. How was it half her family lived in luxury but yet they lived in poverty?

Jessica grabbed her brown hoodie and zipped it up. It did feel good to be wearing jeans and sneakers again. The air was misty with a little bit of cold April rain.

Smiling, her father stepped out of the car. He looked haggard, and thinner. She realized it had been almost half a year since he had seen her.

They embraced. Stephen held his daughter as if she would vanish. Jessica thought he was crying, but she didn't want to look up.

"I thought we had really lost you forever this time," he said, finally releasing her. "Will you please stop going to that awful place? You missed months of school!"

"Dad, I made mistakes, but we need to talk."

"It's okay, Jess, all is forgiven. Don't worry about school, I'm happy you're home. Dinner?"

"Yes," Jessica smiled. "Can we go to Santoros? Just you and me please?"

"Anything you want," Stephen said.

Once in the car, an awkward silence fell between the two. Jessica debated on telling her father the truth, but knew she risked his anger. If she told him at the pizza shop, hopefully he would remain calm.

Hopefully.

The movement and sound of the car felt odd to Jessica, the motion was too smooth and the engine was too quiet. She did not realize how much she had adapted to wagon life.

She ran her fingers along the plastic of the window controls with a strange wonder.

"How is Carrie Anne?" Jessica asked.

"Not bad, all things considered. Her treatment seems to be working. She is a fighter, that's for sure. It gets her down that she can't do as much as she used to, but she's coping. Tonight, she went over to the church. They're having this crafting bible study thing."

"Sounds nice," Jessica was wistful. "I mean that, it's nice, everything Carrie Anne does. I wish Mom would be a little like that, though I haven't seen her since I got back."

"Your mom was worried about you and so was Carrie Anne. And you know, whatever happened there, I don't care. I don't need to hear it. You're back now, and maybe we can revisit this idea of graduation and college?"

"Yeah, I would like to go back to school, it's not too late. I mean, just six months behind. I can catch up if I really, really focus."

Even as she said the words, she knew it was a farce. She had screwed up badly.

"Glad to hear that, Jess."

They drove into the little village of Autumn Valley and found parking outside Santoro's Pizza.

"Can we eat upstairs?" she asked.

"Of course," her father replied.

As they entered the tiny pizzeria, Jessica relaxed as the garlic and tomato sauce wafted through the air. She didn't realize how badly she missed being an earth girl.

For once, she had gotten her fill of Centernia.

Looking through the glass barrier, a dozen hot pizzas were prominently on display, each one more alluring than the last. Her stomach growled as she debated between Buffalo Chicken and classic sausage and mushroom. She opted for both, and a slice of Hawaiian.

In all the months with the Circus, she had not craved pizza. Somehow, the minutes waiting for their slices to crisp became an excruciatingly long time

Jessica took her bottle of soda from the cooler, appreciating the cleanliness of the restaurant refrigerator.

The pizza was soon served onto paper plates placed upon plastic trays. They took their food to the upstairs seating area. The large windows were decorated with spring flower decals and a neat little line of white LED lights.

As Jessica had hoped, there were no other patrons upstairs.

Jessica bit into the pizza, savoring the cheese and the sweetness of the tomato sauce. The crust had the perfect tiny bit of crunch.

"That is so amazingly good!" she gushed over the decadence of the pizza.

"I know," her father agreed. "It's my favorite restaurant."

"I missed home. Dad, I didn't know how much I would miss it until now."

"Well, I am very glad you came back," Stephen smiled.

"We need to talk. I actually really need your guidance, because I've run out of people who can help me."

Stephen took a sip of his orange soda, face creased with concern.

"You are not going to like what I have to say," Jessica said. "But please, please for once listen to me. I spent the past six months with the Holy Circus. I went to Polaris Academy and was rejected, so I went to the Auroriates hoping that their healer could teach me. Then along the way, I fell off a bicorn into a river, and luckily the Auroriates I was looking for saved me. So I stayed with them, but they weren't truthful about their healer. Now I have no one."

"Jess, you're talking crazy gibberish to me."

"Stop lying, please stop lying. Dad, I *know* you know these places and these people. You know them better than I do. I met Saurin Bane at Polaris, he told me about you, *the real you*. I saw photos and I don't doubt that you are Savartos Sarkisian."

"Well, I guess this is the end of dinner," Stephen set down the soda bottle and stood.

Jessica reached out, anchoring her father's hand to the table.

"No, you need to listen. I need your help because I'm the same as you." Her voice dropped, "I'm a blood mage. I'm untrained, and my powers are backwards. Carmelina Lightsong won't teach me. I have no one."

Stephen glanced around uncomfortably and sat down.

"Jess, I can't go through that Gate. Did Saurin Bane explain that? I am marked as a criminal. I am trapped. Do you hear me? Not a choice, *trapped.*"

"But, please, no one has explained anything to me. I healed myself once, and now nothing. And worse, I accidentally hurt myself. I even made a needlewasp explode once. I'm on the wrong side of blood mage and I don't know how to fix it."

"Jess, that's a lesson for you. Stay here. On earth, you can't hurt yourself or anyone else."

"But I can't help anybody, either!"

"Sure, you can, with your smarts, you study. You can be a doctor, a bioengineer, so much you are capable of."

"But..."

Stephen took his hand back as he sat at the table, crossing his arms.

"Dad, I'm telling you something no one else knows. I'm really getting scared that I may hurt someone accidentally. I can't control my powers."

"I can't teach you anything from here. You need to go back to high school, forget them all, forget about that crazy woman's son."

"What? Nico? This has nothing to do with him!"

"Really. Your mother told me all about him. Six months with him alone with those circus freaks, and you're telling me he's not anything to you?"

"My *friend.*"

"I wasn't born yesterday, Jess."

His insinuation was infuriating.

"Okay, sorry I asked. Sorry I asked you for any help at all!"

"I cannot do anything."

"Even if I was sleeping with Nico, what would it matter anyways? I still need guidance. The mages are stopping you from crossing the Gate, but not from talking to me. You're Savartos Sarkisian, you are a blood mage of Polaris, and you're my father. I need your help."

Her father spoke his next words carefully.

"I wish I could help you Jess, but I buried that part of me."

"They told me you killed a classmate. What happened?"

Stephen glanced around, but the room was still empty.

"I can't believe you're asking me this. You want the messed-up truth, Jessi? Your cousin Teren is a Sinari, do you understand what that means?"

"I've always known."

"Well then you know the laws. Danyelle was my friend, and she found out the truth about your cousin, and she was going to tell the council. I stopped her, then I refused to let them scan my mind, because then I knew they'd find out about Teren. Justen and Trix were two of my best friends and I would never let anything happen to their little boy. I refused to confess and then I was sentenced to death."

He paused.

"I really thought I was going to die, and on the darkest night of my life Saurin Bane and your mother, and Justen and my brother got me out and brought me here. That's where I've been ever since. I didn't say goodbye to anyone, not your grandparents, not your uncles or aunts, not even my gryphon."

"Ravenwolfe."

Her father nodded.

Jessica felt a chill in her spine, followed by a clammy coldness that ran down her shoulders. Her throat went dry as she stared at the now-cold pizza.

She didn't expect her cousin to be involved, and she didn't expect the awful hurt in her father's eyes.

"I am Stephen Ravenwolfe. And that's it. If you really can't accept that, then maybe you should go back to Centernia. Stay there, and never bother me again."

"Dad, I'm sorry, I'm sorry you went through that, but…"

"No. Listen to me. I am done with Centernia, and I won't help you."

"But I want to use my powers and help Carrie Anne."

"Blood mages can't cure cancer, believe me, I tried."

"But other people…"

"No. I never want to hear about that place again."

The finality of his words darkened her heart.

"Okay, I get it," Jessica stood. "Forget, forget I ever asked you for help."

Jessica abandoned her dinner and stormed away.

"Where are you going?"

"We're done talking," she said. "I'm not asking you to cross the Gate, I'm asking you to talk to me. If you can't confide in me, help me, then why should I ever tell you anything again?"

Stephen didn't follow as Jessica ran down the stairs and through the pizza shop. The door slammed with the tink of the bell as she escaped into the cold April night.

***

Nico found Sienna with Reese, tending the gryphons by the light of the lanterns. As he approached, the leopardess turned, leveling a crossbow at his chest.

Nico held up his hands.

"I hate the idea that a Sinari is lurking around," his second-mother apologized, lowering the bolt.

"I hope we kill her," Reese tried to muster authority in his tiny form.

"I know," Nico nodded.

Sienna set the crossbow into the holster on her back and continued tending the gryphon chicklets. The bucket of entrails sloshed and spilled.

"I'm surprised Jessi left you," Sienna said. "Though she seemed very friendly with that blonde mage."

The woman's tone was callous.

"She isn't with Jared," he replied defensively.

"Well she's not attached to you," Sienna replied.

Nico was taken aback.

"Oh come on, your beds couldn't have been further apart and you hardly spoke. We all knew, I just assumed eventually...you know."

Nico wasn't certain how to respond, feeling embarrassed and foolish. He had spent months holding Jessica at an arm's length.

Now he missed her terribly.

He needed to return home.

"Sienna, I came to ask you about my father," Nico said.

"What do you wish to know?"

"The Mark of Corvalian, how did he get it?"

"Wasn't easy," Sienna replied.

"Yes, but how did he do it?"

"Reese, can you go back to camp and get more fish?"

The boy nodded. Climbing off the gryphon's back, he picked up a bucket and ran towards the center of camp.

"The Mark of Corvalian is administered by stones, but I believe they react badly to mages. If you're thinking about masking your presence, it may not go so well."

"How badly?"

"He didn't say. Your father went north and stole the stones from a place in the mountains. He brought them back to Aurumice, but I have no idea where he hid them."

"Are you certain they're in the castle?"

Sienna nodded.

"Thank you," he said.

"You're going to go look for them, aren't you?"

"I am starting to see that it may be my only chance at evading the mages and Zia."

"You know they're not meant for people like you."

"I'm not a mage anymore," Nico snapped.

"I doubt that. I've never heard of a mage losing their gifts. I think you're either lying to me or lying to yourself, about more than the stones."

"If the mages or Briken will kill me anyways, then what does it matter? If I have a chance at escaping them and having my life again, I'll take it."

"You know I can see behind your plan. Your friends leave, and now you realize you belong with them, not us."

Nico was startled by her words.

"Don't look so surprised," Sienna gave him a small smile. "I knew Aurumice would always pull you back. Your Aunt hoped otherwise, thinking if she could keep Jessica here, she would be able to keep you. I knew it would never work."

Sienna stood and gestured to the gryphon.

"So do you want a bicorn or would you rather be dropped off?"

***

Jessica walked for an hour aimlessly, trying to piece together her thoughts. The village of Autumn Valley was quaint, dotted with little specialty shops and eateries, but every person Jessica passed felt like a ghost.

The teen considered texting Lee, but that friendship was so broken she had no hope of repairing it. She considered texting Ashlin, but the girl was too young to drive.

With her mother working, Jessica had one option left.

She sent a message.

Jessica she curled up on a green metal bench. She tried to figure out what she would say, but her mind could give her no answer, other than the truth.

Thankfully, it didn't take long before a blue sedan pulled up to the curb.

Carrie Anne climbed out of the car and threw her arms around Jessica.

"You're back! Oh, my goodness, I missed you!"

"I know. I was wondering if you could give me a ride back to my house?"

"Of course! Did you just arrive? Where were you?"

"It's a long story," Jessica said. "Can you bring me home?"

"Oh goodness, your mother will be so happy to see you. I need to call your father."

"Don't bother, I just left dinner with him."

"Dinner?" Carrie Anne was confused. "But he didn't tell me you were back."

"I just arrived, and we had a fight over dinner."

"Oh, well let me call him and we'll make it right."

"No, no, please, Carrie Anne I would really appreciate a ride home."

Jessica opened the car door. Her thoughts were jumbled as she tried to figure out the best thing to say.

"Of course, whatever you need. I am just happy you're here," Carrie Anne climbed into the driver's seat. Jessica sat in the perfectly clean car. She didn't know how Carrie Anne remained so meticulous, even while dealing with her illness.

"How are you feeling?"

"Wonderful," Carrie Anne replied.

"No, I mean, with the cancer."

"Oh, it's just the meds, that's all. They make me feel sick and not want to eat."

"I was worried about you."

Carrie Anne nodded, driving.

"How are you?" the older woman asked.

"I'm okay," Jessica responded mechanically. "It's nice to be home."

"Can I ask why your father is upset?"

"It's complicated," Jessica said, looking at the businesses as they passed by on the highway. All the electric lights twinkled in the cold air. She had forgotten what the world was like with so many lights.

"Have you talked to your mother?"

"Yes, just a bit ago. She's happy I'm back."

"Can you tell me where you were?" Carrie Anne asked.

"I just got into a fight with my mom, and I needed to be on my own a bit, to clear my head. I was with friends."

"Are these people you met online?"

"Yeah," Jessica said.

"You know that can be dangerous."

"Yeah, but I've known these people a while. So, they just let me crash at their place. I did research for college. I just tried to figure it all out. I even went to church, a whole bunch, my friends are pretty religious people."

"Oh, that's good, good. I hope you found clarity," Carrie Anne encouraged.

Jessica could tell that that her step-mother was choosing her words very carefully.

"How's Ashlin doing in school?"

Carrie Anne seemed much more comfortable with this topic. She talked about all the clubs Ashlin participated in, her grades, her teachers. Jessica was able to stay silent and nod as Carrie Anne filled the silence.

They exited the highway, and drove down the older side streets where the houses were smaller and not so well-kept. Arriving at the little blue house, Jessica felt a burst of shame. The driveway was crumbling and had more cracks and sinkholes than Jessica remembered. It probably wouldn't last another winter.

"Thanks, I'll call you later," Jessica said, giving Carrie and a quick hug and climbing out of the car. "We'll have dinner this week."

She scurried up the driveway into her house, refusing to let Carrie Anne say anything more. Unlocking the entrance, the musty odor from the basement hit her nose. Closing the door, she turned on the light, shaking her head. The hall was dim, only one of the lights in the hall fixture still worked.

Jessica stood in silence, feeling bad for leaving her step mother so abruptly. She just couldn't deal with the kind woman's questions. Any more pressing and she knew she would say things she would regret.

The doorbell startled Jessica.

She opened the front door slowly.

Carrie Anne was on the porch.

"Did I forget something?" Jessica asked.

"Yes, to actually talk to me," Carrie Anne was visibly annoyed. "You ran away for six months, that deserves an explanation!"

"I can't tell you where I was."

"Why not?" Carrie Anne demanded. She peered in past Jessica, seeing the strange shelves full of objects from Aurumice. "What's all that in your living room?"

"Just junk from garage sales."

"Jessica, please let me in, it's cold outside."

"I shouldn't…my mom will get mad."

"I don't care." Carrie Anne pushed the door opened and stepped in the hallway. Jessica could have shoved her back, but feared hurting her stepmother.

Carrie Anne walked into the hallway. The disgust was clear on her face as she peered around. From the dirty carpet to the hole in the wall Nico had punched years ago, the house was in bad shape.

"Yeah, I know, it's not the nicest, "Jessica stated, "but it's home."

"Oh Jessi, I had no idea….is your mother here?"

"Mom?!" Jessica called out. There was no response, as she expected. She glanced at the clock, it was only ten.

"Yeah, she's still out working," Jessica said.

Carrie Anne was drawn to the living room. She searched around for a light, when she found it, her disgust turned to curiosity.

"What is this stuff?"

The shelves were fairly well stocked, and Jessica noted a lot of old items were gone, replaced by new ones. She hoped that was a sign things were well with the side business.

Carrie Anne picked up a sword, surprised at its weight.

"You have money for this and your house is in such bad shape…?" Carrie Anne asked, marveling at the blade.

"It's for selling, not for keeping," Jessica said.

"This all came from garage sales?" Carrie Anne set the sword back in place.

"Yes, and online ads. We re-sell things."

"How interesting. These things are strange oddities," Carrie Anne was drawn to the animal bones, "Like from the movies Ashlin likes."

Jessica didn't know how to respond.

The blood flowers were still brilliant. Some lay on the table next to the vase, dried and pressed.

"What a beautiful plant," Carrie Anne said. "Is it real?"

She touched the petals. It gave the distinct tink as the pollen moved inside of it.

"Is it a chime?"

"It's a blood flower," Jessica explained. "From South…America…?"

"Jessica, where were you?" Carrie Anne asked again. "And if you have some issue with your mom, just come live with me. We'll deal with the custody issue, I don't care. I don't want you running away again."

Carrie Anne picked up one of the delicate drying blood flowers.

"I missed you. I thought you were dead in a drug house somewhere, or someone had taken you. It's not okay, you can't run away like that! Please, move in with us. Your sister needs you and so do I and so does your father."

"Carrie Anne, I'm sorry," Jessica said. "I'm really sorry. I was safe, I was with friends."

"You could have called."

"There were no phones where I was."

"How is that safe?"

"It…" Jessica had run out of lies. "It's impossible to explain."

"Stay with us and you can have anything you want! We can get you a car, new clothes, a new violin, a new computer! What about a trip to Europe? Backpacking Europe is very lovely! The old-world towns are so quaint."

"I can imagine, but you've never seen Castle Aurumice. You've never seen the Starlight Desert, or Katanzarko city, Polaris Academy, Watersglade or the streets of Yellow Valley ."

Carrie Anne tried to follow what Jessica was saying.

"Okay, if I tell you where I was. If I take you there, and I promise it's safe, and I promise it's amazing. If I take you there, do you swear not to tell my mother or my father or Ashlin? It's our secret?"

Jessica was tired of playing by her parents' rules.

"Take me there?" Carrie Anne said. "Is this some sort of drug thing?"

"No," Jessica smiled, liking the idea more and more. "No drugs. You keep my secret, and I'll start going to school again."

"Of course I'll keep your secret."

"Alright, follow me," Jessica said.

Carrie Anne set the blood flower on the table, expecting to walk to the front door. Instead, Jessica led her to the basement. Jessica flipped the lightswitch and walked down the stairs.

The wooden steps creaked.

Carrie Anne hesitated at the top of the stairs. She noticed the padlocks on the door. A dozen locks were hastily attached when Lily had tried to prevent Jessica from going to Centernia.

"Yeah don't worry about those locks. That was an old thing. Please, trust me. I can't explain, and if I did you'd think I was nuts. But I can show you."

Carrie Anne timidly walked down the steps, clutching her winter coat, still wearing her purse and winter boots. She looked around suspiciously at the cardboard boxes that filled the basement.

"Why is the floor all wet?"

"Well that's another problem," Jessica said, taking her stepmother's hand.

"I have wanted to show you this, don't be scared," she embraced Carrie Anne, wrapping one arm around the woman.

Jessica took a step, and threw them both into the cinderblock wall.

Colors swirled as Jessica lost her sense for a moment and her body was broken up between dimensions. They stumbled through the other side into the barn store room and Jessica breathed a sigh of relief.

Carrie Anne trembled violently, staring at the floor, terrified. Jessica had forgotten how terrible it was to Travel for the first time.

"Sorry," she said. "I know what was scary, but I could never have prepared you for it. You'll get used to it."

"Was I in hell?" Carrie Anne asked, "I couldn't see, I couldn't scream!"

"It was just the in-between," Jessica said.

"Is it gone?"

"Yes, it's just what happens when you Travel."

Carrie Anne looked up, noticing she was in a barn store room for the first time.

"This is my secret. There is another dimension to our world, it's called Centernia. It's an entirely different place, a different planet. You get to it through these dimensional Gates, invisible in our world, but very real."

Carrie Anne stood slowly, Jessica offered her a steadying hand.

"I don't understand."

"Here, follow me, this store room is a bit ugly."

Carrie Anne trailed after Jessica.

"It's like the C.S. Lewis books, except without the wardrobe," the teen explained.

"How is that possible?" Carrie Anne asked.

"The world is bigger than we knew. I've been coming here for years, my mother for years before me. That's why our house is so cruddy. We live here most of the time."

"In a barn?" Carrie Anne looked around.

"No, here," Jessica pushed the barn doors opened a few inches, allowing the sunlight of the stable yard to beam in. "In Castle Aurumice."

***

Carrie Anne could not believe the color and brightness beyond. The barn was in the shadow of a castle unlike any she had ever seen in a book or movie. The castle seemed to be both made of stone architecture, yet rooted to the ground like a tree.

Carrie Anne stepped forward to get a better look.

"We can't be seen," Jessica warned. "I'll get in trouble for bringing you here."

"Oh?" Carrie Anne retreated. "Is that some rule of the king?"

Jessica grinned.

"Oh no, there is no king at Aurumice, the monarchy was disbanded years ago. They live by a sort of diplomatic rule? But the leaders come from same family? Everyone is free to do as they wish, to leave or to stay. It's more like a hippie commune but with a ball room, and a trained militia."

"Why will you get in trouble?"

"My mother and cousin won't be happy with me, or my dad."

"What are those beasts?" Carrie Anne could see tall creatures, the size of horses. They had two horns on top of their heads and were colored in intense hues.

"Bicorns," Jessica said.

"Are they magic?"

"No, but they're pretty interesting. They can see in the dark, they eat mice sometimes. They're really smart but really stubborn. I have one, though I haven't seen her in a while. Her name is Frostfire."

"What are those people?"

Strange cat-like creatures were carrying buckets from barn to barn. Two were striped like tigers and reminded Carrie Anne of werewolves.

One was tall and thin, her ears shaped like those of a lynx. They wore clothing and walked like humans. The lynx-eared one seemed very pretty.

"Castlefolk," Jessica said, "Ailurians. Most people here are somewhere in between cat and human. Then there's caprasians, they have curved horns"

"I don't believe any of this," Carrie Anne whispered. But she knew she was not dreaming.

Stepping away from the door, Carrie Anne looked at Jessica, her mind traveling back in time. All the odd conversations, the weird occurrences.

"Your friends," she said, "the ones from Halloween…"

"That wasn't makeup," Jessica explained. "Well, actually we added makeup to Nico to make him look fake."

"Your mother knows about this?"

"So does my father. Carrie Anne, this is why I need your help. When I left home, I went to a place called Polaris Academy, to learn how to be a mage. They rejected me, not because I can't do it, but because of something with my dad."

"Because he's a normal person? What's the word? A muggie?"

"No, that's not how this place works," Jessica laughed. "He's a mage too, but mage strengths don't work on earth, only in Centernia. When we go through the Gate, things get weird. It's like because we don't belong here, we can influence the world with our minds. I want to learn, but I need my dad's help, and he doesn't want anything to do with me or this place, but he's from here."

Carrie Anne looked around the barn, seeing a hay bale she sat down.

"Are you okay?" Jessica asked. "You look pale."

Carrie Anne tried to sort through her thoughts.

"I can't believe this is happening."

Her mind raced back to the days when she met Stephen. He was odd, he was charming, there was something about him that felt foreign. There were lies, and things that didn't make sense.

But he loved her and took care of her.

"Please don't be upset or go crazy. I really need you Carrie Anne. This is the secret I wanted to tell you. I wanted to tell Ashlin too."

The door creaked open and Jessica jumped. The lynx-eared woman walked in. She was incredibly exotic and beautiful, wearing a purple dress. Her hair was pulled back upon her head and tied in a floral patterned scarf. Each of her ears were adorned with a dozen different earrings.

"Ah! You're back! What are you hiding? Is Nico with you?" the woman asked. She had an interesting accent.

Carrie Anne shrunk back, fearing the strange cat woman.

"Savina, please don't tell my mother. Give me a chance to figure this out."

"Who is this?" Savina questioned. "A visitor from your demon-world?"

"Yes, but I'm having a problem with my family, and I need to deal with it. This is my...dad's wife. This is Carrie Anne."

Carrie Anne trembled, not sure if the stranger was going to attack.

"I am Savina. Are you feeling well? You seem pale."

"Me?" Carrie Anne questioned. "Are you talking to me?"

"I don't know what you're doing, but I'm getting this woman something to drink, then I'm summoning Teren."

"Oh no, no, no, please...."

"You worried the castle with your circus trip and now you ask this? No! Teren needs to know."

Savina left the barn.

"Stay here," Jessica ordered. "Just please don't move."

Carrie Anne sat, looking at the barn. Farm equipment hung on the walls. There were no animals and appeared to be a storage shed.

Jessica returned with Savina and a familiar face from years ago.

"Teren," Carrie Anne said. She instantly felt calmer.

"Ah, welcome to Castle Aurumice," the pale young man greeted. He clasped her hand.

"I am certain this is surprising for you, but you are our guest."

Jessica carried a wooden cup.

"Here, this is javeilla, they made it fresh this morning."

Carrie Anne took the cup. She drank the tangy sweet liquid.

"That's amazing, I've never tasted that flavor before."

"It happens a lot," Jessica said. "Pretty awesome, a whole world of food nothing like back home. And Aurumice has amazing cooks. It's where I picked up my barbeque skills, and my knife skills, and my riding skills."

"How did you find your trip across the Gate?" Teren asked.

"Terrifying," Carrie Anne replied. "I have never been so scared in my life. I couldn't see, I couldn't talk."

"Oh, the first trip across the Gate can be like that," Teren said. "It gets easier, to the point you barely notice. You just hop right through."

Carrie Anne believed his reassuring words.

"So, what is your plan now, cousin?" Teren turned his attention to Jessica.

"Yell at me all you want. I didn't have one. I got into an argument with my dad, and then I called Carrie Anne, and she followed me to my house and kept asking me where I was, and I just couldn't lie anymore."

"I imagine you were even more worried about Jessica than we were" Teren said. "She gave us a fright for a few months, but, I can forgive her for that. She rescued a lost friend of ours, and I am eternally grateful for her sacrifice."

Jessica seemed surprised at his words.

"Rescued from what?" Carrie Anne asked, sipping the drink slowly. Her heart rate returned to a steady rhythm. Her breathing came easier. The tension and knots in her back relaxed.

"That's a really long story," Jessica said.

"That it is," Teren agreed.

"So, if I understand this right," Savina said. "You're Jessi's second-mother, the one who's sick?"

"Yes," Carrie Anne said. "I'm her step-mother."

"Teren, you know..."

Teren held up a hand, silencing Savina.

"Mrs. Ravenwolfe, I would love for you to be a guest and tour Castle Aurumice. We have different customs here, divorce simply is not looked upon favorably. So, I would think it wiser to have a new identity for you, perhaps aunt would be most appropriate. But we need a little time to work on that. For now, it is best if you return to Earth, and when the time is right, you will return to us?"

Carrie Anne nodded, completely smitten by the young man's words. She felt a little flush to her cheeks. He was easily ten years her junior, and Jessica's cousin. The layers of awkwardness were ridiculous but yet she was enamored.

"Do you feel well enough to return?" Teren asked. "If Jessica could escort you home?"

"Oh, yes," Carrie Anne said. "though I'm sad to leave. I don't know if it's just clean air, but I feel better than I have in a very long time."

"We will arrange a proper visit. Jessica?"

Jessica stood and Carrie Anne handed her the empty cup. The girl set it on the hay bale.

"Back this way," she pointed.

"Safe journey," Teren said.

"Blessings of the goddess to you," Savina moved her hands in the air, much like the Catholic Sign of the Cross, but different.

Carrie Anne followed Jessica, her fear of the Gate gone.

***

Teren waited a few minutes, then crossed his arms.

He kicked a rock across the floor.

"That girl will be the death of me."

"You were being incredibly charming there," Savina said "I could see it, that was overkill."

"I had to," Teren said. "Carrie Anne was terrified to go back. Had to convince her to be calm and leave quickly. If Aunt Lily had seen her, this barn would not still be standing."

"How will you keep her away now that she knows about our world?"

Teren threw his hands up.

"Stop asking me for answers to impossible questions! You ever notice none of these problems are mine? They find me. Broken Nico, angry Kaity, irrational Lily, impulsive Jessica!"

Savina picked up the cup.

"Well, by the goddess' blessing, I seem to stay off your trouble list," she leaned close. "By the way, you may thank me later for keeping you aware of strangers in your castle."

413

Teren opened the barn door, allowing her to pass in front of him. "Savina, I really would be lost without you."

CHAPTER 35

Carrie Anne returned to her home. She set down her purse and coat on the bench next to the door, her bones weary.

The house was quiet. The light was on in Stephen's first floor study.

Carrie Anne walked upstairs, collecting her thoughts. As she walked across the plush carpet, she wondered if it would give way and she would slip between the threads of reality.

She opened her daughter's bedroom door slowly. The girl lay tucked beneath covers in the darkness.

"Mom?"

"Oh hon, I thought you were sleeping."

Ashlin sat up, "Where were you? You didn't answer me."

Carrie Anne walked into the room, past piles of papers and clothing. She sat at the edge of her daughter's bed.

"I'm sorry, the volume was off on my phone. I didn't hear it."

"Dad and I called the church, you weren't there. Then dad went out and drove to the coffee shop. He was looking for you all night!"

Carrie Anne understood how Jessica lived her life just a bit more. It was very easy to slip away to Centernia and forget everything else for a little while.

"I was with your sister," Carrie Anne said.

"Jessi is back!?"

"Yeah, and she's doing well, better than I thought. And I think she's had quite the adventure, but I think she's home to stay."

Ashlin rested her head against the pillow. Carrie Anne couldn't help but notice that the girl still slept with her plush purple pig. Ashlin had that stuffed animal since she was two. Now her toddler was a teenager, and each moment passed through the hour glass. *Teach us to number our days, that we may gain a heart of wisdom...*

"Mom? What's wrong? Did something happen to Jessi?"

"No," Carrie Anne reassured. "I had quite the evening learning about your sister's life. I don't think I really knew her before."

"Will you please promise to not turn the ringer off on your phone?" Ashlin said, taking her mother's hand. "Dad and I were really, really sure something bad had happened to you."

"I promise," Carrie Anne brushed her daughter's bangs to the side.

"You're acting strange, even for you."

"I want you to promise me something, too."

"What kind of promise?"

"Promise me you'll never forget that there is so much to this world that we do not understand. There is so much more out there. Places and people you don't even know exist are all around us, so many you can't even imagine them."

"Please don't talk like this, it's really morbid," Ashlin said.

"Oh Ash, I don't mean it that way. What I'm trying to say is *be grateful, for everything in life*. Now I need to talk to your father. Can you fall asleep now?"

"Yeah, now that you're home."

Carrie Anne leaned forward and kissed her daughter's forehead.

She stood and walked out in the hallway, closing the door gently, as she had done for over a thousand nights before.

***

"Stephen, Jessi needs your help." Carrie Anne walked through the French doors into the little home office.

Stephen sat at his computer, trying to bury his worry in work. His office was his sanctuary of books and tasteful art prints of the western United States.

He refused to look up.

"Stephen, I am talking to you," Carrie Anne repeated.

Staring at the cells of the spreadsheet, the lines and numbers became a blur across the screen.

His wife crossed her arms.

"Stephen?"

Stephen knew he was being rude, but he had a sinking suspicion that the conversation was about to turn very uncomfortable.

"Where have you been?" he finally asked. "You have ignored all of my messages."

"I was at Jessica's house."

"Doing what?" Stephen's eyes stayed glued to the computer screen, though his hands had stopped moving. He didn't want to hear what his wife had to say.

"Having tea."

He glanced up.

"Having tea until midnight? Ashlin was nearly hysterical worrying about you, and I didn't appreciate the short notice to pick her up from practice."

"Well, we went on a little adventure, then had tea."

"Why were you at my ex-wife's house?"

"I was there because I was worried about our daughter, and I invited myself in, and then Jessica was kind enough to show me the basement, and the Gate, and then Centernia."

"I can't deal with this right now." Stephen stated. "I don't want to be involved. Whatever they told you, just forget it."

His wife wasn't satisfied with his answer. She reached across the desk and slammed the laptop lid closed.

"I know who you are. I know *what* you are, and I know about Centernia. You need to stop this lying, and more than anything, you need to talk to your daughter."

Stephen shoved his desk chair back, furious Jessica had betrayed the Gate.

"Will you please trust me when I say this is something you should not get involved in?" he pleaded.

"Stephen, my understanding of the world changed in one night, and you want me to ignore it?"

"What do you want me to do? The situation is more complex! Jessi is dealing in things that are more dangerous than anything else she's ever dealt with! It's not fun, it's not games. There may be a castle but it's no fantasy world."

"Stephen, look at me. You have got to stop running. I admit, I don't understand what this magic portal truly is, and I don't understand how it even exists. But if Jessi is dealing with something dangerous, you need to help her."

"If I help her, I will get pulled back in. I know it, and that has consequences for this family. We need to move, far away from the Gate, far away, maybe to another country. It isn't safe for Ashlin."

"And you're going to abandon Jessi?" Carrie Anne's voice was sharp. "If you abandon her, I will abandon you because that is not the type of man I want to be married to."

"Stop talking like that!"

"I am serious. You sound like a monster."

"Lily will look after Jessica. We're selling this house."

"You and she are the most backwards parents I have ever seen! Jessica is asking you for help, she has always been asking for help, and you just shut her out in your own selfishness!"

"She doesn't listen!" Stephen argued.

"Because you lie!" Carrie Anne wasn't angry, she was betrayed. Her pleading gaze stabbed holes through his heart.

"This is not right," Carrie Anne continued. "This is not how we chose to be a family. We built everything on the truth! We always told Ashlin to tell the truth, to trust us and we would never lie to her! And you have treated Jessica completely the opposite. You lied to her and she ran away. She wants to trust you, she wants you to be her father, and you just are acting so incomprehensibly! You lied to me! If the situation is so dire what can possibly make things worse?"

Stephen wished he could run out of the room, but he had nowhere to go.

"I have spent the past thirteen years of our marriage trying to respect the boundaries you and Lily established. You're both ridiculous. I am doing whatever Jessi needs, and this is the start."

"Carrie—"

"And it's more than Jess, it's Ashlin too! If I'm gone, who does she have? Who? She barely knows my family, yours is a joke. She needs her sister!"

He couldn't handle the hurt in her voice.

Stephen approached her, leaning against the mahogany desk. Arguing wouldn't work, he had to be honest. He took her hands.

"There are people in that world who think I am criminal, and rightly so. I can never cross the Gate again."

"But why lie to your daughter? Why are you turning her away?"

Stephen looked down. For so long he had been angry. It was easier to hate the place that betrayed him, cast him aside, than it was to admit how terribly he still ached to be home. He thought of his brothers and sisters, his parents, aunts and uncles, his cousins, his friends. He longed for Ravenwolfe and the days riding the wind across the treetops through the land that knew magic.

"I want to go home," he choked, "but I can never go back. Carrie, that world is like nothing I can describe to you, and for as much trouble as it brings, it's wonderful. I wish you could see all of it. And as soon as I let myself think of my life as Savartos Sarkisian, I don't know what that means. He was a son of Castle Nova. He was a healer who could knit flesh with a thought, and he was the one who loved Lily. What does that mean?"

"But he, *you* are Jessica's father. And right now, she needs the father who understands Centernia."

His hands trembled, but she held tightly.

"Are you sure?" his voice was very soft. "This is a box I didn't want to open. And helping her might mean other people and things might come through that Gate. The rule of law there is almost incomprehensible. Ashlin will be pulled in. Our lives are never going to be the same."

"But you haven't been able to stop it by pretending it isn't real. So, help your daughter instead. You're Savartos Sarkisian, and that's okay."

Her words resonated in his heart.

He had never heard his wife speak his real name.

Leaning forward, he kissed her forehead. She wasn't content with the kiss instead embraced him, bringing her lips to his. Carrie Anne had a wisdom and spirit that continued to amaze him, and he prayed he could hold onto her.

"Okay, how do I do this? If you've talked to them, what do they want?"

"I think Jessica just wants to understand you."

"I don't want to share."

"You want her trust, you have to try to meet her in the middle. Stephen, my heart cannot it take it if she leaves again."

"Alright, give me a little time to think this through and what I need to say to Jessi, and her cousin. It's complicated, and I just need to think."

***

Jessica counted down the minutes until her mom arrived home, panicking over her foolish choice. What compelled her to bring Carrie Anne across the Gate? It was stupid, so very, very, stupid.

After they'd crossed back through, Jessica had fixed Carrie Anne tea and answered her questions. The more she talked, the more the teen realized she had opened Pandora's box.

Sitting on the worn couch, she tried to figure out what to do. She was lucky Savina saw her before anyone else did. She breathed, remembering the prayers of the goddess to calm her nerves.

She exhaled.

But Teren knew, and Teren would help her out of the mess. He always did in the end.

The door opened, and Jessica jumped.

"Mom!"

Her mother took off her coat, revealing the uniform of a fast-food restaurant. Jessica felt the sting of shame as she realized her mother lost a good job for her.

Lily embraced her daughter and Jessica could smell the grease of fryer oil. "I missed you. Why the hell were you with the circus so long?!"

"I didn't know they didn't send my letters. Or they got 'lost' or whatever bullshit answer! I thought you guys were still mad at me."

"No, we stopped being mad at you months ago."

"Oh good, glad there's a limit on immortal embarrassment."

"Your cousin fixed it, and it pretty much was the talk of gossip until Talinda and Deremy were caught in the wine cellars, which broken Talinda's engagement to Ren. And then Corwin and Kaity had a falling out and left. And somewhere along the way it just became old castlefolk news."

"They left?"

"Yes, but I'm sure they'll return. Kaity loves the castle too much and I doubt the mages will treat Temi the same way we do."

"Mom, I am so sorry I went to Polaris behind your back. It was a mistake."

"Yes, Jared told me what happened in Polaris."

"Yeeeeeeah…..about that."

Lily smirked, shrugged, and walked past her daughter.

"Tea?"

"Sure. I actually had dinner with dad before you came home. I confronted him."

"Oh, my God, Jess, what did he say?"

"I would say he didn't take it too well, got really upset."

"You know why he lives here and not there?"

"He told me about his friend trying to betray Teren."

Lily washed a plate that had been sitting in the sink, shaking her head.

"It was bad Jess, really bad."

"Is that why you divorced him? Because he killed that woman?" Jessica asked.

Lily set the plate into the drying rack.

She wiped her hands on the back of her black jeans.

"No, no not at all. It made me fall in love with him more. Your dad made a difficult sacrifice when he fought Danyelle, and I'm grateful to him," she said, "and so was your aunt."

Lily had never been grateful to Jessica's father for anything.

"I'm happy you're home."

Jessica nodded, still feeling guilty for telling Carrie Anne the truth. Her mother seemed like she was in a great mood, as soon as the woman found out, the peace would be decimated.

"Are you going back to Aurumice tonight?" Lily asked.

Jessica shook her head.

"I just need to stay here. Honestly, I want to watch a movie, and eat popcorn and pancakes, and just be here. What day of the week is it?"

"Friday. Did Nico return with you?"

"That's another story."

"If you'd like to tell me what happened, let's go to the grocery store, and you can tell me on the way there."

CHAPTER 36

Aunt Dahlia had not been happy with Nico's decision to leave, but couldn't stop him.

Sienna brought him to the edge of the forest north of Aurumice. A quiet return seemed wise.

"If you change your mind, I will be in staying in Trabalis a few days," Sienna said as he climbed from Zastrugi's back. "I need to warn the local temple about Casimirio."

Nico paused a moment, not sure what to say to his second-mother. If it had been a different time, he would have invited her to the Castle, but they had both become outsiders to Aurumice.

"Sienna…thank you, for everything."

"Like I told Jessi, I would never turn my back on castlefolk."

Sienna bid Nico goodbye, and her gryphon launched into the sky.

With a light pack on his back, he started the day's trek to Aurumice. He attempted to obscure his identity in the garments of the Holy Circus, still fearing detection.

It took him a while to find the path through the autumn forest. Closer the castle, his memory served him better. He needed no map, trusting large landmarks of his childhood as he walked through the undergrowth. His bad eye was just a little bit better, and he was able to open it enough to see blurry forms.

The imbalance was annoying, but it was a sign of improvement.

He had walked a quarter of a day when he heard the rustling on the path. Immediately he thought of Zia and ducked behind a tree, drawing a short sword.

To his surprise, a large blue bicorn pushed through the trees, snorting and sniffing the air.

Moontower immediately found Nico, knocking him over. Nico dropped his sword and dodged the sharp horns as Moontower coated his hair with slobber.

"Old friend," Nico chuckled. "You've come to greet me."

Moontower appeared to be in good health. His coat was covered in dirt and burs and his mane and tail seemed to not have been brushed in months.

"Would you mind giving me a ride back to the castle?" Nico asked, climbing onto the bicorn's back.

The climb up was not as easy as he had remembered. He hoped he hadn't made a mistake as he gave Moontower a light squeeze with his legs. The creature stepped forward at an easy pace and Nico relaxed.

As they traveled through the forest, a shiny blue speck in Moontower's mane caught his attention. It buzzed, trying to burrow into the bicorn's hair.

A needlewasp.

It was the first he had ever seen near his home.

Nico plucked the bug and flicked it away, recalling his dream. Bicorns usually had a strong resistance to the bacteria that infected people, but Nico was not eager to find out if Puce fever was one of them.

They traveled cautiously towards the castle, taking the long route to avoid the usual guard patrol paths.

When he could go no further on the bicorn, Nico dismounted and bid his friend goodbye.

"No worries," he said. "I will see you again."

Drawing his hood tighter, Nico carefully moved through the forest, ever watchful for the guard. Avoiding the stable yard, he approached the side of the castle from the north. There was little activity, the doors were heavily bolted, but Nico knew a way in. There was a hidden door through a garden alcove, behind a dry fountain. From there, he was able to access the passageways of the castle. Like most raised in the Aurumice, he knew about the secret network of tiny hallways. But Nico was different from most children. He knew there were hidden passages within the already hidden passages. There were certain triggers, hidden buttons and levers that gave him access that would allow him to be undetectable.

As he wandered through his home, he couldn't shake the feeling that something was a little different.

He traveled downwards, through staircases. His first goal was to take food from the storerooms, then go down to the chamber of the Azure

Lake. From there he would begin his search for the Corvalian Stones and freedom.

***

Teren watched the dinner hall, wondering how his cousin was handling her family on earth.

Jared approached, hands in his pockets.

He leaned towards Teren. "You need to fire the guard. They're not very good at keeping intruders away."

Teren allowed his senses to stretch out, listening for the strange cacophony of Zia. Nothing seemed out of place.

And then Nico's apprehension hit him like a strong, low tone.

"Hmmm," Teren nodded. "Where is he?"

"Already inside. I would say going for the cellars. Shall we greet him?"

"He knows where we are. Let him find us when he's ready."

***

The subterranean passages of Aurumice were so different from the underground mines. Instead of suffocating darkness, Aurumice was a cozy den. Of course the underground chambers were cold and musty, but there was a familiar presence in the air. The faint smell of wine barrel casks permeated upper passages. Dried fruits and meats mixed in with the earthy aroma, creating a pleasant medley.

It felt right to Nico.

Glowstones illuminated his path for a while, until he reached a passage without them.

He lifted a glowstone torch from the wall and continued deeper into the darkness until he reached the false generator room.

The massive machine whirred with the trundle of gears and the rumble of pressure. Nico walked past the noisy loud machine to a tube set into the wall. Climbing through a small hatch, Nico entered the chamber that had been his favorite room, the Azure lake.

425

Closing his eyes, he realized how deeply connected he was to the castle. It was home, how could he have forgotten that? Nico's heart beat faster with a sense of relief and almost…joy?

Memories swirled back to him. In his mind's eye, he recalled the first time he had seen the Azure Lake. Misa had discovered it as a child, then brought her companions down to explore. They had tried to go swimming in the crystal-clear water and had a nasty surprise as they found the water icy. Their cries and laughter echoed across the cavern walls.

Another memory bubbled up from the depths of the lake. When Nico's blue fiery powers had gone wild, his mother had carried him down to the Azure. He was no danger to anyone in a massive cavern made of stone. With his mother's guidance, he had learned to bottle up his powers.

Walking forward under the glittering glowstone ceiling, he came to the lake's edge. He knelt at the shore, his knees sinking into the soft mossy bed. There was something in the cavern that he could not describe. Inhaling the smell of frigid stone, there was purity and power in the foundation of Aurumice.

Dipping both hands in the water, he lifted them carefully, intending to drink.

Instead, his hands glowed blue as a familiar tingle returned. The light danced through the water.

The sensation both frightened and delighted him. He didn't know what had caused his mage strength to vanish, it seemed Azure Lake would draw it back out.

Nico watched in awe, ready for the inferno to cover his body, as it always had. Instead, the energy lingered on his palm, under his control. The young man twisted his hands around, the blue magic moved like a ball from fingertip to fingertip. He smiled, for the first time since he was a child, his mage gifts were entertaining and delightful.

Nico played with the tiny magic ball, moving it from hand to hand with a calm rhythm. In the back of his mind he recited the prayers of the goddess, the more he prayed, the more in control he felt. The rhythm of his breathing, the movement of the magic, it was all in time.

Eventually exhaustion over took him, and he fell asleep on the mossy bed.

CHAPTER 37

Saturday had rolled by in a strange calmness, melding into Sunday and then Monday. Jessica received one text from Carrie Anne, stating her father was no longer mad.

She also wasn't sure what to say to her step mother. She regretted her impulsive choice to show Carrie Anne Centernia and doubted her father was no longer angry.

Jessica tried to ignore her worry as she watched TV. For three days, she lounged around in sweatpants and allowed the real world to soak back in.

Occasionally, the teen did leave the couch to help sort through their online orders. Their sales were steady. It wasn't nearly enough to fix the hot water heater, but it was still something.

Things were very calm, until Jessica's cell phone buzzed on the kitchen counter on Monday evening.

"Jessi, what did you say to Carrie Anne?"

The teen looked up from her burrito.

"Mom, don't be mad. It's been a really nice weekend, do not be mad."

"What did you not tell me?" Lily asked.

"Just don't be mad."

"Did you tell her the truth? She said here that she talked to your dad about helping you, and he's sorry he lied about his past? What does she know?"

"Not much," Jessica said.

"Did you tell her about Centernia?"

Jessica set her plate down on an end table. She grabbed the TV remote and muted the volume.

"Yes," she replied, staring at the TV.

"Oh, my God Jessica, what were you thinking?! Did she believe you?!" Lily threw up her arms.

"Not at first, but then, I sort of forced her to believe."

"Did you bring Carrie Anne to Centernia?"

"Yes."

"Why?! This is a sacred, unbreakable secret and you broke it!!!!"

Jessica jumped to her feet. She knew the peace between them could never last.

"Mom, I have kept this secret for years! I lied to Felicia Lee so damn much it broke our friendship and I won't let that happen to Carrie Anne! She worried about me and I wanted to prove to her that I had a reason for being gone!"

"You had no right!"

"Did you ever tell anyone about Centernia? Did you?!"

Lily hesitated a moment.

"Someone else knows," Jessica said. "Who else knows about the Gate?"

"I didn't tell anyone! You should never have brought her there! How stupid are you!? What did those circusfolk do to your head?! You stayed with them for months and threw away high school!"

"A bicorn rolled over on top of me, and then I fell in a river, and the circus saved my life."

"While you were running from *the Nova mages* of all people! Oh God, Jessica, I don't know how to fix this!" Lily slammed her fist on the table.

"Mom, I'm eighteen. It was my choice."

"You're eighteen and stupid."

"Carrie Anne has cancer, I wanted her to see something amazing."

"You made an entire castle worry and you're concerned about one woman! You should have cared more before you decided to stay away for six months!"

"I don't want to fight about this," Jessica.

"Jessica please…"

"No, I don't want to fight," Jessica ran down the stairs to the basement.

"Come back and talk! You're just like your father!"

Jessica hopped through the Gate, trying figure out how to allay her mother's anger.

Lily followed her through the cinderblock wall.

"I don't want to talk to you if you're just going to yell at me!" Jessica shouted.

Jessica regretted going through the Gate in her bare feet as she crossed the rough floor.

"I'm really trying not to yell." Lily insisted, following Jessica as the girl climbed ladder into the barn. She didn't want to be trapped in an argument with her mother in the long tunnel into the castle.

"Can you understand why I wouldn't want Carrie Anne to know? What this could do? You didn't think!"

"Please, mom," Jessica held up her hands, "I get you think I'm crappy at making choices. This is just something I had to do."

Jessica reached for the barn door, but her mother grabbed her wrist.

"Jessica, I don't want to take an argument into the middle of the stable yard again!"

"Then stop lecturing me and let go."

"Not until you stop and actually talk to me."

"You're yelling at me!"

"I'm not yelling!!!"

"YOU ARE!!!!" Jessica wrenched her arm from her mother's grasp with the pop and crack of bone.

At the same time, Jessica had a moment of stillness, seeing the bone split in her mind's eye.

Lily shouted, stumbling back and grasping her forearm. A lesser woman would have been in tears, but Lily gritted her teeth.

"Why would you do this?!" Lily shouted.

Jessica was horrified. Panicking, she turned and ran.

***

Teren sat at his desk, sorting through the never-ending pile of documents. A familiar presence poked at the back of his mind. Nico was near.

"I know you are in the walls, why would you bother hiding from me?"

A panel next to the fireplace slid open. Nico emerged, his identity obscured by a cloak and the mask of the Holy Circus.

"Jared and I could have gotten you into the castle without detection."

"I changed my plans after you left," Nico leaned against the arm of the chair. "My sister told me that the Stones of Corvalian are in the castle, and Sienna confirmed it. Jessi had suggested it before, but I was a self-absorbed idiot."

"Where do you think your father put them?" Teren asked. "I would assume something of that value would be in a clever place."

"I have no idea what they even look like, let alone where my father may have hidden them."

Teren pondered this, tapping his pencil absentmindedly on the desk.

"Are you mad at me?" Nico finally asked.

Teren was surprised.

"Why would I be angry?"

"Because you worked very hard to free me, and when I finally was free, I did not even send you a message."

"To confess Nico, I thought you may be a little angry with me. I ran away from Aurumice when your father came back, and things went to hell."

"You needed solitude."

"Yeah, I was in an abyss after Misa died. I walked through that Gate so I couldn't hurt anyone."

Nico's eyes grew distant.

"You're thinking of the other Sinari, aren't you? Zia is nowhere close. Her emotions are very distinct to me."

Nico darkened.

"Sorry, I should not have mentioned her."

"How often do you listen to people's emotions?" Nico asked.

"Depends on how busy I am, maybe a few times an hour I sweep the castle," Teren replied. Mentioning his habit, he let his mind reach out across the halls. He expected to encounter the mundane mix of the day.

Instead, he sensed the maelstrom of his panicking cousin.

***

Jessica dashed barefoot through field, running for the woods.

Her vision blurred, her ears pulsed strangely and her heart was beating faster than she had ever felt. Trembling, she ran to the edge of the pasture were the bicorns grazed.

Jessica could not quell the panic as she sweat profusely, gasping for breath. She had been ignoring all the signs. She wasn't a blood mage healer, she was something else.

Crouching on the ground, she held her head. The pressure was so intense, she thought it would explode. She opened her eyes. Looking at her arms, she realized they were pulsing with a purple-red light.

It was the same hue she had been seeing for months with the circus.

She had thought it was magic of the world.

But it was her own.

"Jessica!" Teren's voice cut the night from the end of the field.

Her cousin must have sensed her panic.

"Stay away!" Jessica shouted. Teren was not alone, followed by an Auroriate.

Jared ran into the meadow from an opposite path.

"My mage strength is out of control!" Jessica warned. "Don't come near me!"

They continued to walk towards her until they were about twenty feet away.

"I can't make it stop! Listen to me!" Jessica tried to warn them. "STAY AWAY!"

All three fell to their knees, gripping their sides. The bicorns bellowed, stampeding into the woods.

"No! No! No! I don't know how to make it stop!"

The Auroriate convulsed, Jared howled, and Teren gritted his teeth so hard the veins on his face bulged.

Jessica was trapped in her own maelstrom.

Teren reached out.

A warm soft fluffy blanket cradled Jessica's mind. The terror was gone, the anger was gone, and she was left in a cuddly cloud. She fell to her knees in exhaustion.

Motionless, the trio lay sprawled out in the dirt.

"No, no, don't be dead…"

"Holy goddess tits, that was awful," Jared rolled onto his back in the wet grass. "It felt like you were squeezing me from the inside and pulling my veins in different directions."

"I'm sorry. I'm so sorry!" Jessica cried.

The Auroriate recovered first, crawling to her.

"Your eyes are red... are you hurt?" he asked.

"You came back," Jessica recognized Nico's voice.

"Are you hurt?" Nico repeated.

"Me? But I nearly killed you."

Jessica's brain argued with her body. She wanted to panic, but her emotions remained calm.

"I think you damaged my spleen, I don't know what a spleen is, but I think it's damaged!" Jared called out.

Nico placed a reassuring hand on Jessica's arm.

"I'll hurt you," she warned. "Please don't touch me. I don't want to hurt you."

"Hey! Still dying over here!" Jared called out. "I've got hurts in places that shouldn't be hurt!"

"Blood storm," Teren sat up slowly. "That is what just happened, completely normal. We're fine. There is nothing wrong with you, Jess, you just need to learn."

"Normal my ass!" Jared croaked.

"I attacked my mom before I ran out here," Jessica explained.

"Jared, check on Lily," Teren requested.

"Oh damnit," the blonde-haired boy grumbled, sitting up. "She's okay Jess, well, mostly. I see Fentalon, he's helping bandage up her arm. But she looks better than I feel right now."

"Oh good."

"What did she say to make you angry?" Nico asked.

"I told her I brought Carrie Anne to Centernia."

"You did what?!" Jared chuckled, then moaned in pain.

"Why do you think it's funny!?" Jessica protested.

"Why would you do that?!" Jared laughed again in spite of himself. "Oh god, my sides hurt. But why? Why did you tell Carrie Anne?"

"Because I'm an idiot and I ran out of lies."

"Your secret was yours to tell," Nico reassured.

"Yeah, well, ever since I crossed that Gate it wasn't, it's my parents' secret, and now I messed up, I messed everything up. I'm going home," Jessica said. "Where I can't hurt anyone."

"Please, stay," Nico encouraged. "I'm sorry I told you not to use your powers. You need to learn. Don't make the same mistake I did."

"Why did you come back to Aurumice?"

"I thought about what you said, and realized you're right. The mark of Corvalian can keep me away from the mages, and I found out that my father stole the stones and hid them in the castle."

"The mage assassin thing?" Jared asked. "You have them in *Aurumice?!* No wonder Nova hates the castle."

"My father stole them about thirteen years ago, I suspect the mages are unaware where they are hidden."

"We will find them," Teren promised, standing. He offered a hand to Jared.

"Are you actually okay?" he asked.

"I feel like an elephant sat on me," Jared said, "but I'll live."

Jessica felt Nico's eyes on her.

"What?" she snapped.

"I'm worried about you."

"Now? Really? Now you're worried about me? This isn't new. I've screwed up a lot with my family. I left Jared bleeding to death to chase after you, then I left high school. For six months you didn't care about any of this, and *now you're worried about me?*"

Jessica climbed to her feet. "I'm going to go talk to my mom," she stumbled a little as she walked, her balance unstable.

"Jessi, I'm sorry!" Nico called out after her.

Teren and Jared remained silent.

She shook her head, leaving her friends.

***

Lily sat in front of the fireplace, drinking a tea sprinkled with pain killers. She stared into the flames.

A knock roused her from her thoughts.

Fentalon opened the door.

Jessica stood outside.

"I need to talk to my mom, and also I wanted to apologize to you for my rudeness."

"You have caused a lot of trouble," Fentalon said.

"Talon, let her in!" Lily yelled.

"I'll be outside if you need me," he said.

Fentalon pulled the door closed, leaving Jessica standing alone. Her daughter looked like she had been through hell, her eyes red, her arms blotchy.

"Are you okay?"

"No," Jessica was reticent. "I'm really, really not."

Lily gestured to the chair across from her.

Jessica walked in, and took a seat gingerly.

The girl was an echo of Beatrix. Different hair, different eyes, but the weight of the universe rested on her shoulders. Lily felt terrible. Jessica's absence destroyed her yet she couldn't last a few days without screaming at her daughter.

Why did she fail so badly at being a mom?

"I'm sorry," Jessica said. "For everything. I know you're mad, and I didn't mean to hurt you."

"You didn't hurt me Jess, I twisted wrong."

"No, no you didn't. I saw your arm break, I felt it break! But I meant more than just your arm. I should never have run away with the Auroriates."

"Don't worry about the arm, I'm worried about you."

"Me? But—"

"Look, I know sometimes I am not the best mom, and I struggle with your dad."

Lily looked at the mug of tea, struggling with the words.

"Jess, I'm not mad at you. I deserve this, it's like Madiernian balance for what I did to your shoulder years ago. I still hate myself for that, you know?"

Jessica unconsciously reached for the scar of the castlemark.

"I justified in my head at the time," Lily continued, "because I realized you wouldn't be raised in Aurumice. You would need to go to kindergarten, and then I'd be forced to explain a tattoo. So it made sense to burn it off...but I think it was really because I didn't want to see it. And that was selfish and crappy, and what you did to my arm is fair. You deserved to hurt me."

"Mom, I didn't see it that way..."

"I should help you get back to Polaris, you need it. You're like a baby nightflight ready to fly, and me keeping you tied down isn't going to end well for the village."

"I really didn't mean to hurt you, Mom, any of the ways I hurt you. I shouldn't have run away, or told Carrie Anne or hurt your arm. I think that was my mage strength gone wrong. You look really bad, should we go the ER?"

"I don't have health insurance, Jess, so I can't."

"That's my fault, too, isn't it?"

"I should have listened to Saurin Bane and brought you to Polaris myself."

"Can we start over?" Jessica pleaded. "I don't want to argue with you, not again, and I really mean, never again. I need you."

Lily gave half a smile.

"Me? You got an entire castle who has your back. The castlefolk gave you hell for what you did to Wadjette, but when you went missing, they searched for you."

Jessica nodded.

"I should go home, I don't want to accidentally hurt any of them."

"You know now to be cautious. When my lightning abilities manifested I wanted to run to earth and never come back, but I learned to control them. You'll learn too, and maybe now your father will help you."

Lily laughed in spite of herself.

"What?"

"I know I said I'm angry you told Carrie Anne, but I wish I could have seen your father's face when she confronted him. Sorry, I can't help it. For so long he's made me shoulder everything Centernian, and I feel like the world is less lopsided now."

Lily felt her eyelids droop.

"I'm tired and these herbs are making me sleepy. I should rest."

"Alright, and I did want to apologize to Fentalon. Was that him accepting my apology?"

"It didn't really sound like it, but in his way, yes, but I'll talk to him. And if he's mad at you, then he's going to be mad at me, because I'll take your side over his."

"Do you think you'll ever marry Talon?"

Lily smirked shook her head. "The truth is, and this sounds really bad coming from me, your parent, but he and I are just friends with benefits. What they say about pure ailurian men is true."

Jessica raised an eyebrow.

Lily's eyes continued to droop. "You're eighteen now, may as well talk to you like you're an adult. Happy belated birthday, by the way. Did you celebrate it at all?"

"Oh that's a story," Jessica replied. "Mom, you're falling asleep sitting up. I think I'll go now.

"Yeah, we'll talk later."

Jessica began to walk away.

"Wait…can I hug you?"

"Yeah, of course…"

Jessica hugged her mother carefully then left the room.

CHAPTER 38

A few days later, Jessica knelt at the base of the hot water heater in the musty basement. Her mother leaned against the cinderblock wall, cradling her bandaged forearm.

"Mom, I am worried about your arm."

"I can't afford it, Jess. I had Dr. Onyxgrove look at it."

Jessica grimaced at the thought of the castlefolk doctor.

"But he sucks. Google could tell you more than he could."

"What do you want me to do?"

"I don't know," Jessica said. She looked at the base of the hot water heater.

"Forget about me, can you fix it?" Lily asked.

"Wires I'm good with, plumbing I'm really not. You're going to hate me for saying this, but maybe I could borrow the money from Dad and Carrie Anne to replace it?"

"I don't want to ask them for help," Lily crossed her arms.

"But I really think they can afford it."

"Just because they live in a nice house doesn't mean they actually have a lot of money. Some people are just better at managing their credit cards than others."

"Yeah, but you should see my college fund."

"You have a college fund?"

"Yeah, it's what my dad was using to try to convince me not to go to Centernia. It had a lot of zeros," Jessica climbed to her feet.

"He really said that to you?" Lily asked.

"Yeah, he did," Jessica said. "I know the money exists. He showed me a bank statement. I don't know what to do about college."

"I want you to graduate high school first, then move on to that question."

Jessica wiped her hands on her jeans and began to walk up the stairs.

"Is that why you stayed away?" Lily asked. "It wasn't just for Nico, or waiting for the healer. You bought yourself more time by failing your senior year."

Jessica stopped on the stairs.

Her mother was right.

"How did you choose?" Jessica asked.

"I followed my heart," Lily replied. "And it seemed good at the time, but when we locked the Gate, I had nothing. The magic isn't stable, Jess. You don't want to be on this side, thirty years old, and no chance at a real job."

"I know, Mom," Jessica continued up the stairs. Lily followed.

"And Nico isn't really the type of person you want to tie your life to. I think you figured that out when you left him behind. That was wise."

"What's that supposed to mean?"

"It's not him, but Centernian men, or women for that matter, aren't worth it. Not worth splitting your life in half."

"He came back already," Jessica stated as they stepped into the kitchen. "He's hiding in the castle."

"Oh."

"Mom, I didn't stay with the circus because I thought I could sleep with Nico. I went to the circus to help Carrie Anne. It's not my fault they lied to me about learning how to be a healer."

"You didn't suspect they were lying a month or two in?"

"I was dumb. I didn't want to believe it, just like I didn't want to believe that my mage strength is backwards."

"It's not backwards, it's just not what you expected it to be. You've taught yourself so many things, Jess, you can learn this. Sometimes mage strengths are funny. You have one great moment where it clicks, and you spend years chasing it again. You will figure it out."

Her phone glowed on the kitchen counter top. Jessica picked it up and read her messages.

"This is weird."

"What?" Lily asked.

"Dad invited us to dinner, at his house. And my cousin too."

"Strange."

Jessica held up the phone.

"Amazing," Lily said, "but I can't go. If they see my arm, they'll drive me crazy…"

"Can't you lie to them like you tell me to? Remember when I gashed my forehead falling off Frostfire? Told them I hit a countertop. They bought it."

"Your father didn't."

"Okay, well…"

Lily wrestled her hands together.

"Jess, this will be the most incredibly awkward dinner ever! I can't go."

"So, me and Teren are going to go alone?"

"He's much better at social tact than I am."

"But he'll be pretty much blind, so to speak, because it would be here, on earth. Why does dad want to talk to my cousin?"

"I would guess this is a step towards mending the past."

"If this is a step towards past mending, are you sure you want to decline?"

"Let me think about it."

***

In a quiet corner of the castle, Nico opened a ceiling panel. Peering down into the darkened office, he carefully made his descent to the floor. Below him was a bear statue, frozen on his hind legs, jaw open. Nico climbed down onto the creature's head, steadying himself on the wall. The ornate crown molding actually had a perfect spot for a hand grip. As Nico descended, his leg trembled unsteadily and he begged the goddess that he wouldn't slip.

Gripping the bear's head, he lowered himself onto its arms and then was able to make the leap to the wooden floor. In his better days, he could have easily leapt from the bear's head to the ground.

Securely in the room, he listened. A quick glance assured him the door was locked and likely had been for a better part of a decade. Dust coated everything in the room, mingling with spiders' nests and rodent droppings.

The office was small, about fifteen feet across and ten feet deep. It had no window and just a few books on the shelves, left by its previous occupant. His father had never been much of a reader but he liked the impression the books gave. A small cold fireplace was tucked into a corner, with a cluttered desk before it. Two wooden chairs were positioned by the desk, on it were a small statuary of the goddess, placed on a corner and a lamp on the other. Prayer beads hung, draped from the lamp.Nico's eyes adjusted to the darkness of the room. He hated the castle without electricity, it was strange. It worried him that Trabalis was being so demanding about something they had ignored for so long.

He explored the room, opening desk drawers and searching for any sign of the Corvalian stones. If he found them, he hoped the magic worked as castlemarks did—you placed it to your skin and the magical imprint emerged.

Nico found a small arsenal of weapons, an array of odd objects, but no indication of the stones. The small study was too obvious a location.

Nico wiped away and dust and bug carcasses and sat in his father's chair.

The old leather creaked.

Pondering in silence, he picked up one of his mother's pearl combs from the desk drawer. She had worn the elegant little hair piece often.

Nico's mind wandered to the past, half out of unbidden nostalgia, and half out of hope his memory would surface the location of the stones.

Malachi had been an eccentric man. He'd lived for drama, theatrics, and a good joke. He'd been brash and bold, unafraid to say what others wouldn't say, which often got him into trouble. From what Nico understood, it was these very qualities that had drawn his reserved, regal mother to the vagabond. Where others had, whether through shame or fear, tried to hide their thoughts from her, he'd delighted in the idea that she could read minds. Their courtship had been brief and shocking to the circus and castle alike, because Malachi had done what no other person had ever done. He had *invited* Elina to read every one of his thoughts and memories.

Within a few days, they knew everything about each other, and formed a bond with a depth that few could imagine.

It was difficult to believe they both were gone. In stray moments, Nico wondered if he was crazy and was misremembering reality. How could they both be dead?

He had cried rivers for his mother, but hadn't truly ever mourned his father. A part of him believed it was an elaborate joke. But he'd seen the stab wound, seen the dead body, but it couldn't be his father.

Something still didn't add up. Why did Malachi trap Kaity, and why was Corwin so furious and fearful that he would draw a weapon? At the time it had been drama and theatrics, but Nico felt like he was missing something.

The answer was eluding him, like everything else... the location of the stones, his freedom, a meaningful rapport with his family and a real relationship with Jessica. Everything just seemed inches from his grasp!

He was thoroughly done being tossed at the whim of the universe.

Nico set the hair comb on the desk. Running his fingers across the tines, he sent a tiny wave of magic through the metal. It glowed briefly. Little balls of energy appeared, trailing after his fingers.

Collecting the energy beads, he scooped them up, forming a larger ball. He grinned, delighted at his ability to command the energy. Whatever took his magical abilities, the gentle re-emergence had given him the chance to control his strength.

I need to show Jess...

He been an awful friend while marinating in his misery.

She had every right to be frustrated with him.

Clenching his fist, the energy disappeared.

A noise in the hallway caused him to jump. He ducked under the desk, heart beating wildly.

But no one came to find him...no castlefolk, no mages, no circusfolk, not even the maddening Sinari woman.

The room was undisturbed, like a sarcophagus.

Crawling from beneath the desk, he was disgusted and annoyed. Why was he wasting his time hiding in his own castle?

The world had thrown him in hell, again and again and again, but he still clawed his way through in spite.

Climbing to his feet, he looked around his father's office.

He wasn't a ghost, why was he acting like one?

CHAPTER 39

Paisley Mae snapped her fingers, creating tiny sparks. She had been traveling on Obsidian for days. It was her first mission, and the novelty had quickly worn off.

The little group of mages crested a hill.

"Can we stop for lunch—"

The girl's words faded from her lips as she looked around in horror.

They had come upon a farm. Each sheep was bloated and red, covered in oozing sores, more than half of them were unmoving. Those who still had strength bleated painfully. A few stray insects fluttered from creature to creature.

Paisley fought the urge to wretch.

She had never seen the effects of the needlewasps.

"Fan out to assess the extent of the damage," Scottswen ordered. He was an older fire mage and leader of the party. "I will go north, Santino and Meladry go south. Zapaisley, take the farm house, see what the residents know. The rest of you go east."

The mages split up. Paisley Mae warily eyed the sheep as she cut through the pasture, urging Obsidian to keep his distance. The buzzing of the needlewasps made her skin crawl.

What a lousy first mission.

The door of the neat little wooden house was open, swinging eerily in the cold air.

Paisley Mae dismounted, carefully looking around for needlewasps. She left Obsidian loose, he was well trained and would not wander.

She stepped onto the porch.

"Hello?" Paisley Mae called out. "I am Zapaisley Maeve Sarkisian, mage of Castle Nova. We come offering aid."

Needlewasps struck the glass of the window, confused on how to escape. They became caught between the folds of the embroidered curtains.

She rubbed her fingers together, ready to call the flames to protect her. She tried to remain calm, knowing it would be easy to set the little home on fire.

"Hello. Mages of Castle Nova are here. May I enter?"

Paisley Mae stopped.

The family lay on the floor of the kitchen, as bloated and punctured as the sheep in the pasture. The grey-furred ailurian had her hand on her son's back. The father was sprawled out in front of the cold fireplace, his eye sockets shimmering strangely.

Needlewasps burrowed through his eyeballs.

A needlewasp flew by Paisley's head and she slammed it into the wall, squashing it with a crackle. Its blue blood stained her gloved hand.

She ran from the farmhouse in time to hear the other mages shouting.

Buzzing reverberated through the summer day like the growl of a demon. Over the horizon, an undulating unholy mass of blue emerged. At first it was as big as a house, then two, then three.

Paisley Mae shoved her fear aside, this is what she was trained to do. She climbed onto Obsidian's back then urged the bicorn towards the swarm. Raising her arms, Paisley Mae called fire to her hands.

CHAPTER 40

The Pennsylvania evening was dark and drizzly as they rode in the black sedan to Stephen's house. Jessica filled the silence by explaining her plan for finishing high school.

Teren sat in the back seat. Like his cousin, he wore comfortable jeans and a sweatshirt. The dinner invitation had been so strange he couldn't resist accepting. It was a welcomed change from Nico's never-ending mope train through the castle walls.

Staring out the window, Teren found Jessica's conversation with her father interesting. Without his abilities, he couldn't discern how they actually felt about what they were saying, but he listened to the subtle inflections in their voices.

"Teren, how is the castle these days?" Stephen asked, jarring Teren from his concentration. What an oddly casual question.

"As well as can be expected, sir," he replied, "in debt, disorganized, and in disrepair, but the stills work, so I suppose we are alright."

Arriving at Stephen's house, Carrie Anne greeted them at the door like an excited chittering mouse. Ashlin was nowhere to be seen.

A warm aroma of earth spices tickled Teren's nose.

The house was spacious, bright and clean. It was clear to Teren that his Aunt's house was a hovel in comparison to the little estate.

They were seated at the dinner table, set with a meal of pasta and a meat Carrie Anne called *Italian braciola*. Teren was served a glass of water and was a bit puzzled why there was no wine with such a rich meal. Then he remembered he was just barely old enough to drink alcohol by the earth laws.

"Carrie Anne, did you get new candle holders?" Jessica commented. "They're pretty."

In the center of the table, two wooden candleholders were carved into a familiar bird design.

"Those are not mine, your father took them out of storage," Carrie Anne replied.

"Gulian candles," Teren unfolded his cloth napkin. "It's a symbol of welcome in the south of Madierna."

"Oh," Jessica blinked. "I didn't know you had anything from Centernia."

"I buried it," Stephen said. "Literally, I buried it, in a box. But I dug it back up last night. Felt like some sort of grave robber out in Southpine Park. Snuck out there at three am with a shovel."

Carrie Anne smiled and reached out her hands for grace. "Stephen? Would you like to lead the blessing?"

Teren followed the tradition, eyes darting as he tried to figure out the custom.

"Oh, let me say it," Jessica interjected, "I got really good at preaching when I was with the Auroriate circus."

"Glad you learned something with those charlatans," Stephen said.

Carrie Anne ignored her husband's comment. " That would be lovely, dear."

Jessica glared at her father, then continued.

"I also learned how to pick pockets, but anyways," Jessica cleared her throat. "Bless us, O Lord, or Lady Goddess, whichever face you choose to take. And bless these your gifts, which we are about to receive from your bounty. Thank you for health, and for this opportunity that I never imagined would happen." Jessica's voice cracked. "Protect those who are not here at this table this evening, we ask this in your name, Amen."

They echoed the Amen.

"That was beautiful, dear, thank you," Carrie Anne picked up her fork. "I noticed you said goddess. Teren, what is your religion?"

"Actually, despite being raised in Castle Aurumice, where our religion is typically that of the Goddess Aurora, I do have a great deal of respect and understanding Christianity. I quite admire Jesus Christ, and I have found him easier to understand that than Aurora."

"Oh, have you read the Bible?" Carrie Anne seemed pleased by his words.

"My mother made sure I understood my American heritage, and she loved Christmas."

"Oh, how wonderful. Do you have Christmas trees?"

"The castle decorates trees, but in a different way. Our winter is different than yours. Centernia seems to be one season off from earth."

"That's very interesting. Tell me more about your world."

Teren explained as much as he could. Jessica contributed, but she let him take the conversation. His younger cousin was still nervous, waiting for her father to speak. Stephen said very little.

Finally, as their plates where cleared, Teren sensed the topic was about to turn. Stephen leaned forward more, about to interrupt the flow of conversation, but stopped.

Whatever he had to say, he was fighting with it.

Carrie Anne stood to brew tea and load the dishwasher. She shuffled the plates and glasses around in the strange little machine.

"Sir," Teren said, "I feel like you have been wanting to say something. If you wish to talk to Jessica, I would be happy to go for a walk."

"Oh no, no, I asked you both here because I need to talk to both of you." Stephen said. "First thing I need to say is Jessica I will help you, though things are tricky between me and your mom and Centernia and I need to explain. If I explain honestly, it involves Teren. It's not right to talk about a person without them being present."

"Me?"

"Yes. You."

Teren was not accustomed to surprises. Unknowing was strange.

Stephen crossed his tattooed arms.

"I don't know what you know or remember about me, but I was a friend to your parents. We had a mutual acquaintance, Danyelle Orion. She figured out what you are, and I stopped her."

"You saved my life," Teren interrupted as the memory suddenly resurfaced— his mother's pleading with another mage, a barking dog, a fight. Until that moment it had been hazed over with the clouds of time. He knew someone was there, but he had no idea it was Stephen.

That changed everything.

"It was never my intent to hurt Danyelle, I just needed to stop her..."

"Sir, I know you sacrificed a great deal, and for that I am eternally grateful!"

Stephen was visibly relieved that he did not need to retell the painful story in great detail.

"I did what I had to do. Your parents were two of my greatest friends. I'd known your father since we were kids. I met your mom the first time she visited Polaris, and she was amazing."

"How did you save his life?" Carrie Anne smiled curiously.

Stephen hesitated a moment.

"It's complicated."

"I'm sure Jessi would also like to know."

"Carrie, I killed a woman. The details don't matter. I was trying to stop her from making a decision that would have put my nephew's life in extreme danger, so she died instead."

For once, Carrie Anne was silent, not sure how to respond.

"I'll explain more at some point, but I need to say something. If this Pandora's box is open, then I need to say something I have needed to say for over a decade."

He cleared his throat.

"Teren, the reason I invited you here was to apologize, and maybe have a little chance at forgiveness, because your aunt won't forgive me."

Teren nodded.

"I didn't save your mother's life, and I should have," Stephen said.

"How?"

"That night when your father locked the castle under the forcefield and Elina lost her mind. I should have been there. I'm a blood mage, I could have easily saved your mother that night, but I stayed here."

"Everyone takes a piece of blame that night," Teren replied. "It's not your fault."

"No, no, no, you don't understand. Lily begged me to save Beatrix, but I was too afraid of going back through the Gate. I was convinced the mages would kill me. These fugitive marks forever make me a target for anyone who's ever studied in Polaris."

"The city was crawling with mages that day," Teren said. "They would have sensed you and known."

"Yeah, but your dad made that forcefield. I could have probably made it through and back. But Jess was really young, and Lily was always in Aurumice those days, I was the only one she had," Stephen's voice cracked. "I couldn't leave her. But Teren, if your mom had lived, I don't think any of this would have happened. Aurumice would have never been stuck for ten years under that forcefield, the castlefolk wouldn't have suffered in Rockwood, there would have been no tax debt to throw Nico in Briken. Jessi wouldn't have wound up with the circus. Lily wouldn't have divorced me. *Everything is all my fault.*"

Teren allowed Stephen's words to sink in. Jessica was staring at the table, clearly uncomfortable. Carrie Anne seemed dumbstruck, her face white, her lips pressed into a thin little line as if she was afraid to even breathe.

Teren considered his next words very carefully.

"Uncle Stephen," Teren said. "You did not kill my mother. Elina did. And knowing my mother, she was grateful for your sacrifice till the moment she died, and I will forever be grateful as well. "

Not a day went by that Teren didn't think of his parents, and knowing a little bit more about their lives brought back pain and wonder in the same breath.

"In fact, if ever you could tell me more about my parents, I would love to hear it. I am afraid to talk anyone in the castle about them. I'm supposed to be their strong leader, but I don't have the strength to ask them anything."

Stephen nodded.

"Teren, your mom used to sing, all the time, and she would quote pop songs, and she never cared who heard her. Never tried to hide that she was from Earth. She liked to sing that Beatles song, *Here Comes the Sun*, to annoy your aunt. I don't know why it annoyed her, but Trix and Lily fought all the time. Anyways, every day that I'm up early enough to see the sun rise, I think of your mom. I really, really miss her."

Stephen paused, and Teren waited for him to continue, completely in awe. Dinner was turning out to be the most delightful surprise he had experienced in a long time.

"Your dad was another one of my best friends. He was so maddeningly stubborn. If he got a crazy idea in his head, no matter how complex it was, nothing could stop him. You know he had cancer? That's what his lung issue was, and I could not figure out how to beat it. I tried so many different ways to heal him, and I just keep failing, but he kept fighting it. Never met anyone as determined. Jessica, this is how I know you just can't beat a cancer but..." Stephen looked at Carrie Anne as if he had forgotten she was in the room. "I....Teren, maybe tonight it's too much, but yes, sometime, let's have a beer and I'll tell you some really, really great stories."

"Yes, absolutely," Teren felt different, as if he had been missing something for years and didn't know it was lost. There was no one Teren had truly regarded as elder kin. The shadows swept away, Stephen was his uncle, and it was heartening to rediscover a piece of his family.

Carrie Anne hands were shaking as she held the empty teacup. She slammed it on the table, and walked towards the door.

"Carrie?" Stephen called.

She turned.

"I don't know who you are," she said to her husband.

"Carrie, I wanted to tell you, but I didn't know how."

"Five minutes ago you said you killed someone and brushed it off as casually as if you forgot to take out the garbage!?" Carrie Anne shook.

"It's complicated."

"And now you're talking about how you think about some other woman every day? How can you have this thought, every time the sun rises, and not even mention her to me?!"

"Carrie, Trix was my friend, Lily's sister, we weren't like that."

"But everything! You've never mentioned these people once, or that you killed someone, and cancer isn't beatable?!"

"No! No! It's not like that. I'm a healer in that world, but we don't have radiation and chemo, and here you *can* beat cancer. Please, I didn't mean it that way..."

"If you're a healer, how did you kill that other person? Like shot her? How?"

"Well, technically I burst her carotid artery from the inside."

"What are you even talking about?! This, I don't get it! This is just nuts."

"Carrie Anne," Jessica stood, "I know this sounds really bad, but if you understood Centernia you would…"

"Jessica, shut up, this doesn't concern you."

The teen recoiled as if she had been hit.

Teren hadn't expected the maelstrom from Carrie Anne. If he had been home, he might have dampened her fury to help his Uncle.

"Who are you?" Carrie Anne looked at her husband. "Are you actually from here? Did you go to school here?"

"No, I never went to high school."

"But how do you have a job without a diploma?" Carrie Anne was perplexed.

"A lot of trickery, forged documents. It's easy to convince people if you know how. I did what I had to do for you and Ash. I had to get money. At the time there was a society here, on earth, and it was made up of mages and mage-kin. They were very, very good at making money and official papers."

"What else is a lie about you Stephen?" Carrie Anne persisted.

"Honestly? Everything that didn't matter. My social security number, my birth certificate, my college degree. But, I was good at numbers, good at finance, good at mimicking everything I saw. The work was real, and I did it for you!"

"What about what you said about your family? You said your father died of lung cancer, you said your mom was in a car accident!"

"No, my parents are alive. I told half-truths. When I talked about my dad's lung cancer, I was talking about Justen."

"So Ashlin has grandparents, and you didn't mention it?!"

"And aunts and uncles."

Carrie Anne's face was so red she looked as if she might explode.

"One more thing, Stephen, one more thing I *need* to know the truth about. All those years ago, Lily was mad at you, Lily wanted to divorce you, not the other way around. *She left you*, and then you met me. *Did you actually love me?"*

"Yes, Carrie, please, no, that wasn't a lie!"

"I don't believe you," Carrie Anne grabbed her jacket. "I need space. This is crazy."

The front door opened and slammed.

Stephen made no move to stand.

"Dad," Jessica said. "I'm sorry. I've never seen her that mad."

"Give her a minute. Everyone has every right to be mad at me."

***

Carrie Anne hadn't gone far. She sat on a little bench in her rock garden in front of the house. Her arms were folded and she sobbed softly.

Jessica walked out into the crisp, night, putting on her gloves.

"Leave me alone," Carrie Anne looked towards the road. Her breath made little clouds in the air.

Jessica put the jacket on her shoulders.

"I can't believe this, I can't believe any of this. This is insane!" Carrie Anne leaned forward, her head in her hands.

"I know, I know it's strange. I didn't know any of it until Misa showed up in my house a few years ago."

"Jess, you're too young to understand this, but marriage is built on trust. I should be the one person in the world he confides in and he couldn't even tell me his real name! I should have known he was a liar. When he didn't tell me he was married, I should have walked away then and taken Ashlin with me."

There was a time Jessica wished Carrie Anne *had* left, not stealing her father and bringing Ashlin into the world. But that was a young Jessica, angry and alone.

"But he's been by your side for the past fourteen years," Jessica pointed out.

"If your mom had invited him back, I don't think he would have stayed," Carrie Anne looked up, her makeup streaked. "Leave me alone."

"But…"

"Leave me alone," Carrie Anne repeated.

"No," Jessica insisted. "Listen to me. My father hasn't changed, not one bit. What's different is that you know more, but it doesn't change anything about him, and you know more about me. He's not leaving you. Everything he did was for you."

Carrie Anne took a deep breath, considering her words.

"Give this a chance, please. Teren needed to hear what he said today, it matters to him and to us. Please, now give me a chance to know my father for who he is, because Savartos Sarkisian is the father I need right now. With that identity comes all of his past, *but it's still him.*"

Carrie Anne was quiet for a while as her tears ceased.

"Wise words for eighteen."

"Thanks, I usually fail at wisdom, but I'm learning."

CHAPTER 41

The bicorn's hooves pounded the ground, sweat poured from its black and white striped body as it raced down the dirt path. His rider refused to relent, urging him forward. They dashed through a meadow then down a path that was wide but unkempt. Rocks and weeds littered the path. Still they galloped on, past stone towers and tall walls.

The massive rusted gates were open as they entered a grand garden that encircled the entrance of Castle Aurumice. The landscape was brimming with unkempt plants and old statuary, as if the entrance had been abandoned.

Paisley Mae reigned in Obsidian and dismounted. The moment Paisley's feet touched the ground, she lost control of her mount. The bicorn ran for the pond, fell to his knees and plunged his head into the cold water.

Paisley Mae stared up at the double doors, searching frantically for the best way into the old castle. There was no bell or attendant. She swallowed hard, her throat prickly with ash. It was faster to stop at Aurumice instead of racing all the way down to Trabalis, but now she regretted it.

She screamed for help.

It was maddening that the castle was undefended and seemingly unoccupied.

A young man approached, face spotted with patches of cinnamon brown and black. He lazily held a crossbow over his shoulder. His casual demeanor was a farce as he was clearly well armed.

"Can I help you?"

"This is Castle Aurumice? I need to get in!" Paisley Mae frantically paced.

"Well, that's the front door, but this side of the castle is only used for parties."

"I don't care! I need to find Jared Evansi, or Jessica. I'm a mage of Polaris and the entire city is in danger!"

As she spoke, five other individuals approached, dressed similarly to the young man. She realized it was a uniform and they were a guard. Everyone held weapons centered on her. The others were much less friendly than the first guard.

A commanding black pantheress approached.

"I would say fetch Jared, but knowing him, he's on his way."

"Hey!" a window opened far above them. "Let her in! That's Paisley Mae, she's with me!"

***

Jared sprinted down the staircase, tripped on the last step, gathered himself and ran to the side entrance door. He lifted the heavy bolt and ran through the door and out into the courtyard. He already knew through Penrik's eyes that Paisley Mae looked terrible. She was covered in soot, her hair a wild mess, her usually carefree face creased with worry lines.

As she met him in the courtyard, Paisley Mae grabbed Jared by the shoulders.

"We need to warn Polaris! I need fresh bicorn, or a nightflight if you can find me one!"

"What happened?" Jared asked, "Wadjette, you have some water?"

"We failed, Jared! The mages failed. The swarm was too big, we started to burn it, and there were needlewasps everywhere! My power is gone!"

Wadjette handed the girl a jug of water. She drank, though her fervor didn't relent.

"Explain again," Jared said. "Catch your breath, and come inside. Pen, can you tend to that bicorn for us?"

Paisley Mae handed the jug back to Wadjette.

"Jared, I don't have time to go inside. I need to get back to Nova, I've lost my power!" Paisley Mae snapped her fingers, trying to call fire to her hand. When nothing happened, she tried again, gesturing wildly. "There was a swarm, and we were supposed to just toast it, and it didn't happen. I was with Santino and Scottsven and the others! They didn't make it out!"

The news was chilling. Santino was the water mage who served the guard of the Club Underground. Jared had known him for years.

"There were fields of livestock bloated with wasp larvae and there was this dead farm family, and it was horrible! The swarm was much bigger than we thought, I swear it was easily half the size of this castle! Castle Nova needs to know that needlewasps are poison to mages!"

Paisley Mae faltered and seemed pale.

She sat down on the ground.

"I feel really cold."

"You got bit by those things?" Jared asked. "Or stung, or whatever they do."

"Yeah, it's not bad though." She rolled up her sleeve, revealing a red speckled arm.

"Oh God, Pais, you're going to get Puce fever. We need to get those eggs out of your arm before you go anywhere."

"Eggs? They laid their eggs in my arm?!"

"The back of your neck has little red spots too," Jared said.

Paisley Mae grimaced.

"It's Puce fever," Jared explained. "I know someone whose brother got it. It was bad, really bad, the kid nearly died."

He helped Paisley Mae to her feet. It was obvious the girl was deteriorating rapidly.

He blinked, trying to figure out where Jessica would be. She and Nico would know how to treat the illness.

"Wadjette, bring Paisley up to my room. I'll be up as fast as I can."

***

Standing in the secret passage, Nico observed Jared's room through the amber eyes of the wall-mounted chimera statue.

The unconscious girl's uniform bore the dragon signet of Castle Nova. It was bitterly ironic that a mage had come to Aurumice just as he had found the strength to stop living like a specter.

Jessica picked at the girl's right arm with a tiny knife, removing the unmistakable needlewasp larvae. Jared hovered. Savina murmured prayers of the goddess as she worked on the left arm.

"Will you not do that?" Jared glared at the cat woman. "I feel like we're at a funeral."

"For some people, prayer is focus, and hope. If you prefer, I can leave."

"Don't fight," Jessica said. "It's not helping."

"Are you sure this is how to treat this? Just poking and stabbing into her arm?"

"When's the last time you saw puce fever?"

"It just seems wrong."

"Look, this is what Nico taught me!"

Jared glared directly at the chimera statue.

"Will you get out here and bloody do something! Paisley Mae isn't going to turn you in to Polaris, but if she dies, I will!"

Nico hesitated, then slid open a wall panel, entering the room.

Savina jumped to her feet and tackled him.

"You idiot, this is where you belong, not with the circus!"

"I'm sorry, Vina." He held her tightly. "Things have been bad."

"Doesn't matter, this is your home!" Savina cradled his face lovingly. "What happened to your eye?"

"It's better than it was."

"This is a charming reunion," Jared growled, "but we need your help, now!"

"I will. Who is the girl?"

"One of my oldest friends, and a mage whose powers just vanished."

"Unbelievable." Nico thought he was the only one. "What happened?"

"She was sent by Polaris to fight needlewasps," Jessica replied. "But then she was stung and lost her fire magic!"

"Are you certain?"

"That's what Paisley said and it makes sense since the same happened to you. Briken was crawling with these things!"

The thought was frightening. Nico had convinced himself he had been the cause of his own loss.

But it was the needlewasps of the Mine all along.

"I wonder if it's like some sort of neurotoxin," Jessica theorized. "Like the part of your brain that makes you a mage, it disables that. Well, if there is a part of your brain that makes you a mage. I don't know, I'm just guessing."

"Well, it may not be permanent," Nico reassured.

"Well thanks, good to know, if she lives." Jared glared. "Are you going to help us or not?"

"I am here to help," Nico excused himself to the small washroom to clean his hands then pulled up a small chair beside Savina.

He glanced at Jessica. There were unspoken words between them, but it was not the time. Her eyes made it clear she understood this as well.

"Let me show you," Nico settled to work, taking a slender knife and lifting the girl's arm. Savina had removed two needlewasp egg sacs, but there were eight more.

"She didn't put a pain killer on that spot..." Jared warned.

Nico ignored him. Working quickly, he jabbed down with the knife. Making a small vertical incision he was able to deftly lift out the wiggling maggot. Paisley Mae stirred in her sleep but did not wake.

"It renders you unconscious before the seizures. You need to work quicker," Nico said. "She may hurt for a week, but it's better than being dead."

They worked for a while, painstakingly removing each tiny maggot.

"Thank you for this," Jared said to Nico. "Paisley is one of my oldest friends."

"I owe you," a knock on the door interrupted them.

Nico froze, ready to flee.

"Come in," Jared called.

Nico relaxed as Lily walked into Jared's quarters, her arm still bandaged. She paused for a moment, regarding him with a smile.

"Glad to see you've come back."

"Mom, I think you or Jared need to go to Nova, no way Paisley can ride like this," Jessica said. "I think we got all the bugs, but she'll be out for a day."

Lily glanced over at the three little silver plates covered in bloody tissue and wriggling maggots. Each tiny worm twisted frantically, searching for their warm fleshy home. Lily blanched, taking a step back.

"That is the most disgusting sight I've ever seen, and do you smell it?"

Savina nodded.

"The goddess makes some terrible beasts."

"The smell isn't the maggots," Nico explained. "It's the necrotized tissue."

"I can't believe I'm saying this," Lily closed her eyes. "Can you put those *things* in a jar? Some people need extra convincing."

"Yeah, I'll get a jar," Jessica stood.

"Lily, a bicorn is too slow," Nico said. "Sienna is still in town, and she has a gryphon. I am certain I can convince her to fly you to Nova. If you can fly with that arm."

Lily smirked. "Flown with worse, no worries."

"Do you think Nova can stop it?" Jessica asked. "If needlewasps can poison mages, then what will kill the bugs and stop the fever from spreading? They don't have pesticides here, not like at home."

"I don't know, Jess, and Aurumice should prepare regardless," Lily said. "Tell your cousin, the castlefolk should know to be on guard. And while I'm at Nova, I'll see if I can convince Corwin and Kaity to return. Nico, you think you can get a few circusfolk to fly out this way and scout?"

He nodded.

Lily turned to Jared.

"Are you coming with me?"

"I'm staying here until she wakes," Jared replied. "And I imagine the gryphon will fly faster with fewer passengers. I'm confident you'll convince Castle Nova that this is too big for them to ignore."

CHAPTER 42

Castle Nova was not receptive to the news.

"You must be mistaken! Mages cannot lose their power!"

Lily left the council chamber of Nova, the words of the bureaucracy stinging her ears.

"Yes, the loss of the mages is a great tragedy."

"Did you see this swarm with your own eyes?"

She had traveled with Sienna without rest.

"How could five mages be killed by insects?"

"I fail to understand how that jar of whatever is a threat."

Begged audience with the council, but her words fell on deaf ears.

"But these are just needlewasps."

"The Council of Nova and the Mage Consortium does not have time for trivial issues."

"Zapaisley Maeve is young, she probably was nervous."

"We are investigating the situation."

"Mages do not lose their power."

"Yes, Lady Vance, we value your concern."

"Thank you for your time."

The mages were thoughtful, reasonable, caring people of action. She didn't understand why when they were grouped together in a council that they seemed to lose all common sense!

Lily walked through the halls, exhaustion hanging on her shoulders. After the rapid flight, Lily had run straight for the council. She hadn't eaten and barely had a chance to breathe. Stepping out into a courtyard garden, Lily was at a loss for what to do next. Drawn by the sunlight, she walked mindlessly along the crystal cobblestone paths among the exotic plants.

Lily's arm still ached terribly and she worried that it was not healing correctly.

The bitter irony, two blood mages in her family and neither could help her.

"Why do I worry every time I see you?"

Lily startled at the sound of the voice.

Saurin Bane stood beside her as if appearing from thin air.

Her old mentor was a Shadow Runner, an elite group of mages skilled at evading detection.

"Can anyone hear me?" Lily asked.

"My ears are around, but they are no threat. You may speak freely. What did the council say to you?"

"Needlewasps in the north just took out five mages, the only one who survived was Zapaisley Sarkisian. She ran right to the doorstep of Aurumice, so of course I have to help."

"Paisley Mae?" Saurin raised an eyebrow.

"Yes, teal hair, fire mage."

"Ah. Speaking of the Sarkisians, I wish you had told me about Jessi's father. It would have given me a chance to introduce the idea to Lady Lightsong sooner. Instead I was forced to do damage control."

"It's not really a topic I like talking about," Lily defended.

"Well I fixed the issue. Jessica is free to come to Polaris. You're welcome."

"Well thank you, but that's not my biggest problem at the moment."

"Is he well?" her mentor inquired.

It took a moment before Lily realized he was referring to her ex-husband.

"Better than I'm doing right now," Lily gestured to her arm. "Look, forget about my family. There is a swarm of needlewasps north. If they turn south, Aurumice is in trouble."

She pulled the jar of now-dead maggots from her satchel and handed it to Saurin.

"This is what my daughter and her friends pulled out of the skin of that little fire mage. Saurin, she *lost control of her abilities.*"

"This is troubling," Saurin looked at the jar. "How many insects was she fighting?"

"It didn't matter. *She lost her power,* and she's not the only one. I know another mage that it happened to. The council can't bury its head in the sand! No force in this world has ever stopped a mage."

"They are not. You need to think of the bigger image, Lily. Why is the council dismissing you?"

Lily bristled, she hated it when Saurin knew the answer but made her guess.

She looked out into the garden, taking a deep breath before she spoke.

"Okay, if they know about the needlewasps and the mages, and then they're ignoring it…then… there's more to the story."

"And…?"

"Saurin, people will die, quit with the riddles!"

"Think, Lily. The mages have been the ruling force of the continent for hundreds of years, not because they're wise or kind or have divine providence. They control Madierna because they can flatten people and roast them alive in the blink of an eye. If common people knew needlewasps could stop mages, Nova would lose its political strength."

Lily was stunned.

It was so obvious.

"Polaris Academy and Castle Nova are at odds," he explained. "The Mage Consortium at Nova wants it quiet, until they can figure out the source of the insects. The Council of Polaris wants it dealt with before the threat gets too big. They sent Zapaisley and that team, not Nova. I suspect Polaris does not know the mages failed their mission."

"We should go to the Council of Polaris then?"

Saurin heaved a sigh.

"Polaris is not supposed to send mages into the field without Castle Nova's very explicit permission, you know that. This is bad, and the fallout will be bad."

"Saurin, I don't care about the politics between the stupid Academy and their Castle. I care that people are going to get hurt. You need to help me."

"I'll get who I can," Saurin Bane handed the jar back to Lily. "I have favors to call in."

"They need to be in full black dragon armor so they don't get stung, with helmets and face masks," Lily said. "We also have aerial aid coming from the Auroriates."

"Oh this will be an amusing venture. Mages flying with the Circus."

"At this point they've been more helpful," Lily replied. "Anyways, I need to go find Corwin and Kaity, do you know where they are?"

"The cottages, on the far side of Polaris."

***

Lily took the shuttle carriage from Castle Nova to the campus of Polaris Academy. Everything seemed as pristine as when she had last seen it almost two decades ago.

She easily remembered the way across the campus, through the commons, past the dormitories to the cottages. A quaint little grocery shop was positioned at the edge of the network of neighborhoods and she stopped there to ask for directions.

Knocking on the door of Kaity and Corwin's cottage, Lily looked at the neat little hedges and hardy rows of rainbow flowers. Everything smelled the same, looked the same, and her heart longed deeply for the past. Gazing towards the student dorms, she remembered her days and nights running around with friends. It was a life she wished she had never left behind.

She remembered forging her friendship with the Sarkisian brothers. Tigard was brash and bold, much like Malachi, but legitimately charming. Trixie slept with him more than once. Lily always politely declined, her eyes and heart locked onto Savartos.

She wondered what ever happened to the gryphon Ravenwolfe.

A surprised Kaity answered the door of the cottage.

"Lily, what's wrong?"

"I'm sorry, I can't just pay a social call?" Lily gave a wry smile as Kaity gestured and invited her in. Corwin was seated at a tiny desk in the small living room.

"Why are you here?" he stood. "Did something happen?"

Temi looked up from her stacking blocks. The child grinned, recognizing Lily. She jumped to her feet, pointing to the air expectantly.

"Nothing happened, yet, but it will," Lily gestured in the air, manifesting a tiny cloud of snowflakes. Ice was painful and her head ached immediately, but it was worth the grin on the child's face. Temi danced in the little snow flurries.

"Please, sit, can I get you something?" Kaity asked.

"Yeah, some juice, or anything," Lily replied, sitting on the couch. Temi climbed up beside her, expecting more weather tricks. Lily gestured again, cascading little ice crystals across the child's hair. Temi giggled, her hands in the air, she wiggled her fingers like falling snow.

Lily mimicked the gesture.

"Is this the sign for snow?" she asked the tiny girl.

"It is, we've been working with a psychic mage to teach Temi her signs quicker, and we're using some of those sign language books Jessi brought for standardization," Corwin explained. "Polaris is good for Temi."

Kaity hurried back to the kitchen and returned with a brown mug of juice.

"Thank you," Lily took a sip, then focused her attention to Corwin. The man looked oddly nervous, but Lily ignored the anxiety and continued.

"You were right. You were so right and Aurumice is so sorry for it. The needlewasp threat is real, and they can take power from mages."

"No!" Kaity was in disbelief. "That's impossible! *How?!*"

"I don't know, but I saw it with my own eyes. Paisley Mae, she's a Sarkisian, a little fire mage."

"I know Paisley, she burned down the Library of Sarestina," Kaity said. "And she's Jared's friend, so no surprise she's trouble."

"She fled to Aurumice with dozens of stings filled with these disgusting maggots," Lily pulled the jar from her satchel and handed it to Corwin. Temi followed the jar, intrigued.

"How did she lose her power?" Kaity repeated. "Paisley is fierce."

"She's not the only one. Nico's come back to Aurumice, but he's in trouble. He also lost his powers, stung in Briken."

"Really? He's free?!" Kaity was overjoyed. "Corwin, we have to go home. We have to go see Nico."

"Yeah, he's home, but in trouble," Lily swallowed hard. "Jessi said he got into a tangle with the mages. A slaver bought him, a Sinari woman in an airship. Mages went after the slaver, and in the middle of the skirmish, Nico killed a mage.. He's been hiding ever since."

Corwin thought quietly.

"I didn't hear of any mages dying," Corwin commented. "I know the ship you're talking about, they have it behind the nightflight stables on the west side of Nova. It's a beautiful piece of equipment."

"You know how the mages cover things up, especially in anything with a Sinari."

Kaity shuddered.

"I hate their kind, and I hate the thought of one of them running loose."

"That's another problem for another day. Look, I know your pissed at the castlefolk, but Aurumice needs you both. There's no telling where the swarms will spread. Corwin, what do we need to do to stop the needlewasps?" Lily set her mug on a side table. It was difficult to find a spot as it was piled high with rolled maps and papers. She shifted a few aside and continued. "I was thinking of freezing them."

"Freezing won't work," Corwin warned. "They have anti-freeze in their blood streams. They thrive in cold. They're also fairly resilient to heat, but pure fire will destroy them."

"Okay, that risks setting a forest on fire. What about drowning?"

"Excellent lung capacity."

"Damnit!"

"This is why I was ordered by the Polaris Academy to study them. They are the most puzzling thing I have ever seen. Definitely a cross-breed between a traditional frost wasp and the normal needlewasp."

"This is bad, and I am worried," Lily picked up her mug, careful not to spill it on the maps. As she shifted one aside, she noticed it was marked as Aurumice. She paused, looking more closely at the papers.

Corwin handed the maggot jar back to the Lily and paced.

"I just don't have all the research yet. But I assure you, there is something odd to them! Talon destroyed everything I was working on, that nearsighted stupid idiot—"

"He's sorry," Lily was distracted.

All the maps were of Aurumice.

"Why do you have these here?" she asked. Castle schematics were something they guarded closely. Teren gave Jessi hell for forgetting a bag of her electrical maps in the stable yard.

"I was researching this very problem," Corwin said smoothly. "Aurumice has many weaknesses and strengths against the wasps."

Corwin selected a map of the continent out from under the pile of castlemaps.

"Where was Zapaisley Maeve fighting the wasps?"

"It was a farm near Maaria, near Chissa Peak. Jessi said they were up in Greypoint and Red Clay a month ago."

Lily looked over his shoulder at the map, noticing a pattern.

"They're following the River White," Corwin stated.

"Which means Aurumice is in their path, and Trabalis, the Yellow Valley…right down to Katanzarko."

"The Council is being foolish."

"How odd," Kaity was looking past Lily out the window of the cottage. "Why is an Auroriate here?"

Lily's heart dropped. She had intended on keeping Sienna away from Kaity and Corwin. She didn't think Sienna would follow her here.

"Oh no, no, no, Kaity don't open that door," Lily warned. "They brought me, it was the fastest way to get to here."

"She seems to be looking for you," Kaity said, standing. "Why…"

Sienna knocked.

It was clear Lily was not going to be able to make it back to Aurumice without watching the train wreck happen.

"You two stay here," Lily said. "I will handle this."

She opened the door.

"This is not the time," Lily told the masked Sienna.

"And this is not your concern," Sienna said, pushing the door open. She glanced around the small living room.

"Hello."

"You!" Kaity stood, instantly bristling. "When I said I never wanted to see your face, I meant it! You have so much nerve coming here after betraying our father to Trabalis! If it wasn't for Corwin, he would have never made it out to safety. You're a rock-sucking whore, and I know about your bastard children!"

"If it wasn't for Corwin, my *husband* and the father of my three children would be alive."

Sienna removed the mask, addressing Corwin directly. "You have a lot to answer for."

"You disgust me! I can't believe I'm hearing these words!"

Kaity's words confused Lily, how did she know about her sister?

"You're the one lying with my leftovers," Sienna said calmly as if she was commenting on the weather. "And let me assure you, Malachi was twice the man of Corwin. Speaking of, how is your daughter with the broken ears?"

In response, the objects in the room quivered and levitated.

Lily frantically debated if she could ice the room before it got out of hand. Or she could crack lightning. Every option seemed likely to ignite the powder keg between the widow and the kinetic mage.

"Ladies, please. Kaity, don't destroy the house," Corwin pleaded.

The objects fell with a clatter and the breaking of glass.

"I want to know why you killed my husband," Sienna bared her teeth.

"Sienna…" Lily tried to warn.

"What gave you the right?! You took a man from four children, and you sentenced Nico to the Mines of Briken with your stupidity! Why?!"

"I regret it!!!" Corwin trembled.

Temi peered around the corner, watching the confrontation with wide-eyes.

"I'm so sorry Sienna, I regret it every day. I was angry, I was scared, and tired of Malachi always destroying and taking everything from me."

"I didn't leave you for Malachi!" Sienna raged. "I left you because you were pathetic and spineless and I didn't want to be tied to a lap-dog of the mages. Though apparently, my little sister has no problem being a mage bitch."

Without warning, Sienna was thrown against the wall.

"You bloody shunt, I will show you what it means to be a mage!" Kaity shouted.

"Your husband took everything from me! And I don't believe you or trust you!"

"Sienna I am sorry," Corwin pleaded through tears.

"ENOUGH!" Lily shouted, thunder exploded in the sky above the little cottage, shaking the walls.

"Next one will be in this house! Kaity! Put your sister down, now!"

Lily stood in the center of the room, her mind reeling as she tried to untangle the mess of blame.

Kaity hesitated, then slowly she relented.

"First," Lily turned to Kaity, "How did you know about Malachi's other children? How would you know and Nico not?"

Kaity hesitated.

"He told you, didn't he?" Lily asked. "He told you and you got angry, that's why he was frightened enough to imprison you."

"Yes, yes that was the truth. Malachi destroyed the castle," Kaity glared. "And was going to do worse."

"It was the mages of Nova who constantly harassed Malachi!" Sienna argued. "They didn't like that their precious psychic chose to marry an Auroriate leader. And I didn't scheme to be Malachi's second-wife, it was by the blessings of the goddess that I saved him, and he in turn, saved me."

"I can't stand hearing about your disgusting goddess," Kaity spat. "Aurora is a fake myth, used to drain the coffers of the people."

"How dare you!"

"ENOUGH!" Lily had lost all her patience with the sisters. "This is not the time to fling words at each other. You both know we don't have time. If Corwin's right and the needlewasps are following the River, Aurumice is in trouble and Nova is being stupid. Both of you have right to be angry, but both of you need to understand that there comes a point where you need to leave the past in the past!"

The sisters watched Lily intently. Corwin trembled in the corner. Temi continued to watch from the door. As Lily spoke, she saw the echoes of her own past coming back to haunt her.

"You need to listen to me," Lily's voice cracked and she bit back tears. "I fought so much with my own sister, over stupid things and things I thought mattered. Now Trixie is dead and gone and I can't apologize. I fought with my husband. I put so much blame elsewhere and I have been angry for years. What did that bring me? I destroyed Aurumice— the forcefield, the exile, Elina's death was my fault, it's all on my head and I kept making it worse."

"We need to get Saurin Bane, round up as many mages as who are willing to defy Nova and follow us back to Aurumice. *You both will help me.*"

CHAPTER 43

As the sun rose, light filtered into the tower room.

Jessica lay on her pile of mattresses, unable to fall back sleep. Projects and plans filled her mind, tangled in the worry of the wasps. She hoped her mother would return soon. There was too much that could go wrong at Nova.

Jessica wished she had someone to talk to freely. Unfortunately, Jared was likely with Paisley Mae and Teren was busy creating a strategy to protect the castle.

Before Jessica could change her mind, she left her room. Making her way through the castle, she slipped into a wall panel and walked through the dimly lit shadow hallways. She could hear the bustle castlefolk going through their early morning routines. Pans in the kitchen clattered and someone yelled angrily.

Jessica slipped past the storerooms descended into the dark cellars of Aurumice. She crossed through the secret passages, past the generator room, through the hatch, to the Azure Lake. As she entered the ancient chamber, she marveled at the starry walls and glowing plants. She had been in the room hundreds of times, but it never got old.

Nico stood at the edge of the water. He juggled light orbs, chanting a prayer of the goddess in the language of the Auroriates.

Jessica's breath caught in her throat and nervousness returned. Nico seemed so peaceful, like his old self, surrounded by home. For a moment, she thought she was caught in a dream, but her own feet had brought her there.

After a moment, the energy orbs vanished, and he turned to face her.

"If Aunt Dahlia saw your juggling act, she would have never let you leave the circus," Jessica commented.

"Who says I wasn't practicing for the circus?" Nico replied with a smirk.

"When did your powers return like this?"

"It started a few months back but I didn't realize it. When I came home to the Azure, it became much stronger. I have no idea if Paisley Mae will be the same, but I am hopeful she will also regain her strength."

"I think she's just grateful to be alive, and Jared's grateful too. This whole thing has gotten ridiculous and I'm worried that my mom and Sienna haven't come back from Katanzarko yet."

Nico didn't reply, extending his left hand.

The energy danced across his fingers.

"I am concerned, too, but there is nothing we can do right now but wait."

"Waiting sucks," Jessica watched the tiny glittering sparks. "Why do you think you have this control? You didn't used to be like this."

"Not certain. My mage strength is still coming back gradually, I think this gave me a better chance to control it. I'm older, more disciplined."

Walking away from her, he stood at the water's edge. Holding out an arm, he closed his eyes and breathed deeply. He murmured prayers of the goddess under his breath. The sphere grew to the size of a small deer before dissipating.

"That's beautiful," Jessica was enamored.

"Stay back," he warned. "I will not let you be burned again."

"You know you're not a fire mage, right?" she recalled her conversation with Paisley Mae, "You never were."

"What do you mean?"

"Nico, that's just pure energy. It's not fire."

"But I set things on fire," he argued with her.

"Yeah, and one electric spark can send a whole house up. You should go talk to Paisley Mae, she really is a fire mage. Fire mages need something to burn, and they can burn themselves. That's not you. Also, fire mages glow red, you glowed blue."

"What am I?"

Jessica shrugged.

"We need to figure that out. That is, if you stay. Teren has told me you were just here to look for the Corvalian stones."

"Yeah, I don't think my father really hid them here," Nico said. "And if he did I don't know if I'd ever find them, or if it's worth it."

He looked upwards to the ceiling of the Azure as if arguing with himself.

"Jessica, in truth I came back for you. To what end I don't know. I fought this so much. I'm sorry for everything these past few months, and I swear I will make it up to you."

"You were in a bad spot, I couldn't leave you. I never would."

"You should have for the way I treated you."

"Are you going back to your family?"

"No, I don't want to go back to the Circus. I want to try to hide here a while, I don't think the mages are really tracking me anymore. I don't know what got in my head these past few months, but it wasn't me. I'm sorry."

"Uh, the Sinari? She got in your head."

Nico shook his head.

"Yeah, she did more than that," Nico murmured. "And I hate myself for that too."

Jessica reached out and grabbed his four-fingered hand.

"What are you doing?" he eyed her warily.

"Telling you that I don't care, and you need to forgive yourself for. Misa, your father, the castle, me, whatever."

"But—"

"Everything."

She kissed his hand, not sure how he would react.

When he remained wordless, she kissed him again, then again. She nuzzled the stump of his missing finger, then kissed his hand again.

Nico stopped her kisses, cradling her face. Then, timidly, he brought his lips to hers.

"Every single day in the mines," he whispered. "I never stopped thinking about you."

She stole a kiss before he could change his mind. His lips were dry and sweet. She hesitated, remembering their last kiss.

His magic had burned her.

This time, he had control.

Nico kissed her again, wrapping his arms around her.

"So strange…it's like being with you draws my magic out. I feel it, but I can control it now."

Jessica was so giddy she thought her heart might burst from excitement. Her mind raced, wondering how far things would go.

"So, so sorry to interrupt this," Jared stepped into the cavern.

Nico released her abruptly, embarrassed.

"You have crap timing," Jessica glared.

"Ah, payback, my dear friend," Jared smirked. "And you can't be angry with *me*, I'm only the messenger. Your mom and Sienna….who I suppose is really your mom," he pointed to Nico. "So your mom and your mom…"

"*Kilati* mother," Nico angrily corrected, no doubt also displeased with the interruption.

"Regardless, they're back," Jared said. "Now pay attention. While you two were making out, the grown-ups were having a discussion upstairs—"

"It was one kiss!" Jessica bristled.

"Shhhh, this is important! Nova has their heads shoved so far up their bums they basically ignored *everything* Lily had to say. But Saurin Bane came through and a handful of mages should arriving shortly—"

"Mages of Polaris will be *here?*" Nico was concerned.

"They should be kinetic mages, you should be fine. I still have more to say. Sienna sent for aid from the Circus because nightflights would be helpful. And speaking of helpful, Teren wants the radio project up and running. So both of you are on that."

"Really?" Jessica grinned. "That means I get to turn the power back on, right?"

"Sure, let's just go with yes on that one. Jess, you're also supposed to tell your dad to send medical supplies. And then, since you're home, your mom also wants you to check the mail and bring the trash to the curb."

"Wait, wait, wait, you want a working radio and me to get stuff from my dad by *when?*"

"A day? Two? Sienna is scouting the wasp situation now. Oh, also, Corwin figured out the wasps are following the River White, so if we fail, every city from here to Katanzarko is very much screwed. Questions?"

CHAPTER 44

A dozen riders from the Holy Circus arrived a few hours later, their expressions hidden behind their masks. Their nightflights and featherwings delighted the castlefolk and sent the chickens fleeing in terror. Jessica hurried to set up the radios with Nico, installing antennas and repeaters as quickly as they could. She really, really wanted to try to kiss him again, but there was no time.

The mages arrived as promised, racing in on bicorn. Saurin Bane and his tiny entourage of four were led to the dining hall to discuss strategy against the insects.

Jessica was so busy trying to make the radio system work, she hadn't considered the enormity of the situation until the mages and circusfolk were gathered in the dining room with the castlefolk. There was not an empty seat and the room was louder than a middle school cafeteria.

"We welcome you to the castle," Teren said as the mages arrived, "and who do we greet?"

Saurin Bane introduce the mages. Atheenaraas was a blonde-haired water mage, soft-spoken. Renzie and Nile were fire mages. The last mage was Leaf, the mage Jessica met in the club underground. Today he was considerably less bright, wearing the uniform of the mages and bold green eye makeup and lipstick. He was a rock-shaper mage.

Saurin Bane was an interesting figure. For all his influence, Jessica knew very little of him, other than he was an ally to Aurumice. Many of the elder castlefolk greeted him warmly, others kept distant. Saurin Bane made no indication of his own abilities, but Jessica did not want to interrupt to ask.

Paisley Mae was awake, but alarmed.

"That's it?" she said. " Do they not understand how serious this is? I lost my powers, don't they care?!"

"I know, but bureaucracy moves slowly."

"But mages are dead!!!"

"Nova is sending and investigation, or so they say."

"Why didn't they care?!"

"Because sometimes people can't believe what is in front of their eyes," Saurin told the girl. "Or they prefer it not to be true."

"Where is Jared's Aunt Kaity? I thought she was supposed to be here? She's such a great kinetic mage, she could just smash those bastards into the ground."

"She will be here soon," Lily told the girl. "I hope."

Paisley Mae seemed crushed, but Jessica was optimistic. She had never seen so many people in the castle ready so quickly to take on a cause.

The mages sat down with maps and the circusfolk, discussing their options. Jessica was a little annoyed that they just didn't leave immediately. How hard was it to just suit up, fly in and toast some bugs? But Saurin Bane, Sienna and Fentalon were cautious, planning a strategy that wouldn't accidentally set the forest on fire.

They would leave before dawn, just as the needlewasps were waking and taking flight.

Jessica was frustrated she wasn't enough of a mage to help with anything more than the radios.

"This is good," Wadjette came up beside her, speaking softly. "Saurin Bane is a wise leader, my father trusts in him, I can tell. And this wouldn't work without the Holy Circus and Sienna. Thank you, Jess, and please thank Nico as well, for bringing the Auroriates to us."

"How did you know...?"

Wadjette smirked.

"First of all, your cousin told me Nico was free of Briken months ago. Now my guards tell me he is hiding in the castle walls."

"Really?"

"Jess, they're more than idiots with swords."

"No, I never doubted them! The guard is pretty awesome, and it's because of you," Jessica said. "You really do a lot, I admire how you lead. You put so much work in, I don't think you're thanked enough." She paused. "I never apologized for hitting your knee, it was pretty terrible of me."

Wadjette shrugged.

"Have no worry, it healed," she smiled, "Speaking of which, did you learn how to use your blood mage abilities?"

"I like how casually you ask that, but no," Jessica replied, rubbing her arm out of reflex. "And actually they're sort of backwards. I hurt things instead of making them better. I'm pretty useless."

"First time I held a crossbow, I didn't realize the trigger was so sensitive. I sent a bolt through a barn window and almost hit Penrik. I stuck to swords and staffs for a long time after that."

Jessica nodded, seeing the wisdom in her words.

"You have other skills that are invaluable," Wadjette continued. "Is your communication system ready? I want to be the first to learn."

"Yeah, I'll get everything. The portables are simple, just turn one knob, press one button. I even got headsets that should fit under the armored helms. Only thing I don't know is how long the batteries will last. I wish we had more time."

"The mages know what they are doing. If the goddess smiles upon them, they will get a good rest tonight and destroy the insects before midday meal."

Jessica shook her head. "I still think tomorrow morning will come too soon."

CHAPTER 45

Stephen stared in the bathroom mirror. He studied his portrait carefully, wondering when he had become so old.

Turning away from the mirror in disgust, he hit the light switch as he entered the master bedroom. Carrie Anne was already in bed, reading serenely.

Stephen placed his robe on a chair and joined her.

Carrie Anne closed her book, smiling.

"These past day has been so different. It felt good bringing supplies to Jessica."

"Yeah, kid doesn't ask us for anything for years and she tries to bankrupt us in one day."

"You know Stephen, since Jessica came home I have felt more like myself and almost forgotten I was sick. When this whole wasp situation resolves, I really want to go back and see that world."

Stephen sighed.

"Of course you do."

"What?"

"I want to go back too," he finally said. "I want to see my home again. I want to race across the sky. I want to feel that surge of power, to knit flesh together with my hands."

"That sounds amazing," Carrie Anne was enamored with his words. "Tell me more."

"I wouldn't know where to start, but it is amazing, but there is a darkness. I mean, we just spent the day helping Jessi prepare for a swarm of killer insects. They don't have hospitals or ambulances or even firetrucks. If things go wrong, they will go very, very wrong, and it still doesn't sit right with me."

"But they have magic, isn't it better than all of those things?"

"It's still limited to people, and people make mistakes. I can't shake this feeling that they're underestimating the problem. No matter what they do, they aren't really prepared."

"Jessi seemed confident."

"Yeah, but, she doesn't know what she's really in for. I wish I could do more for them."

***

Lily sat in a chair by the window, unable to sleep. She tried to review the map in her mind, keeping landmarks clear. She didn't travel north of the castle very often.

The door to her bedchamber opened. It was Fentalon.

She placed her teacup on the windowsill.

"I didn't think you were joining me this evening."

"Everything seems calm. Our visitors are settled, the livestock is inside. I believe there is a high chance we will eradicate this threat."

"Then onto the next problem."

"I don't see many problems on the horizon."

"Talon, Nico is hiding in the castle, hiding from the mages ironically enough. Once these wasps are exterminated, that will be my problem. Probably will just let him hide in my house."

Fentalon stripped out of his armor, neatly placing it on the chair.

"Aye, I see how that would be a problem. How did he get on the wrong side of a mage fight?"

Lily drew her knees to her chin.

"I don't know, bad luck. You don't seem surprised."

"Everyone in Aurumice knew Nico escaped Briken. Your daughter shows up alone? Anyone who was castlefolk would be daft not to think he wasn't near by."

"Nico came to find the Corvalian stones. Do you have any idea where Malachi may have hidden them?"

Fentalon paused, his bare back facing her. She watched his muscles as he breathed slowly in the darkness.

His silence told her everything.

"You know where they are," she said.

Fentalon approached, sitting on the edge of the bed.

"Those stones are dangerous."

"They may be Nico's only chance at freedom."

"I don't know much about mages, but what happens if a mage is marked Corvalian? I think the answer isn't a good one."

"Talon, please," she reached for his hands. "Where are the stones?"

"Once the needlewasps are gone, I will show you."

***

Teren stared at the ceiling, counting the wooden joists silently. Savina curled around his form, buried beneath blankets.

"I know you are still awake," she murmured. "You need to sleep."

"I know, but I am thinking through our plan for tomorrow. It's the best we have, but I am still worried."

"It's a rare day that Nova mages work alongside of the Holy Circus and Aurumice. Have faith Aurora is guiding us."

"But what if it's too much for them?" Teren asked. "What if we miscalculated everything? What if the wasps overwhelm us? Or what if they turn out to be nothing at all and we look like fools?"

Savina sat up.

"Teren, stop worrying and sleep," she ordered.

A knock on the door interrupted their conversation. He called for the visitor to enter, knowing it was Jared.

The blonde-haired man walked into Teren's room, closing the door slowly behind him.

"I was having trouble sleeping, and I didn't want to drink," he stated.

"You are welcome here," Teren replied.

"I was really, really hoping you would say that," Jared sighed in relief. "I have a hundred things going through my mind but I just can't be tired for tomorrow."

"I'm surprised you're not spending the evening with your mages," Savina commented.

"As much as I curse out you stupid castlefolk, I think I prefer you to the stupid mages."

"I also am having difficulty sleeping," Teren told him.

"If you stopped talking you may have an easier time of it," Savina pointed out.

Jared's eyes flickered briefly.

"Stop surveilling the castle," Teren ordered. "It's not helping you sleep."

"Need to earn my keep somehow," Jared replied, stripping out of his shirt.

"You do more than enough," Savina reassured. Teren noticed how intently his lover stared at Jared.

"Do you want to be marked as one of us?" Teren asked. "For all you've done, it's more than an overdue honor."

Savina leaned on Teren's chest.

"As much as I hate you, I would love to see the castlemark on your back."

"Thanks, Vina," Jared replied. "I will very seriously consider the offer."

"We will discuss this after the wasps," Teren assured. "I just need to say the word 'party' and Kaity will magically appear."

"Will you let me plan the menu?" Jared asked. He glanced away, his eyes flicking to white.

"You're doing it again," Teren pointed out. "Stop watching the castle."

"I can't help it," Jared said. "The rate at which you people hurt yourselves is astounding."

"Relax," Teren encouraged. "We need your focus tomorrow."

"You should take your own advice," Savina snapped, turning over and burrowing under the blankets.

***

Nico knocked on the wooden door, nervously holding a leather satchel.

There was no answer

He opened the door.

"Jess?"

"I'm here, come in," the girl called.

The windows of the atrium were darkened.

Jessica had on a single dim lamp, creating reflected patterns across the glass floor. Most of the room was enveloped in darkness. Curled up in a chair, Jessica double-checked the settings on each of the radios, creating labels with tape. Her desk had become a command center, the largest system attached to an antenna just beyond the domed ceiling of the atrium. They had calculated that the height would give them furthest reach, but it was still less than ideal. They would need repeaters placed away from the castle to carry the signal, but that wouldn't happen in time.

Everything felt rushed.

Nico set the satchel on a table, and took off his jacket, setting it on the back of the chair.

He regretted doing so immediately, afraid she would get the wrong impression, but he didn't know what the right impression was.

"I am surprised you are still awake and not sleeping."

"I'm reviewing our notes. Trying to make sure I've talked to everyone, charged everything I can, got backup batteries. I think the mages understand how to use them, the circusfolk I'm not so sure about. Nico... I feel like this is a dumb idea, and it will backfire and then the castlefolk will just complain that I don't know what I'm doing."

"Jess, you're doing more than any of our governments are doing right now. They are simply hiding their heads as if nothing is wrong."

"Speaking of hiding, this also came today, with the mages," she held out a letter.

Nico opened it and read it slowly.

"They are accepting you to Polaris Academy after all?"

"Saurin Bane said I could wait until I graduate high school."

"That is not far off."

"Yeah, but I'm not sure I want to leave Aurumice."

"You need to learn what you can do, Jessica. Don't be like me."

"You can make magic energy balls. You know what I do? Cause bruises. Then I made a needlewasp explode, once."

"You didn't tell me that. That may be useful."

"One bug. It was back at Briken, you weren't very talkative."

"I'm sorry about that," he picked up the jacket. "Sorry, I shouldn't have intruded on your space. I'm sorry…. something has been weighing on my mind."

"Stop saying I'm sorry."

"I was an idiot—"

"Nico, you don't need to apologize to me again."

"No, no, I do. I feel like I need to give you something. I wanted to make you something, really, really meaningful, and this was the best gift I could think of. Jessica, you are a greater friend than I deserve."

Nico opened the satchel, removing a heavy worn book and a wooden box.

"You've had that scar far too long. Please, may I restore your castlemark?"

She hesitated. "Won't that wake the entire castle?"

"I think at most it will give them a wild dream, and make them feel connected. If anything, it will be a very good thing for Aurumice. It was an ancient tradition to do a Mark Ceremony on the eve of a battle."

"Why are you doing this?"

"You don't want a castlemark?" he panicked, afraid he had misjudged.

"No," Jessica said. "Aurumice is my home, and I've hated that scar for years. I didn't think it could be fixed."

"It can, if you will let me."

"Will the others be upset if there is no big ceremony?"

"Not every one is a spectacle."

Jessica reflected on this, then stood.

"Okay, how do we do this?"

"Your shoulder please?" Nico's hands trembled as he set down the ancient book and opened the box. In it was a small cube carved with the Mark of Aurumice. To the casual observer, it seemed ordinary. The wood, however, had been infused with a powerful magic.

Jessica nodded, turning away from him. She pulled off her sweatshirt, revealing a thin white camisole that left her shoulder exposed.

"Do you want me to say the ritual speech?" Nico asked.

"Well, my mom already made a promise on my behalf eighteen years ago, but I wouldn't have changed it. Aurumice is my home, and I would do anything for the castle."

Nico steadied his hand on the back of her neck as he carefully pressed the wooden cube into her shoulder.

Red light engulfed the mark.

Jessica gasped.

Nico's vision clouded as suddenly the room dissipated as the traditional dream vision appeared.

They were witness to another mark ceremony, in the same room. It was a time long past, when the room was still an aviary.

Nico found himself above the scene, sitting on one of the perches meant for the large birds. Jessica likewise sat on one beside him.

Below them was a curly haired woman, Jessica's Aunt Beatrix. She wore a green gown, cut low at the back. Nico's mother held the signet stamp. Uncle Justen stood by, so did D'Artagnan, their large white dog. Nico's father stood near, as well as man he did not recognize. The stranger was mostly human, his hair curly and dark.

"Oh, this is a good vision," Misa's voice said. She appeared floating between them.

Nico startled, even in the magic of the mark vision Misa seemed out of place. The girl wore a white and blue gown that shifted with a hundred small rainbow fish swimming throughout the folds of the fabric.

Nico's eyes had a difficult time comprehending the dress, was it fabric or were the fish real? How were they swimming through something so flat and flowing?

"Your dress..." Jessica breathed. Wriggling in harmony, the rainbow fish were completely enchanting.

"I know, I took inspiration from the floor." Misa gestured down. "Isn't it gorgeous?"

Pulsing, the aquarium was alive with color. The beautiful glass of the present day was nothing in comparison to the radiant life of days' past. Red and orange, green and purple, feathery fins, stripes and spots in a tropical symphony. So many aquatic creatures lived in the floor tank. Nico felt like he could just fall off the perch, slip through the glass, and be lost in the beautiful aquarium forever.

"I like mark ceremonies," Misa continued.

"Misa, you're not part of this vision, are you?" Jessica was delighted to speak to her cousin.

"No, I just fell into it."

There was something different about Misa, as if she were more vibrant than the rest of the vision.

"Are you really here? Are you in the castle magic?" Jessica asked.

"Yes, and time is my biggest problem"

"You're running out of time?" Nico questioned.

"No, I have no time."

"Your time is gone?"

"I don't remember time, I know it's a thing."

"How can you forget time?"

"No, there is no time," Misa repeated, looking frustrated. "I can't grab onto it."

"I understand you!" Jessica shouted. "You're in a plane without the boundary of time?"

Misa stepped off the swing, the pretty room faded and they stood on a void of white and blue.

"No time…. time is important and I can't find it, because it's not here?"

Misa was dejected.

"I'm going around and around and I'm tired," Misa sat in the nothingness, her shoulders hunched, "but I'm glad you're both here. I try, I try to find you all! It's like a spinning wheel and jumping in and hoping I hit the right point. I jump blind, and then when I do talk to one of you, I fall through the reality. I like making these dresses, because I feel like they weigh me down to the point where you are."

"Why didn't you tell us sooner?" Nico asked.

"I was trying! I couldn't remember the thing I forgot!"

"Misa, we will find a way to help you," Jessica promised. "I'm a mage now, and Nico is more than a fire mage. He's an ethereal mage. The castle, the Gate, the marks, it's all tied to you, and we will untangle this knot!"

"You will?"

"Don't be sad," Jessica comforted. "There's a lot of people who love you, and would do anything for you, and still do things in your name. I'll wake up and tell them."

"Really?"

"Please don't be sad."

Slowly, the blue and white void changed to a beach at sunset. The air was salty and birds flew across the water, skimming down and picking up fish.

"Just keep jumping into our dreams," Nico encouraged, "and we will help you."

The beach beneath their feet disappeared and the water continued to lap onto the dark nothingness.

Fading slowly, the dream vision disintegrated as the room reappeared. The energy in Nico's castlemark faded.

"Nico, I saw my cousin!" Jessica jumped.

"Jess, it could have been just the mark magic, it draws echoes of the past..."

"Nico! Why are you denying it!? You heard her. She's real and she needs our help. Her soul is still there, because she's a dreamspinner, she got caught in the in-between. She's in the etherspan, I know it! Nico, please believe me!"

"Jess, I believe you. I've known for a long time, because Misa saved my life."

"You knew?"

"Yeah, Misa was always popping in my dreams in Briken, keeping me sane. After my fight with that mage I tried to kill myself with fangberry poison. Your cousin wouldn't let me die. She made me wake up, and I threw up the poison. It was enough to save my life."

Jessica looked at him intently, and he felt uncomfortable.

"Nico, you know there is nothing you need to hide. I will never judge you, even for trying to kill yourself."

"What if I believe we will fail at helping Misa like we fail at everything else?" Nico asked. He held up his hand. "Forgive me, Jess, but my life has been a string of broken hope."

Jessica grabbed his hand, without hesitation she kissed it.

"The world isn't fair, but it doesn't mean you need to lie down and let it crush you."

She trailed small kisses across the back of his hand to his wrist, across the scar where a mining blade had cut so deep it had touched his bone. A warm tingle stretched through his body and he felt an odd clarity. Yes, the universe was awful, but at that moment, Jessica was in front of him.

No matter how terrible and withdrawn he had been, she never left his side. Nico leaned forward, tentatively kissing her bare shoulders up to her soft ear.

"Thank you," he whispered.

He felt her body shift at his words. She kissed his ear lobe and breathed deeply. He had no idea such a gentle whisper could travel through his entire body. Jessica ran her fingers across the silky fabric of his shirt, unbuttoning it slowly.

Nico's mind raced.

This had not been his evening goal, but now that Jessica started, he wanted her to continue. Jessica pulled the fabric away, his chest was muscled and scarred, a battlefield of pain.

She kissed each one of his scars. He leaned, and her kisses trailed up his neck to his lips.

"Call your power," she requested.

"Why?"

What an odd request at that moment.

"You burned me once, prove you can never do it again. Call your power."

He hesitated.

"Just do it, please."

He moved a foot away from her. With his right arm extended, he generated a glowing ball of blue flame, four inches in size and perfectly controlled. The light illuminated the room, casting feathery shadows and reflecting across the glass floor.

Jessica approached slowly, then allowed her lips to touch his. They were dry and soft. His lips barely moved, he was tense and fearful.

Shifting, Jessica kissed him a second time. With each kiss, he relaxed, still holding the energy orb. His arm dropped and the ball began to fade.

She withdrew.

"Do it again," she commanded.

Calling the orb, Nico extended his hand. This time he let it break apart into three smaller orbs, letting the magic roll around.

Jessica kissed him again.

The three energy spheres vanished.

"Again," she pressed even closer. She clearly liked it when the energy was near. It enhanced the already enjoyable sensation of her body against his. He didn't know if it was the danger, or the energy itself.

Extending both hands, he called his power again, this time twisting his fingers so that the orbs became jagged like crystals. It was an exhilarating sensation. He never dreamed he could be so close to someone and be able to use his powers with such control. All of his shame and guilt evaporated, replaced with elation.

"Don't move," she said, her open mouth pressed against his. She placed her hands on his bare chest. Running her hands across his shoulders, she reached outward.

"What are you doing?"

"Don't move," she stated again. "Trust me."

She ran her fingers along his biceps, across his forearms. He closed his eyes. She rested her hands on his wrists, inches from the energy.

He opened his eyes, looking at his hands.

"Are you satisfied?" he asked. "Can I lower my arms?"

"I'm not satisfied," Jessica smirked.

"I can do more," he took on the challenge in her words. He raised his hands above his head and called forth an energy sphere that completely encased them. It shimmered like an iridescent bubble, pulsing with its own inherent harmony.

Jessica was enamored, and the grin on her face made his heart burn with greater intensity.

He released the magic. The energy dissipated, avoiding Jessica like a flurry of butterflies. He wrapped his arms around her body, pulling her even closer.

"That wasn't the satisfied I meant," Jessica said, "but it was amazing."

"Do you want to...?" he glanced downward.

"I…"

"Not tonight," Nico answered his own question before she could finish her sentence. "I want to know you first. If your kisses feel this amazing, then I can't even imagine."

He cared for her too much to be a clumsy desperate fool.

Jessica nodded and she kissed him again.

Nico wanted every moment to last as long as possible. Every minute seemed a minute closer to dawn. He kissed her neck, and let his lips trail down her chest. Her skin was so smooth and soft. It didn't seem right that such a creature would ever want him, and with such ferocity.

He nuzzled her stomach and she laughed, leaning back onto the smooth aqua glass.

Nico carried her to the low bed with the white sheets. His knees sunk into the soft mattress as he set her down. Nico searched Jessica's face for any sign of disapproval. He had so much to learn about her.

Her green eyes were on him, very intent.

"Can you do it again?" she asked.

Now it had become a game.

Nico generated a little orb. He curved the lines of the energy, forming a tiny flower. He balanced it on the tip of his fingers, holding it inches above her face.

She smiled in wonder.

He let the flower melt away.

"Someday," Jessica said. "Someday I'll have control of my blood mage powers like that, and I'll show you what I can do."

Jessica reached up, cupping the side of his face in her hand. Rubbing his cheek against her soft palm, he sighed in contentment. Nico kissed her wrist, then ran his kisses down her arm, across her neck, across her body to her soft belly. Jessica giggled with delight.

CHAPTER 46

Before the dawn, Nico woke. He looked down at Jessica. She curled around him tightly.

Reluctantly, he untangled himself and left the warmth of the bed.

Finding his shirt, something nagged at his mind.

The tower room had one white door leading out to an old staircase that wrapped around the exterior. Nico opened the creaky door and walked outside to the curved balcony, hopeful he wouldn't wake Jessica.

The sky was still enshrouded in night and the air chilled with the scent of coming rain. The tower was far above the majority of the castle, giving him an impressive view of the darkened and overcast landscape.

There were no stars.

The wind was bitter cold.

It reminded Nico of Briken.

Calming himself, he inhaled the clean air.

He was free and he was safe.

If anyone hunted him, Nova mage or outlaw sinari, he could escape to Earth. Raising his hands up, he called his magic. Drawing the orbs together, he fanned the energy outwards, creating a cone, and then a bubble as tall as himself. He had made several by the time

Jessica opened the door. The girl was wrapped in a blanket, buffering herself from the cold.

"I thought I would find you here."

"I was just practicing."

Little droplets of morning rain struck the surrounding rooftops.

"What are you practicing?"

"The giant orb last night. I wanted to do it again, see how much control I could have. Could I create a protective orb? Maybe even put a forcefield around the castle?'

"You're considering helping the mages today?"

"I know, it's crazy and stupid," he said, following her back inside the cozy tower. "And untested."

"You've been practicing your entire life," Jessica let the blanket drop as she searched for a shirt. Nico averted his eyes in respect.

Jessica walked over to the mirror, craning her neck to see the castlemark. The symbol was a little intertwined figure eight.

"It looks different than some of the others. The core shape is the same, but other marks are fancier."

"People have additions made," Nico explained.

"It's weird, it tingles, like there's more magic there than before."

Jessica dressed, then covered the mark with a jacket.

Nico slipped into his boots.

"You think we could trust Saurin Bane with your mage problem?" Jessica asked. "Would he believe that a Sinari made you kill that man?"

"I would rather not take advantage of all Saurin has done for us."

"I wish Polaris Academy had accepted me sooner," Jessica said. "Maybe by now I could heal."

"Your father is helping you. I am certain within time, you can."

"Yeah, but it's not enough," she sighed. "I should go down to the stable yard, make sure no one has questions about the equipment. You'll be around?"

"Yeah," he nodded. "In the walls, I won't be far."

She paused at the door, about to speak, but then moved on.

***

At the stable yard most of the castlefolk were already gathered and ready to leave. Jessica felt different, and despite the gravity of the day, her heart was light.

Dawn was beginning to warm the eastern sky.

The rain had stopped.

Jared was putting on a pair of gloves. He wore a suit of close-fitting black dragon armor.

"Good morning, Sunshine!" he beamed.

"Hi," Jessica said, "you got any questions?"

"How was *your* evening?"

"Uneventful?"

Jared hooked an arm around her shoulder, walking her away from the gathered group.

"Really, not all interesting? Nothing interesting? Your *solitary* sleep was restful?"

"Oh, my god, you didn't," her hand went to her forehead. "Really? Have you no shame?"

"I'm making sure everyone is okay. Though, seemed like you had a lovely evening. Surprised you stopped when you did, but seemed very exciting nonetheless."

"For the love of everything that is holy, can you not do that ever again?!"

"I was doing my rounds. I didn't intend to see anything."

Teren walked by, holding a map. He glanced at Jessica, and gave a chuckle, shaking his head.

Jessica's face flushed with embarrassment.

"Seriously can I have no secrets around here?"

"I said nothing," Teren held up his hands innocently. "How's your shoulder?"

"Her shoulder?" Jared seemed confused. "Why would her shoulder...?"

"It's great," Jessica replied. "More normal than it's been in a long time."

Jessica answered questions about the radios as they waited for everyone to arrive. She was hopeful she would see Kaity in the crowd, but it looked like the leopard mage would not be there in time to fly.

Jessica approached her mother. She wanted to wish her good luck, and say something meaningful, but she struggled with the words.

"Hey," Lily greeted her. "Did you have any odd dreams last night?"

"Yeah, about that," Jessica crossed her arms, "that may have been my fault."

"Oh, your mark was restored?" she asked.

Jessica nodded.

Lily smiled.

"Good, I know it was all my fault, but I'm glad it was fixed."

"Yeah," Jessica nodded. "So, I know this mission is a little dangerous, very dangerous. So, I wanted to wish you good luck?"

"Jess, don't worry about it," Lily said. "I have faith this plan will work and I am proud of everything you do."

"Thanks, mom," Jessica said, hugging her mother. "Be careful, please."

***

As Teren waited, he reached out with his mind, sensing the nervous emotions around him. Then he hit an unexpected cacophony, like a symphony preparing for a concert.

Zia Casimirio

Teren grabbed Jared's arm.

"I need your assistance, come with me."

"Wait, what now? We're going to take off soon as the others get here."

"Follow me," Teren repeated, nearly dragging Jared into a tool shed.

"Look, last night was fun, but is this really—"

"I need you to do that merge trick again," Teren commanded. "The Sinari woman is nearby, I can sense her but I need to know *where* she is."

"We don't have time for her!"

"Jared, she's a danger to Aurumice and a danger to Nico. We need to know where she is, and you need to be able to know what her eyes are like so we can track her."

"I disagree, but I'll help you," Jared held out his hands.

Teren held tight. The urgency was so great.

He reached out, and sensed the maelstrom of emotions. He was aware that Jared's presence was near, likewise reaching out.

This time it didn't take long, she wasn't far.

And then he saw the front hallway. Zia was in the far side of the castle, near the ballroom entrance.

"Great!" Jared was pleased. "I'll tell Fentalon—"

"No, we go alone. Let's grab Rosin and Ember and be back as quickly as possible."

"Alone? That's stupid."

"Sending the guard would be foolish. Sinari are only dangerous through the people they control. She can't control me, and I need you."

"I feel like I should be gravely insulted here."

"You can be insulted after we find her."

***

Zia had not gotten far. The cloaked woman had entered the castle through an old servant's door near the grand ballroom. Jared and Teren were able to take a small passageway and trail her silently.

Thankfully, it was a quiet and unoccupied part of the castle.

Teren opened the backside of a large idyllic landscape painting and stepped into the hallway behind the intruder.

"Are you lost?" Teren asked.

Zia startled, and replied with a sharp knife blade.

Teren was quick to react, he spun with her momentum and throwing her off balance. She rolled across the decorative carpet, but sprung back with her blade. Teren dodged the weapon and tried to pin the woman's arms but she locked her legs around his torso. They tumbled to the hard floor. Spiny barbs on her knees dug into his sides like claws.

Teren cried out. She met his cry with an elbow to his face. Blood trickled down his nose and she wrestled free, bringing the knife to his throat.

Jared ran in terror.

Oh no you don't...

He squashed his friend's fear.

"Why did you save me?!" Zia demanded.

"I wanted to have a conversation," Teren replied smoothly as he could, ignoring the knife and his stinging nose. "I have never met anyone like you, and I imagine you could say the same."

Zia twisted Jared's emotions back to fear.

"I don't believe you!" she spat, pressing the knife into Teren's neck. The blade was sharp and drew a thin line of blood, but she didn't dig deep enough to harm him.

"You are a very skilled fighter, so I should have more than a bloody nose. I have never met another of my kind, and I imagine you have experienced the same. It would be foolish to let this opportunity pass, and you are no fool, Zia. You wouldn't be alive if you were."

Teren sent a wave of confidence to Jared, freeing him to draw a crossbow.

Zia was quick to react.

"Teren is using you," she addressed Jared. "He thinks you're nothing and useless! You should kill him and be free."

Jared's hand trembled.

"That was a very poor attempt," Teren stated, calming his friend's emotions. "Jared, you are vital to this castle and one of the most cunning mages I have ever met, trust in my words."

"I'm getting really, really tired of this game," Jared shook his head, refocusing his crossbow on Zia.

"You're a mage?" Zia grinned. "Well, you would be interested to know that your friend here is a Sinari."

"He is?" Jared questioned in mock disbelief. "Why, I had no idea."

He fired the crossbow.

Zia shrieked, dropping the knife and clutching the back of her calf. The wound was shallow and stuck in the muscle instead of the bone.

"This is foolish, Zia, I want to talk!" Teren cried out.

The black-haired woman recoiled, her hand over the bloody wound.

"Talk?! He just shot me!"

"And I'll do it again, bitch," Jared replied. "You messed with Nico, and then he stabbed me, so this is a fair repayment!"

"Your friend was a broken shell when I found him. I fixed him! You should thank me!"

"He crashed without your influence, hardly a fix," Teren climbed to his feet.

"Not my fault your friend is weak."

Teren pulled a handkerchief from his pocket and offered it to Zia.

"What's that?" she eyed him warily. For someone with a bolt through the calf she appeared relatively calm.

"You're bleeding all over the floor. It's very difficult keeping this castle clean."

Zia's glared up, her black hair obscuring her eye. Her emotions were like a symphony tuning for a concert.

It was exciting.

People rarely made Teren feel excited.

Zia accepted the fabric begrudgingly.

"Why are you here?" Teren asked.

The black-haired woman pondered this a moment.

"I prefer not to share."

"I'll let Jared shoot you again," Teren replied. "But I would really rather talk. There is a swarm of needlewasps just north of castle. I do not have time for you."

She considered it his words, then relented.

"The Circus owes me. I freed your friend, and they denied me my payment, then they sold me out to Castle Nova."

"Sounds like the Circus I know," Jared commented.

"Zia, I want to thank you," Teren said. "We couldn't have freed Nico without you, and for that I am eternally grateful."

"It really wasn't a charity case," Zia replied.

"You did what we couldn't do, regardless you deserve my thanks. Now, that wound doesn't look too terrible. May we help you remove the bolt?"

Zia wasn't in any condition to run, and nodded warily.

"Jared, I'll stay with Zia, you go get the medical supplies."

"What? Wait. We're going to help her right here? The nightflights are going to leave any minute and you want to deal with her?!"

"I think she would prefer if neither the Holy Circus nor Castle Nova knew she was here."

Jared was stunned.

"Are you sure? She's not messing with your head?"

"No, it's okay."

Zia seemed likewise surprised when Jared left the room.

"Are you stupid?"

"No, curious," Teren replied. Yes, he was foolish, but he had to know more. Animosity was not going to win Zia over. "Do you have questions for me? Anything, I would love to hear your thoughts."

He knelt beside her. He could see she had tiny lines at the corners of her eyes. She was older than him, but not by much.

"How many people can you influence?" she asked.

"Many," Teren said, "I've never counted, but to varying degrees. More than you can, I would wager by that crowd at the circus. You couldn't control more than two or three at once."

"How many animals?"

"Animals?" Teren leaned forward. The thought had never occurred to him. "None."

"Really? You can't sense the feelings of animals?"

"No. Wish I could. My mother was a beast speaker."

"This is so strange," Zia leaned forward. "I see your face, I know thinking of your mother saddened you, but I can't feel the sadness. It's so odd."

"You've never encountered those marked by Corvalian?" Teren asked. He also wanted to ask if she had ever crossed a Gate, but thought it wise to keep that topic off the table.

"Yeah, in the Auroriates."

"How did you get mixed up with them?"

"I'm a freelancer, they are just one of my clients," she smiled. "Look, it wasn't my intent to mess with your friend's mind that bad. He seemed nice enough, but I wasn't happy that his family screwed me out of my compensation, and now they have a death mark on my head. Not to mention they caused me to lose my airship to Castle Nova."

"Airship? I thought that Graveer had destroyed them all when they attacked Madierna."

"And I thought electricity was outlawed at the same time, but this castle has a lot of lightbulbs."

"We are not very good at following laws," Teren replied, "I'm sure you can relate."

"What do you intend to do with me?"

"I have a proposition for you, Zia. I will work to make your Holy Circus problem disappear and get your lost payment. It's fair, you freed Nico, you should be compensated for that. In exchange, you stay away from Aurumice and my friends until I say otherwise. And yes, you could kill me, betray me, but I think we have learned that allies would be a wiser path at this point."

"You better thank the stars that was a wooden bolt and not metal," Jared returned, handing the pack to Teren. "And that I have fantastic aim."

Zia remained silent and winced as Teren carefully removed the bolt and bandaged the wound. He kept a careful watch, still not trusting that he wouldn't find another knife at his throat.

"My airship," Zia said, "in trade for not selling your Sinari secret, and I want my lost payment."

"Jared? You are more familiar with Castle Nova"

"Oh no, no, no, don't promise that. I'm already in enough trouble with Polaris."

"We will see what we can do about your airship," he told Zia.

"And a fresh bicorn out of here, now."

"Rosin is outside. She's mine, take her."

"Teren, are you out of your mind?!"

Teren offered Zia a hand. She hobbled, unable to completely put weight on her leg. He led her outside as Jared paced, swearing frantically. Teren quieted him with an overwhelming blanket of calm. The man instantly stopped, blinking as if stoned. It was surprisingly more effective than he had intended.

Dawn had come, blanketed in dark clouds.

He helped Zia upon Rosin as it began to rain again.

"There is a tavern in Yellow Valley called the Bear and Bucket. You will meet me there in three moon turns," Zia stated.

"I look forward to it," Teren gave Rosin one gentle pat on the shoulder and hoped it wasn't the last time he would see the mare.

As soon as Zia was out of sight, Teren returned to Jared, releasing him from the blanket of subduing calm.

Jared grabbed Teren by the shoulders and shoved him against the wall, enraged.

"Don't you ever do that to me again!"

"Sorry."

"What are you doing? You just made a deal with the devil! She's going to destroy you! And Aurumice! There's reasons there's laws against her!"

Teren glared.

"You trust me."

"But you're different!"

"No, I'm not. Why did you shoot her in the calf when you could have done much worse?"

"I'm not...I...damnit, Teren!"

"Exactly, if we hand her over to the mages and Auroriates, she would be dead. We could either kill her, or make an ally of her. There is no in between."

"Damnit! I hate you so much!"

"Now we have a swarm to deal with."

CHAPTER 47

After the nightflights took flight, everyone took position. Fentalon, Wadjette, and the guard patrolled the grounds, making certain every creature and person was inside the castle.

Teren used Jessica's tower room as a communications center, maps spread out across the table.

Their plan was simple. The mages flew with the circus on their aerial mounts, trying to stay above the swarms. They didn't know if the nightflights could fly higher, but it was as good a strategy as any. Jared flew between the team and the castle, keeping eyes on everyone who didn't have a radio. On the ground, Wadjette had communication.

"This equipment seems complicated," Savina commented as she sat beside the maps. "What more is there than find the insects and destroy them?"

"Because they're deadly and unpredictable," Jessica replied. "Look, you can go downstairs and help patch the windows if you prefer."

Savina shook her head, curling her foot onto the chair.

Teren stood, and paced across the glass floor.

"What's wrong?" Jessica asked.

"Nothing," he said. "Nervous. We have no second plan if this fails."

Jessica shrugged it off, waiting for the team to check-in when they reached the swarm.

"So I heard you had a good night last night," Savina commented.

Jessica glared at Teren.

"You told her."

"No, Jared did. I told him not to."

"Can we not talk about this now?" Jessica pleaded with Savina.

"I'm bored," the tall woman replied. "I heard this was your first romantic encounter, is that really true?"

"They will reach the wasps any minute," Jessica avoided eye contact. "Let's talk about that instead."

"No, it's a sincere question. Have you been drinking lunarcha tea? I doubt you could handle a little one of your own."

Jessica cringed. Teren chuckled.

"Yes! Not that it's any of your business either, and *you*," she glared at her cousin, "you quit laughing! It's weird, you're all being weird."

"I'm looking out for you," Savina persisted. "But really, six moon turns out in a tent by yourself, and never once? Not even a little?"

"I'm going to kill Jared for talking to you," Jessica said. "And no, never once. Nico was miserable. It wouldn't have been right."

"Maybe he would have been less miserable sooner."

"Can we just pay attention to the radios?" Jessica asked.

"What is there to do?" Savina asked. "We're just sitting around listening to people talk, and they're not even doing that."

Realizing she was on the wrong channel, Jessica quickly switched the dial, her face flush with embarrassment.

"Well, was it good?" Savina persisted. "I have always been curious what type of lover he would be. He always rejected all of my offers."

The radio cracked to life. Lights indicating the signal strength illuminated.

"We're coming on the first swarm," Lily's voice was calm through the slight static of the radio. "And I hope to Aurora that's the biggest one we see."

***

Jared flew alone, trying to survey the scene.

Most of the insects were to the north. He flew south of the castle, halfway to Trabalis. He reached out with his mind's eye, looking through the vision of the people. Things seemed relatively calm, as they were blissfully unaware of the horror unfolding to the north.

He felt a crawling sensation at his cheek and quickly swatted it away, relieved to see it was just a normal beetle. Jared pulled the nightflight into a tight turn and headed back towards the castle.

***

Black dragon armor was very protective, but it wasn't very warm. Lily had hoped riding with Sienna and Zastrugi would be more comfortable that riding on a leathery nightflight, but she was wrong. Chilly winds battered the gryphon, stinging the inside of Lily's nose.

Thankfully the rains had stopped and the clouds were rolling away. The sun was just beginning to crack its orange light across the forests and rushing river.

Like a behemoth sentient cloud, the swarm of needlewasps shimmered across the horizon. The waves shifted like undulating mass, stretching as far as Lily could see along the River White. Buzzing vibrated through the air. Lily cringed, it was like bees and mosquitos crossbred to create flying nightmare fuel.

She prayed they weren't already too late.

And that their mounts could withstand the bites and stings.

The nightflights flew the lowest, their scaly hides were thick. The armored Zastrugi flew high above.

On Saurin Bane's signal, the nightflights dove in first. Renzie unleased the first blanket of fire across the swarm. The tiny insects exploded in a vivid flame cloud.

The warmth from the aerial blaze was welcoming, warming Lily's joints.

Renzie dove in again, releasing more beautiful fire. Paisley Mae joined, her powers weakly returned. The nice thing about fire was that it spread.

"Lily, you're up," Saurin's voice crackled in her ear. The signal was weak, but good enough to hear.

Lily gestured. Knowing the insects were ice-resistant, her goal was make the air difficult for flight. She concentrated the insects into tighter bunches so the fire mages could take them out more quickly.

Nile and Athenaraas worked with their fire and water in tandem to poach the insects that were close to the treetops. Hot steam was released into the air and they flew higher to avoid the broiling cloud.

It seemed that their plan was working.

They had successfully grounded four batches of swarms in blazing, steamy clouds of fire. The smell of the toasting insects was pleasant, like fresh baked coconut.

Lily inhaled deeply. She wished she could have used wide-spread lightning, but it was too unpredictable. She would have a headache from using her ice powers, but at least the insect death had a pleasant byproduct.

Reinvigorated, she tossed out another blast of ice, accidentally catching Zastrugi's tail. The gryphon yowled like a cat who had been stepped on.

"Will you mind where you're aiming?" Sienna warned. "Unless you want us both thrown to the ground."

Lily apologized.

They continued to work, taking out more and more of the blue cloud. A quarter of the mass had been eradicated by the time the sun had fully risen

Lily felt ill.

It was a different sort of ill, not just her ice headache.

Concentrating, she realized she could no longer feel the air particles with her mind.

"I'm losing control," Lily said into the headset. Blood began to drip down her nose.

"Did you get stung?" Sienna asked.

"I don't know, at least I don't think so. Not like a bee-sting stung, that's for sure."

"What do you mean, Mom?" Jessica asked.

"I can't make ice, there's nothing there. It's like I'm back in Pennsylvania with a migraine."

The flaming swarm went wild. It merged with the other swarm and exploded across the sky, setting fire to the treetops. Birds panicked and escaped their homes.

"I'm not feeling right," Renzie's voice came over the headset. "My fire is fuzzy."

"Stay your course," Saurin Bane encouraged. "Atheenaraas, extinguish those trees before the forest catches. We have made significant progress!"

"Yeah, but that's just the first swarm," Jared chimed in. "I'm flying ahead, you got a lot more coming."

"Saurin, I can't feel the water! I can't stop the fire."

***

"This is what I feared," Teren murmured. "They should flee."

"But if they don't try, what else do we have?" Jessica said.

"We could evacuate, to your world."

"No!" Jessica said reflexively.

"We have an escape door, just the castlefolk would use it. Jessica, when my father made the forcefield, they all suffered for his folly. It won't happen again, not because mages thought they knew best!"

"But that would change everything!"

"I'm not discussing it with you," Teren said. "I am telling you. If this all goes to hell, the castlefolk will go through that Gate. You and your mom won't stop it."

"Okay, okay! I will agree with you," Jessica couldn't believe the situation had escalated so quickly. "But we have to try this, my house can't hide all of the castle. Well, maybe, but, just give them more time."

"Hey!" Jared said over the radio. "Kaity is back! She and Corwin and Temi are coming up from the south."

"Fly—here!" Saurin shouted, the signal broken up. "We — that forest fire. Leaf is— but— Kaity's skill. We need Kaity."

"She won't have armor," Jessica said. "She'll have no protection from the wasps."

"I got this! — stable yard!" Jared replied.

"Can you fix that awful noise?" Savina leaned in, annoyed with the static.

"Well maybe if you people had given me more than a day's notice!"

"I have Kaity right now on my nightflight. Can someone come back for Corwin and Temi? Cloudspark has the cart and she's—— seeing some wasps in the castle yard, we don't have time!"

"Racewind and I will meet them, where are they?" Wadjette's voice chimed in.

"The orchard road."

Savina's hands went to her lips, murmuring prayers of the goddess.

Teren went silent.

"Don't worry about the castlefolk," Jessica reassured. "Just because the bugs are in the stable yard, doesn't mean they'll get in."

***

Wadjette met Corwin and Temi on the path. They turned Cloudspark loose from the cart. The gelding would follow on instinct. Racewind was a much stronger and larger bicorn and could carry the three.

Temi was delighted to see Wadjette.

"Ah, little one, I missed you!"

The leopard child signed excitedly, unaware of the danger ahead.

"I'm happy to be home," Corwin interpreted for his daughter. "And happy to see Racewind."

Temi gave the bicorn an affectionate pat.

"We need to get inside, the needlewasps are close. Hold tight," Wadjette ordered.

Racewind galloped down the path through the orchard. His hooves thundered over the little bridge, down through the empty meadow.

In her peripheral vision, Wadjette could see the trees becoming obscured by a blue cloud. Shimmering blue clusters emerged from the forest. It started as a few spots, then needlewasps emerged by the thousands. By the time they reached the first barn, stray insects buzzed in Wadjette's ear like little mosquitos. Temi squealed and Corwin cried out.

Seeing nothing but wasps ahead, Wadjette directed her mount into the goat barn. Reaching down, she slammed the door closed behind them.

The dreaded hum was muffled.

Wadjette pressed the button on the radio.

"We can't get to the castle! We're in the goat barn!"

***

"Who's trapped in the goat barn?" Saurin asked.

"I have Corwin and his daughter with me," Wadjette said, "We're okay for now, but there are a few wasps in here."

"I'll help them! We're close," Paisley Mae said from her crimson nightflight. "We can fly to the stable yard."

"You shouldn't break with the plan," Lily cautioned. "We need you here! We're already in trouble!"

"Who will help them if we don't?" Paisley Mae disregarded the elder mage's warning. "I won't let a mage child be hurt!"

"Paisley Mae! You're still injured!"

"Drop me off," the girl told her circus partner. Not wearing a headset, he couldn't hear the argument.

"Paisley Mae!"

"I am going to destroy those suckers," she promised, hopping off of the nightflight's back. The needlewasps didn't seem so dense. Paisley Mae let lose a blast of fireball at the largest group. Insects flared up through the air. Her circus companion flew higher, hovering far above the fire storm.

"You idiot! You shouldn't be on the ground!" Jared shouted. Needlewasps dove at Paisley and she swatted wildly. Everywhere she turned was another tiny demon.

She had made a terrible mistake.

"Here!" a female voice called from the barn. "Come here!"

***

"Wadjette, what's your status?" Jessica asked. "I couldn't hear you over the static."

"Jessica, the wasps came out of the forest."

"Where are you?" Jessica felt helpless in the tower aviary. They had not secured the barns.

"We're in the goat barn with Temi, Corwin and the fire mage! Is there any way you can help!?"

Tinks at the ceiling caught their attention. Jessica looked up as she realized little sapphire wasps were striking the glass. They had grossly underestimated their threat. Savina jumped to her feet, ready to flee.

"Were those windows repaired well?"

"Yes, I had Jiberty help me months ago. It's all sealed."

The needlewasps continued to tink against the glass dome.

Savina murmured and prayed.

"It's a nightmare."

"Fly up," Saurin commanded through the radio. "Let's regroup and attack again. Who still has their full strength?"

None of the fire mages were feeling normal.

"I think you're flying all too low," Jared said. "You're putting yourself at risk."

"Sienna and I are way above—it's not the stings," Lily said. "—feel awful. I think it's the air!"

"Can you fly higher?" Jessica asked.

"The smoke is everywhere." Saurin pointed out. "—impossible to avoid breathing."

Jessica's mind raced, thinking back to Briken, where the insects plagued the land freely and black clouds swallowed the sky.
Think, think, think

A gentle touch on her shoulder made her jump.

It was Nico.

"Have you been listening to this?" Jessica asked.

"Yes, that's why I came out of hiding. The situation sounds dire."

"I'm out of ideas," Jessica gripped her hair.

"Evacuate everyone to earth," Teren stated. "Before the insects find a way into the castle."

"Yeah but that doesn't help Wadjette and Temi and Corwin!" Jessica said.

"They might be lost, but it will save everyone else!" Teren replied.

Nico placed a hand between his arguing friends.

"Jess, if your mom is right and it's the air, then we need to filter it for the mages. Ask Sienna if the Holy Circus brought the gill masks, the ones they use for the shows."

"Sienna, do you have the circus breathing masks?" Jessica was hopeful.

"Yes, but they're back on the ground with our gear."

"Can you get them for the mages? It might be defense against the poison."

***

"Kaity wants to go down to the stable yard," Jared said.

"No! We need you to the north," Saurin cautioned. "We can't afford anyone else to change plan! Concentrate on the larger swarm. Everyone stay north."

There was a pause.

"Kaity said that's her daughter and you can go to hell."

Lily listened to the argument.

"Sienna, we should—"

"Fly to the stable yard and ignore Saurin Bane? I know," Sienna signaled to Zastrugi and the massive beast altered course. The insects seemed to swarm in tight clusters. Lily gestured. Nothing happened.

In desperation, she tried to send a blast of lightning.

Nothing.

"I'm done," Lily said. "I can't do anything, I'm sorry."

"Lily, you look like you're about to fall off that gryphon," Jared's voice commented. "Your vision is getting bad."

"My powers are totally gone."

"Aunt Lily, get inside," Teren commanded.

"But…"

"We don't need more casualties. Land, and get inside."

***

"*More* casualties?" Jessica slammed down the microphone. "No one's dead yet!"

"Wadjette is terrified right now," Teren paced around the atrium furiously. "I've seen that girl stare down six sting lizards and control her fear! They are in dire trouble."

"Wadjette? What's your situation?" Jessica asked. Nico rested his hand on the back of her chair, leaning in to hear the response.

"—wasps are getting in and the roof is creaking."

"I'll go out there," Nico stated.

Jessica closed her eyes, knowing he would volunteer.

"You?" Teren said. "Even if you could withstand the wasps, how will you bring them to safety?"

"He's gotten good at energy fields."

Nico gestured to his right, creating a perfect energy orb as tall as himself.

"It's different from what your father used to do, but I think it will work well enough."

"And if you're wrong?" Savina asked.

"He doesn't have a choice," Jessica replied.

"We don't have any spare armor," Teren warned.

"I'll either be fine, or dead," Nico gave a smile, "I've already been dead once before, hoping for fine."

He pulled up the cloak of his hood, placed on his mask of the Holy Circus and walked away, leaving his friends behind. Savina and Teren seemed frozen, but Jessica jumped to her feet and chased after him. She grabbed his arm.

"You're not leaving like that!"

"Jess, we don't have time, I will come back!"

"And if you don't?"

Nico hesitated.

Jessica refused to release his hand.

"When Trabalis took you, you left me with a necklace and years of questions! You will *not* do that again."

Reaching forward, Nico leaned close to her ear.

"Jessica, please, you've always known the truth."

Reluctantly, she released his hand.

CHAPTER 48

Sienna reached the gear, grateful the dragon armor and her own traditional mask protected her face from the wasps. The field wasn't as bad as the stable yard, but the wasps buzzed around her, landing on her protected arms.

Lily helped as she grabbed all she could from the supplies, frantically popping the slimey gills into the chambers of the special masks.

"I pray to Aurora this is enough to filter the toxin," Sienna said, gathering the masks into a satchel.

"It will work, Kaity is still well enough to fight."

***

Nico traveled through the castle, approaching the back entrance.

He paused at the top of the staircase in the white foyer, overlooking the entrance and the tapestry of the goddess Aurora.

Familiar panic began to creep up along his spine. His arm trembled as the darkness of the mines wrapped around his heart.

It was hopeless.

He would fail.

Nico closed his eyes.

No.

And then the mages would discover him, chain him, and take him back to Briken.

No.

At this moment, he was free, and at this moment, his dear friends were counting on him.

Nico descended the stairs through the empty hallways. He stood at the door, pondering how to keep the wasps out.

He generated a bubble of energy outside him, sealing the door. Generating a second bubble around him, he opened it.

The insects swarmed, but veered away from his power. Those that didn't sizzled and fell.

Stepping out in the stable yard, Nico was enshrouded by only a cloak and a mask. Reaching out, he maintained the forcefield. He wasn't quite certain what he would do once he reached the barn but he was hoping he would find his answer when he got there.

The wasps flew frighteningly close, but deflected from the energy sphere as if it were glass. Insect carcasses fell in his wake.

A nightflight circled frantically overhead. The wasps around the goat barn behaved erratically, as if an invisible hand kept slapping them down and away. It was effective, but not consistent. As soon as the hand waved through, wasps filled in.

"Who's down there?!" Kaity's voice was frantic in his ear. "There's someone down in the yard, a barrier mage."

He needed her help, and he needed to tell Wadjette to not touch the energy sphere.

"Kait, it's me."

"Nico? How are you doing that?! That's not fire!!!"

"I'm not a fire mage."

"Temi's in the goat barn with the others, can you get there?"

"That's where I'm going," Nico stated steadily. It wasn't easy to maintain concentration. The wasps were frantic with their deafening hum.

"Wadjette are you there?"

"Yes."

"Stay away from the energy ball. Am I clear? It could kill you if you touch it, tell the others."

As Nico reached the door, he flattened the sphere against the wood and created a half-bubble. He opened the door carefully.

"Follow me, stay close, and do not touch the sphere."

Corwin carried Temi as they entered the giant orb. The little child clung to her father, in awe of insects.

"Thank the stars for you!" Corwin said. "Thank the goddess!"

Paisley Mae hesitated, terrified.

"Are you certain that energy will hold? I almost died once!"

Nico expanded the orb as sweat dripped down his back.

"It's alright, I have control."

He had never tried to maintain concentration for so long.

They walked slowly through the stable yard. The needlewasps continued to deflect from the orb. The buzzing grew louder and more angry.

"This mask makes everything smell better," one of the mages commented from the sky. "Are we ready to take another pass?"

"One at a time," Saurin said over the radio. "Slowly. If we're wrong about the masks and we all lose our powers, Trabalis will suffer out folly."

Nico was confident in their new strategy, and it lifted his heart a little bit. He continued to walk. The others remained silent, acutely aware of his deep concentration. Only Temi was oblivious to the danger, marveling at the crystal orb and the tiny insects that bounced off of its surface.

Nico coughed and the sphere fluctuated slightly. Paisley Mae flinched, white with fear. She grabbed onto Wadjette.

"Have faith," the Wadjette assured.

They reached the wooden door to the castle, Nico again formed a half-sphere.

"Go ahead and get the door," Nico advised, his voice strained. Wadjette carefully opened the door to the castle. Beyond it, Jessica waited with Fentalon and a group of castlefolk.

Nico found his strength diminishing as he allowed the sphere to shrink around them.

As Corwin and Temi approached the door, the child reached out, enamored with the crystalline appearance of the energy sphere. Her tiny spotted hand innocently stretched upwards, inches from the energy. Nico panicked, throwing the energy outward and destroying the orb.

The needlewasps descended.

Wadjette didn't realize what was happening as she crossed the door, Paisley Mae pulled them inside.

Paisley Mae threw the door closed, her phobia taking hold.

The slam echoed across the stable yard, quickly engulfed by the deafening buzz of the wasps.

Nico stumbled forward, no longer able to see as hundreds of tiny needles stabbed his skin, pumping their eggs into his flesh.

***

"Why the hell did you do that?!" Jessica shoved past Paisley Mae to get to the door.

"No!" the fire mage argued. "You'll kill us all!"

Paisley Mae threw a small fireball, singeing the top of Jessica's hand. Her skin reddened and immediately blistered with searing pain. The sting welled up with Jessica's anger.

"You god damn mage, I'll strangle you from the inside if you try that again!" Jessica reached for the door. Beyond the wood, her mind's eye could see the red purple glow of millions of wasps.

"Paisley Mae!" Jared's voice shouted through the headset. "I know what you're doing and I will fly down there and kill you myself if you don't open that door!"

Jared's voice was all the distraction needed.

Fentalon grabbed Paisley Mae from behind, bringing a knife to her neck.

"Attack Jessica again and I'll slice your throat," he warned. "This isn't Polaris. This is Aurumice."

"Jessi," Paisley Mae pleaded. "If you open that door, you'll kill us all. He's just an Auroriate and not worth it, he's already dead."

Jessica concentrated on the wall of wasps beyond the wood. She could see Nico's form, the outline of his veins, the blood congregating in his heart and through his vital organs. Nico was barely five feet beyond the door, his heart still pumping, blood flowing to his brain. He lived, incased in a thick blanket of tiny little wasps.

The purple-red light of the insects continued to dance. Jessica narrowed her eyes, focusing on the tiny little bodies in the air. She imagined them popping like miniature grapes. To her delight, as she concentrated the wasps exploded, each speck of blood dispersing like a raindrop hitting the pavement.

"Don't open the door!" Paisley screamed. "You don't know what you're doing!"

Jessica ignored the mage, concentrating on the wall of insects beyond.

Time slowed as the insects fell to the ground in her mind's eye. Touching the wasps with her mind was as real as if she had squished them with her finger. It felt like the resistance of pushing two opposing magnets together.

As Jessica cleared enough space in the swarm, she grabbed the metal handle. Depressing the button, she shoved the heavy door open.

Beyond in the chaos, she saw magenta explosions, but everyone else saw a shimmering waterfall of blue blood as the creatures perished. In the maelstrom of buzzing, an opening was pushed through the air as the needlewasps died.

The teen lunged forward, grabbing Nico and dragging him inside. His body was still covered in wasps, as she was fearful to use her powers too close to his skin. She couldn't distinguish between the vicious creatures and his capillaries.

As Nico crossed the threshold, Fentalon released Paisley, shoving the girl to the side. He seized the door, pulling it closed.

Blinking, Jessica could no longer see the glow of the insects, the poison of the blood rain dampening her abilities. A flurry of commotion erupted around her. Paisley Mae fled with half the room. Corwin carried Temi out of harm's way. The remaining castlefolk stayed, using anything they could find to crush the tiny errant bugs. Blue stains covered the carpets and walls as they worked in a frenzy to kill the insects. Thankfully, needlewasps were not intelligent enough to dodge the books and bare hands that smashed them.

Jessica frantically brushed the insects off Nico, but they stuck everywhere. She tried to flick them off her hand but they gripped like velcro, burning her body with their sting.

Jessica cleared the wasps away from his face. He looked up at her in agony, his eyes so swollen they were barely able to open.

Nico reached up, his hand brushing against Jessica's cheek.

He wanted to speak, but he was unable to form the words.

His arm fell to his side and his eyes rolled back.

"Nico?! Nico stay with us!" Jessica cried out.

Needlewasps continued to dig into Jessica's skin, but she told herself that she would dig them out later. Her left arm was going numb, but she refused to think about it as she crushed the tiny insects with her hands.

The swarm in the room quickly thinned, and a handful of people came to Jessica's aid to kill the insects that surrounded Nico. The more needlewasps they cleared off the young man, the more seemed to emerge. They were forced to rip off his clothing to release the insects that had gotten trapped beneath the fabric layers.

Swelling engulfed his body leaving his face barely distinguishable.

Nico's breathing was most terrifying of all, unable to draw enough oxygen as wasps flew out of his mouth. His tongue swelled like a fat purple slug.

"Can you heal him?" Fentalon asked Jessica.

Jessica was at a loss.

She closed her eyes, placing a hand on Nico's wrist. It was hot and swollen with fever. His skin had an odd wet texture as pus and fluid oozed from the wounds.

Jessica closed her eyes, trying to find a center of healing. Updates from the sky above chirped in her ear from the headset. The mages were turning the tide against the wasps, but Jessica didn't care. She threw her headset to the ground and fought to clear her mind.

Instead of clarity, her thoughts were a jumble and she hated herself for every choice she made since becoming a blood mage. She should have stayed in Polaris and insisted the mages teach her.

"Jessica, try to heal him," Fentalon encouraged her. "You can do it."

As she opened her eyes, Nico's breathing was still labored, and his body continued to redden and swell. Tiny black specks began to emerge from his skin.

"Talon, I just can't."

"You're all the hope he has right now."

"Jessica," Lily was at her side, her face red with exhaustion as if she had run from the other side of the castle.

"She's trying to heal him."

"She doesn't have the training. Jessica, listen to me carefully. If you can't do it, please don't hate yourself. Just say goodbye."

"Goodbye?" Jessica looked at her mother.

The older woman was not saying the words in malice.

Lily had lost all hope, from too many years of not saying goodbye.

"Be grateful you can tell him that you love him, and accept that."

Jessica watched Nico's labored breathing.

She wasn't ready to let him go.

Nico went into a seizure, twisting uncontrollably like a terrifying bloated puppet as his organs failed.

Jessica turned to her mother.

She locked eyes with the older woman.

"I'm getting Dad."

Jessica climbed to her feet, looking around the room. There were only castlefolk around.

"It's not worth asking. Your father wouldn't save your aunt, and he won't help Nico!"

"Then maybe he will tell me how to heal."

"But he can't!"

"Talon!" Jessica ignored her mother. "You tell the castlefolk to keep every damn mage of Polaris away from the Gate. No matter what! If they go looking for a fugitive mage, you lead them in circles and do whatever you need to do to keep them away."

"We'll do it, I swear we will," Fentalon promised her.

Jessica glared at her mother.

"Bring Nico to the edge of the Gate."

Lily shook her head.

"Fine, but you're just going to be disappointed."

Jessica ran.

***

"Jessica?" Teren spoke into the radio. "Jess, what's the update?"

No response.

"What happened?"

He knew the answer already.

It was bad.

Terror and silence.

"Jessica, is anyone down there? Answer me!"

"Teren," Jared's voice crackled through, "Go to the house, now!"

"What does that mean?" Savina asked. "What house?"

"Jessi's house. The Gate, we need to get to the Gate," Teren abandoned the radio. Sprinting out of the room, Savina was close behind him.

***

Jessica stumbled through the Gate and leapt up the basement steps of the suburban house. Her right hand trembling violently, she grabbed her phone and dialed her father's number. Her left fingers felt like fat swollen sausages.

Bringing the phone to her ear, she waited the eternity through the ringing.

One ring, two rings, three rings....

Don't go to voicemail, don't go to voicemail.

The phone clicked as her father said hello.

"Dad, I need you more than I ever needed you before, so please, please, please listen to me. Nico was totally covered in needlewasps. He's not breathing right and the wasps went down his throat and he's having seizures and I don't know what to do!"

"Jessica, calm down," Stephen said. "Where is he?"

"They're bringing him to the storeroom under the barn. Dad, I don't know how to heal him, you need to tell me how."

"I can't just tell you over the phone! It takes years of practice and focus!"

"Then please, please, come and save him."

"Jessi, you know what will happen if I cross over to Centernia."

"I know, but I swear the castlefolk will protect you. The guard already knows to keep the mages away from the Gate."

"Jess, the mages will know I'm there. They will kill me."

"The castlefolk won't let that happen! Even Fentalon swore they will keep the mages away. Nico's dying, please, help me."

***

Stephen lowered the phone, pressing the mute button. He sat across from Carrie Anne in their living room, cradled in the heaven of weekend.

Ashlin was in the kitchen, mixing a batch of brownies.

He could hear Jessica's voice screaming into the phone, muted and far away. The suburban living room was calm and peaceful. The floors were freshly vacuumed and a chirpy spring bird sang beyond the window.

"Who is it?" Carrie Anne asked.

Stephen looked past his wife, watching the thirteen-year-old sloppily heap the gooey chocolate batter into a brownie tray. It was Ashlin's first foray into baking and she seemed very pleased with herself. That morning they had received uplifting test results for Carrie Anne's cancer.

Stephen looked at the phone.

He could hang up, and slam the door on Centernia forever.

"Stephen? I can tell it's serious."

He closed his eyes.

Or he could help his daughter and return to the chaos and magic.

"Stephen?"

"I need to go, but I might not come back."

"It's bad?"

"They need my help."

Carrie Anne placed a hand over his.

"If you're asking my permission, you don't need to."

Looking up again, Stephen watched Ashlin scrape the bottom of the bowl with the rubber spatula. He wanted to save every last lingering moment of normalcy, but knew it was futile.

Stephen brought the phone to his ear.

"I'll be there."

Disconnecting the call, he took a deep breath. He hugged Carrie Anne, then went into the kitchen. Ashlin was licking batter off her finger.

"What's going on?" she asked.

Stephen hugged Ashlin and kissed the top of her head.

"Nothing. Take care of your mom. I need to leave."

He grabbed his jacket from the hook in the hallway, picked up his car keys, and ran out of the house.

CHAPTER 49

Lily waited alone in the darkened cold store room. She pulled a blanket over Nico as the boy shivered from fever. Thankfully, he did not have any more seizures. The sight terrified Lily, resurrecting painful memories.

Rapid footsteps caught Lily's attention. The fight with the needlewasps had dulled her powers, but she still carried a short sword and her anger.

Thankfully, Teren ran into the room, followed closely by Savina. Her relief turned to more anxiety as she saw the pain on her nephew's face.

"What happened?!" the young man choked, falling to Nico's side.

"He was caught in the swarm," Lily said. "The others made it to safety, he didn't."

Savina immediately broke into hysterical sobbing.

"Jessi ran for her father, didn't she?" Teren asked.

"That's her hope," Lily replied.

Teren cradled Nico's head in his hands. The pale man's face was contorted in a strange expression, fighting to keep down his own grief.

Lily knelt beside her nephew, quietly watching.

"Teren, listen to me, I know you're trying to help Nico now, but if Jessi comes through that Gate with her father, you need to help keep the mages away. Can you focus on that from here? Can you make them frightened if they come near?"

Teren nodded.

"I'll know if anyone gets close," he said, running his fingers through Nico's hair, picking out stray needlewasp legs and wings.

"Is he there?" Lily asked.

"Yes. He feels terror, and anguish and hopelessness, but I want him to feel loved."

***

Jessica sat at the front door, using a small paring knife to pick needlewasp eggs out of her arm. It was an unseasonably warm spring day. She heard the distant hum of an early lawnmower, or maybe it was someone burning the gas out of a snow blower. Why was everything so damn normal while her world was falling apart?!

Blood trickled down her arm. Her cuts had been large and sloppy, but she was furious at the tiny monsters invading her skin. Every minute waiting for her father ticked by in agony.

A delivery truck drove by, oblivious to the terror surrounding Aurumice.

Stephen's Mercedes peeled around the corner, passing the truck on the left and pulling up the uneven driveway.

The car was barely in park as Stephen dashed out.

"Jess, your arm!" he placed a hand to her forehead, concerned she had contracted an infection.

"Dad, I'm not bad. Nico is worse."

"Where is he?"

"On the other side," Jessica explained, expecting an argument.

Stephen ran ahead of her, racing down the stairs.

***

The Gate shimmered.

Lily looked up to see a sight she thought she would never see again.

Stephen appeared.

He wore jeans and a black t-shirt, his hair grayed and his face aged and gaunt. Time shifted as Lily recalled the days when she had known him only as Savartos.

Jessica followed her father, her arm reddened with bloody welts.

Focused, Stephen knelt beside Nico, wordlessly placing his hands over Nico's neck and face.

Long moments passed.

Nothing happened.

Nico's chest barely rose.

Lily closed her eyes, praying to the deities of earth and Centernia.

Nico's face slowly shifted from purple to a warmer red. His mouth opened and his breathing strengthened from shallow pulls to heavy gasps.

Jessica knelt beside Lily. The girl watched intently, her face a mixture of wonder and fear. Lily put her arm around her daughter's shoulders. She wanted to tell the girl that she was proud of her for everything she had done, but said nothing for fear of breaking Stephen's concentration. Everyone else in the room remained silent.

As Nico's breathing returned to normal, Stephen shifted his focus to the individual needlewasp stings. Very carefully he held his hands over Nico. The wounds would well up with yellow pus and the tiny eggs would appear. Each pod of poison was chased with a tiny rush of blood as the small wounds closed.

***

At first, Ashlin shrugged off her father's absence, but as the brownies cooled she took notice.

"When is Dad coming back?"

Carrie Anne was trying to find a way to distract herself. The TV was maddening, the computer was boring, her mind raced as she wondered where Stephen could be.

"Something for work dear, it's important."

"Then why did he forget his phone?"

"Oh, darn," Carrie Anne said, "well, he won't be happy about that."

Ashlin held up the forgotten phone, playing with the buttons.

"Why was that call from Jessi's mom's house? Why are you lying to me?" "What's going on with my sister?"

"Your father will explain."

"Mom, that isn't fair."

"Ashlin, I can't tell you!"

"Why do you lie too! They all lie! Jessi, my father, her mother and now you?!"

***

519

"You feel that? That humming in your head?" Kaity's voice came over the radio. "There's a marked mage nearby! A criminal!"

The mages murmured in agreement.

"It's closer in the castle," Leaf said through static. "I can feel it, in the castle."

"We need to finish our work with the wasps," Saurin Bane advised. "Just a little more."

"But you know the laws!" Kaity argued. "Whoever they are, we need to find them now!"

"Lady Kaity Cosette, our loyalty is to the people. It wouldn't do them any good if we protect them from a fugitive and they die from wasps, now would it?"

***

The healing process was long and painstaking. After a while, beads of sweat appeared on Stephen's forehead as the fatigue began to show.

Jessica stood briefly, her joints aching. She was certain she had fever but she refused to say anything to her father.

At last, Stephen sat back on his heels, breathing deeply.

"Nico should recover," he reassured. "He'll sleep for a long while, but he should be okay."

The room heaved an audible sigh of relief. Jessica threw her arms around her father, still in awe that he crossed the Gate.

"Thank you, you have no idea what this means to me."

"It's okay, Jess, I know. Now let me see your arm before you get an infection."

Jessica held her arm out. The few eggs that remained in her skin popped to the surface with no pain, her wounds healed.

"Thank you."

"I wish I could help the others, but you all must know my time here needs to be very short."

"Goddess bless you!" Savina gushed with gratitude.

"Thank you!" Teren echoed, "You have our eternal debt. Whatever Aurumice can do for you, we will."

Jessica's father nodded. As he began to walk away, he paused, and looked at Lily.

"Your arm," he said. "Please, may I help you?"

Lily nodded.

Stephen knelt beside her, carefully taking her hand in his left and placing his right on her shoulder. Lily breathed deeply, looking up at the face of her former lover as his magic laced up her arm and across her back.

Stephen lifted his hands, letting them hover above her skin.

The pause was quick. Had it been two strangers, Jessica would not have noticed, but these were her parents.

She saw the truth through one look.

The years of twisted hatred and bitter blame had not destroyed all that they had been.

Stephen slowly stood.

Lily moved slightly, as if readying herself to stand, but remained frozen in place.

Stephen took a few steps away from her, his expression twisted to sadness as he vanished into the wall.

Lily stared long after he was gone.

EPILOGUE

Jared peered into the toaster oven, standing in the Vance kitchen. "As long as I live I will never eat microwaved burritos again."

"We're going to be eating a banquet in an hour!" Jessica replied from the half bath. She stood in front of the mirror while braiding her hair, dressed in a formal gown.

"But it's *my* Mark Ceremony, I can't be hungry!" Jared replied as the front door opened.

Several weeks had passed since the needlewasp swarm. The gill masks had proven effective in preserving the mages' powers. They were able to turn back the monstrous tide before the swarm reached Trabalis. The threat diminished, the mages turned their focus to locating the renegade.

Of course, the mages couldn't locate Savartos Sarkisian.

He was back home, eating brownies and arguing with a teenager.

The Auroriates wanted no part of the hunt, and their duty complete, returned to their troupe.

The needlewasps were still present across the land, but word of their danger spread rapidly. It became a daily routine to check for the malicious stings and dig out the eggs.

It was time for life to return to a new normal.

"We can probably give Cookie a recipe to make burritos in Aurumice."

"No, no, no, he'd use the wrong meat, and substitute cucumber for tomatoes. Jess, you just don't get it, do you? Earth food tastes so much better."

"You're just wrong. I would rather eat in Aurumice any day."

"I agree with Jared," Stephen entered the kitchen. "I think it's the water. Earth water has less impurities, so it makes all the food better."

"See, it's not just me," Jared grinned as the toaster dinged.

"Hi, Dad."

"I know you're leaving for the ceremony soon, but I stopped by to bring back the books I stole from the castle....oh, about twenty years ago. I think you may gain some insight as to what happened to your dreamspinner cousin." Stephen placed the grocery bag full of priceless tomes on the table. "Is Nico around? I marked some passages he would find interesting."

"Yeah, he's upstairs," Jessica clipped her hair up. "He got bored and he tried to fix the hot water tank, because that's still broken, and then the upstairs tub started leaking, so he's trying to fix that too."

After healing, Lily offered Nico sanctuary in her home until they found a more permanent solution. For the first time, Nico was inclined to take it. Jessica wasn't sure how long the peace would last, but for the moment, she enjoyed having him around. It felt like having a real, normal friend again.

"Do I look okay?" Jessica turned around. She had selected a red gown with a classic single-shoulder style, proudly displaying her castlemark.

Jared sighed.

"Passable."

"I hope you spill salsa on your new white jacket."

"Jess, you really look great. Wish I could see this party."

"Well, someday, Dad."

"We'll see," her father was forlorn for a moment, then smiled. "I actually also came here to bring something to you, speaking of that hot water tank."

Stephen pulled an envelope from his jacket pocket and handed it to his daughter.

"What's this?" Jessica peered inside, hopeful.

"I know people don't use them much anymore, but it's a checkbook. It's tied to the bank account with your college fund, but I think you and your mom could use the money now. Use the money how you'd like, you know what you're doing, Jess."

"Dad, this is amazing…" Jessica was astounded. "I don't know what to say."

The basement stairs creaked with the sound of footsteps and the door opened. Lily ascended the stairs in a green dragon gown. She hid one arm behind her back.

"Are you both ready?" her mother was truly smiling.

"Lily, have you tried this toaster oven yet?" Jared grinned. "It even has a convection setting. I didn't know what a convection oven was until now."

"Well, thank Carrie Anne," Lily said. "Glad someone's using it. I rather eat at Aurumice."

"See, it's not just me!" Jessica said. "The food just tastes better."

Lily noticed her ex-husband.

"Oh, I didn't know you were stopping by."

"Just dropping off a few things," Stephen replied. "Those old books, and then I gave Jess access to a bank account so you can get things fixed up."

"Stephen, you don't need to do that, but thank you," Lily was still smiling. "Jess, where's Nico?"

Nico walked down the stairs into the front hallway.

"Here," he said.

"But, Mom, this is from the really big bank account."

"Stephen—"

"This house and this Gate are my responsibility. Let me help."

"We'll talk about it later. Nico, there is a guest waiting for you in the castle, and you are required to attend tonight's ceremony."

Lily revealed her hidden arm, tossing pile of formal clothing at Nico.

The young man seemed wary.

"It's not a trap," Lily reassured him.

"How do you know no one will betray me?"

"Trust me, no one will betray you to Trabalis or the mages tonight. Get dressed, we're going."

***

Lily led them into the castle to the grand ballroom.

Nico was nervous and vulnerable, unable to fathom what protections Jessica's mother had been able to secure.

"Would it be better if I wore the attire of the Holy Circus?" Nico asked. Jessica was at his left arm, she looked as anxious as he felt.

"Look, if the weather witch says you're safe, you're safe," Lily reassured him.

The sound of people and music spilled out into the hallway. The electric lights illuminated the room, in blatant defiance of Trabalis. Despite his fear, Nico felt the power and grandeur of the massive chamber.

Jared followed behind them.

"Ah, now this is a party."

"Glad you could join us this evening," Teren approached, holding a glass of wine.

"Me too," Nico replied warily. Teren took him by his right arm.

"You have a visitor, two in fact! I think you will be most pleased."

Two men stood by the dessert table, dressed in the formal attire of Polaris Academy. As they neared, Nico realized he knew both guests. One was Saurin Bane. The old mage spoke to Kaity, who was three glasses too far into the wine. The other man was biting into a cracker, laughing flirtatiously with Savina. His face was gaunt, his hair black streaked in grey.

"I don't believe it," Nico murmured.

"Ah, there you are!" Saurin said. "I have someone to introduce you to, thought I believe you have already met under much less cordial circumstances."

The stranger swallowed the cracker and wiped his hand on his pants.

"Tigard Sarkisian," he said, bringing his hands together in the traditional greeting of Madierna. "You tried to kill me."

Nico was so stunned, Jessica had to nudge him to respond. Nico bowed his head.

"I am so eternally sorry! I cannot begin to express how much I regretted attacking you!"

Tigard waved his hand.

"Nah, that little Sinari bitch has been a thorn in our side for a while. She's messed with many people. You're not the first, won't be the last."

It was clear where Saurin exuded decorum, Tigard took a more casual approach to life.

"How did you survive?"

Tigard shrugged.

"I'm a bit of a *mazjilie*, and some of that is blood mage. Can't heal anyone else, but I can keep my own blood in place long enough to pull together a carotid artery."

"A mixed mage! Oh thank Aurora! And once again, I am so sorry."

"Sir," Jessica interrupted. "If I may ask, you said your last name is Sarkisian? You're a relative of Zapaisley Maeve?"

"Yeah, my niece," Tigard said, chuckling. "Heard she almost killed Nico. See? The universe balances."

Jessica nodded. Nico knew she wasn't asking about his relation to Zapaisley. The man was her uncle, and he didn't know it.

"So if I didn't kill you, why did mages chase me in the Yellow Valley?" Nico asked.

"Trying to find the Sinari woman, but you panicked. My colleagues searched for you in the river for two days before they gave up."

Nico couldn't believe the words.

Teren glanced around.

"Well, everyone is here, and this song is ending. We can begin?"

Jared clapped his hands together, excited.

"I'm ready to join you castlefolk."

"Oh, we have something else planned first," Kaity grinned, leaning onto Teren. "Something so much better."

"Are you upstaging my mark ceremony?"

"Lord Bane, if you please," Teren gestured to the small stage. He offered a hand to Kaity.

"Dear, can you find that Polaris propriety for about two minutes?"

"But I want to celebrate now!" The leopardess complained walking up to the stage. The buzz of the crowd quieted. Nico noticed that every one of the castlefolk was in attendance, though oddly none were approaching him.

As she stood upon the stage, Kaity quelled her carnival grin into a proper smile.

Jessica leaned up to whisper in his ear.

"Nico, I don't know what that man is going to say, but I think it's going to be a big deal considering how drunk Kaity is right now." Jessica's breath was warm and pleasant. The woman could have whispered anything and Nico would have been excited to hear her talk.

"People of Aurumice," Kaity began. "Teren and I stand before you with one of our brethren. For those of you who may not remember this man, he is Saurin Bane, High Mage of Castle Nova, and marked castlefolk. He led the mages against the needlewasps and we welcome him back tonight."

A cheer rippled through the crowd.

"Castle Nova is buying our silence," Teren whispered low enough so Jessica and Nico could hear him. "We stay quiet about the needlewasp toxin, and they are making our problems go away."

"Which problems?" Jessica asked.

Saurin Bane stepped forward and Teren didn't have a chance to reply.

"My words tonight will be brief. The real reason we are gathered tonight is to welcome Jared Evansi as one of the castlefolk, but the news I bring will impact every one of you."

Saurin Bane's rich voice reverberated across the ballroom from the chandeliers to the marble floor.

"As most of you have heard since the crisis with the needlewasps, Nicoveren secretly returned to Aurumice. He had been purchased as a slave from the Mines of Briken, and was fortunate enough to escape. Slavery is illegal in our lands, his freedom was not sanctioned, and the moral integrity of the Mines of Briken has been called into question and investigation."

The demeanor of the crowd shifted ever so slightly. Jessica grabbed Nico's hand, entwining her five fingers into his four. Nico's heart beat fiercely as he listened.

"During the crisis of the needlewasps, Castle Aurumice acted when no one else would, protecting the city of Trabalis. Though there were many deaths across the land, the choice of Aurumice saved many lives. In addition, Nicoveren's unquestionable heroism saved the lives of mages of Polaris as well as our own castlefolk. This act is not to be overlooked by Castle Nova."

Saurin Bane reached into his pocket and pulled out a rolled scroll.

"This document confirms the forgiveness of the debt incurred by Castle Aurumice during the ten years the forcefield encased the castle and stretched across the River White. By the forgiveness of the monetary debt, Nicoveren has been freed of service to the Mines of Briken."

Cheering erupted throughout the ballroom. Nico trembled, unable to believe Saurin's words. Jessica grabbed Nico from his left side as he was tackled from the right by Savina.

Congratulations rained upon him. He never thought he would truly be free, but for the first time, the world was kind to him. In the midst of the laughter, his eyes traveled up to the crystal apex of the ballroom.

Nico silently thanked Misa.

He promised to free his friend from her own prison.